DON'T ASK, DON'T TELL

Don't Ask, Don't Tell

A Geek Growing Up Gay in the 90s

JAY T BAILEY

Flatscan Publishing

This is my story, unabashedly honest and unapologetically raw. Still, this is a work of fiction, and I reserve the right to embellish, exaggerate, omit, and fabricate certain aspects. Names have been altered and obvious events have been changed to maintain the privacy of everyone included. All depictions have the element of veracity behind them and are included to show how they helped influence the man I have become. Memories are tricky things; we often misremember certain things, and memories often change as we share them. Additionally, if anyone recognizes themselves and recalls events differently, please remember that we each had separate perspectives of the same events and of course will have different recollections. For those of you who know me well, you may be uncomfortable with some of the things you will read about my life, but that's on you. I will no longer discard pieces of my life in order to make those around me more comfortable. Finally, if I offend anyone with my words, too bad. As much as I am tempted to pre-apologize, I am aware that would be specious.

For Crystal and Keith Bailey,
without you this story wouldn't be possible.

I

HOW DOES YOUR GARDEN GROW?

Chapter 1

AND WE'RE FINE

Summer, 1994. San Antonio, Texas.

It was seven months after *"Don't Ask, Don't Tell"* became the official stance concerning gays in the military and I came out of the closet. I must admit it was mostly a story-book occasion; especially considering it was 1994, about a month before my eighteenth birthday and about two months after I graduated high school. I only lost one friend and my parents were incredibly accepting. Ironically, the only person who asked me if it was a "phase" was my sister. A lesbian. A lesbian who never really had to come out. The first person I told was the dungeon master of my *Dungeons & Dragons* group. Oh yeah, I'm that kind of a geek. Okay, to be fair, yes, I'm a geek, but Murry, he was "that" kind of a geek.

Murry and I were never particularly close, but he was an energetic, little goblin of a man who was dedicated to providing his company an incredible gaming experience. Unlike every other previous gaming group I had been part of, this one was a sizeable fellowship, so that was an amazing feat. Gaming was so important to me, and the experience was so ridiculously fun. Mostly because of Murry. Everyone that slew an evil wyvern, died a horrible death, or stopped some nefarious vampire's diabolical scheme in Ravenloft on those worn out couches and chairs – *I swear they were made of burlap and brillo pads* – had a connection with Murry. Murry plain rocked, once you looked beyond the stereotyped exterior.

When I say goblin of a man, I can't think of a more appropriate metaphor. He was maybe three-feet tall *–okay at least five feet, but he stood with a slight stoop which evaporated another few inches.* He was in his mid-twenties, with the hairline of a seventy-year-old, and Trump's repugnant comb-over. I understand it sounds cliché, but his glasses were quite literally held together with duct tape, and they constantly slid down his pock-scarred nose. His enormous ears were offset to the degree of Sloth from the *Goonies,* and they caused his large, black-framed, thick-assed lenses to hang at the most awkward angle. His undead pallor, round belly, spindly arms, and giant feet only contributed to the stereotype; one point to his favor: at least he showered. *Seriously, he was that kind of a dork.*

When I came out to Murry, I was terrified about how he would react. About a week before, I had my first gay experience, and it changed my life. And I am the kind of person who refuses to live a lie, so I had to tell someone. Once I had accepted this aspect of my identity, it was time to kick that door down. So, of course, you tell your best friend or your mother. Maybe a sibling or cousin. Someone you are close to, right? Nope, the logical choice is clearly your dungeon master.

After a rather short gaming session, my recently divorced, twenty-four-year-old, co-worker, and first-ever roommate took off to conquer his fifth or sixth piece of tail that week – *can't say I blamed them, he was hot, Human Torch hot.* I took advantage of any opportunity to spend time with him; his personality may have needed some work, but damn Dan was beautiful. We had ridden to Murry's together, but he was gone long before I realized.

I was without a ride. San Antonio is a giant city, but its mass transit sucked. Murry being the perpetual pleaser quickly offered to give me a ride to Amanda's apartment, to which I had a key; and who we all knew to be working that night as she had missed *D&D*. I didn't want to go to my place; I was certain Dan would be ass up on some woman on the couch, and as much as I usually enjoyed catching that glorious spectacle, my mind was consumed by my similar experience with Jerry five days earlier.

I didn't plan to tell Murry, but it happened before I put much thought into it. I knew Amanda always had some beer and booze, and drunkenness was calling to me like a new-born fawn that lost sight of its mother. I never asked where she got the hooch, as she was only eighteen, but there was always a drink to be found in that miniature, one-room efficiency apartment. I hadn't a single objection to partaking in her liquid wares. When he was curious about why I was going there rather than home, I invited Murry in for some drinks. I'm sure I was looking for some good old-fashioned liquid courage, and I was all but exploding with the need to share; because I really started guzzling the beer, and perceptive Murry realized something important was percolating in my mind. He started asking questions.

"What's up, man? You've been off in la-la land all night. You're usually an intense gamer." Murry eyed me through those glasses – *those glasses.* He had an intense presence that peaked in one-on-one conversations, especially if he could involve *D&D* in the agenda.

I took a shot of Jim Beam and shrugged my shoulders. I handed him a Shiner Bock and opened one for myself. Half of my beer disappeared before he could adjust his busted specs and refocus for the next question. He liked to ask questions. *I think it's a DM thing.*

I looked at him and belched loudly – *it's something I do.* "Excuse me," I quickly muttered. Before he could begin to form his next question, I downed the rest of that beer while pouring my next shot of Beam. *My multitasking functions can outpace Rosie the Robot when I decide to use them.*

A few more shots, a six-pack and about twenty minutes of rather benign questions, and Murry finally got to the point. "Does this have something to do with Gretchen's party?"

I shook my head, burped, and apologized, "Excuse me," for the forty-second time. I often belch when drinking beer or soda, but I will say *excuse me* every time – *Mom was always big on manners.*

For the past month, the entire gathering had been teasing Amanda, Dan, and me with the vigor of a pack of rabid bunnies from *Holy Grail.* All three of us were caught naked in the shower outrageously drunk. *That one doesn't count. Amanda tried to kiss me once, but eww she was my best friend, and some lines I will not cross. Sex with friends is near the apex of that list.* I had secretly wished that something would happen with Dan, but we were interrupted before things could get juicy.

For the first time since I met him, Murry got right to the point. His aim was off target – *Green Arrow, he wasn't* – but he didn't drag it out, "So you and Dan finally fucked, huh?"

He's lucky I was reaching into the fridge starting in on the six-pack of Natural Light. Amanda had the worst taste in beer, but she did keep Shiner Bock specifically for me. I spat the last of my Shiner Bock all over the interior, and I didn't bother cleaning it – *not that she'd notice.* That question cut, but my reply was as sharp as a +2 vorpal sword.

"Fuck. I wish." I couldn't hide the smile on my face. That thought often entered my head when I was alone in my room – yeah there was the internet, but porn over dial-up is nothing you want to experience. *Plus, I only watch if I'm wasted.* He might have read me right, but he was wrong about Dan. Dan was a wholly straight, misogynistic, douche bag with blond hair, blue eyes, excellent nose – *I have a thing for noses* – killer abs, ass for days, and a great dick. He was also a silent homophobe. He was the only person whom I had considered a real friend, that I lost when I came out.

"So, you're gay?" The endless questions. Especially since I felt my outburst had settled the matter.

I dodged the inquiry with the reflexes of Cat-Woman. "Why do you think Dan and I fucked?" I opened my second pack of Camel Lights for the day. *I chain smoke when I drink.*

"I dunno. You're both so attractive and outgoing, we all thought there was something going on between you two. And after Gretchen's party..." *I'm not ugly by any standard – I thought I was at the time – but trust me I was nowhere near Dan's level.*

I quickly interrupted with an answer I had been saying like a knock-off Discman stuck on repeat, since that night in the shower with Dan's naked chubby hanging in my face, "That was a Dan and Amanda thing. I don't even know how I got sucked into it." It was the absolute truth, so it follows that no one believed me.

"Yeah, I believe you," *sue me, I guess one person believed me.* "So, you're gay?" *Again, with the questions.* The alcohol had performed its duty better than any henchman, and it was time to be honest with myself and with Murry.

"More like bi. I met this dude, Jerry." Although it would be some time before I told my sister, I guess she was right about one thing. I did go through a phase, the 90s obligatory bi-phase – *don't misunderstand, "bi" is by no means a phase for everyone, but in the 90s almost every gay man I knew had a "bi" phase before "becoming" fully gay. It was a gentle transition into coming out of our personal closets.* It lasted all of a few days; the exact length of time until I next talked to Amanda.

My trepidation in telling Murry was ridiculous, we're talking a twentieth level bard casting a *Confusion* spell ridiculous. He asked so many more questions. Most answers seemed obvious, but I happily humored him. Excitement and relief began an epic battle through my body – I had finally told someone.

He told me he was honored that I told him first, but he warned me it might be better to keep it to a select minority in our fellowship. It was the 90s after all, and that wasn't my first real-world experience with *don't ask, don't tell*. Those weren't just some political buzzwords, and this policy wasn't simply a military thing. This concept shaped my entire young gay life in so many ways and still affects me to this day.

Chapter 2

R3WIND

Mid-1970s. Montana. Alaska. Texas.

With a couple of exceptions, my childhood was *Absolutely Fabulous.* No, not the drug-fueled, crazy antics of two, rich, middle-aged British women, but it was wonderful. My dad was an enlisted man, and my parents were terrible with their finances, but my sister and I never lacked anything we needed. Sure, we had Payless shoes, and K-Mart was the origin of the bulk of our clothes, but they were clean and the proper size. By no means were we rich, and often we bordered on destitute; not that my parents ever gave us the slightest indication.

Mom dropped out of high school and was a stay-at-home mom with odd jobs throughout the years. My mother is one of the strongest people I know, and most of the time she supported me in whatever I chose to do. We weren't white trash, and we weren't impoverished, but we weren't quite middle-class – *upper-lower class? Is that a thing?* Dad is a smart man and incredibly dedicated to everything he does. Family, life, work, hobbies. My nature is akin to his, but he never really seemed to have the drive to push forward. He has always been content to be a worker, and I have always felt he wasted his potential. He could have done anything, but don't misunderstand, he is the greatest man I know.

Dad grew up in a small town in Northern Montana in a very conservative family. Mom's roots are in the over-soaked Portland, Oregon area. Her family is also on the conservative side – *I'd say a seven out of ten compared to my paternal side's nine.* My parents might lean conservatively but compared to much of my extended family they may as well be hippies. That they found each other and made their way alone out into the world at a very young age is fitting; and when Dad, at twenty, married his seventeen-year-old bride and joined the military, I believe they both desired to escape their families. After a year of marriage, Mom gave birth to my sister. Two years later I joined the cacophony of humanity; our family was complete, and to my parents' credit they have managed to forge a continuing forty-five-year marriage that still appears healthy.

For the bulk of my early life, like many small children, I was enamored with my mother. She was my world, and for the most part, I would do anything to see her happy. She was affectionate and attentive, and she always had a way of making me feel special. I loved to ask her philosophical questions that absolutely drove her crazy. *Mom, if your favorite color is red and mine is blue, if we exchanged eyeballs would our favorite color change? How do you know that I really exist? Couldn't I just be in your imagination? If Dad were someone else, would I still be me?* And really tough ones like, *why do you love me?* She would always just laugh and smile that authentic grin that warmed my insides like I could breathe dragon fire. She would tell me they were great questions, but she rarely had an answer for me. Except for the last one, to that, she always had an answer: *"Why do I love you J.T.? Because you are the greatest son anyone could ever ask for."* I'm telling you she was – *and still is* – an amazing woman.

Part of what made Mom so wonderful was that she was a bitch. She was loyal to a fault, protective to the nth degree, intimidating when necessary, and vicious when confronted. Mom spoke her mind without a single reservation and didn't care if you were offended – *a trait I am happy to have inherited.* She is quite possibly the most powerful person I have ever met, and she is worthy of the admiration exhibited to Captain America. She was most definitely not the type of person you wanted to cross, and when you did get on her bad side, all you wanted to do was slink away and hide in the sewers like some kind of mutant Morlock.

She was dedicated to raising her children well and was as quick with punishing bad behavior, as with offering the needed hug after a miserable day. She gave her entire self to her commitment to providing my sister and me with all the tools we needed to be happy, productive adults. *Mom, if I have never told you, thank you for all your sacrifices.*

Dad has always been a man of few words, but when he did speak up, I guarantee you'd stop and listen. Like Mom, he was loyal and dedicated to his family, and it was always obvious that he loved me. However, I don't know if he ever particularly liked me– *the two of us have entirely different interests and never quite clicked on a friendship level.* Still, when the chips are down, my dad is the first person I turn to for advice and help. I have aspired to be as much like him as possible, and I can think of no better role model. Dad is the most reliable person on the face of the planet; a true superhero. Just like Colossus, he would gladly give his life to save his own from the Legacy Virus.

He has the worst case of resting bitch face I have ever seen, and that scowl coupled with his extreme reticence to speech caused every single friend who ever met him to ask: *Does your dad hate me? Why is he so scary? Is he as mean as he looks? I don't have to talk to him, do I?* I swear they thought he was Dr.

Doom. Once any of them got to know him though, thoughts like that were quickly discarded. *My dad's a teddy bear.*

I could write an entire book about my parents, they are such interesting humans, but that's not the story I promised. What I have shared though is essential and suffice it to say I inherited what I find to be the best of their qualities. I'm loyal and dedicated. I can be quiet and thoughtful, but just like my mother, I am scarier than Galactus if you piss me off. I'm also an unapologetic bitch, and I will speak my mind without any care to consequences and will always stand up for the things I believe in. I've often wondered why bitch carries such negative connotations when used to describe a woman. Think of a female dog; all her qualities are admirable.

Chapter 3

IN THE BLOOD

Summer 1994. San Antonio, Texas.

Murry couldn't seem to follow his own advice. After sharing with him and beginning to come to terms with a fundamental shift in perspective, I promptly passed out on Amanda's couch. He immediately called her at work and disclosed to her what was mine alone. The first person to confront me, however, was not her. I didn't see her for a few days, as we were working opposite schedules, and there were no cell phones – well there were, but they were large bricks, and only the wealthy owned them.

There were still payphones on every corner, and everyone had a pager; it's how we communicated. Every group of friends had tons of codes that followed their own number. *For example, mine was 09, so if I was hanging at Denny's drinking coffee and I wanted Amanda to get me cigs, I would dial her pager and press 091111115 – all the 1s looked like individual cigarettes and the 5 an "s." I would call again and hit 09332 – not sure where that one came from, but it meant "meet at the Denny's by Gretchen's". If you added a 911 at the end, it meant to hurry the fuck up. See kids, we had texting long before you "invented" it.*

I awoke and called Dan for a ride long before Amanda returned home – she was going through her "slut" phase, so who knows where she spent that night. *Don't misunderstand, I don't believe in slut shaming. More power to anyone who uses their own body in any way they desire.*

She spent the next few days paging any applicable code followed by endless 911s, and we played endless rounds of phone tag during this period. I had no idea that Murry had told her anything, and I thought she was being needy. *She could be so clingy.* Nothing felt out of the ordinary.

It seems Amanda had as few reservations concerning boundaries as I did when attacking her liquor. She took it upon herself to tell Dan, and she later revealed she only thought it was fair he knew since we lived together. When she told Dan, she hadn't even talked to me about it yet.

After a double shift (including graveyard) at I.H.O.P, I finally walked through my apartment door around noon. I was exhausted and on my second day of a hangover after my bender with Murry. The air-conditioner was blasting, and I wanted to curl up under my thick-down comforter. I would have dashed to my bed like Quicksilver if my feet didn't feel like Jell-O. I had just stripped out of a uniform that smelled like waffles and grease – I was too tired for a shower – and lied down naked in an igloo of an apartment. Then I heard the dead-bolt turn at the front door.

In seconds Dan was pounding on my bedroom door, and I was on my feet stark naked when he rolled in like the Juggernaut – *since that day, I've never been able to sleep nude.*

"What the fuck! Are you fucking kidding me?" he said when he saw me.

I thought he was just giving me shit about standing there with both hands covering my cock and balls, and I didn't even notice the anger in his voice. The air-conditioner was blasting on my ass and upper thighs, and I hate to be cold. "Fuck, man.

I've been working the last thirteen hours. Go away. Need sleep. So cold. Blue Knight needs blankets badly." *Yes, I geek-speak from my mouth too.*

He shoved me on the bed and screamed, "I should kick your ass, man. I should fucking kill you!"

"Whoa. What the fuck is going on?" I started dressing as soon as I got back on my feet. I had no idea where this was going, and in no multiverse did I think he had heard I was gay already. It hadn't even been forty-eight hours since I had admitted it to anyone, and less than a week since accepting it myself.

"Yeah, put some fucking clothes on, faggot. I don't wanna see your dick get hard when I kick your ass. What the fuck man? That's why you like to watch me on the couch, ain't it?"

I wasn't about to remind him that I always went straight to my room, or that he was *always* on the couch fucking. He couldn't bring himself to use his bed – *I think it was the only thing he had left after the divorce.* And under no circumstance was I going to point out the number of times he had asked me to join in. I still hadn't pieced together that gossip amongst our fellowship jumped minds faster than the Stepford Cuckoos.

"Slow down, Dan. I don't know what you're talkin' about. I sure as hell am not going to fight you." I really wanted the situation to simmer down. Dan's eyes were seething as he watched me buckle my belt.

"Amanda fucking told me," those eyes, I'd never seen anything so crazed – if he flashed a giant smile, he would have looked like the Joker. "That's why you weaseled your way into the shower, isn't it?"

"That was a Dan and Amanda thing. I don't even know how I got sucked into it." Yes, I spoke to him in the third person, I honestly had been repeating that phrase so much it was automatic.

"Fuck you! You wanted to suck my dick. Admit it."

He wasn't wrong, but I was starting to lose my cool. And I still was in the dark. "You're the one who dangled it in my face when we held the door closed. Looks like you're the fag to me."

"You better watch it, or there's gonna be a good old-fashioned gay bashing in your room."

"Bring it on bitch. Maybe I'll let you suck my dick after I kick your ass. You may be pretty, but you ain't too bright." *Whoops, wrong words.*

He came at me with the ferocity of Wendigo. He was out for blood.

I'm not a fighter, in fact, this was the only real scuffle I had ever participated in, and it didn't last long. As Dan charged looking like he was going to tackle me, I swung wildly with my right hand and connected with his left eye. His momentum carried us into my dresser, and I smacked my head rather soundly. With my ears ringing, I began swinging wildly at his face while kneeing him in the stomach. He caught me with a right hook on my cheek and cut me with his ring – *I still have a small scar beside my nose from this brawl* – and my righteous fury ignited. The dynamic was quickly reversed, and I found myself on top repeatedly punching his face. And as quickly as it started, it ended. He was curled up covering his face, and I was spent. I just stopped.

Calmly, I stood up and quietly told him, "Yeah, I'm gay, bitch. And you just got your ass handed to you by a faggot."

Scurrying to the door, he turned to me with a look that dripped hatred. He had a swollen lip, bloody nose, and a light, greenish color starting to surround his left eye. "You tell any-one about this, and I'm gonna tell 'em you're a faggot. And I'll tell them you suck my dick while I'm sleeping. I'll destroy all of your friendships." Another dose of *don't ask, don't tell*, and it was a hard pill to swallow. Dan was an asshole, but the two of us had been friends.

Neither of us told any of our friends about this incident as far as I know. The last words he said to me were, "Get your shit and get the fuck out. You got 'til the end of the day."

"Fine by me." I wasn't on the lease and I sure as hell wasn't going to spend any more time with him than necessary. Those eyes indicated he was seriously considering grabbing a knife and stabbing me.

Chapter 4

JE NE M'EN SOUVIENS PAS

Summer 1981. Malmstrom A.F.B, Great Falls, Montana.

My first encounter with the dreaded *don't ask, don't tell* atrocity happened at an extremely early age and is one of my earliest memories. It was a terrible event that occurred the summer before I started kindergarten or maybe the summer before that, and to be honest, I didn't even realize I had buried it until I was in my mid-thirties – *we're talking levels of denial bordering on Mr. Fantastic's belief he is a good family man.* In fact, as I write these words, there is exactly one person I have shared this with, my mom. And to be completely forthright, I would never even have talked to her about it if I wasn't seeking clarification. Even my partner of almost twenty years will be shocked when he reads this chapter – *but I promised truth.*

I was molested by a neighborhood, teenage boy multiple times when we were living in Great Falls, Montana at Malmstrom Air Force Base. I don't remember the boy's name, and I'm not sure I ever knew it, but I will never forget his face. He had dark hair cut in a short, military style. He had a prominent brow with thick eyebrows that came very close to becoming a caterpillar. He had a pointy chin and razor-sharp cheekbones. His lips were plump, and they were the color of a soft-pink rose petal – *women pay all sorts of money on this particular shade of lipstick.* And his breath always smelled of Doritos and Shasta Cola. All-in-all he was a relatively normal looking boy of fourteen or fifteen, but his otherwise forgettable and mundane appearance housed a monster that even the Justice League of America would consider a challenge.

We lived on base, and it was the early 80s; parents weren't quite the overly watchful creatures we find today. The neighborhood was quiet and safe – *well, mostly* – and it was filled with kids that often played near their house without a parent boring a hole in the back of their head like Cyclops without his ruby-quartz visor. It really was a different time, and the fact that we lived on a military base provided an extra level of comfort and security. Except for this one boy, I have never had any other nefarious encounters on a base. *And before you ask, no, I don't blame my parents for "letting" this happen.* I wouldn't trade a single thing from my childhood – *not even this.*

My mom was always very attentive and checked on me regularly when I was outside playing; additionally, there was almost always a mother with her head poked out a window or door keeping an eye on all the neighborhood ruffians. *For those of you who aren't military brats, there is something you must understand about neighborhoods on bases. Base housing was generally for the soldiers who had families; the single men and women typically lived in the barracks or off base. There were only so many houses to go around, and those with families got preferential treatment. This simple fact meant that every home in the neighborhood contained at least one child, and as such there were lots and lots of kids – think Multiple Man in a demolition derby.* Every parent knew the other parents were also keeping an eye on the meandering vagabonds, but of course, kids learn how to recognize when there is no adult supervision.

I was never allowed to go farther than two houses left or right from 49 Birch Street, and under no circumstance was I to cross the street. And I followed my parents' rules – which served me well my entire childhood – I learned that if I did what was expected, I was given more freedoms, and I liked autonomy. It is quite unfortunate that the boy in question – *let's call him Mephisto* – lived two doors to the left of our duplex, so within my approved exploration zone.

Even as a small child, I was never one to want for companionship. *I strike up conversations easily and am quite personable. I listen intently when people are talking to me, and I engage with them – my mom calls it the gift of gab.* While I have had tons of acquaintances over the years – enough to fill a dozen bags of holding – I have had few friends. I was also entirely content to be on my own and gifted at entertaining myself. I liked to explore because I have always been inspired by the most innocuous things.

Seconds before my first encounter with Mephisto, I had already become great friends with his family's dog. He was a giant, fluffy, lovable Saint Bernard, and the moment we laid eyes on each other we were buddies. When Mephisto came running into the yard hollering at my newest, best friend before I could pet him, I quickly understood he wasn't a friendly dog. *But I have met many mean dogs in my lifetime that have loved me the moment we met. I think he was the first, and I really wish I could remember his name. I do recall he was a boy, though I'm not sure how.*

I quickly apologized for getting – *hmm, Sasquatch feels right* – in trouble. I asked Mephisto if it was okay if I played with that magnificent beast. He told me he would have to ask his mom, but I should probably go home, so he didn't get in trouble. I apologized and headed off to look under a bush that had caught my attention before my first, fateful gaze at that pup.

I could be quite dogged when I wanted something, and I wanted to play with Sasquatch desperately. So, the next time I was allowed outside to play, I marched right to Sasquatch's house and rang the doorbell. Mephisto's mom answered, and after a somewhat confused conversation, we arrived at an agreement. I was given permission to play with Sasquatch, whenever I wanted, after she watched over our first interaction. It was as wonderful as my second encounter with Mephisto was terrifying.

Looking back, I find it humorous that a Saint Bernard would ever need a doghouse, especially considering he was usually in-side the family home. Sasquatch had his own giant condo nes-tled up under a large pine tree with an entrance that couldn't be seen without some bending and stretching. Some days later, I ran to what was *–for sadly a short time –* my favorite spot on Malmstrom Air Force Base. And of course, I was disappointed when I didn't see Sasquatch waiting for me; but once I had spotted the doghouse for the first time, I always checked it if I didn't see him in the yard.

This particularly warm and windy, summer day was an average one for the area. The grass in the yards was green, and there were dandelions and clover flowers littered through-out the bright fields. White fluffy clouds wandered across the enormous firmament. *There's a reason they call Montana: Big Sky Country.* After poking my head in what became my first personal hell, I scurried away from the tree and turned around smacking face first into Mephisto's crotch. Mephisto wasn't an obvious demon, he was actually incredibly friendly and started chatting with me. I thought he was fascinating, as kids his age don't generally talk to a four-year-old that isn't family. *My first impressions of people are often wrong, and this was no exception.*

He convinced me to go into the doghouse with him, and rather quickly he had his erect penis poking out of his unfastened, button-fly Levi's. I noticed the tip was the same pink as his lips. When he told me to stroke it, I didn't understand, so he grabbed my hand and gave me quick instructions. That wasn't enough; he convinced me to put it in my mouth. *As a kid, I liked to make people happy, so I don't think he had to try hard.* He proceeded to jam it down my throat until my throat was raw, and he had finished. My throat was in agony, and I was sure that I had done something wrong, but Mephisto hugged me and told me what a great job I had done and how proud he was of me.

Praise like that went to my head, and confusion quickly overwhelmed me. He was quite clear that I was to tell no one what had happened, but I don't remember exactly what he said. I only remember that I was scared to death that if I revealed this encounter something awful would happen – *and I don't want to fabricate a convincing argument. That's a headspace I don't want to travel in.*

There were a number of these "sessions," and they generally went the same way. My throat always hurt horribly, and the cum that coated it only made it sting worse, but he still somehow made me feel both ashamed and happy that I had pleased him. And the draw of Sasquatch always brought me back to that yard. These encounters never lasted more than four or five minutes, and if not for that I'm sure my mom would have discovered this monster. *And he would be dead, and I would have grown up with an incarcerated mother.*

Finally, we got caught in the act, and the confusion about this incident was what elicited my questions to my mom. *Once this memory began to bubble its way to my surface thoughts, I had thought it was my mom who had caught us, but after talking to her, I have come to realize it was Mephisto's mom.* I remember her being extremely angry and yelling at both of us. After admonishing Mephisto all the way to the back door of his house – *I'd like to think she was smacking the shit out of him, but that doesn't seem right* – she came back and had a little conversation with me. She told me calmly that this was all my fault and if I told anyone about it, I would never get to play with Sasquatch again. So long as I maintained my silence, I would be allowed to play with him, and she promised Mephisto would never touch nor talk to me again, *a promise I am happy she kept.* That sounded like a win-win to my young ears. *I don't know that I blame her, after all, she was a mother looking out for her own.* "Don't ask, don't tell", more than a decade before Clinton uttered those loathsome words.

A not so fun fact about me. As a child living in Great Falls, I came down with strep throat numerous times – and numerous is a gross understatement. Additionally, after we moved from there, every time I have returned to the area and spent more than a day, I have come down with the same illness. I now wonder if strep throat can be a psychosomatic occurrence.

Chapter 5

WOUNDED

Summer, 1994. San Antonio, Texas.

Reeling from my first physical altercation, dealing with a growing lump on the back of my head, and feeling unbalanced due to sleep deprivation, I began packing my things. Luckily, I was young and only brought *important* items with me when I first left home; the bulk of my possessions never left my room thirty miles west of San Antonio. I had no clue what to do. The only thing I knew for certain was that I didn't want to go home.

When I had decided to move out, Mom was adamantly against it. It was Dad that had convinced her that I should be able to make my own way. *My parents are great and all, but I wanted freedom.* I would have lived on the streets before I tucked my tail and went home, especially considering it hadn't even been sixty days. I sure as hell wasn't going to tell them what had happened between Dan and me.

I had been paging Amanda constantly once I heard Dan leave the apartment, and each of them was followed by countless 911s, but she never called me back. *Typical.* She was my best friend, however, and I did have a key, so I figured I would take my stuff to her teeny-tiny apartment and make my next decision after getting away from the monster I had been fantasizing about for months.

By the time I unloaded my car, I was exhausted both emotionally and physically – *it was like I had just discovered a mutant power that went out of control.* I threw myself onto her disgusting couch, and I think I was asleep before I landed. I was out of Dan's within a few hours – *and I'm slightly embarrassed by my pettiness. I dropped my key in the garbage disposal and left the front door wide open, hoping he'd be robbed* – so it was late afternoon when I finally caught some much-needed shut-eye. It didn't last long though, Amanda was home from work by five.

All of my possessions were scattered around the apartment, I hadn't bothered stacking them neatly, so when Amanda pushed open the door with her giant ass, she didn't notice anything. *Amanda's ass should have had its own zip code. It was huge, and it was a huge source of her self-esteem. She loved her large posterior and used it to great effect.* She had picked up some guy at work, and they were wrapped up in each other as they stepped in. She was facing the outside world and promptly fell backwards over a box pulling the guy right down on my Super Nintendo, destroying it in the process. *That Nintendo was my Mjolnir. I became lost without it.*

"What the hell was that?" She quickly scanned the room and noticed the piles as well as my body lying motionless on her couch. She shook me by my shoulders and didn't realize I was already awake – *sleep had become an elusive dream.*

"Oh. Dan didn't take it well, I see."

I may be bright when it comes to school, but I could be rather dense when it came to social concerns. Even though during our altercation Dan screamed at me that he heard about my sexuality from Amanda, I was still confused about the entire matter. I still hadn't pieced together that Murry had told Amanda, and Amanda, Dan. When packing, I tried to decipher the puzzle – *it was like one of Murry's campaigns. Empty room except for an hourglass, and a single door with three locks. Go!* – but I think the lack of sleep was working against me – *at least that's the story I'm going with, then I don't look so stupid.*

"Huh?" I replied in a fog. I then noticed the guy who was clearly grossed out by Amanda's poor housekeeping skills. "Who're you?" I asked.

Before he could open his mouth, Amanda interrupted, "Don't worry about him. He's just here to fuck. Hopefully, he lasts longer than the last guy." Yeah, she was blunt like that. If she brought a guy home and it was just for sex, she wouldn't bother talking to him. To her, it was just a piece of meat. "I take it Dan was upset, huh? Did he kick you out?"

In my mind, Amanda still didn't know. It was like I was in some parallel universe. "Yeah. He kicked me out. I don't wanna talk about it. I just wanna sleep."

"Oh, we're going to talk about it." After a brief pause, she added, "After I'm done with this hot piece of tail, we are so talking." *She had the worst taste in men, at least physically. In no multiverse would I have characterized this troll as a hot piece of tail.*

Her apartment was a reverse of the Tardis. It looked large from the outside but was about the size of a bright blue "call box" inside. Amanda's little apartment had a bedroom. *Sort of.* It was a separate room, about the size of a walk-in closet, but there was no door separating it from the "living" space. *The only reason to enter that lair was to get to the tiny bathroom.* There was no expectation of privacy in that shoebox, not even in the bathroom. Even with the shower running.

It wasn't the last time I would have to hear some guy grunting on top of her – *but damn this guy was loud, and he was really into the dirty-talk.* She was wrong about him though, he didn't last longer than the previous. Within a couple of minutes, he got quiet, and she started laughing at him. "I thought you could go forever. That's what you promised when I sucked your dick at work. You said it might be small, but you knew how to use it. Get the fuck out of my apartment. Waste of my fucking time is all you are."

Her laughter never stopped. *Yeah, she wasn't very nice to men once she got what she wanted out of them. I thought it was one of her greatest strengths.* It was easy for our friends to judge Amanda's behavior, for the most part, they were all repulsed by her objectification of men. She had complete control of her sexual life, and she didn't buy into outdated patriarchal ideals. If Amanda were a man, she would have been praised by this same group of ultra-dorks.

Grabbing two beers, she brought them back to the couch, and lifted my ankles, rotated my body, and dropped my feet to the floor. She flopped down as she handed me a longneck. "I'm pretty unhappy with you," she said quietly while avoiding my gaze.

"What? Why? I'm sorry I brought all my shit here, but I wasn't sure where else to go, and I had to get out of there."

"Not that, jackass. You can stay here as long as you want." She grew silent, staring at her beer.

"Umm, okay. I'm lost and so goddamned tired. What the hell is going on today?"

"Seriously? Murry? You told Murry before you told me? Do you have any idea how that makes me feel?" *Yep, she was playing the victim card; after being the catalyst for my first fight.*

"I didn't mean to tell Murry. It just kind of happened," the pleaser in me was creating excuses.

"He told me you were bi," she finally looked at me for the first time. Initially, I was expecting her to freak out like Dan. I thought for sure I was going to lose all my friends. The expression on her face, however, spoke volumes. I could tell she was hurt not to be the first, genuinely hurt. I don't think she ever considered how I was feeling, but it was quite evident that my being gay changed absolutely nothing between us.

"To be honest, I think I'm gay. I don't think girls are for me."

"But you've had girlfriends. Skye and I were pretty good friends, and she told me y'all had sex all the time."

"So? That's just sex."

"Then how do you know you're gay? If you do girls, you're straight."

I just looked at her. I wasn't sure how I should answer. At the time her argument seemed logical, but she didn't know about Jerry. I knew I was done with women.

"Oh wait. You met someone, didn't you? Did you get busy with some guy? Why haven't you told me, and don't think I'm letting you off the hook about not telling me first. I thought you were my best friend, that's not what best friends do." *Nope, instead, they guilt trip someone who is going through a complicated time and make it all about themselves. Looking back, I can't believe I didn't tell her exactly which hole she could shove it in, but I was happy that someone I cared about didn't seem to care that I was gay. Instead, she was mad that I hadn't come out the "correct way."*

I probably should have been mad at Murry as well for sharing what was mine alone, but I really didn't care; I had been working myself up trying to decipher a way to tell Amanda, so I didn't have to stress over that any longer. I still hadn't realized that Amanda told Dan either, or at least I squashed it down. I didn't want to open that can of worms, and if I brought it up then, she likely would have gotten defensive. Amanda on the defense was like Gandalf confronting the Balrog – *you shall not pass.*

Chapter 6

MISUNDERSTOOD

1980s. Montana. Alaska. Texas.

Siblings have complicated relationships – *rarely are they as picturesque as Sue and Jonny Storm's* – and growing up in the military complicates this dynamic. My sister truly is incredible, but she has her own skeletons. She was at the same time my best friend, worst enemy, biggest supporter, and the partial root of all my insecurities regarding body issues. But most importantly, she was always there.

Although Dad wasn't forced to relocate often, we did move several times especially when we were young kids. But growing up in the military meant someone was always leaving. Friendships in the military were short-lived and quickly made, but they burned brilliantly for a short time – Jubilee and her firework powers. *I treasure every friend I have made, and just because we fall apart doesn't mean they weren't important. One becomes accustomed to letting go of them, it's the nature of growing up in the armed services.* But my sister, she was always there.

She has some fantastic qualities, and when we were younger, I thought she was the coolest thing on the planet. She was my Bat Man. I always thought she never cared what others thought about her, I was wrong, but she was excellent at giving that impression; I aspired to be just like her in that respect. She also has a huge heart that she hides behind a resting bitch face she modeled after Dad's. She has a soft spot for orphaned creatures, both the animal and human ones. She was always quick to bring home a stray pup or kitten that was moments from death's embrace; and as we got older, our holidays were often joined by some friend of hers that had been disowned by their family – *usually, because they were gay.* Mom and Dad always made them feel welcomed, and Mom was quick to pick up an extra present or two, so they had something to unwrap on Christmas morning. My sister has always had a need to fix people; she surrounds herself with some of the most broken people I have ever met, and she puts her entirety into repairing them – think Forge meets Cyborg. *When I say her entirety, I really mean it. When she has a project – read person – that is worthy of her attention, she will ignore all her other relationships.*

Most of the time my sister and I got along rather well. *We always have.* I endeavored to make her laugh as often as I could. *When she genuinely laughs, she is at her best; it's when she lowers her guard and stops worrying about keeping the cool façade.* Making her laugh was one of my greatest joys, and I think I had a knack for it.

She liked to tease me mercilessly, and as often as she could. I learned at an early age that this was mostly done out of love, so it rarely got to me. If she wasn't teasing me, I figured I had pissed her off. She also knew how to push my rage button. She could enrage me as easily and often as the Thing says, *It's Clobberin' Time.* That, however, was a two-way street. I could get under her skin without an effort, but still, we hung out regularly; so long as she wasn't obsessing over some friend or love interest.

We suffered from the most one-sided case of sibling rivalry ever. With few exceptions, the things she excelled at were things I found abhorrent. She was great at sports and was a hipster. It didn't matter what the current fad was, she was on top of it, but unlike most hipsters, she actually was cool. I was always a nerdly little dork of a kid – *Brainy Smurf levels* – and I never competed with her. For some reason, she always had to be better than me at anything I did apart from school. *She is not stupid, she is quite insightful, but school was not for her.* In this area, she never challenged me. It was the only thing she allowed me to feel good about.

When we lived in Alaska, we both took up skiing, and we both owned the slopes. I can't remember a single skiing trip where I didn't get told a few hundred times by her how much better she was. It was constant.

Truth be told, I may have been a better skier; and if I was, it wasn't by much. Assuredly, I was far more daring than she. I attacked every jump I saw, would ride the slopes on one ski while the other was propped over my shoulder, ski backward, and sit on the back of my skis regularly as I flew down the mountain. Once when we were taking on a black diamond slope at Alyeska, I even flew off a forty-foot cliff because I thought it was a jump. She never performed those shenanigans, but she could ski as well as –*usually better than* – anyone else we encountered. Any sport she played, she was one of the best on the team. *I did tell you she never had to come out of the closet, didn't I.* For me it was never about which of us could ski better, we skied differently. For her, she needed to continually remind me how much better she was. I think she liked telling me this more than she enjoyed the skiing.

She did this same thing in so many other ways too. Anytime I started to excel at anything – *through determination that would outshine Frodo* – she would begin to tear down my confidence. She loved to point out anyone that was better than me if it wasn't herself; this was a common tactic. There was one thing she often said, to my friends and hers alike, and over time it really started to affect me.

It all started one Halloween when she was in junior high. I don't remember my costume, but hers I recall with complete accuracy. That year she dressed up as a mobster, complete with bowler hat, pin-striped suit and tie, and a patchy little mustache that she glued on meticulously. She spent hours in front of the mirror, perfecting the illusion. Sure, the fake lip-crawler looked fake, but that didn't detract from the image. She practiced strutting and sitting and standing like a man, and sure, it was overly dramatic, but she pulled it off. She looked like a teenage boy costumed as a mobster.

We were going to some rec-center dance or party or some other silly event geared for the age group, and she was dedicated to convincing everyone she was a boy. I don't know if she was successful – we didn't spend any more time than the car ride there together that night – but she told me something that would be repeated to this day. She stared me down and said, "I make a better-looking guy than you do." This wasn't a phrase meant for my ear alone, nor was she stingy with it – oh no, she would tell this to anyone who would listen. Her friends. My friends. People we had just met, "Don't you think I'm hotter than my brother? I make a better-looking dude." I never understood this obsession. *Still don't.* The only thing as consistent as the question was the typical response. Uncomfortable silence.

I was a late bloomer and didn't experience my first crush until high school. *Yeah, I had girlfriends and my first kiss in junior high, but it was all an act that I was replicating by watching my friends.* Once I became concerned about body image, my sister was right there to squash any budding confidence like a poor Goomba caught under Super Mario's butt. *You have a huge ass* – to be fair, I did have a bubble butt that suddenly vanished in my mid-20s – *Your face is ugly, you wish you had my face. Those zits are huge. You could never get a hot girl.* You get the idea. This was an almost daily occurrence, and it didn't take long before I believed her. I think she saw it as the innocuous teasing she had been doing for years; to that I was immune, and I don't think she knew how it affected me. I thought I was the ugliest guy on the planet. *I know, I know, tons of adolescents feel the exact same way, it was just that I was hearing it from my own brain and from my sister's mouth at the same time. Easy sell.*

She wasn't a monster though. As quick as she put me down, and as often as she teased me, I was her Danger Room, and hers alone. She could destroy me all she wanted, but she never was the type to share. She was fiercely protective if anyone teased or mistreated me.

One of my earliest memories was at a playground on Malmstrom AFB. Mom let her take me there, and I wanted to go on the big slide, a feat I had yet to perform. I followed her up the ladder; and after she reached the bottom, I became petrified and started crying. I locked up and just stood at the top, gripping the bars. She tried to encourage me to slide down, but I was on the verge of hysterics. The boy that had climbed up behind me eventually got tired of this nonsense, and he pushed me over the side. *Okay, it was a big slide to me, but it couldn't have been very tall because I quickly got to my feet.*

Once my sister realized I wasn't hurt, she stood at the bottom of the slide and waited for the little bastard. Once he reached the bottom, she beat the living shit out of him. She then calmly grabbed my hand and walked me home without saying a word. *She really was my Bat Man then. I often get the impression that she thinks I judge her, but she's wrong. Although she can make terrible decisions, they are hers alone to make. I don't judge her. I love her.*

Chapter 7

FALLING APART

Summer, 1994. San Antonio, Texas.

Amanda and I sat on the couch and chatted for quite some time, and every few minutes she would bring up how hurt she was, and she didn't seem at all concerned about what had happened earlier that day at Dan's apartment; evidence of our altercation was evident. She didn't ask, and I never told.

I sat and listened to her talk about how me being gay affected her. At no point during this conversation did she ask how it affected me – *to be fair it was more of a supervillain's monologue since I never spoke.* After a few beers and a shared joint, I finally fell asleep as she was droning on about how her parents were going to react, who we – *we, not me* – should tell at *D&D*, and what guys she brought home were going to think about her having a gay roommate. Selfishness, Mr. Freeze style. Fortunately, she had gotten it out of her system by the time I woke up.

I headed towards the bathroom and stepped right on the used condom that I assume was dropped by the troll, after the verbal lashing, he took from Amanda. *Gross.* Amanda never cleaned. *Never.* I doubt that would be the only used condom found if I decided to excavate her "bedroom" – I avoided that place like the Savage Land. Hopping the rest of the way on one foot, I fell in the bathroom smashing into the stackable washer/ dryer combo that dominated the cereal-box-sized lavatory. *I'm a klutz. At least this time it was the front of my skull. The other lump, caused by the collision with my dresser after being attacked by Dan, was starting to make me look like Mojo Jojo.*

Stepping out of the shower, I realized I had forgotten to grab a "clean" towel. My only concern, pre-shower, was: wash foot. I eyed the towel hanging on the back of the door and shivered; I didn't want to share Amanda's. Channeling Longshot's luck powers, I opened the dryer and found a load of fluffy, clean towels. Not entirely lucky, I discovered the load in the dryer only contained hand towels. Searching, I finally found one that barely wrapped around my waist. Exiting the bathroom, I grabbed the towel hanging on the door to drop over that condom. *I wasn't touching it, and I sure as hell didn't want to step on it again.*

I was digging in a box for some clean boxers when Amanda and another guy walked through the front door. Like being caught in a tractor-beam, my eyes started on his feet, meandered their way up and settled on his nose. Damn! What a nose, it was perfect and became the standard of comparison when Amanda and I checked out guys. I don't recall a single other detail, and his name became Nose.

"He is cute," Nose whispered – *loudly* – to Amanda. *I might not slut shame, but I'm not going to hop into bed with some dude offered up by my slut friend.* She was never good at giving presents, she always gave what she wanted to receive.

"Um, what?" I was feeling very self-conscious standing there in nothing but a small green towel that barely covered me; it provided even less coverage than Namor's costume.

Amanda rolled her eyes at Nose and turned to smile at me. "He's bi. You can go first if you want?"

"Or all together?" Nose chimed in, eliciting another eye roll. *She really didn't like it when the meat talked.*

"Um, what?" *I really need to stop repeating myself.*

Nose walked towards me and reached for the towel.

"Um, what?" *Where did she find these guys?* "No, no, no, no, no, no. Just no. You two have fun, but no." The fourth person to learn I was gay was a stranger, a stranger who's only lasting impression is that of nasal perfection.

"Yeah, I'm outta here. Freaks." *Maybe he wasn't as bad as I initially thought.*

"No work tonight?" she asked as she started stripping out of her clothes. "I need a shower," *truer words have never been spoken.* She completely ignored Nose as he left. She retrieved the towel I had dropped on the floor, noticed the condom, and kicked it under her bed. *I was wrong, she did clean.*

I found some shorts and a t-shirt. My boxers were buried somewhere in the dragon's hoard – *freeballing it is.* I wanted another beer. In the past three days, I imbibed more than all my high school years combined; pot had always been more my speed. Channeling Longshot again, I was excited to see a twelve-pack of Shiner Bock. I downed one, belched loudly and grabbed the Jim Beam bottle, a dirty shot glass, and another beer, then headed to the couch to sulk.

The past twelve hours had been surreal, not to mention coming out to Murry just days before. Exposed to three people without my consent or knowledge. Got in my first fight. Lost a good friend. Whacked my head – twice. Face cut and scarred. Packed and moved. Stepped on a used condom. Almost got molested by the sexiest nose I have ever seen. And still, no one had asked me about Jerry, and that was all I wanted to talk about.

Amanda exited the bathroom with that disgusting towel wrapped around her head and a stained robe. "Grab me a beer, and tell me about this guy you met,"

Finally...

Chapter 8

THE KILLER INSIDE

Various, 1980s – Early-1990s. Montana.

I've only hated one person in my life. True hatred. Compared to Mephisto, she was Thanos, her evilness was on a galactic scale. She hated me too, and she hated me first. I will never know why, but we both put on our happy faces when around the family. Most would characterize her as a bitch, but as I said those are all positive traits.

To put it simply, this extended family member abused me whenever we were alone or out of earshot from the rest of the family. Physical. Mental. Emotional. The trifecta. It wasn't a constant thing, but it was insidious.

She is almost solely responsible for all my insecurities that aren't image related. She loved to tell me that I would never accomplish anything. I would never be anyone. I never finished anything I started. I was worthless. She wished my mom had an abortion – *from a staunch conservative*. My dad wasn't my real dad. Mom never wanted me. You're dumb as shit – *she never used curse words unless we were alone* – you only get straight A's because you're a suck up. You only do anything to show up your sister.

After visiting for my sister's graduation, when we were forced to hug goodbye, she whispered, "Don't think we're coming back here for yours. You'll never amount to anything; this world would be better if you were dead." She then flashed her forced, weaselly, more-frown-than-smile, smile my way and climbed into the RV.

I was not at all sad when I learned she had died.

Chapter 9

SILLY FOOL

Summer, 1994. San Antonio, Texas.

It was about twenty minutes before the end of my shift, and I hadn't made shit for tips. Tuesday graveyards were the worst. At least the cook and I got along since we were the only ones on shift. Our little I.H.O.P was by all the strip bars, and weekends were money, but Tuesdays were a waste of eight hours.

Except for the cook, there wasn't another soul in the restaurant, and I wasn't at all upset to be sitting at the counter listening to 99.5 Kiss FM, smoking cigarettes and drinking coffee. Brian, the cook, was sleeping in the storeroom – he worked three or four jobs to support his growing family.

Seventeen minutes to go. *Don't think about it, or it's going to happen.* There is nothing worse than getting a rush of blue-hairs five minutes before your replacement arrived. Especially since the day bitches – *that's what they called themselves, you go, girls* – would never let you transfer tables. Nothing like being stuck there until six, for two bucks if you were lucky.

When I heard the door open, I thought *fuck, here we go.* Turning around I was happy some old fart wasn't standing there.

He was about six-feet-tall – *right at my height* – with short-cropped, brown hair, a chin goatee, cheerful eyes, nice lips, ears that were slightly oversized and turned forward a touch. And his nose? Very Roman, and very large. *It wasn't quite Nose's nose, but I'd give it a nine.* He had an average body, not quite thin – *that I later found out was covered with the perfect amount of downy hair.* He was in great shape, but not overly muscled. He reminded me of Josh from *Clueless. That wonderful movie wouldn't make its appearance for another year, but when I watched it, my first impression of Josh made me instantly think of Jerry. Maybe that's why I've always had a thing for Paul Rudd.* When I turned towards him, he smiled. His smile lit up his face, and I felt like I was going to puke. The attraction was instant – Magneto playing cupid.

I just stared at him for what felt like an eternity, and he just stared back. It should have been awkward, but it wasn't. After a minute – *fine, five seconds, maybe ten* – my "extensive" server training took control.

"Smoking or Non?" I asked.

"Huh?" *That smile.*

"Do you want a table? Counter?" I couldn't stop myself from reciprocating with a goofy grin.

"Can I smoke at the counter?" The smile hadn't begun to fade, and he smoked. *Sexy – hey, it was the 90s.*

I theatrically looked all around the restaurant and replied, "I don't think anyone'll care." *I can be a smart ass when I'm nervous.*

"What time do you get off?" the smile turned a touch sideways, but I was oblivious.

"At five, unless I get a table that keeps me here," *whoops, didn't think that one through.* His smile disappeared, and he turned to leave.

Quickly, "That came out wrong. It's usually some old hag. I wouldn't mind sticking around," *whoops, did it again. That sounded desperate.* I was flummoxed. I'd never attempted to flirt with a guy before.

Apparently, he had more practice. "You want to grab some breakfast when your shift ends?"

I glanced around and gave a sour look. I never could keep my emotions off my face.

"Not here," he added. *Smooth.*

My goofy grin returned, and his luminescent smile reached a higher magnitude – *Dazzler in a war zone.*

"I'll tell you what, I'm going to go to Denny's on Wurzbach and I'll grab a table in smoking. I'll wait 'til six to order in case you get stuck here. Join me if you want, if not, that's cool."

Not that Denny's. That's our Denny's. I didn't want to bump into a comrade and get stuck talking about griffins or centaurs, nor did I want to explain what I was doing there when I didn't sit down with them. It wouldn't be out of the ordinary to find someone there. Geeks, like goths, tend to drink coffee all night. *Fuck it. I don't care.*

"I'll be there." *Did my voice just squeak?*

He lit up a cigarette and headed towards the door.

"Wait. What's your name?" I asked him.

"Jerry," he replied standing in perfect profile, which highlighted his nose – *wow, what a nose.*

My gaze swung compulsively from the clock to the door, and every time a car passed, I glared at it with a vehemence I usually reserve for when I'm driving. Seven minutes to go. Clock. Door. Evil car. Door. Clock. Clock. Door. *No, Goddammit, a car just pulled up.* For once, Latisha was early, it was 4:56. As soon as she clocked in, I jetted out the door faster than Cannonball. I didn't even wait for her to check my side work.

When I pulled into the parking lot and glanced at my watch it was 5:22 – *stupid stoplights, I swear I hit every red light on the way there.* I yanked off my work shirt and rooted around my back seat for a clean-ish superhero tee. I had a vast collection of comic book t-shirts. I painstakingly combed specialty shops in the mall and consignment stores. Before the numerous summer blockbusters and shows like *Big Bang Theory*, superhero attire was not readily available. Comics were still a geek thing – the most notable pop culture icon being the comic book guy from *Simpsons* – I may not have looked the part, but I flew my geek flag with pride. Back then, I was superbly unique – *memorable anyway* – because of my dress, -- *especially in the "gay" world* – now everyone thinks they are a fanboy because they've seen *Deadpool 2.*

Like a werewolf on Adderall, I thrashed around bare-chested tossing colorful rags until I found one that was fresh. The Green-Lantern symbol on a white background. I smiled. I liked the way that one looked on me. After my sister moved out – about a year and a half earlier – I had started to regain some self-esteem.

After wiggling into the shirt, I frowned at my black, work pants, but I didn't have any jeans or shorts in the car. At least I was wearing my Doc Martens. I lit my fifth cigarette since my shift ended and killed it in a couple drags. I had no idea what to expect, but I saw him sitting at a table from my parking spot, so I knew he was there. I hadn't seen any cars I recognized either. *I still felt like I was going to puke. That sensation hadn't retreated since the moment I laid eyes on Jerry.*

Chapter 10

AMERICAN DREAM

Early-1980s – Mid-1990s. Great Falls, Montana. La Coste, Texas.

My mom often told me that everything I did came easily to me. I never thought this fair though; it dismissed the amount of work I put into anything I find interesting. Those things, I usually attack with an intensity – Wolverine slaying ninjas levels of intense – and I get good at them from sheer determination. I'm terrible at most sports and have absolutely no musical or mechanical aptitude. In fact, there are tons and tons of things I'm not good at. But I don't do them, as they simply hold no interest for me.

Back in the early 80s as a small child, I was obsessed with Sesame Street. I absolutely loved to learn things, and when I started showing off the lessons from the TV screen, my parents realized I was a bright kid. No genius or anything, but I liked to learn, and I enjoyed school. *High school was awful – even Peter Parker fell victim to those horrible years – but I still enjoyed class time.* I changed schools a few times, but we didn't move often; at least compared to many other military families. I thought it was a fantastic upbringing, and I got to live in some very cool places – *hell, San Antonio still feels like home, and I have no family there, nor have I lived there for almost two decades.*

In the second grade, I met my first best friend: books. On the first day of class we were handed a copy of *Charlotte's Web*, and we were told to read the first chapter that night. I secretly read that book while we were learning math or something – *I wasn't paying attention to the lessons.* I enjoyed the novel, but I didn't find it particularly challenging. When I told Ms. Winters, I had finished it after last recess, I don't think she believed me; she stood there and quizzed me. She must have been satisfied by my answers, as she piled about half a dozen books in my bag and told me to bring them back to her after I had finished them.

I brought all the books to her the next morning, and I don't remember what they were – *I believe Curious George was in the mix.* When I placed them on her desk, Ms. Winters smiled and said I didn't have to bring them back every day. She informed me I could return them one at a time. I told her I finished them. Last night before dinner. Again, she tested me, and more intently than the day before. She just looked at me, her jaw was hanging slightly askance, and her head cocked to the side. After first recess, she took me to the library before heading back to discuss Wilbur and his spider friend with the other students. She introduced me to the librarian and told me to look for some books that sparked my interest and to bring them to her so I could check them out.

When Ms. Winters returned, I was sitting at a child-sized table with my arms folded and a scowl on my face. I was trying to be Jean Grey and use my telepathy to convince the librarian to let me take home the books I had chosen – *although it would be a few years before I was introduced to the red-headed Phoenix, my young brain had already conceived of telepathy, it just didn't have a name for it yet.*

The librarian explained that everything I picked was far too advanced for me and I would never understand them, but those were the books I wanted, and I was stubborn. I refused to even look at anything else, and the two of us had been arguing for some time.

Ms. Winters picked up the single hardcover and two paperbacks and scanned the titles. *The Adventures of Dr. Doolittle, A Wrinkle in Time,* and *Animal Farm.* She looked down at my pouty exterior and shrugged her shoulders. She looked at the librarian and said, "What's the worst that could happen? He might actually understand them." After dinner that night, I picked up *Dr. Doolittle* and didn't put it down until I was finished, and when Mom told me it was time for bed, I had just finished *Animal Farm.*

The next day, I marched up to the giant desk I always wanted to sit in and plopped the two tomes down. I looked Ms. Winters right in the eye and said as supremely as I could manage, "I did understand them." She had me explain everything I had learned, and when my limited vocabulary stumbled around ideas of communism and revolutions, she muttered, "I'll be damned."

But it was Dr. Doolittle learning to speak the language of animals that fascinated me. My young mind became convinced I could teach myself, just like Doolittle had. I became a fixture in the library at Loy Elementary and made friends with the librarian. She constantly helped me find new books, and she asked me many questions. She smiled and hugged me when I disclosed my plot to learn the secret language of animals. I started to spend from first recess until lunch with her every day and did so until Christmas break. Ms. Winters told her I was learning far more there, and I was light years ahead of my class when it came to Reading.

I was unaware, but my parents had met with Ms. Winters and the fifth-grade teacher Mrs. McMurray, and it was arranged that I would spend the first half of my school day with the class one year ahead of my sister's. That part of the day was dedicated to reading, writing, and English. After that Christmas and until I graduated from high school, I never used the same reading material as my classmates. Never. I either went to higher classes, or I was relatively self-directed. Consequently, I became friends with every librarian in the half-dozen schools I attended.

We never did learn the secret language of animals, but we sure tried. The Loy librarian attempted to impart some wisdom, which I ignored. She told me when I started spending half of my day with the fifth grade, I would be better served remaining quiet. She told me they wouldn't like a little know-it-all. It took me about a month to process what she had told me; I had never thought of myself as a know-it-all. I just liked to read, so when teachers' asked questions about literature, my hand would shoot up in the air faster than Mighty Mouse; I was excited to show off a strength. Like my sister in Little League.

I quickly became *that kid,* and I was rather small. I never got beaten-up, because I would run to my sister or a teacher and tattle – *that didn't help with matters at all.* Teacher's pet was not a stereotype I wanted to wear. After those lessons, I learned to closet my nerdy self from the other students. Another self-imposed *don't ask, don't tell.* Don't get me wrong, I was still a nerd, I just wasn't *that nerd* anymore – *well, I was. I just hid it better.*

Without Ms. Winters, Mrs. McMurray and the Loy librarian, I could have easily slipped through the cracks. The support and challenges provided by these three women shaped me into an avid reader, and I never once thanked them or the countless other teachers and librarians that recognized an aptitude unique amongst their endless throngs of adolescent zombies.

The rest of my schooling was completely average – Rick Jones average. Junior high was awkward, to say the least, and high school was spent finding a clique, avoiding bullies, and of course, crushes. I only had one of each.

For most of my time in high school, I never quite found my clique. But there were some notable standouts. Like my friend Miguel, a guy basically obsessed with perfection – *at least that was the impression I always got from him* – I always looked forward to the classes I had with him, and as neither of us were very athletic I will always have a fond memory of winning first place in our gym class, doubles, tennis tournament – *we even beat the coaches.* I always tried to break him out of his shell, but I was never able to talk him into going bungee jumping with me – *oh, and by the way, Miguel, you will never teach my children anything.*

We all had a bully in high school, and mine was relatively mild. I loathed him, but it was never physical. He constantly asked if I was a faggot, and always asked if I wanted to suck his dick. He must have been more perceptive than I realized, but I had those feelings squashed down so deep, even the Mole Man couldn't find them. *Years after high school, I often wondered if he too was secretly gay and projecting his desires.*

It wasn't until my Junior year that I started to really notice guys. Although I had a steady girlfriend once I got my first car – *a year long relationship that ended when she and my best friend slept together* – I was completely enamored with a classmate, and it wasn't her. Chris was on every sports team, even tennis and golf, but he wasn't at all a douche-bag like the other jocks. He was also quite intelligent and graduated in the top ten of our class. *Intelligent might be a bit of an overstatement, but he was determined.* I think he had one of *those dads.*

Chris was tall – one of the tallest in our class. He had loose straw-colored curls on the top of a short, simple hairstyle. His inquisitive, penetrating, green eyes sat too close to the bridge of his nose – *it wasn't bad, maybe a 6.* He was thin but muscled, and his patchy "beard" made me jealous – *I couldn't grow a beard until my early thirties.* He dressed like a jack-ass hick, but I went to school in a farming community in small-town Texas, so that wasn't even slightly unique. His tight wranglers hugged his ass and cradled his package. He was either hung, or he stuffed.

As I explored my own body those years, I always fantasized about making that discovery. In the geekiest of ways. *A favorite daydream would be stopping time and undressing Chris to find out. This quick little fantasy would crop up whenever I noticed his giant package, and I noticed it a lot.* Yeah, I was suppressing those feelings like Tony Stark does with his for alcohol, but the first time I ejaculated, we were together in the gym locker room, and I had discovered that there were some things tight jeans simply couldn't conceal – *at least that's what was happening in my head the first time I explored my sexuality and my body.*

When I discovered he was seeking help with his Chemistry homework, I quickly offered to tutor. At the time I really didn't like the class. I was maintaining an A, but just barely; and I was starting to get lost. That was until I had the proper motivation. I studied my ass off so I could help Chris with his homework. And I did the same our Senior year in Physics. I hated that class even more, but I really liked seeing him outside of school every few weeks.

Nothing ever happened, and we never became friends. It was always about studies. I think he caught me staring at his dick on a regular basis, but he never said anything. Too bad. I think I would have been happy to keep that secret in the closet.

Chapter 11

IT'S ONLY NATURAL

Summer, 1994. San Antonio, Texas.

As I stubbed out my cigarette in an overflowing ashtray, I opened my glove box and grabbed a package of spearmint Certs. Popping one in my mouth, I looked up and saw him from across the restaurant watching me. His face was aglow with that mesmerizing smile, and my face quickly reached Firelord temperatures. *What was I doing? Was I imagining that he was flirting? No way he's interested in me, he's perfect. Oh my god, I'm going to puke.* Trying to fight my nausea, I waved like a little school girl – *oh yeah, that was sexy* – and I realized my goofy-ass grin had returned in full force. *Relax. Breathe. He's watching you. Open the door, and get out of the car, and for God's sake think about some grandma, or you're going to walk in there with a full-on erection.*

"I wasn't sure you'd come," this time I did notice the change in his smile – it developed an animalistic undertone.

I sat down as quickly as I could – *the old nag had left my mind the moment her job was done* – and my blood flow rapidly changed directions with the change in his smirk. I didn't know what to say, so I swallowed my breath mint and dug in my apron pockets for my cigarettes – *are you kidding me? I left my apron on?* My hands were trembling slightly when I produced my cancer stick. By the time I had it in my mouth, he had his zippo waiting. *Holy shit, this is happening.*

My mind was racing far too rapidly for my tongue to formulate words, so when the server stepped up and asked, "Want some coffee, Jay?" I was grateful for the diversion. Still unable to speak, I just nodded at Nicole. Nicole was about sixty and had lived a hard life, but she had a soft spot for our *D&D* group. *Whoops forgot about Nicole. I hope she's not a gossip.*

"I didn't know you were famous," the wolf-like qualities had left his face, but his smile still beamed.

"Yep, I'm a Chippendales dancer." *Did I just say that?*

"I believe it." Dammit, the primal aspects returned to his face, and I needed to keep some blood in my brain to carry a conversation.

"Here ya go sweetie," holy shit, I hadn't even noticed Nicole's return. "What no pile of books and all those dice this morning?" Blankly, I stared at her, and I think she worked out what she was witnessing; she gave us space. Usually, Nicole would just sit down and chat with our fellowship when she wasn't busy, or any of us when we came in individually.

"You boys ready to order?" *Thank you, Nicole.* That was the distraction I needed to think clearly again. *I think I'm going to puke.*

"I'm starving," Jerry replied, and ordered a bunch of food. I don't remember a single thing Nicole brought him. *I remember my order clearly though. Dollar sized pancakes and a side of bacon.* Neither of us ate much, but I did finish my bacon. I guess my body understood it was going to need the extra protein.

Nicole shoved her pencil behind her ear, "Pretty slow. Shouldn't take too long, and I'm sure you boys wanna get out of here." *Did she wink at me?*

"So, are you family?" Jerry casually asked me.

"Huh?" That was the best reply I could think of.

"Family. Are you family?" he repeated. *Damn, now he was going to think I was stupid.*

"I'm not sure what you're talking about. I did understand the words."

"Smartass," he said, but his smile was still plastered. "How old are you?"

"I'll be nineteen next month," I lied; I added a year. "You?"

"I just turned twenty last week. You don't know what family means?"

"The only thing that comes to mind is the mob, but I doubt that's what you're asking."

His smile drooped a little. *What did I say?* He watched me for a bit and fiddled with his silverware. His gaze bore through me as he said, "I'm bi."

Without a moment's hesitation, I replied, "Me too." I'm sure my grin had reached an all new height of absurdity, and his returned with that bestial quality.

"So, what's family?" I asked.

"It's code for gay," he chuckled, then quickly added, "Or bi."

"Oh." When he said he was bi, my brain was drained of blood. It was like daydreaming about Chris in Physics class. Forgetting to leave the apron in the car turned out to be a blessing. I didn't want him to notice the stiffy hiding below my pens and ticket pads.

"I'm guessing you've never been with a dude before then?" he asked me.

"Why do you say that? Because I didn't know what 'family' meant?"

"That's not an answer." *Smooth.*

"Yeah, I've been with a guy before. Just one." *I lied again, I thought he would leave if he knew how inexperienced I was.*

Nicole was right, we didn't stay there long. When I mentioned my roommate was out of town, and I could use a beer, he laughed and said it wasn't even 6:00 am. I reminded him I had just gotten off work. I told him Dan usually had a six-pack or two and asked if he wanted to come have an early morning cocktail. *I was trying to be smooth like him, but that was far too obvious.*

"That could be fun," he said gazing into my eyes. *I still felt like I was going to puke.*

We argued over the bill, but I let him pay when he agreed to let me leave the tip. I dropped a twenty on the table hoping to buy Nicole's silence. While he stood by the register waiting for Nicole to finish taking an order, I excused myself and headed to the restroom. *Holy shit. This is going to happen, and Jerry is way hotter than Chris. Oh my God, I'm going to puke.*

I barely made it to the stall before the bile ejected from my throat. *I hope he didn't hear that.* The restrooms were right by the register. Fortunately, I shoved my Certs in my apron pocket earlier when I got out of the car.

Jerry climbed into his beat-up Toyota Tacoma and told me he'd follow. It only took us about ten minutes to get to my apartment. *This time I hit all the green lights.* Before I could turn the deadbolt, his mouth hungrily found mine, and there was the cliché trail of clothes leading to my bedroom. There wasn't even a detour through the kitchen. *Guess I didn't need the beer after all.*

The details of the next few hours are mine alone. I did learn several things about myself that morning though. The moment Jerry kissed me, I was electrified. The way his stubble rubbed against my cheeks was magical. It was at that very moment I accepted that I was gay. Nothing had ever felt so right. As his hand reached down my pants, his reaction was astounding. *Finally, a body trait to be proud of. Yep, I'm a victim of the patriarchy too, but still, that was a first, and it made me happy.* I also realized that I enjoyed sucking dick when consensual. The last thing I learned was that I wasn't ready for anal sex – *HIV and AIDS still hovered over the gay community like a murder of crows.* That was a line I wasn't prepared to cross, and Jerry may have been disappointed, but he was understanding.

He called in sick for work at about 8:00am, when we were taking a much-needed breather. We fell asleep around noon with half of Jerry's body draped over mine on my single-sized bed. We awoke about 4:00pm, and I promptly followed his example and called in for my shift. We showered together, and it was immensely more satisfying than my fantasy of Chris. After *that* shower, we took turns in that tiny stall, so we had a chance to clean up.

When he took his turn, I ordered a couple pizzas. I was starving. When it arrived, and I opened the box to reveal pepperoni and black olives, he said, "Yum, my favorite." *This guy was perfect.* We didn't leave the apartment the entire day, and we were all over each other until we were both firing blanks. We finally fell asleep again around midnight, and Jerry slipped out sometime before my eyes creaked open the next morning. There was a note taped to the bathroom mirror that read,

Morning Sexy,

Here's my pager # xxx-xxxx

I'll be out of town until this weekend. I should be back by Sunday, Monday at the latest. We should go bowling. Do you bowl?

Yesterday was so fucking hot, can't wait to do that again.

Page me.

Jerry

Chapter 12

RECOGNIZE

Early-1990s. La Coste, Texas.

Once I got my first car, my life changed. We lived in a small town thirty to forty miles west of Lackland, AFB (San Antonio, Texas), and I went to a small high school attended by the bulk of Medina County. There were about one hundred students in my class, and it was the first time I had lived off base. It was an entirely new experience.

Everyone had been going to school with each other since kindergarten, and everyone knew everyone's business. New students were viewed with suspicion and curiosity. It took me some time to find friends. I had been accustomed to military schools and the easy comradery. I was friendly enough with several students from varying cliques, but I spent most of my free time nose deep in David Eddings, Piers Anthony, Robert Heinlein, Orson Scott Card, and countless other fantasy and sci-fi authors. Until I started working.

I was able to get a job bagging groceries at the Lackland commissary. It was a perfect first job, and I was allowed to start when I was fourteen. My sister was also a bagger, and before I started driving, we would ride together.

There was no schedule, other than day and evening shift, except for weekends, those were free-for-alls and could be worked by anyone. If I didn't feel like working, I didn't have to. While working, I could take breaks whenever I wanted. I worked every day and rarely took breaks. I quickly discovered I could make great money if I worked hard. Baggers worked for tips only and were considered self-employed. Pay directly reflected how hard you worked.

By the time I turned sixteen, I had enough money saved to buy a "junker." My sister was driving a '79 Mazda 626, but I wanted something newer. Under pressure from the family, I was convinced to buy that car from her so she could get something else. It wasn't really what I wanted, but I didn't want to make my family unhappy with me. It was beat-up and bright silver, and you needed a flat-head screwdriver combined with a key to start it. It burnt about a quart of oil every few days, so there was always a case of 10w-40 in the trunk for refills. I named her Silver Sable – from the Marvel character of the same name. *All my cars have had names, and the majority have been superheroes. Vehicles are females in my mind. Always. We have all ridden around in a woman for roughly nine months, and the amount of time in cars dwarfs that. The Transformers always seemed "off" to me.*

Although I was without close friends, I had several acquaintances that I spent time with when in school. Julie was such a person, and over high school, we grew close – *not quite close, but comfortable.* We were both personable and got along with most of our peers, but we learned neither of us had any real "friends." It seemed that we were drawn to each other by this common experience. We were more than friendly, but not quite friends. Friend-ish maybe?

At the beginning of our Junior year, I started driving. No more bus. It helped that I loved driving – *still do. Except in traffic, but that's not driving.* I offered to start collecting Julie before school, even though she lived in the next town over, and I would have to leave forty-five minutes earlier than if I had gone directly to the school.

Julie had started "seriously" dating Eduardo, "Eddie," the summer before, and after she realized my route to her house took me right by his, she requested I pick him up along the way. Julie's mom gave me gas money, so I was happy to oblige.

Eddie was two grades behind me, but he was a couple months older than me. He had one of *those mothers* and had no stability until he moved in with his grandma at age 10. He had gotten a couple of years behind in school. Turns out we had a great deal in common. Not only did we both enjoy comic books, but we were also both die-hard X-Men fans, and we both enjoyed tabletop RPGs.

Eddie, Julie, and I became a tight-knit little group, and Eddie and I spent as much time without Julie as we did with her. Our rapid friendship was much more what I was accustomed to.

Eddie's first decade of life with his mother had taught him certain "skills," which his grandmother had been attempting to correct. *She always thought I was a good influence on him.* We began going to a handful of comic book and gaming shops on a regular basis and became regular fixtures. It was where you found gaming groups.

After returning to my car after I bought a game manual and suffering from buyer's remorse – *I couldn't decide among four different Palladium settings but only had money for one* – Eddie lifted his shirt and produced the other three I had been examining in the store. He handed them to me and said they were mine. He said it was a thank you for never asking for gas money.

On the drive home, he must have been aware that I was uncomfortable by his larceny. He did an adequate job convincing me that what he had done wasn't really "wrong." Mostly, I really pitied his early childhood, where he had learned such skills from his mother, but it also helped that I really enjoyed spending time with him; and he assured me if he were ever caught, he would take the entire blame. He was never caught.

He didn't start shop-lifting every time we went to a store, but he did start doing it on a more and more frequent basis. I convinced him to keep his sticky fingers to himself unless I was buying something. He agreed with no reservations and convinced me to further arrangements. I would buy something he wanted, and he would steal a couple somethings I wanted. *I'm not proud of this, and I am equally to blame, but we figured we were merely screwing the proverbial "man."*

Just down the street from Eddie lived Skye. She was in Eddie's class, and just like Eddie, she was two years behind where she should be. Skye was behind due to a childhood illness that she had conquered, but it had set her at a disadvantage for her education. She and Eddie became friends over the years, mostly because of their shared experience of being older than the other kids in their class. Their friendship was much like mine and Julie's. Not particularly close, but a shared bond due to similarities. Eddie asked if I wouldn't mind also taxiing her to school in the morning.

Before long the four of us were always together. Julie and Skye became fast friends, much like Eddie and me. They instantly bonded over a love of old Western movies and quickly discovered they had much more in common.

Skye and I were practically forced into dating each other. It seemed to make sense since the four of us had become our own clique. We got along wonderfully. She had a laid-back nature, and she was very comfortable to be around. Skye was funny and always had great one-liners, she was smarter than she gave herself credit for, and she and I shared a similar interest in books. She trusted people far too easily, and because of this, she had a pregnancy scare at fourteen with her first boyfriend. She had been burned by guys and didn't want a boyfriend.

I had begun fantasizing about Chris regularly, and the thought of a girlfriend hadn't even crossed my mind before Eddie and Julie's prompting. The two of us resisted for a month or two, but after Skye realized I wasn't one of those guys that were trying to get into her pants, she developed a "thing" for me. Although I wasn't attracted to her – *obviously* – we had become friends, and with Julie and Eddie, we had the dynamic of The Fantastic 4. So, the two of us started dating.

Eddie and Julie eventually got to the stage where they couldn't keep their hands and mouths off each other. Skye began to follow suit, but I stopped her by explaining that "public displays of affection" made me uncomfortable. *Yes, it was an excuse, but it wasn't really a lie. PDA does make me uncomfortable. I don't mind holding hands and hugs or a peck. But if tongues are involved, please take it elsewhere.*

We did start getting hot and heavy when we were alone though – *hormones...* -- and I always told Skye that I wouldn't pressure her to have sex – *and I never did.* I told her she only had to let me know when she was ready. *My secret desire was that she would never be ready.*

She eventually decided she was ready, and I wasn't. I knew I didn't want to have sex with her, and I knew that I fantasized about Chris when I masturbated, but I was not ready to accept I was gay. I told myself that sex with Skye would prove I wasn't gay. Once we did have sex, my dick would go flaccid unless I was thinking about Chris. I always wanted her to go down on me, and I wanted to take her from behind. She never wanted to do either, and we didn't have sex regularly. That arrangement seemed to work for both of us.

Although I hated the sex – *well, that's not entirely true. It felt good, but it was only possible when I was thinking about a man* – I loved having a girlfriend, and I genuinely cared for Skye. I enjoyed the love notes, phone calls, talking about hopes and dreams, confiding secrets, and sharing yourself on multiple levels. Sex was part of it, but for me, it was the smallest part – *mostly because Skye wasn't a man.*

I didn't realize that sex was more important for her, and my reluctance coupled with my desires in the bedroom caused her to resent me. She felt like I wasn't into her – s*he was right, and I'm sorry to have deceived her.* After a month or two of celibacy, I tried to initiate sex, for the first time. Before I had always found excuses when she was the initiator, the most common being a forgotten condom – *I knew I wasn't ready to be a father* – and she grew very silent.

I understood something was wrong and after some pressure – Colossus bending steel levels – she disclosed that she had slept with Eddie. My inner monologue thought, *"Oh well, now I have an excuse to end it."* Although it was fake, it seemed like the right thing to do, so I put on the angry face and yelled at her, even though I wasn't really very angry. She got defensive and turned it around on me. She even accused me of being gay – *I wasn't ready to face that truth, and it infuriated me.*

I told her we were done, and I wasn't nice about it. I stormed out of her house and drove up the street, parking in front of Eddie's. It was shortly after midnight. I hadn't quite processed how angry I was at Eddie. I didn't know what I planned to do when I rang the doorbell. His grandma answered and looked me in the eye.

She reached out and put her arms on my shoulders and said in a thick accent, "You got the devil in your eyes. I don't know what he did but promise me you won't kill him." As soon as she was given a verbal assent that I wasn't homicidal, she woke Eddie and brought him into the living room. I said nothing, but I punched him in the face. Once. And I left. I never spoke to him again, but I did see Skye once more. *I ran into her at a party I attended with Amanda. She had heard through some rumor mill that I was gay and wanted answers. She was incredibly nasty in her questioning, and regardless of my sexuality, I wasn't the one who had been unfaithful. Among many other horrible things, I told her that I wasn't gay when we were together; but after she had fucked my best friend, I could never trust a woman again, so my only option was to become gay. I made her cry a great deal that night. I sometimes feel bad about it.*

Chapter 13

A NEW KIND OF LOW

Summer, 1994. San Antonio, Texas.

I waited until Tuesday to page Jerry, I didn't want to look desperate – *I could have saved us both some time if I had, though.* I was out-of-this-world-happy when he called back in less than five minutes – Shi'ar galaxy out-of-this-world. He said he was excited that I had paged, and I could see his smile through Amanda's old rotary phone. He mentioned he had started to give up hope that I would contact him and asked if I wanted to go bowling.

"Of course," I replied far too quickly, and that time I'm certain my voice squeaked.

I had my very first date with a man. It was marvelous, even though I didn't bowl well. I scored an eighty-two, while Jerry finished somewhere in the two-hundred and thirty range. He was a fantastic bowler, and his ass looked amazing as he approached the foul line with the bowling ball in hand. The first time we got "too close" to each other, the guys one lane over noticed and started flashing us the evil eye. We both got the message and *butched* it up. Neither of us was willing to deal with that nonsense when it was just easier to portray the "bro." After two games, we hightailed to his sister's vacant apartment.

After our second date – *the movies. The newest Police Academy. Seven, maybe? Terrible.* – I introduced him to some of the fellowship at *the* Denny's, and he sat there patiently as the rest of us talked excitedly about last week's game. I anticipated an accepting attitude to my geeky side – *seriously, geek culture was not a "cool" thing then* – and I thought he wouldn't judge because he knew what that felt like since he was bi. I was wrong, he reacted in an all-too-familiar way.

We left Denny's and returned to Amanda's. I had started keeping the place clean – *okay, clean might be an overstatement, but cleaner* – so wasn't mortified at the idea of bringing Jerry there. Amanda was at Denny's, and I paged her a message to stay out late – *0987, upside down the 87 looks like "L8."* As soon as my hand replaced the phone receiver on its base, I had him on the couch, and I was unbuckling his belt in two seconds flat. After we finished, I came to realize that he really wasn't into it. And when he headed to the kitchen to grab a couple beers, I knew something had changed.

"What's up, man?" I asked as he handed me a Shiner Bock – *he was perfect, he didn't have to ask my beer preference.*

"I don't think this is going to work," Jerry replied.

"Huh?" My heart was shattering as quickly as Professor Xavier's dream.

"Dude, your friends are weird. Really weird. And watching you with them made me realize you are just as strange. You're so damn cute, I didn't see it. Sorry man, nerdy guys just aren't my thing."

My emotions were churning. He thought I was attractive, that was a relatively new emotion, but I felt like I wanted to cry. I wouldn't let myself though, growing up a military brat teaches you quickly to withhold tears. I really thought we had a connection. He finished the beer and looked at me with a smile that didn't seem real. It wasn't the smile I had fallen in love with instantly.

"We could try being fuck buddies. Sex with you is intense, but I don't think we'll get along as friends."

I shrugged my shoulders, chugged the last of my beer and belched. That time I did not apologize. Jerry got up and left, and I cried for the first time in years.

What I did next, I'm not proud of. Like my encounters with Mephisto, I have never disclosed these events. I stalked him – Blade after a pack of blood drinkers, stalked him. Whenever I wasn't working, I would drive by his sister's place to look for his truck. I would check the parking lot where he worked, and the bowling alley. When I saw him, I would hide, and I would follow to investigate his activities. I was careful enough to use Amanda's car, he would never recognize it. I was obsessed. I thought I was in love. And I was hurt.

I started writing him letters. Lots of them. Letters of anger. Letters of love. Letters that described our sexual antics in astounding detail. Poetry. Pictures I drew. The works. He always left his windows cracked on the old pick-up truck so I would slip them in whenever the opportunity arose. Which was often. I even missed the next *D&D* night to follow him around. Eventually, he had enough, and I got to see him for what I thought would be the last time on my birthday. I was at work, I couldn't find a replacement. He walked through the front door, and he had what appeared to be about four hundred folded notes gripped tightly in each hand – *did I really write that many?*

As I walked to the lobby, he spotted me, and the scowl on his face was terrifying. He threw the notes at my feet when I approached.

"My sister read all of these. I'm not out to my family. At least I wasn't."

My face turned as red as Superman's "underwear."

"We've known each other all of two weeks. Tops. We've been on two dates where we barely talked. All we did was fuck." He was not using his "inside voice."

"Um. Sorry?" I didn't know what to say.

"Sorry? Sorry? Just leave me the fuck alone. You're a fucking freak. All we've done is fuck. Stupid *Dungeons & Dragons* dork. Go roll some dice up your ass!"

He turned and stormed out of the restaurant, leaving all the notes behind.

The only other employee on shift was the cook, but I had about a dozen tables that all craned their heads like prairie dogs once Jerry's voice escalated. I don't think I have ever been so embarrassed, but I discovered two critical things. First, I would never again play stalker. Lesson painfully learned. Second, my geek nature was as acceptable as it was in the "straight" world; so, not at all. Yet another aspect of my life that I would continue to keep closeted. *Don't ask, Don't tell* indeed.

II

FRICTION, BABY

Chapter 14

SPEEDING UP TO
SLOW DOWN

November 1994. San Antonio, Texas.

Ah, The Candelabra. Café or Coffeeshop, or some other surname. To me, it was always just The Candelabra. It was the Saturday after Thanksgiving, 1994, and I had discovered my Sanctum Sanctorum. The Pacific Northwest may have already started to become inundated with coffeeshops, but this was my first experience, and it was unique in South Texas. It was nothing like walking into a Starbucks today. It wasn't filled with identical, boring, mass-produced tables and chairs, and there wasn't merchandise everywhere.

The Candelabra was housed in the bones of an old craftsman in the "gay district" of San Antonio – *what I mean by "gay district" is the part of the city where most of the gay bars were located; at least they were back then.* The square footage was quadruple what you would find today, and it was filled with numerous, eclectic, sitting areas. Bistro style tables with little chairs. Couches and armchairs. Bean-bag chairs. Low benches. Coffee tables. Bookshelves. A long counter at the coffee bar with a half dozen bar stools that couldn't be more mismatched.

The most diverse collection of puzzles, books, games, maga-zines, and dozens of daily newspapers from around the coun-try arranged throughout. It wasn't designed to encourage you to buy an eight-dollar coffee and get the hell out, instead, it was warm, cozy, friendly. They wanted you to stick around.

Whoever designed the seating arrangements was a genius – Brainiac levels. No matter where you sat, there were plenty of people around, but it still felt intimate. You could sit curled up with a book in what felt like a private corner under a softly lit, oversized, hanging lampshade alone in prose. But it was easy to join conversations anywhere in your periphery. Intimacy in a crowded space is not an easy atmosphere to create.

Ah, the coffee. *Coffee is life. It is the perfect beverage. Sure, I'll partake in a thirty-two-syllable-ridiculously-confusing-to-order-sugary-creamy-barely-coffee-flavored coffee drink from time to time, but I like my coffee plain, black, and ice cold. One of the owners, Ben, turned me on to iced coffee, and I have never looked back.* Not only lattes and macchiatos – *although I had no idea what they were, nor how to pronounce them* – they also provided a daily selection of five or six different "regular" cof-fee roasts. And they rotated frequently. It was here I developed my palate for the nuances of the varieties, but I never became a coffee snob. If all I can find is Folgers Instant Decaf, I'll drink it happily. Bad coffee is better than no coffee.

Best of all, the place was gay-friendly. I even recognized several guys from the bars – one of them I had fooled around with. There were also many gay men I didn't recognize – I didn't know there was such a thing as "gay" places that weren't sweaty, dark, packed, smoky, blacklight-lit bars and nightclubs. Coffee, check. Comfort, check. Games, check. Gay men, check. Best friend by your side so you don't look pathetic. Check-ish. Amanda was with me that evening, due to ship out for the Navy in a few days. This was our last night together for quite some time.

"Told you, you'd like it," She loved I-told-you-so's.

"Yeah, you were right. How'd you hear about this place, and why am I just learning about it today?"

"Mom told me. She was the escrow agent for the gay-couple when they bought their house." The Candelabra was owned by two couples. One straight; one gay.

"Oh." I wasn't sure what to say. I may have been accustomed to goodbyes. But this was the first time I had to say goodbye to a real best friend.

She fiddled with some little, wooden, puzzle box, looked up at me, and asked, "Why are we being so awkward? This is weird. It was like my last night at Murry's."

"Yeah? I don't know. What would we be doing if you weren't leaving?" I snatched the puzzle box out of her hand.

"Bitch. Give that back." Bitch had become my pet name.

"Eat a vaj. You weren't even trying." After her single excursion to a gay nightclub, she *loved* being told she was a lesbian.

"We'd be sitting out on the patio at the table right by the door. Then we could smoke, and still be close enough to feel the air-conditioning. We could see the whole place and check out the meat."

"Then why are we sitting in here?" I opened the puzzle box and found a key with a note that read, "find the box." In a smaller script, "please don't take the key home – Candelabra."

I tossed her the open box, after removing the key. "Hm, wonder what this is for?"

"Oh, a mystery," she replied after I showed her the key. My head had already begun to spin around like the Red Tornado. Hidden all over were dozens, maybe hundreds, of little treasure chests with tiny keyholes. All the perfect size for the key I had found.

I picked up the closest box and was shocked when it popped open. I assume the expression on my face was telling.

After a peal of laughter that turned many heads, Amanda said, "Dumbass. The key will open every box. The trick is to find the right box. I thought you liked to read."

I could feel my ears burning. At least one of the guys watching was cute. I grabbed my coffee, the key, and tried to channel the Invisible Woman as I walked to the indicated patio table doing a better impersonation of the Red Skull.

She joined me with as many boxes as she could carry, and after setting them on the table, she snatched the cigarette I had just lit out of my mouth. "Start opening." *Nothing.*

After a few cups of coffee and endless boxes, Amanda nudged my arm. "Check out the nose."

I looked up and followed her line of sight. "Nice. Seven, seven point five. Oh, holy shit, check out the blonde behind him."

I didn't know it, but I had seen my first boyfriend for the first time, but it was incomparable to the first time I saw Jerry. No instant, animalistic chemistry.

"Day'um," she replied. *We had rating systems for everything. Some were simple, but for men, we had gotten more inventive. In ascending order: umm; no; meh; hmm; do-able; nice; yum; damn; day'um; wow.*

"Agreed. Looks like they're together," I muttered.

"No way, the nose is straight. And the other one would be out of his league" she answered without much thought.

"Not what I meant. Came in together. Friends, maybe?" I explained.

"We should say hi. Day'um is gay. One for each of us?" *Some things never change.*

I shrugged my shoulders. I'd prefer if it were only the two of us. But at least we had gotten through the awkwardness of earlier.

Chapter 15

BLACKLIGHT

September 1994. San Antonio, Texas.

Every customer that watched Jerry deliver his verbal bitch-slap left a terrible tip, and my last table sat there until 11:00pm; an hour after my shift ended. *Happy birthday to me.* I grabbed a cup of coffee and sat down in an empty booth and lit up a cigarette. The place was empty, and I was lost in an emotional shame spiral – *Vertigo meets Stacy X.* I had already paged Amanda to let her know I was stuck at work – *09008, or "BOO" up-side-down.*

I sat there for an hour and drank far too much coffee. Pity party, table for one. Literally. I watched the graveyard cook arrive for his shift and heard a whoop of joy from Brian. On his way out the front door, he noticed that I hadn't left. He asked if I had a change of clothes with me. *Yep, even jeans and shorts.* He told me to get changed, and he called his wife. He didn't say where we were going, he just told me to follow him downtown.

We arrived at a parking lot just west of downtown San Antonio, it was near SACC (San Antonio Community College), but I had never been there before. It took us some time to find empty spaces, and then each other. There were numerous obviously gay men and women in sight, not to mention the gaggle of drag queens that stepped out of an old station wagon. *Where am I? Where's Brian?*

After noticing that many of the people I could see were "dressed up," I looked down at my t-shirt. Voltron's face on a light blue background. Not my favorite, but it was the same color as my chucks – *have those ever gone out of style?* Baggy jeans, and a baseball cap – *a prized possession. It had the X-Men symbol in yellow on a solid navy blue. It even fit my pea-sized head perfectly. Hats have always been tricky, but I feel naked without one.* I felt comfortable but dressed "wrong."

We found each other and headed towards some place he called Moondust. Brian told me he knew the guy who worked the door; and if I flirted with him, he probably wouldn't check my I.D. *Even if he did, some of the nightclubs, this one included, were 18+, minors were just branded with giant X's across the tops of each hand in ultra-super-duper-wide-tip sharpies. They were impossible to remove.* Brian assured me he would be able to sneak me drinks regardless. He was under the impression that I needed to be drunk. I have no idea how he knew it was my birthday.

We had to walk a few blocks to get there, and when we rounded the corner, I saw the entrance. There was a long line of people that seemed to be stereotypes in the flesh. Cowboy, goth, grunge, Tejano, club kids, old, young, black, white, brown, lesbian – *both the butch and lipstick varieties with everything in between* – yuppies, gym rats, soldiers, drag queens. It was amazing to view such a variety of people – *and this was the first time I realized gay crossed all the artificial boundaries we use to separate ourselves.* Still, it all looked manufactured. It was like Halloween; everyone appeared to be in costumes.

There was a small parking lot in front of the main entrance. The building looked like a nondescript warehouse. There wasn't a single window, and if it weren't for the music and flashing lights pouring out of the wide-open double doors – *not to mention the line about fifty deep* – it would have been as invisible as Wonder Woman's jet.

We walked the wrong way – *towards the front of the line.* Over the music, I heard Brian call out, "Hey, Jerry." *Um, what?* The three-hundred-pound, five-and-a-half-foot-tall, Chicano bouncer that looked like a Hell's Angel motioned for us to cut the line. Many frowns and some bitching from the queens had me looking down the line as Brian was nudging my ribs.

"This is my friend, Jerry," Brian said pointedly.

"Hi," I was trying to look at everything at once when I heard Brian and had already forgotten I was supposed to flirt.

"Today's his birthday. It's been a rough one," Brian explained, when I didn't follow his lead.

"First time here, cutie?" The voice was completely unexpected. There was too much "gay" inflection for the face.

I just nodded. On the top of my right hand, Jerry pressed the same ink-stamper that he had used on Brian, branding me as an adult of legal drinking age. Brian grabbed my arm and shoved his way to a bar that sat in a tiny nook beside the coat check just to the right side of the cashier, where we paid our ten-dollar cover. We were standing in a big room with several standing-height tables along the walls. There were black lights everywhere casting a strange fluorescent glow on everything, and it was packed shoulder-to-shoulder. The room was large, but not large enough for the building.

After some shoving and shouldering, we finally made it to the bar that was wide enough for maybe five people. We waited for ten minutes for the bartender to get to our order.

When he pointed at me, I told him, "Shot of Beam and a Shiner Bock." He handed me a Bud Light and poured some brown liquid into a shot glass.

"It's his birthday, get him another," Brian chimed in.

He poured me another shot, and handed me another beer, and said dispassionately "Happy Birthday."

Brian showed me around, and I was right that the first room was too small for the building. The building was large, but the tour was short. There was only one other accessible space. To the left of the blacklight room, through a narrow opening, I saw an immense room; the bulk was filled with a dance floor about the size of my high school gymnasium, and there were so many people they were difficult to distinguish. It looked like a giant slime monster composed of countless shirtless bodies, and the music was loud enough to shake my fillings. Brian pointed at his watch, waved goodbye, and screamed into my ear, "Have fun." I barely heard him.

It was time to explore. First things first. Restroom. The dance-floor room seemed unlikely to house my destination, so I walked back to the blacklight room and noticed an opening on the far wall that ended in a long, skinny hallway. I was unaware there was another path to my destination and headed towards the hallway. But walking through the blacklight room was – an adventure, to say the least.

There was a slight break in the sea of humanity, a flowing current in the tide of people – *and just like Aqua Lad, I jumped in feet first.* With a beer in each hand, I pushed my way to the slowly moving section, and as soon as I hit the wall of people, my body became public property. Five steps into the throng and my ass had already been squeezed a dozen times, and my dick was fondled constantly – *maybe it was time to rethink my freeballing practices.*

Trying to keep the beers from spilling while fighting off hands coming at me from every direction put my multi-tasking skills to work – *if only I had Armor's kinetic shell.* I needed a free hand, so I downed a beer and belched loudly enough to garner some attention over the loud thump, thump, thump of the heavy bass. This drew some dirty looks from a group of nelly hipsters, but also caused the hand on my ass to retreat. *Sweet.* The solitary hick in his far-too-bright, white, cowboy hat, with a pot belly that would put Dr. Druid's to shame, laughed and called out, "Damn, that was sexy." *Um, what?*

With a renewed determination and a liberal application of knees and elbows, I traversed halfway across the room before again coming to a halt. While stuck in a glowering brood of businessmen, one leaned over and whispered in my ear, "Meet me in the bathroom, I wanna see your cock." *Umm, what?* I reached behind and grabbed some wrist attached to a hand that was down the back of my pants with questing fingers. *Um, what?* As I threw the hand away from my posterior as forcefully as I could, I balled mine into a fist – I was ready to punch someone. Unfortunately, I had no idea who the hand belonged to.

Finally, I made it to the hallway and saw a long line of men along each wall. I asked the nearest person which line was for the men's room. With a dirty look, he said, "Both," then muttered, "Fucking breeders. Go to your own club." *Umm, what?* I noticed the line on the left wall was moving faster, so I lined up – the shots, beers, and endless cups of coffee needed to be ejected, and soon was a requirement. Standing there, wishing the line would move occupied my attention, so I didn't notice the whispering yuppy in line behind me. It wasn't long before he made his presence known.

This hallway was just as crowded as any other part of the club I had seen, and the space between the two lines was narrow enough that everyone exiting the bathroom had to rub up against those waiting their turn – *at least people stopped grabbing my crotch. There seemed to be a silent understanding that those waiting to piss were hands-off.* Since walking into the club, at no point was I not in constant contact with someone, and I quickly became accustomed to the constant jostling.

Amongst the constant sliding of bodies, I finally noticed a pattern.

Every few seconds it felt like someone was pressing a half-eaten roll of Mentos firmly into my lower-ass-upper-thigh, and it was starting to develop into a rhythmic pattern copying the bass line of the overly-loud, terrible music. I turned and saw the yuppie smiling, as he was dry humping me. "Damn, you got me hard already." *Umm, what?*

I scooted my lower body as far away from his as I could – it wasn't far – and he responded by pressing even closer. *What the fuck is going on?* That clean-shaven, Hispanic, businessman may have been cute, but I was already ten steps past annoyed. When I reached down and grabbed his dick, his eyes widened, and his smile deepened. Until I started squeezing. Hard. His smile quickly faded, and his eyes showed panic – *can't say I blamed him. I'd be scared too if someone was squeezing my cock that hard.*

When I started laughing, he grabbed my wrist and leaned towards my ear telling me in a tone that dripped venom, "Whatever. I bet yours is smaller." That wasn't what I was laughing at, but my new-found mirth reached a volume that temporarily drowned out the music. One last eat-shit-and-die look and he left the line. *Good riddance.*

As the line moved forward enough to grant me a peek into the restroom, I finally deciphered the mystery of the two lines. The slow-moving one was for the single stall; the other – the one I was in – was for the urinals. There were two rows of them at a right angle in the corner, and they were packed tightly together. There were no partitions, and they looked like they were designed to allow everyone in there to watch you piss. Hell, there were even mirrors in front of the urinals, angled to view right at crotch height. *Um, what?*

When it was finally my turn, the only open urinal was the one closest to the corner, that I had noticed remained vacant, but I practically sprinted to it. Sighing in relief, I whipped it out and glanced in the odd-angled mirror deciphering that from this position my dick was on complete display to the entirety of the room. Reflections of reflections of reflections. Everyone in there either turned and stared directly at it or one of the mirrors that showed it clearly. Instantly, I felt like I was Ghost Rider; my face was on fire. *Not that anyone would have noticed. They weren't looking at my face.*

I finished, shook it, hid it away, zipped my pants, and high-tailed it as quickly as I could. At least my bladder was relieved. I had had enough of this birthday, so I shoved my way back through the blacklight gauntlet – once again experiencing bod-iless hands groping every inch of my midsection – and when I saw the exit, my elbows honed themselves into spearheads.

Making a mad dash towards the salvation of a relatively empty parking lot, I was infuriated when my upper arm was grabbed by some hand. I turned around ready to swing.

"Whoa! Everything okay, cutie," Jerry – *the doorman* – asked. The look on my face answered his question before I could open my mouth.

Jerry pulled me in for a hug. A friendly hug. He whispered, "Don't worry, you'll get used to it." He planted a quick kiss on my cheek and patted my ass softly – like a coach's swat. He hollered out, "We'll be seeing you again. Soon." I channeled my inner Northstar and flew out the door.

Um, what?

Chapter 16

BEAUTIFUL MISTAKE

November 1994. San Antonio, Texas.

There were dozens of open chests piled around our patio table, and we had drawn a small crowd. Three or four were standing behind me watching over my shoulder. Amanda had recruited the other patrons to help find more boxes. All the obvious ones had been brought to my little throne – *normally I hate to be the center of attention, especially in a large crowd, but this was a group effort now. Thundercats, Ho!* Everyone was bursting with curiosity wondering what I would find, and all four owners were watching with obvious merriment.

"Excelsior!" I exclaimed – *Thanks, Stan Lee. Best battle cry. Ever.* I triumphantly held up a small, laminated business card with the words, "You're a winner!" in bolded, block lettering.

There was a feeling of listlessness that traveled through all the patrons. Everyone had gotten involved, and most seemed disappointed by the simple card. I thought it was amazing. The scavenger hunt was boisterous, and I now had proof of my winning status. The card got passed around, everyone wanted to investigate it. I guess they were looking for some hidden meaning – *why couldn't they just accept that I was a winner?*

Before the crowd dispersed back to their own lives, Rachel, one of the owners, walked over with a bus-tub to collect the boxes. "That card gets you free coffee for life," she said with her oh-so-cheery grin. This was followed by happy murmuring and even a few claps. I guess everyone preferred that they had contributed towards a "real" prize.

After the congregation dispersed, Amanda turned to me and said, "That was fun. I'm glad we found a place for you before I leave."

"Yeah, even without the free coffee, I think I'd be coming back on a regular basis. Might even be good for studying."

"Are you ready for your first semester?" It was starting to feel awkward again.

"Yeah. I think so anyway. "I hope IS is the right major," *I had no idea what I wanted to be when I grew up. Since I liked school, I thought teaching would be a good route, and the Interdisciplinary Studies degree was the most flexible.*

"I still can't believe you paid tuition out of your pocket."

"Stop being awkward. I don't wanna do that again." Her laugh was forced. We both grew silent and lit up cigarettes in unison.

The beautiful blonde and the seven-nose walked up, and blondie asked Amanda, "Can I bum a smoke?"

Amanda eyed him, eyed me, eyed the nose, eyed me again, and said, "Sure. Join us. I'm Amanda. This is Jay. He's gay."

The blonde eyed me, the nose, me again, then Amanda, "I'm Mike. This is my brother Gabe. He's gay too."

The tips of Gabe's ears were instantly red, "That wasn't awkward," he said waving sheepishly.

Amanda and I squealed with laughter. Gabe and Mike just scrutinized us.

Amanda explained, "Jay just told me to stop being awkward seconds before you walked up."

I smiled in apology to Gabe. "That's how she always introduces me." Gabe was attractive, definitely a *yum – two steps below his brother.* He was shorter than me, but not by much, dark brown hair that rode that messy-neat line perfectly, dark brown eyes, and somewhat-pouty lips that always left a serious expression on his face. Gabe had an average build but walked like he had the proverbial stick in his ass. His smile helped to erase his seriousness, but he appeared to share it far too infrequently.

He looked at me with a silent thank you, "Well Mike's never done that to me before. I was taken aback." When he glared at Mike, I saw his nose from the perfect angle. I changed my mind, his smile and his nose moved him up a rung. He was now a *damn.*

I noticed neither had a beverage and since they had helped find the box, I offered to buy them one. Amanda held out her hand, palm up, "I'll go get 'em. What do you guys want."

"Just coffee. Black," Mike replied.

Gabe held his chin, and looked like a young Doctor Strange, "I'm unsure. Hot chocolate, maybe? Coffee sounds delightful though. But I need lots of cream and sugar."

"Then get up off your ass, and come on," she grabbed his hand and pulled him to the counter.

Mike reached for the ashtray, and said, "My brother thinks you're hot. He noticed you when we walked in. He saw your t-shirt right away."

"That's cool," I replied, as nonchalantly as possible.

"Do you think he's attractive?" he probed.

"Yeah, he's cute. He seems so serious though"

"Nah. He's just nervous. I drug him here, he didn't want to come. After he told me he was gay, he went to a club on his eighteenth birthday. He said he never wanted to go back, and he would just be celibate for life. He wouldn't tell me what happened, but he didn't know how else to meet dudes."

"I can relate to that. Bars can be tiresome, but you do become accustomed. Amanda found this place and drug me here tonight. I love it."

"Why'd she have to 'drag' you then?"

"She's leaving for boot camp in a few days. Our last night together," I stated, as my face developed a sad countenance.

"Oh, dude. I'm sorry. We'll take off so you two can hang."

"No. It was getting awkward. If anything, she's looking to get laid before she's stuck with her family for two days and then boot camp."

"Oh, yeah?"

Amanda and Gabe returned, and she asked, "Oh, yeah. What?"

Mike and I shared a laugh at her expense. Gabe continuously stirred his coffee and blew on it to cool it down. I kept thinking, *it's just coffee. Drink it.*

Amanda looked right at Mike, "So, you like to get your dick sucked?"

Gabe was looking at me when she said it. I ended up with a coffee stain on my favorite Spider-Man tee. *Dammit. I take that back. Don't drink it.*

Amanda again held out her hand, palm up. I dropped my keys in them and said, "I want my change back, bitch."

"I am so sorry," Gabe apologized to me. He even grabbed some napkins and started wiping down my chest.

I removed his hand, "All good. It happens. Especially with Amanda around."

"So, um, you wanna sneak off somewhere too? I have my parents' van," he offered hesitantly while looking down at his coffee cup.

"Are you serious? Yeah, no. I'm not Amanda." *I made them work harder than that.*

He apologized, saying that's what he thought he should do. He seemed sincere, but he sounded like a used-car salesman. He was obviously flustered, and we sat in mostly awkward silence for about forty minutes.

Chapter 17

BURNED

September 1994. San Antonio, Texas.

I hurried back to my car, and I kept my gaze locked a few paces ahead of me. I was horrified, and I wanted to be as far as possible from that overwhelming debauchery. I felt violated and disappointed. *Is this what being gay is like?* As I sat down in my beat-up '79 Mazda, I had a moment of panic thinking I had lost my pager. Thankfully, I checked my work pants before marching back to that hedonistic den.

Six pages from Amanda, all 0401911. *04 was her number. 01 was Murry's. The 911s were for emphasis, real emergencies were just zeros.* I spied a payphone, grabbed a quarter and called Murry's to see if she was still there. She asked where the hell I had been and told me everyone was there, waiting to wish me a "happy birthday."

When I arrived, everything felt odd. Different. I was handed a beer, and everyone demanded answers to where I had been since they anticipated me immediately after my shift ended. I dodged questions with the prowess of a half-elven rogue, but I had this constant awareness that something had changed. I learned Dan hadn't been to play since our melee, and he had been avoiding everyone. At the same time, I had missed a couple game nights; but Murry assured them I just needed some time to myself, which just fetched more questions that he attempted to dismiss.

The gossiping and guessing finally got to Amanda, and she told the entire fellowship that I had come out of the closet. Everyone was there, except Gretchen and Dan. *Besides Murry, she was the only of my friends that I told. She was also the only person from the fellowship except for Murry and Amanda who accepted me without reservations. When I told her later, her response was, "Yeah. Duh. I knew that."*

Eventually, most of the group let me know that they didn't care that I was gay and that it changed nothing. They also made it clear – *some blatant, others more tactfully* – that they didn't want to hear about "gay stuff." When I got annoyed after the third identical conversation, I started asking what was meant by "gay stuff."

It genuinely hurt to hear my friends tell me that I could still be their friend if I didn't talk about a giant aspect of my life, a giant aspect that I knew absolutely nothing about, a giant aspect that was filled with pleasure, confusion, aversion, and suspicion. *Yeah, they don't sound like real friends to me either.* I thought I could work with that arrangement though, as I had no desire to talk about my first night at a gay bar.

Of course, everyone was acting differently. Nothing overt, but subtle little changes. If someone said, gay, or fag, or cocksucker, HIV, AIDs, or anything remotely associated with "gay," then everyone would turn and look at me. Tim who said, "cocksucker," on a regular basis started apologizing each time.

I tried to tell them all to stop. I told them I was still the same person, and that I wasn't going to suddenly start getting offended by the same shit said by everyone everywhere anyway. I told them I didn't care if they made gay jokes or used slurs. Apart from Tim's constant outbursts – *and why is cocksucker an insult?* – it was rare to hear a gay joke, and I don't remember anyone ever saying, "fag," or any other derogatory term much, if ever. *I just don't get it. It becomes infuriating to hear that people don't have a problem with my sexuality. It happens regularly when certain types learn you are gay; they must let you know how cool they are with it. Do I look like I give two shits what your opinion on something that doesn't concern you in the slightest is? When I hear the aggravating, "I'm cool with gay people," I reply, "Yeah? I'm cool with bigots."*

After more drinks, everyone started to act mostly normal. "Fag" suddenly became vogue because I said I didn't care. With alcohol, their demands got more personal, such as the all too familiar: *I don't care if you're gay, but I don't want you checking me out. Don't look at my ass when I bend over. That's just not cool man.* Naturally, I wanted to remind them that no one – male or female – was checking them out, and I wasn't suddenly some sex fiend that was going to molest them. *At least I hoped not. I was starting to worry if that was exactly what it meant to be gay.*

I thought we were done talking about the thing they didn't want me to talk about, but after more alcohol, I was forced to endure another round of questioning. *So, are you going to be the man or the woman? – which had two parts. 1) Whether I wanted a dick in my ass, or my dick in an ass. 2) Would I be the man and go to work or find a man to take care of me. Seriously? It's the 90s, women are "allowed" to work, and they have more than proven they can take care of themselves without a man. I was then asked which gay stereotype I was going to be, funny sit-com next-door neighbor, "rough and tumble" Village Person – and which one – or one of those that had to shove it in every-one's faces, like a "male stewardess." That they only could come up with the three is sad in its own right; even sadder considering none seemed to think I could just be "me" now. It was explained that it would not be acceptable for me to be the third option. They just couldn't handle that.*

There were words of support and encouragement, and a few said they thought it made them open-minded to have a gay friend. Suddenly me being gay gave them some kind of "cred." Before that night was over, I came to realize that the real me had disappeared in their eyes. I couldn't even be the dwarven, barbarian cleric that I had been role-playing for close to a year. Now I was just the gay guy in the corner that they had to monitor.

I bought into the bullshit for another month or so, they were my only friends, and I spent most of my free time at Murry's. Just like everyone else did. As the fellowship became more complacent with my "new identity," I became less comfortable in their company.

I just wanted to be treated as I always had, but they all seemed hung-up on my new gay-candy-coating. I lost inter-est in the gaming, it was like I was playing three characters at once: I continued to be the same old me, but no one saw him anymore; I had to be some easily-understood-quiet-side-show-attraction; and I had to play the character that I loved to escape in. Since the gaming was supposed to be about the third, I thought I could play along. I was wrong.

I maintained a few friendships, but gaming felt awkward, so I stopped going. In silent protest, both Amanda and Gretchen stopped playing as well. Both were angry at the bigoted behav-ior, and the accompanying gossip. I convinced them to return though, and I told them I would start to look for a new group where I would just stay closeted. Gretchen told me it would be better to just be up front, then I could gauge if a group would be a good fit. Amanda agreed with her, but I was convinced they were wrong. *And why should my sexuality be a concern when playing a game that is about playing someone else? Although there may be merciless teasing, most gamers don't give two shits if a guy role-plays a female character. But any character played by a gay guy is automatically gay unless he plays a woman;*

which is seen as "normal." I tried on a few new fellowships, and I followed Gretchen's advice. Results were all too familiar.

That night, no one wished me "Happy Birthday," we just drank and talked about that which shall not be named. I was finally a legal adult, and I had never been more confused in my life. I have come to realize that most of the fellowship really tried to be okay with my sexuality. I hope as they encountered more gay people over the years, they became more accepting and understanding. At the very least no one grabbed torches and pitchforks; and when I stopped coming, I was told that I was missed. I decided I had to learn what it meant to be gay, and I had to learn if "gay" was more than sex – I sincerely hoped it would be – but I was worried I would be disappointed.

Chapter 18

LIKE IT LIKE THAT

January 1995. San Antonio, Texas.

When Amanda and I left the Candelabra, it was surreal. Our last night together was much the same as any other, and I wouldn't have it any other way. We could have sat around boo-hooing, but instead, we finished as we had started. Together, and doing what we enjoyed. I was mad for about ten seconds that she had ditched me, but I changed my mind when she told me that was the most satisfying sex she'd had for quite some time. And she needed it. Six weeks in boot camp without male contact was going to be torture for her.

After I told her about the proposal Gabe made, she laughed and told me I should have gone for it. I explained, yet again that I was tired of casual sex. That wasn't going to be how I found a relationship. I was beginning to think that relationship was a four-letter-word in the "gay" sphere. And I had discovered that when I got horny, finding *that kind* of companionship was a simple feat.

But I had discovered the Candelabra, and that was where I spent the bulk of my free time after Amanda shipped out. I got to know the owners rather well, but without Amanda to force me out of my shell, I tended to sit back and read a book or doodle in my drawing pad. I had become accustomed to men hitting on me at the bars, and I when it didn't happen at the coffee shop, I was unsure how to proceed. Somehow, bar pick-up lines didn't feel appropriate.

Until my first day of college, I spent a great deal of time at the Candelabra, but my hopes of finding something more meaningful than sex with a man were defeated as readily as Cobra Commander. I had the opportunity to meet guys and make friends but instead hid behind a book.

I attended my first day at UTSA (University of Texas at San Antonio) with a great deal of excitement. I had learned a great deal during my semester off, but I was ready to go back to something familiar, and I had always done well in school.

My first class was College Algebra – *which was a breeze. I tested into a higher class, but that was the only math credit I needed. I can do math, but I don't enjoy it.* I stepped into a giant auditorium-style classroom. It sat two hundred and fifty students, and on the first day of class almost every seat was taken. I was early – *I'm always early* – and had my choice of seats. I sat four rows back, and right on the aisle. I grabbed my notebook and began doodling.

"Hi, Jay. Can I sit by you?" Gabe was standing to my right, and his smile was charming.

"Sure. How ya been?"

"Good. First day of classes. I'm happy to see a familiar face."

"Same here." I was in complete agreement, it was nice to see a familiar face. I wasn't sure what to expect.

"So, I really want to apologize again for that time at the Candelabra. That really wasn't me. It was stupid, what I really wanted to do was ask for your number. I'd really like to take you on a date, or just hang out, but I'd rather it was a date. Seriously, that wasn't me, and I have no idea what I would have done if you said yes."

When I smiled, he quickly added, "You don't have to answer now. No pressure." He gave me the prince charming again and put his hand on his chin. Whenever he did that, I thought he looked like a young Doctor Strange, and I loved the illusion.

"What's your schedule look like?" I asked. We compared and discovered we had similar schedules. Algebra was the only class we shared, I can't remember exactly what his major was, but I'm sure it was something Science-y.

Before class ended, we agreed to meet up for lunch during a break. He produced a bagged lunch, and I grabbed a couple slices of pizza from the cafeteria. We found an open table tucked away in a corner.

"Nice t-shirt, I didn't notice it in Algebra," after his eyes did the head-to-toe-and-back-again dance, while I took off my jacket.

"Thanks," I looked down like I hadn't spent hours deciding what to wear the night before. It was a solid dark blue with The Tick's face in the center.

"So, are you really a fanboy? Or do you just like superhero tee's?" he asked as he modeled me an incredulous face.

"Oh, fanboy completely. I'm a dork through and through. Comics. D&D. Video games. And I read all the time. Mostly sci-fi and fantasy. Still wanna take me on that date?" I challenged him.

"More than ever. I like all those things too. I'm utterly," pause, "Flabbergasted."

"Seriously?" I didn't believe him, and I think he reciprocated the feeling. We sat there and played some form of improv Geek Trivial Pursuit. I don't remember either of us stumping the other. Like him, I too was – pause – flabbergasted.

"What are you doing after class," I asked. I had become intrigued. Gabe was a dork too, and he was gay, and he was cute. He still seemed too serious, but once we started talking about books, games, and superheroes, he loosened up some. I didn't have the instant chemistry with him, but I really liked how much we had in common.

"Why? You want to go on that date today?" he asked.

"Actually, yeah. I think that could be fun. Where we going?"

"Well, actually I don't have much cash. I didn't think it would be so soon. I could tell my, um, proposal really turned you off. It was just…"

"I know. And I get it. My first time at a bar was no picnic. It wasn't even that; honestly, I've been getting used to that. I was just bummed that Amanda was leaving."

"Oh?" His face beamed. And then faded, "But yeah, I don't really have enough money to take you anywhere fun."

"This one's on me then. I think I have a good idea."

"I don't know. I said I wanted to take you out," Gabe's face morphed into its naturally serious state.

"Then you better make a good impression, so I want to go out with you again," and I flashed him my goofy grin – *my flirting skills were improving.*

"Ooh. I like a challenge. I'll need to be back here by 5:00. Mike is picking me up after he gets off work. I don't have a car," he stated.

"No worries. I do. I can take you home if we don't get you back here in time. Where do you live?"

"Out by Universal City." *Oh. Damn. I had moved back in with my parents, which was an hour's drive from the university. UC was close to an hour in the other direction. Especially if there was traffic.*

I had a hunch, so I took him to an arcade; a decent one not far from UTSA. I was completely correct with my intuition. Gabe loved arcades as much as I did. We quickly discovered we both loved "fighting games." My favorite was *X-Men: Children of the Atom – naturally. It was a great game that got greater when it became Marvel vs. Capcom –* and his was *Tekken – the first one.*

I ended up spending about twenty bucks on quarters, but that only left five for gas – plenty to get back home on. I wasn't ready for the date to end, but I was out of funds.

"Want me to take you back to the school? Or you do you want to hang out longer?" I was wearing the goofy grin again. I had a great time. He liked to talk smack when he played, but he took it well too. Losing didn't bother him, but he was fiercely competitive. He enjoyed games for the fun of the game and wasn't obsessed with winning. A true gamer.

"Oh. I'm not going anywhere unless you need to get rid of me." He was looking serious again – *boo.*

"Oh, no. It's not that. I haven't had this much fun in a long time. And I just spent New Year's in New Orleans. I just spent all my fun money, and I need to put gas in my tank. I'm not ready for our first date to end."

"That mean I get a second?" he asked, as the gravity of his expression reversed.

"We'll see," I hoped it sounded as coyly as intended.

"I've got a few bucks. I could get us some fast food. If we stick to the value menu. And you get free coffee at Candelabra. I've got enough for one too," he offered.

"Smart. I like it. So long as you don't drag me to Church's Chicken, and you've got your second date."

"Damn. I was just about to suggest Church's."

"Smartass."

He glanced around the arcade, and when he noticed no one watching, he kissed me. No tongue or anything. But right on the lips and embraced me simultaneously; it lasted a few seconds. He stepped back and spun around.

"Let's go get some chicken."

Chapter 19

THE GREAT UNKNOWN

September 1994. San Antonio, Texas.

I told Amanda every gruesome detail of my first night at the bar. She was fascinated, but I don't think she fully believed me. She told me it would be an excellent place to meet guys and explore my sexuality. She reminded me that I had been with exactly one woman and one man, and she couldn't believe that I could be completely sure I was gay. I asked her how she knew she wasn't a lesbian since she had never been with a woman. *The reply? "That's different. Straight is normal."* Sigh.

We argued the point constantly, and she conceded she would have to try sex with a woman. She knew she had zero interest in exploring that avenue, but it was more important for her to be right. She told me she would go with me to the Moondust but thought maybe it would be better to try a week-night, hoping for a smaller crowd. She also suggested we could get high and offered a few options.

Amanda and I had begun to experiment with drugs. Nothing too heavy and on an infrequent basis, and it was always just the two of us, and always at her apartment – *at least at first.*

I really didn't like the uppers – *I already can't sit still for very long, and I like to sleep.* The hallucinogens always left me with a splitting headache the next day. I never tried heroin, but my experience with opioid pain-pills made me feel like Hydro-Man, pure liquid. Alcohol and pot were much more my speed, their effects are easy to control by intake.

On a Tuesday night, when we were both off work, we decided to hit the club. I was extremely anxious to face it again, but I was happy to have someone at my back. Amanda decided she was going to pick up a woman that night, and in preparation procured two tabs of Ecstasy – *we called it "X" back then –* we decided to only take half so we could gauge its effects.

When we got there, Jerry was again at the door, and he remembered me. Both Amanda and I were consequently "stamped-in" as adults. Amanda went to the closest bar and brought me back a beer. I stood and chatted with Jerry for a while. The X had loosened me up enough to feel comfortable. It also helped that there wasn't nearly the amount of people.

Amanda disappeared almost immediately, where the X had me enjoying the sensations of the ordinary – holding the cold beer, feeling the smoke in my mouth, running my fingers through my hair – she had a pressing need to be pressed, and she decided it was time to find a woman.

Jerry was easy to talk to and explained that the dance-floor room was less "cruise-y" than the blacklight one. He explained that most people in that room on weekend nights expected the treatment I had received, and he disclosed that the restroom could be reached without traipsing that depravity. He asked if I had come to see the Tuesday Night Drag Show, and I pretended that I had. I was clueless about the nature of a drag show.

As I had only glanced into the dance-floor room before, I found there was more than just the giant dance floor. There was a large U-shaped bar along the wall adjoining the blacklight room that took up about one-third of the cavernous room.

On the far side of the dance floor was auditorium-ish seating – *two benches, one low one high* – along the entire length of the dance floor. To the far right of the dance floor rested a stage as large as the one in my high school complete with curtains and elaborate lighting. Above the stage perched the DJ booth.

Between the bar and the dance floor there stood numerous standing tables, and all the "seating" was virtually full. I bought a beer and found a spot along the back wall to stand and watch the show. I still hadn't seen Amanda, after she bought me my first beer, but I hadn't been molested once. I was incredibly relaxed and becoming more so with every sip of beer.

When the lights came on, and the show started, I was mesmerized. My absolute favorite gay activity is drag shows. They are amazingly entertaining – *drag shows are the coffee of the gay world. A bad drag show is better than no drag show. And like coffee, drag queens come in a variety of flavors. Some are campy and funny; the comedy queens. Some are glitzy and glamourous; the pageant queens. Same are strange and interesting; my favorite queens. Some are convincingly female; the fishy queens. All are brave and indomitable. All are incredible entertainers, and I think of them as the modern-day heiresses of Shakspearian tradition. They aren't simply men dressing up as woman, they are artists committed to maintaining an illusion. It's not some giant mind fuck, most don't live their lives in women's clothes. And most aren't trying to fool straight men into some sort of gay sex. And for you straight men out there that are afraid you may be attracted to a fishy queen, you should applaud them for their hard work. You aren't suddenly gay and attracted to men, you are attracted to what appears to be an incredibly attractive woman, and it's really no different than many video game heroines. Lara Croft is really just the illusion of a gorgeous woman that was created by a man; not very different than a fishy queen.*

Do yourself a favor and find the nearest drag show and go. Keep an open mind and remember you are there to be entertained, not confused. If you can't find a show, and even if you can, watch RuPaul's Drag Race. Any season. Every season. I'm sure they are streaming somewhere in cyberspace. RuPaul says it best when describing the queens, they possess "charisma, uniqueness, nerve, and talent," and I could write pages about drag shows without doing them justice. Just go. Hey Ru, if you find yourself reading this and looking for a guest judge or make-over candidate...

I watched numerous queens perform and had a few more beers, and the alcohol was exacerbating the effects of the X. My inhibitions were at an all-time low, and as Amanda liked to say, I was inspecting the meat. There was a variety of "cuts," just as the time before, just fewer of each – *except the nelly hipsters. There were more of them. They always seemed to flock the queens.*

After each queen performed once or twice, there was an intermission. The DJ played music and several people danced, but most headed to the bar or restrooms. There was a feeling of randomness as everyone began moving. I still hadn't seen Amanda, but I had been scanning the crowd, and there were twice as many men as women so she would be easy to spot – *to be brutally honest, her ass made her easy to spot in any crowd. The first time I saw Nikki Minaj, I wondered if the two were related.*

When I was scanning the room, I noticed that many men were looking pointedly at me. Not constantly, but frequently enough that I would catch their eye from time-to-time. They were as varied as the Legion of Superheroes. Thin, chubby, fat. Old, Young. Black, Hispanic, White. Ugly, cute. One was even a *wow.* I deciphered quickly that these eye games were the first overture – *and for once, this seemed obvious to me. Maybe it was the X.*

When the crowd dispersed, I moved to a standing table closer to the dance floor which was an extension of the stage for the queens, and how they strolled to and through the crowd to collect tips. It was vacant, and it provided a better view of both the *wow* and the show once it restarted. *And when you go to a drag show, take cash. A lot of it. The queens are rarely paid to perform, and they work for tips. They are one thousand times more entertaining than a good dinner and a movie, so pay them their worth.*

When the *wow* noticed that I noticed that he had been noticing me, he flashed me a quick smile and dipped his black cowboy hat in my direction. He appeared to be in his mid-twenties, Hispanic, with an adorable baby-face covered with a thick goatee and mustache. His nose wasn't great – maybe a four – but not having a nice one did not subtract from his *wow status.* He also appeared to be the "rhinestone" type of cow-boy – *referencing the movie, not the drag show* – he was only dressed the part.

After the noticing came the extended looks. When we made eye contact, we would linger each time slightly longer than before. It was like a game of chicken to see who would look away first, and considering I was feeling as loose and relaxed as Plastic-Man, I found myself really enjoying the experience. *I wanted to talk to him, but I was unsure how to go about it. There are no ridiculous female/male protocols to follow. Don't get me wrong, I discovered many ridiculous protocols that are unique to the gay bars, but we didn't have "traditional" ones to pin us down.*

As the show commenced, I spied *Wow* as he left his friends and walked my way. As he strolled past my table, I noticed him inspect my beer. I turned and watched an amazing ass in skin-tight Wranglers head to the bar. He was just shy of being chubby but proportionate. Stocky or thick would describe him best. I had a similar instant attraction that I had experienced with Jerry, and the X caused me to focus on that. I stared at his ass the entire time he was at the bar, and I believe he stood to present it to its best effect.

I caught him looking pointedly to a friend that he had been "sitting" with, and I saw the friend give him a thumbs up. The friend noticed me noticing and flashed me a thumbs up also. *Odd,* I thought. I saw the *wow* turn from the bar awkwardly carrying two shots of tequila – *I guessed by the lime wedges –* and two Bud Lights. He made eye contact with me, dipped his cowboy hat again, and walked directly towards me.

As he approached the table, he sat down the drinks, extended his hand and introduced himself, Ray – short for Raymundo. He had a thick Texan twang mixed with a touch of a Mexican inflection – it is a very common accent that seems unique to South-Central Texas.

He asked if he could buy me a drink, and when I said sure, he offered me a shot and a beer by sliding them towards me. *I was lucky, and it took me a few years to discover that it is never a good idea to accept a drink from a stranger that you don't take directly from the bartender. Never. Also, never leave your drink unattended nor attended by someone you don't trust. Seriously. Don't do it.*

We made small talk while watching the show and tipped the queens. *I have spent more than two decades of my life as a tipped employee, and I know how much that can fluctuate. I whole-heartedly believe in tip karma. Those who tip well are tipped well in return.* He seemed to be enjoying the show as much as I was and we both kept shuffling our feet to get closer to one another. The beer by its very nature soon had mother nature calling, and as much apprehension as I felt about my previous undertaking, I couldn't postpone any longer.

I explained that I had to use the restroom and asked if he would watch my beer. This trip was nothing like the first. It wasn't as crowded, and the line moved quickly. No one was dry humping my leg, and I knew which urinal to avoid. When I returned, he had another shot and beer waiting. During my journey to the Savage Land, I swallowed the other half tab of X I had been carrying. I was feeling great.

Before finishing that beer, we started full-on making-out during the show; the kind that involved tongues and roaming hands. It happened quite suddenly, and it was amazingly intense. We were pressed very closely – our midsection practically glued together – when the MC grabbed us each by a shoulder and separated us. Neither of us had seen her approach nor heard her comments about those delicious young studs in the corner about to try and make a baby.

She handed Ray the microphone she had been carrying, and we both stared rather dumbfounded; she then reached down and grabbed us both by the dick – *I wasn't quite at full sail, and neither was Ray. Trust me, I was close enough to be an expert, not to mention that our hands had been "exploring."* After letting go, she snatched back the mic and said, "Sorry fellas. I should have let that go on longer, then we could have had a real show."

She kissed us both on the cheek and whispered, "Thank you boys, they were getting bored." We both tipped her a ten, and she kissed our hands theatrically. As she walked away from the table, she said into the mic, "What the hell is wrong with you? Don't follow me with the spotlight, keep it on that hot two-piece chicken." When the spotlight swung back to our location, we had returned to our previous endeavors. We quickly separated, and each of us dropped our hands in front of our cocks, which was met with laughter and, "Thanks, boys. This place would suck without alcohol."

We kept mostly separated after that and watched the show. We played "footsie" and exchanged occasional extended touches, and we carried an engaging – *for a loud club* – conversation. He even asked if I had the X-gene after commenting on my hat. He explained he read some comics when he was a kid. It was challenging to keep our hands and mouths off each other, but we had gotten so much attention there were always eyes on us. His friends constantly pointed and laughed as theatrically as possible.

He asked if I wanted to go grab some breakfast with him. I still hadn't spotted Amanda, so I checked my pager. 0404 – her number twice meant she was home. The second page was 04808 – 808 looks somewhat like a kid's drawing of a top-down perspective of a car, which translates to her availability to come to retrieve me. The last page was 0487 – late. I could stay out as late as I wanted and had a dependable way home.

Food may not have been my first choice, but I was excited to go someplace less crowded with Ray.

Chapter 20

UNDER YOU

Late Spring 1995. San Antonio, Texas.

The first couple of months of my relationship with Gabe were sensational, we even established a *D&D* group where I got my first taste in DM-ing. At the beginning of the semester, I had also started working at a new restaurant. Graveyards weren't going to cut it while I was in school. I was working full-time hours, and Gabe had a part-time job at a game store in the mall. When I wasn't working or in class, Gabe and I were together or talking on the phone.

We got along well with only occasional arguments that usually stemmed from differing opinions regarding Alpha Flight and the X-Men. We spent a great deal of time in his tiny room that was an add-on above the garage. He had a large family with twelve siblings, and he was the eldest; as such he had the only private room in the house. It was like a standard sized room bitch-slapped by a few Pym Particles. It made Amanda's apartment feel like a palace. The slanted roof made it impossible to stand fully erect, and the room was dominated by a single-sized bed, a tiny desk that barely held his state-of-the-art computer, and a low bookshelf filled with Robert Jordan and Star Wars novels.

I was living with my parents again, and the distance made it close to impossible to spend time there – even though it would have been more comfortable and less chaotic – I was already spending three to four hours driving daily. Sometimes more. But I was extremely happy to be in a relationship. It was all the best parts of what I had with Skye, but it was with a man; it felt more honest, more intimate, and more fulfilling. I liked him a great deal, but I desired more chemistry.

Our sex life developed slowly. I think Gabe was afraid to push it after his initial comment. It was unnecessary, but it was rather sweet. It developed in stages, and it was wonderful being able to experience a sexual life at a slower pace. In no way an original discovery, but I learned that sex was much more meaningful with someone you know and cherish.

It got to the point when the subject of anal sex was broached; and once he discovered I had crossed that bridge once before, he began to apply pressure. However, his idea of anal sex only went one way. Gabe made it clear that he wasn't prepared to try receiving – bottom – but he also made it abundantly evident that he was ready to play the top. I wasn't entirely comfortable with this situation, I honestly liked both   the prostate is an amazing gland – and I felt assigning "roles" was silly. I was of a mind that we should just go with the flow and find what felt right, but he was the type that had to classify everything.

The sex was incredible though; maybe not at first but it developed into something wonderful. He was never open to a reversal, but I have no complaints. I was able to discover something about myself that used to feel shameful. I always considered that I was supposed to feel as though I was allowing myself to be violated when engaging in anal sex. I grew up believing that gay men were predators but discovering that side of my sexuality with Gabe felt nothing like that. It was merely two people who cared for each other discovering what felt pleasurable.

I was working as often as I could; we were understaffed, and I was making great money. I was trying to squirrel as much away as possible. I was determined to finance my education myself. I was spending a great deal on gas, and I had bought a brand-new Ford Ranger – *she was medium willow green, manual transmission, and base model. But she was brand new, payments were low, and I was so damned proud of myself to finance a new vehicle at eighteen. She had two names: Trucka and She-Hulk.* But I was thriving at my new job. I was already given bartender shifts, and I was head trainer.

The restaurant was a bar and grill type serving Mexican food and a few award-winning margaritas. There were a couple of locations, and I worked at the newest of the two. We served great food and had excellent wait staff; the managers and owners were also awesome and took an interest in their employees as people rather than workers. It was one of the best jobs I have ever had, and I met my two bestest-best friends there. The other friendships were meaningful as well. I was accepted not only for the gay me but also the geek me. We were a close-knit group, and we ran off those that upset the dynamic.

I was standing at the "chip machine" filling a basket of tortilla chips when Amy, Bo's trainer came running up to me. "Oh my god, you have to trade me trainees. He won't shut up, and he won't listen to a word I say."

"Yeah, no. Where is he?"

"I told him to go take a break. I needed a break. Please trade me, please, please, please."

"No way. He can't be that bad. Ronnie likes him." Ronnie was one of the shift managers.

"That's because he wants in his pants," she explained.

"Is he gay?" I asked.

She let a quick chortle escape her lips. "Have you not talked to him?"

"Not much, but I didn't think he was gay," I admitted.

"I didn't either. But when he found out Ronnie and Jim were gay, he wouldn't stop talking about it. I think he's told me he's gay twenty times in the last fifteen minutes. But he's told me many things in the last fifteen minutes. He never shuts up."

Bo – *short for Bonafacio. All his siblings had Latin names –* walked up and started munching on chips. He never seemed to talk with his mouth full, but he also never seemed to stop talking while eating. *It's one of his magic talents.*

Once he discovered I was gay and out and young, he was glued to me whenever we worked together. He asked me thousands of questions. On so many topics. I didn't like him. He looked down on people who weren't rich and said he only worked to have something to do. He whined continuously that his Jag was being repaired and he was stuck using the pick-up. He only wore Ralph Lauren clothing – *if it didn't have the little Polo guy it wasn't a real shirt.* He constantly made fun of those who lived in trailer parks – *I lived in a trailer park.* He was a smug little bastard that had gotten everything he had ever wanted. Or so I thought.

He was fascinated that I had a boyfriend. He never left me alone. "How long have you been together?" He asked.

"Almost five months."

"Are you the top or the bottom?" he asked.

"None of your business."

"Are you happy with him?" he asked.

" … "

Bo was slowly making inroads, yes, he was a snobby motor mouth who annoyed me, but he was incredibly funny. We worked almost every day together, and he was always talking to me. Tuesday was my only day off, and I made the mistake of swinging by the restaurant after class in lieu of Gabe's house. When I walked through the door, I was *volun-told* I would work. It was only supposed to be the afternoon shift; the evening bartender would be in by five. I quickly called Gabe and told him I'd head over afterward.

That shift was abnormally busy, and the evening bartender never showed. When I worked behind the bar, Bo realized he had a captive audience and would corner me to talk my ear off. Ronnie finally stopped by and offered me a break. I would have killed for a cigarette and listening to Bo rattle on riled my nerves. *It was about 8:00 and my previous cigarette was six hours earlier.*

I sprinted to my truck, and when I opened the door, I saw my pager lying on the floorboard. I hadn't realized it wasn't in my pocket. I lit up a smoke and went through my pages. Almost twenty from Gabe. *Oh shit, he was expecting me by 7:00 at the latest. Twenty in an hour though?*

I stood out there and smoked a few sticks before returning to Bo's endless questions.

Ronnie had been helpful and had cleaned up much of the mess. Two hours until close, and as busy as it was all day, it was suddenly dead. Only a few tables. Bo walked up to his usual spot at the server station and for once was silent. It didn't last long, but he just watched me stacking clean bar glasses for what seemed like an eternity.

"Are you alright?" Bo asked.

"Yeah. Fine. Why?" I answered.

"You look annoyed, and you seemed to be having fun throughout the shift. If anything, I thought a cigarette would improve your mood," he said thoughtfully.

"I guess Gabe is mad at me once again. I was supposed to be over to his place an hour ago, and I haven't had a chance to call and let him know I'm stuck here," I tried to keep the exasperation out of my voice.

"Why would he be mad? You're stuck at work, and if he was worried, he could call."

"He paged." My face screwed up into a scowl.

"So, call him. There's a phone right there. Ronnie won't give a damn."

"Twenty times," I added.

"What?" He thought for a few seconds. "He paged you twenty times? In an hour? Jealous much?"

"It's not that..." I started.

"Bullshit. It's that or something like it. Did you guys have plans or something? Is he expecting a baby?"

I started laughing. "I really don't know what his deal is. I should probably call him back," I said pointedly, hoping he would give me some privacy. Instead, he went and sat at the barstool closest to the phone. This is what he heard.

"Hey. I got stuck at..."

. . .

"What? That's stupid. The other bartender didn't show up."

. . .

"How the hell should I know?"

. . .

"Right. I'll just take off in the middle of the shift and fuck everyone over. This job rocks and I'm making..."

. . .

"What are you talking about? We didn't have plans."

. . .

"You were going to take the *four* of us out to dinner? With what? You're always broke."

. . .

"Oh, of course. You expected me to pay. Shocking."

. . .

"That's why I'm always working. School's expensive."

. . .

"Whatever. I'm just going to head home after work, I'll be stuck here until close, and if I go to your place, I won't get home until two or three. I have my Spanish final tomorrow, and I still have some studying to do."

. . .

"Wow. Are you serious? I don't fucking care. You have two hands, use one of them. I'm not your fucking blow up doll."

. . .

"Fine. Yeah, I'm off Thursday night, and that's fine. I'm not paying for everyone though. I got you and me, but you can buy theirs. Are you still coming to the party with me on Friday?"

. . .

"I don't need your permission to go to the party, and you told me you would come. Everyone wants to meet you."

. . .

"Whatever. I don't care if you don't go. I am."

...

"You're wrong. I really don't care. You don't get to make my decisions, and I sure as fuck don't want to make yours for you. If you want to go, great. If not, don't."

...

"No. I told you I have to study, and it's already going to be a late night."

...

"I don't have anything else to say to you that can't wait until I see you tomorrow."

...

"Just stop. I'll see you tomorrow. I'm not calling you back when I get home."

...

"Whatever. Bye."

Chapter 21

HOLLOW

Autumn, 1994. San Antonio, Texas.

Amanda conceded that I was right, and I could know that I was gay without again sleeping with a woman. She wouldn't talk about her night, except to tell me that she had given it the good old college try, but no dick, no dice. After her affair, she returned to the bar just in time to see the drag queen separate Ray and I; she decided to head home and call up a fuck buddy. Apparently, she had to reaffirm her heterosexuality.

Although she wouldn't tell me about her experience, she demanded to hear all about mine. I disclosed that the sex was amazing, and it included the anal variety. It was my first time, and I liked it both ways. It ramps up the intimacy to a higher degree, and after Ray, anal sex would become something I only shared with those I had a special bond with. That kind of intimacy was not something I was ready to share with a stranger. In my mind sex became separated into two categories: fooling around, and full-on. There were only two things that separated them. Full-on included anal and/or swallowing. Fooling around was everything else.

Without the drugs and alcohol, I doubt things would have gone as far as they did with Ray. I had that all-too-familiar headache from the X, but I wasn't feeling hung-over, so I wasn't complaining. It was one of the few times I touched that drug, but I had a much better experience at the club. I had adored the drag show, so I knew I would be going back. I avoided the weekends for the most part unless there was a show.

Amanda had discovered a hole-in-the-wall bar that didn't check IDs and begun spending her time there. It had a better selection of men than I had gotten used to seeing her with, so that's a bonus. I went with her once, but her, "This is Jay. He's gay," greeting wasn't really appreciated.

That's when I got to experience my first closeted douche-bag. He – *let's call him Denial* – flirted all night and made all sorts of comments about how he's always wondered what it was like to be with a guy. But Denial has never met the right guy. All the gay guys Denial knew acted feminine, but I was just a dude, and he liked it. He didn't realize gay guys could be "normal." Blah, blah, blah. Then as quick as The Flash on crack, Denial is suddenly pissed at me. Like I'm the one that's been hitting on him. What Denial is feeling is my fault, and I'm somehow messing with his mind. Never mind that I'd been trying to avoid Denial's questions all night, and the fact that I had zero interest. Somehow, Denial's attraction to me is me wanting to fuck him. And he's angry and bitter and telling everyone else I'm gay and recruiting – *It wasn't the first time I would have to contend with a "Denial." I did learn to get the hell out when encountering a new one.* As annoying as that experience was, it wasn't nearly as bad as the open hostility, dirty looks, and pointed comments of fag and queer. *Amanda's greeting was getting old. "Don't ask, don't tell" may be an abhor-rent idea, but sometimes it felt safe, warm, cozy.*

So, when Amanda was frequenting her haunt – *which was a nightly occurrence* – I headed to the Moondust – *although I was still working graveyards; so, not nearly as often as her.* Over the course of the next couple of months I got in touch with my sexuality. I went through my first slut phase. I tried on men like shoes. I generally found someone that caught my eye and went home with him or brought him back to our tiny apartment. I only ever fooled around, full-on was reserved for something I hadn't yet found.

During this time, I didn't just ride a carousel of one-night stands; I went on dates with the some. Meeting these guys wasn't only about sex, I was looking for more. I didn't necessarily want a relationship, I just desired something more profound than sex. What I learned was that sex was simply the first hurdle. If the sex wasn't good, then I never pursued anything more meaningful. I was equal opportunity and never developed a real "type." During this time, there were many – *more than I'd care to admit.* I was enjoying the sex, but what I needed was a gay friend. I just didn't realize it.

There were a few notable men along the way, but for whatever reason, it fizzled. I was never sleeping with multiple men simultaneously; it was more that I would move from one to the next. Most would warrant a date, some a few. I have never been the type to juggle multiple partners, it seems like it would require far too much work that is obviously destined for disaster. *Like Skeletor's scheming, the pay-off – even on a rare success – simply isn't worth the effort.*

Whenever Ray and I encountered each other, we would have a repeat of our first night, and it was always intense. But we never really connected on a romantic level, we did, however, develop a friendship. A bar friendship. I also developed a comradery with his friends, so I wasn't stuck alone at the bars while watching the shows and choosing my delectable dessert for the night. And Ray was usually available if I didn't meet anyone else. We had an unspoken agreement to play it hands-off until it was clear neither of us had an interest in another guy.

I developed a reputation at the Moondust in those early days, one that I am rather proud of. I became known as the "comic guy," with various prefixes. I hadn't yet realized that the gay clubs were as clique-ish as high school, and gay men can be such catty bitches. To Jerry and most of the staff, I was the "cute comic guy." The yuppie that had dry-humped me on my first night had been talking shit about me for some time; to his entourage, I was the "revolting comic guy." Some knew me as the "cock-tease comic guy," apparently it got around that I wouldn't do anal. There were a few others, but I only heard the "comic guy" part. *I always wanted to correct them and tell them it was "comic book guy," but I rather liked having some notoriety.*

I had a crash course on being gossiped about, but it never really got to me. I had learned long ago that not everyone would like me, so I didn't waste time trying to change their opinion. It didn't hurt that even the nasty rumors about me never kept me from hooking up with anyone that struck my fancy. I had learned that it was incredibly easy to find sex, so I usually only went to watch my favorite queens and would find something interesting to try on while there.

Although Amanda and I had separate night-lives, we still spent a great deal of time together. When I got home from work, or some guy's place, it was usually between six and seven am, and that was the time she would start her day. She didn't work until noon, but she started her day with a few drinks, and I had begun to end mine in a similar fashion. We would just chill and talk for a few hours every day, and our friendship deepened.

Amanda's trips to her bar became a nightly occurrence, and her experimentation with drugs almost got to the point of "using." I never said anything as I was already a committed "pot head," so who was I to judge – *smoking pot is yet another thing that I don't tell, even when asked.* She recognized that she was on a downward spiral and decided that she needed some direction. Unsure of what either of us was going to do, we decided not to renew the lease on our "shoebox." We had until Halloween, 1994, just shy of a month until everything changed. During that time, nothing changed.

She continued to head to her hole-in-the-wall on a nightly basis, and I went to the Moondust the four nights a week I didn't work the graveyard shift. *There were several awkward encounters when we both brought someone home, that were usually more entertaining than catastrophic – one guy was ready to attack me and one of my "dates" when they walked in on us.*

Within a couple months of my eighteenth birthday, I had had an extensive sexual education. I learned my turn-ons and -offs, and I became comfortable with my body – *I no longer thought of myself as ugly, in my mind I was "average," and that was perfectly acceptable to me.*

My entire existence revolved around working, drinking, getting stoned and getting laid. It was growing tiresome, and I really started to wonder if being gay was just about the sex. I wanted something more, but I didn't know how to find it; so, I continued going through the familiar motions.

Chapter 22

GONNA GET BETTER

Late Spring, 1995. San Antonio, Texas.

When we arrived at the party, Gabe quickly sat in a corner with a scowl on his face. I made the rounds; had a few shots, said hi to everyone and informed those who hadn't yet met Gabe that he had come with me. I grabbed myself a beer and Gabe a wine cooler and went to sit with the pouting princess.

Most came over to meet Gabe, and he put on a fake happy-face and chatted with them all. Whenever we were alone, he whined and whined. He wanted to go home. We would have more fun if it were just the two of us. We could be off fucking somewhere. He could think of a hundred places he'd rather be. I couldn't think of one, but he had stopped asking my opinion on much of anything.

We were sitting on the couch facing the front door when Bo and Kayla, a mutual friend and coworker, walked in. They noticed us and walked over. We had been alone, and I think they could tell I was annoyed with Gabe.

"So, this must be Gabe?" Bo asked. I introduced them all to one another.

Bo looked right at me and said, "He is so not in your league. You're way cuter than he is."

"Hey. What the hell? I'm sitting right here," Gabe replied.

Bo spun to look at him and asked, "What? You don't think it's true?" Kayla started laughing and went to find drinks.

"Well? Are you not going to answer me?" Bo had the friendliest smile on his face. He wasn't acting at all aggressive; it was the kind of teasing done between friends. I think he was giving Gabe an opportunity to brag or something like he wanted to see if Gabe would show off.

"Are you going to let him talk to me that way?" Gabe asked me.

"Are you serious?" I replied.

"You don't think that was rude? If someone said something like that to you, I'd be angry."

"That's because you seem to think you own me. Besides, he was only teasing you. Weren't you Bo?"

"Not really, no. I didn't mean any offense, but c'mon, you are way out of his league. You have to know this."

"What? You have a thing for my boyfriend?" interrupted Gabe, and the way he said boyfriend sounded much more like "property" to my ears.

"Eww, no. No offense, Jay, but no. You just don't do it for me," I completely believed him. "But we'd make a much better-looking couple," he flashed Gabe the cattiest smile I had ever seen, then sat down on my lap and planted a long kiss right on my lips.

We both started laughing. Uproariously. We fell to the floor and rolled around, and nothing we did could get us to stop. He had cut through the tension like a surgeon, and at that moment I met the true Bo.

Gabe was furious, and he stomped out of the apartment. Our laughing was out of control, so I didn't notice. Kayla returned as Gabe slammed the door behind him.

"What'd I miss," demanded Kayla. This brought on a new fit of laughter.

I turned and looked to where Gabe had been sitting, expecting him to be laughing as well. The entire scene was so ridiculous and obviously absurd, I thought he would join in the mirth and come out of his shell. At no point during this interaction did I think anything was "improper." It was good old-fashioned silly fun, and nothing said or done was meant to hurt anyone's feelings. At least that was my perspective.

"Where's Gabe?" I asked while wiping tears from my eyes and holding back further chuckles.

"I saw him slam the door. He looked pissed. What'd I miss?" Kayla asked again.

I looked at her, then the door, then Bo. We both turned to Kayla and shrugged. I didn't think anything was amiss. I hadn't laughed that hard in a long time.

"Aren't you going to go talk to him?" Bo asked.

"No. I don't think so. I'm tired of being the one to apologize. And I didn't do anything wrong," like Sunfire, my blood was starting to boil.

"Don't you think that will piss him off more?" Kayla interjected.

"To be honest. I really don't give a fuck," I answered. Before that point, I hadn't realized what I needed to do. "I'm tired of his bullshit. I'm ending it tonight, he's a prick."

"Oh? Sorry if I did anything wrong," Bo seemed sincere with his apology.

"Are you kidding me. That was fucking hilarious, and if he didn't have a stick in his ass, he would have enjoyed it too."

"Maybe that's his problem? Maybe he needs one." Kayla ruminated. All three of us started laughing.

Eventually, Bo and Kayla convinced me to go and talk to Gabe, but they didn't know me well enough to realize that once I had settled on a course of action, little could turn me –

Nightwing levels of focus. The two however played upon my sense of propriety; I had to do the right thing.

I found Gabe sitting in She-Hulk sulking. When I tried to talk to him, he gave me the silent treatment. I eventually asked if he wanted me to take him home, and his only reply was an icy glare and a quick nod of his head. He stared out the passenger window the entire time. When we got to his house, he still wouldn't look at me; but before opening his door, he told me, "I think we should break up."

I don't think he got the reaction he wanted, because when I told him, "I think you're right," his head snapped around and his chilly countenance transformed to a look of death. He slammed the car door, and later the next week, I didn't see him at our Algebra final. We didn't have any contact for quite some time; whenever we encountered each other, we would go out of our way to keep from interacting.

Eventually, we got over it and were able to become friendly with one another. I don't know if he ever understood why it ended. I always got the impression that he blamed Bo, but Bo never said or did anything to poison our relationship. The kiss had been a joke, and I now believe that Bo knew precisely what the outcome would be, but that was just a catalyst for what I had already decided. Bo presented a situation that would exhibit Gabe's true nature.

I didn't enjoy being treated like property just because he stuck his dick inside of me. I don't know if he ever realized how his behavior toward me changed. I'm not the type of person who will follow orders from someone because he thinks he's the "man" in the relationship.

After our anti-climactic breakup, I turned around and went back to the party, hoping Bo and Kayla would still be there. I was happy when I returned, even though Kayla was wasted and passed out on one of the beds, and Bo seemed bored.

"I'm guessing you didn't make up. You got back here rather fast," Bo asked.

"He broke up with me," I answered with a derisive chuckle.

"That's because he knew you were about to. He had to be the one to end it. That way he could save face." I hadn't realized it, but Bo was right.

"Like it matters. I'm just happy to be done with his uptight ass," I admitted.

"Was it tight?" Bo asked, laughing.

"How the hell should I know. Does he seem like the type that would *allow* such an act?"

"Well, you're better off," he said with a smile. "We should go dancing," he offered.

"What? Now? What about the party?" I quickly countered.

"Everyone is drunk already, and Kayla passed out. We should go be around gay people and dance. It'll be fun. You can forget all about Gabe. Maybe find someone more your caliber."

"I can't dance," I looked at him sheepishly.

"Bullshit. Everyone can dance. Who gives a shit if you look stupid if you have fun? And if you're having fun, then you don't look stupid."

"I haven't been to the bars since school started, I doubt I'll get in as an adult."

"That could be a problem. Especially if we want to bar hop. Most of the smaller places don't allow minors." He grew silent for about fifteen seconds, then snapped his fingers like some cartoon character. "I've got it. Is Jayce still here?"

"I think so. Why?"

"C'mon, I've got an idea." He grabbed me by the bicep, and drug me around the apartment until we found him. Jayce was a part-time bartender, and he worked a business-y type job Monday through Friday and rarely came to parties. He was twenty-four, and his wife just gave birth to their second kid. He worked all the time and spent all his free time as a dad.

Incidentally, he was the bartender that didn't show up for his shift three days previously.

"Hey Jayce, can Jay borrow your ID? We wanna go bar hopping," Bo asked, interrupting the conversation he was having.

He looked at Bo, then me, then started laughing. "Yeah, of course." He turned to me and added. "I don't know why you didn't think of this earlier. Everyone asks if we're brothers."

I hadn't even thought about a fake ID, but I had to admit this was a perfect fix. "Thanks, Jayce. When do you work again, and I'll bring it back to you? Or if you want, I can bring it to your other job or house when I get out of classes tomorrow?"

"Hell. Just keep it. I'll go to the DMV on Monday and get a replacement. It'll give me an excuse to take a longer lunch break."

I took his ID, and on Bo's recommendation memorized all the important information, while I got stoned. Bo whined that I would be demotivated, but I assured him there was no way I'd be relaxed enough to attempt dancing without it. The only statistic that could potentially create problems was Jayce was a few inches taller than me, but it never came up – *August 11, 1970, was my new birthday and I was a Leo. Bo was smart to think of that; it came up more times than expected. Fun fact: I later found out my new birthday was shared by Jim Lee, my favorite X-Men artist of all time.* The best part of the ID was that it didn't expire until less than a month from my twenty-first birthday.

Chapter 23

REARRANGING THE BONES

Autumn 1994. San Antonio, Texas.

Amanda decided to join the Navy. She didn't want to go to college, and she wanted to travel. She knew she needed a change, and it was probably a good decision. She strolled into a recruitment office by the mall and signed up before discussing it with anyone. She was afraid her parents would talk her out of it.

When she took her ASVAB (Armed Services Vocational Aptitude Battery) – *a test to see which jobs you qualify for* – she scored very high, and she had her choice of any schooling. I think her career choice dealt with electronics, or mechanics – *something that sounded awful to me at any rate* – and her tech school was in Florida.

I started looking at colleges in the nearby area. I was considering relocating if I could find a school I could afford. When I brought this up with Amanda, she became obsessed with the idea. She even started researching schools with me. The more we talked about it, the more we became convinced it was a wonderful idea. She was scheduled to ship out shortly after

Thanksgiving, and we had found a few schools that met my criteria.

After consideration, we realized that her schooling would end long before mine; and depending on where she was sent for her first station, it might become troublesome to follow. There would be a likelihood that I would be "stuck" in Florida at a college that I had only chosen because of its proximity to Amanda's school. I wasn't terribly worried about the schooling; I wasn't even certain that college was the right path for me. I had grown up in the military and had great insight into the lifestyle, I knew it wasn't an option for me. I didn't want to be a waiter/bartender forever either, so college seemed like the way to go.

When we were packing our apartment, Amanda proposed to me. In a very casual manner, she said, "You know, we should just get married. I would make more money, and the Navy would move you wherever I get stationed." I didn't need to think about it long, but I made her get down on one knee. It solved the major issues, and we could continue our semi-codependent friendship.

I told my parents almost immediately. They were cognizant that Amanda and I were not romantically involved, but I still hadn't told them I was gay. I wasn't overly concerned about their reaction, my reticence stemmed from not wanting to talk about being gay. So far, all I had experienced was a revolving door of sexual partners. I was still hoping that there was something more. There were no healthy gay relationships to be found in pop culture. The few gay characters on the silver screen were simple stereotypes, and gay-themed movies all seemed to end in tragedy – *I'm looking at you* Torch Song Trilogy *and* Philadelphia. *Of course, there were great independent films and literature that could have provided a more well-rounded view of the "gay lifestyle," but I had no idea they existed nor where to find them.*

My parents didn't think it was a great idea, but they seemed to understand that I had loved relocating as a child; and by marrying Amanda, I could continue with the lifestyle. They supported our decision, so long as I focused on maintaining my education.

Amanda's parents had a very different reaction. They thought it was a terrible idea. They were worried that Amanda would meet "Mr. Right," and he wouldn't want anything to do with her since she was already married. And to a gay man no less. We weren't worried about that, however. Amanda didn't buy into the bullshit that her life would only have meaning with a "real" husband, and she certainly wouldn't marry some homophobe.

Her parents finally grudgingly accepted the arrangement, but they continuously tried to change our minds. When they discovered that my parents were still out of the loop regarding my sexuality, they pounced faster than a Blink Dog. They thought that I hadn't told my parents due to fear of their reaction. Amanda's parents said that they couldn't support the marriage if my parents weren't aware of the entire situation. They thought we would call off the union to avoid a confrontation. They were wrong.

When that conversation ended, we drove out to my parent's. Deep down, I was nervous that they would have some negative reaction, but I reminded myself that they had no issue with my sister, nor her friends. I was happy to have Amanda by my side, and I held her hand when I told them.

Of course, my trepidation was unfounded. My dad shrugged his shoulders, and my mom said, "So?" Nothing changed between us. I was still their son. I was still the same person. They never really asked me about the lifestyle or if I was seeing anyone, and I never told them. I didn't want to admit to them that so far, it was only sex. And if they did try to broach the subject, I would steer the conversation away from it. I didn't know nearly enough about being gay to answer any serious question. *I understand that many people don't talk to their parents about their sex life, but I went out my way to avoid any talk, even about dating. Self-imposed "don't ask, don't tell," but don't ask, don't tell, nonetheless.*

My mother was concerned that if my father's family were to find out, they would disown me; additionally, she was concerned they would disown my father. I agreed with her at the time – *honestly, I believe Thanos would have exploited any excuse to be rid of me* – and remained in the closet with that side of my family. *I am now open with them, but I have spent much of my life keeping this secret which caused me to build walls between us. I am unsure how they feel about me being gay, as it is something that is not discussed, but there is at the least a grudging acceptance.*

My mom also said she would tell those on her side of the family that she thought would be accepting. Her family is large, and I'm sure the news spread farther than she had intended. For the most part, the news was met by a general approval. Some began to treat me differently, and there was even open hostility from a cousin.

Amanda's parents tried to create other excuses, but the two of us were adamant we were going to be married. If they had just kept their mouths shut, they would have been happy with the results. We both started to get "cold feet" for various reasons, but the more her parents tried to separate us from the idea, the harder we fought back. The day we went to pick up our marriage license application, we changed our minds. We were afraid that if we continued forward together, we would continue with the heavy drinking and endless cycle of anonymous sex. We both had to spread our wings, and we had to do it without the safety net provided by the other.

I decided to enroll in classes at UTSA and move back in with my parents so I could save money; and after Amanda left, I spent most of my free time at the Candelabra. But I was too shy to strike up conversations without Amanda around, so when I wanted "company," I would head to the Moondust. That kind of companionship was easy now that I knew the routine. I felt rather lonely without Amanda, and I had cut ties with my *D&D* group. My pool of friends had diminished to virtually nonexistent.

The only associates I had were Ray and his comrades. And we were only bar-friends. Sometimes we would get together beforehand, but it was always a "pre-bar" occasion. Usually a few cocktails at someone's apartment to save money on drinks at the bar. Sometimes dinner. I would offer to share a joint or two, but everyone would say they'd just get lazy. *I'm so often high-strung, marijuana seems to bring me to a nice and comfortable level. Pot rarely kills my motivation. Without it, I try to do too many things at once, and I never get anything done.*

Due to a break-up in Ray's group of friends, I was invited to take the ex's place on their upcoming trip to New Orleans for New Years. They needed a fourth person to keep the costs low. Since I had been saving money since Amanda's departure, I thought it would be a great way to kick off the new year before starting my first semester of college.

Chapter 24

SHUT UP AND DANCE

Late Spring, 1995. San Antonio, Texas.

We never got around to bar-hopping that night. Bo was fascinated by the idea of a gay man who didn't dance, much less one that had never danced. It was evident he was enthralled, as he didn't shut up about it until we got to the bar. And Bo was never one to worry about being in a hurry. I listened to him drone on for close to two hours in amazement. I was stupefied that anyone could say that much on such a minor subject.

As a dedicated motormouth, Bo is rare for his breed. Most people who enjoy talking and dominating conversations generally have very little to say and tend to repeat themselves. Bo rarely does this. He may single-mindedly talk about a very specific topic, but everything he says pushes the conversation forward; and once that issue had been settled, he would move on to the next – *trying to change the subject with him is next to impossible; nothing can stop the Juggernaut.*

I really didn't want to dance; I was afraid I would look like a fool. And I didn't have any idea where to start. My previous dance experience included the high school slow variety and white-people group affairs like the hokey-pokey and the chicken dance. Bo was adamant that I was going to dance, and he assured me – *repeatedly* – that I would enjoy it immensely. He was absolutely certain that it was exactly what I needed.

I was absolutely certain that it was the last thing I needed, and I tried to create excuses. I tried to convince Bo that I wanted to visit the other bars finally, but it didn't work. Bo was never the type to demand things always be done his way, but from time-to-time, his opinion won't be swayed. This was the first time I had experienced it, and all I kept thinking was, *would you please just shut up.* He was not going to take "no" for an answer.

If I didn't have Jayce's ID that night, I probably wouldn't have danced. I needed the alcohol. We waited in line, but it wasn't terribly long. Once we got inside the door, I saw Jerry playing double duty: checking IDs and ringing up cover charges.

"Hey, it's the cute comic guy. Where the hell ya been?" He waved Bo and me by without charging a cover. Looking pointedly at Bo, he added, "Never mind. Looks like you went and got shacked up." He was wrong to assume it was Bo, but right on the money concerning my absence – at least partially.

"Sorry cutie, gotta check your ID. We got busted."

I handed him my new possession and was nervous he would laugh and keep it and kick me out. He looked at it, looked at me, looked at it again and laughed.

"I thought you were one of the ones that got us busted." He held the ID up closer to my face and laughed again. "I'll be damned. You look young for your age, but that's you. I always thought your name was Jay, it's hard to hear in here. Sorry, Jayce."

"You got it right, I go by Jay. Always have." I smiled and placed the ID back in my wallet.

The obviously off duty soldiers behind us started shifting back-and-forth and sighing in evident frustration. "Yeah, yeah,

Mary," Jerry snapped at them. "You two have fun. It's good to see ya."

I walked to the close bar and ordered two shots of whiskey and a beer, and asked what Bo wanted. *He may have had a drink, but I doubt it. He didn't drink much back then.*

"Did he call you comic guy?" Bo asked after we moved away from the tiny bar. Neither of us headed towards the crowd of the blacklight room, instead going the "safe way" to the dance-floor room. There were many people there, but it wasn't nearly as crowded as my first night.

"Yeah. Why?"

"Do you always wear geeky t-shirts? Is that your thing?" He looked down and saw a line drawing of Spider-Man's face in white on a black background. We went and stood at an open standing table. "Do you actually read comics, or do you just like wearing dorky stuff? And why are your clothes always wrinkled? You would be even cuter if you dressed the part." *Oh boy, the materialistic bullshit, yet again.*

Before he could start talking about his oh-so-stylish shirt, I interrupted and answered his questions, "Not always, but most of the time, yes. Yeah, it's my thing. I love comics, and *Dungeons & Dragons* and all sorts of geeky things. Because I basically live out of my car. Dressed what part?" *Okay, I know I shouldn't have ended with a question because those might be the only words I would get to say that night.*

"Really? *Dungeons & Dragons* and comic books? You don't look like a nerd." I was expecting him to say, *huh?* but he understood I had just answered his questions. *Bo and I have always had a way of speaking to each other that rarely requires clarifications, even incredibly vague and misleading statements. When we let our inner mean girls out, we can also talk shit about someone listening to our conversation without them having the slightest indication. It's one of my favorite aspects of our friendship.*

"More geek than nerd, but still, what's a nerd look like?" He painted a picture as though he came out of the closet to Murry as well.

After he finished, I replied, "Well, sorry to disappoint?"

He laughed, then answered, "No it's cool. If that's what you're into, then that's what you're into. I've just never met a gay geek before. Stop stalling, let's dance."

"Let me get another shot or two and another beer." I swirled my almost empty beer in his face to demonstrate.

"Fine. But you are dancing. I promise you'll have fun. Next good song and you're going to loosen up."

Two more shots and another beer on top of the copious amounts of weed I had smoked at the party had me rather relaxed. I briefly wondered if a hit of X would have helped, but quickly dismissed the idea. The day-after headache wasn't worth it.

As I was contemplating another beer, Bo grabbed my arm and said, "I love this song, let's go!" It was a dance mix of Gloria Estefan's cover of "Turn the Beat Around." *I have never been a fan of club music unless I am dancing. But nothing compares to it when dancing.*

My heart was pounding, and I was afraid I would look as out of place as Mammoth in the Teen Titans. Bo found a relatively clear spot in the sea of writhing bodies and started gyrating. I looked around and watched what everyone was doing and copied a couple "moves" that I liked. I closed my eyes and focused on the rhythm trying to replicate a few people. Eventually, I found my groove and just rolled with it.

Bo was right. I loved dancing. And as I started letting go of how I thought I was being perceived, I had even more fun. Bo was also right that the less you cared, the better you looked. I noticed the self-conscious dancers very quickly. They seemed stiff and out of place. It was also easy to spot those that just didn't care. I also noticed that the dance floor was home to the "eye games" that happen when standing around, but the physicality was escalated. And the first time some guy started grinding up on me, I thought, *holy Jebus, not this again,* but when I didn't reciprocate, he moved on. *That was an arrangement I could easily handle, and it was the general etiquette on the dance floor. Sure, sometimes there's the guy that is way too interested and way too drunk and trying way too hard that you just can't shake, but that's a relatively rare occurrence and a small price to pay.*

I also discovered that grinding with someone can be an enjoyable experience without being overly sexual. Although when you find a dance partner that you groove with perfectly, you can't help but wonder what bedroom activities would be like. I decided I would have to make that discovery, but not that night. All I wanted to do was dance.

And we danced non-stop until they turned off the music, turned up the lights, and announced through the loudspeakers that it was time for everyone to go the fuck home. For three hours we didn't leave the dance floor, and except for quick snippets of chatter, I didn't have to listen to Bo drone on about his jag, or his shoes, or his shirt.

I was invigorated. It was like coming out of another closet. Dancing is a freedom that is exhilarating; and for those of you that refuse to dance, do yourself a favor: pull that stick out of your ass, loosen up, and stop giving a shit what others might think about your technique. Dancing is liberating and an innate ability all humans share. Embrace it.

Walking to the car, Bo turned to me and said, "Told you, you'd love to dance." He liked I-told-you-so's as much as Amanda – *maybe more.*

"That was so much fun, and holy shit, I haven't had a work out like that in pretty much ever." I was wearing that goofy grin of mine that refuses to hide when I'm truly happy.

"I was surprised you got into it as much as you did since you told me you've never danced."

"Me too. Did I look stupid?" *Okay, I still cared some about how I looked.*

"Yeah. You looked like you were having a seizure while being electrocuted." He was utterly deadpanned when he said it, and initially, I believed him. *I was mortified and immediately thought I would never dance again.*

He looked at me and laughed. Hysterically. And for much longer than necessary. I punched his arm, and I wasn't gentle about it. *This started a twenty-plus-year-long, systematic, mutually-abusive relationship. We have never fought, though. Never. But he has always whined that I always end things by getting physical. Then he laughs and goes back to his merciless, tortuous teasing. I assume this dynamic is one that could be understood by brothers, but I'm not sure as I only have a sister, and I wasn't allowed to hit her.*

He grabbed his arm overly dramatically and as grumbly as he could manage, "Ow. That really hurt. Do you really think that was necessary?" He looked offended and angry. I stood there dumbfounded and started to stutter an apology. This raised his laughter to an even higher magnitude, and this fit was even longer than the last.

I joined in his mirth adding to his chortles, slugged his arm in the same spot with more force, and told him, "Shut up."

Chapter 25

PALACE HOTEL

Late December 1994. New Orleans, Louisiana.

New Orleans was amazing. It was the first long-distance trip I had taken without my family. We stayed in an old house converted into hotel rooms. I believe there were six units, and we had the two on the upper floor. Each had a little kitchenette and two queen-sized beds. The bathrooms were spacious, updated, and even had a huge whirlpool tub. It wasn't cheap, but it was worth the money. It was in the French Quarter and only a few blocks to a slew of gay bars and clubs. Bourbon Street was close as well. *Someone did their research, without the assistance of Google.*

To avoid any awkward encounters, Ray and I didn't share a room. I shared a room with Paul, Ray's best friend. We had little in common, and we shared a mild, mutual disinterest in one another. Ray was stuck with the recently "divorced" who was on a mission. And that mission was dick. I'm sure Ray was caught listening to a similar cacophony as I did when living with Amanda.

We parked the car in a reserved spot three blocks from our accommodations late in the evening on December 28, with a plan to meet back at the car at 10:00am on January 3. Almost a week in New Orleans, but I was concerned I wouldn't be able to go to the bars with the guys – *this was well before I became "Jayce."*

That fear was unfounded. Not once was I carded. Never at a bar, restaurant, nor liquor store. At some point in the haze of the next six days, I vaguely remember talking to a bartender about it; she told me that bars and clubs made more money off minors than they had to pay in fines, and liquor licenses weren't easily lost. Simple business sense tells you not to card when that leads to profit with little risk.

After unpacking, the four of us journeyed to Bourbon Street for a late dinner and drinks. I had my first shrimp po' boy and was in heaven. It was like discovering coffee; a shrimp po' boy is the perfect sandwich. After food and a few drinks, we wandered around joking and laughing. Being able to carry your drink with you from one place to another was a novel experience that contributed to our wandering nature.

It was crowded everywhere we went, but not suffocating. Eventually, we wandered down to where the gay bars were located; there were many within a three or four block radius. There was a noticeable difference in the general atmosphere once we approached this area. In the touristy "straight" area, all four of us put on the usual disguise and acted more like frat brothers than a gaggle of *homos*. Nearing the gay bars, I was greeted with something new. On the streets, men and women were holding hands, kissing, making out. If I looked hard enough, I'm sure I could have spotted someone getting a blowjob. It was all out in the open, and it was strange and alluring.

After Ray bought the four of us our first round in the first bar, I only saw the others sporadically. Everyone scattered. That first bar was playing jazz at a volume that was unbearable. I watched Ray hit on some guy in the corner and wished him the best of luck. The one-night stands and casual encounters had drained me, and I just wanted to check out a new city. I have never cared much for jazz, so I headed out and walked to the next bar.

I can't remember the name of the second bar, but I have always thought of it as the Video Bar, and it was the most remarkable drinking establishment I have ever visited. There were televisions everywhere. Lined up on the walls, sitting on countertops and tables, all over the place, and they were playing grunge and alternative videos. It wasn't terribly dark in this bar, but the sheer number of screens could brighten it up to daylight levels or leave it pitch-black for a second or two between videos. There were small spotlights above the cash registers; otherwise, the entirety of the lighting originated from the videos on the screens. It was an intriguing effect, and the music selection was exactly my taste. I didn't need to see any of my other options that night.

I sat at the bar enjoying the vibe until the constant shifting of lights coming at me from every angle got annoying. I wandered around and found a small outdoor courtyard with a long low bench. There were three other people out there, and the two that saw my arrival on the patio grew silent. I rubbed my eyes vigorously, so they would acclimate to life without constant motion, as I sat down on a low bench opposite from the others. I lit up a cigarette as the strangers resumed their conversation of hushed whispers.

I could only make out a few words, but pot was one I heard repeated often. I promised the guys I wouldn't bring any with me, but I really wanted to get stoned. I was feeling slightly on edge being in an unfamiliar city and currently flying as solo as Dare Devil. I sat back and watched the three of them as covertly as possible.

Two were standing facing towards me, and the third was facing away. He had a hood up, and I didn't get a good look at him when I stepped outside. The other two were obviously a couple, in their mid-thirties, they were dressed like twins, and had the same hair cut along with the same Van Dyke goatee. They were separated in height by about six inches, and both had dark brown hair. One was white, the other Hispanic. They were *that* type of gay couple. The type where neither seems to have an individual identity. This couple is customarily two hipsters with the current fashionable haircut, facial hair, shoes, and clothes.

I found it odd that I was attracted to the third guy, as I only had a view from behind; and to be honest, it wasn't anything special. He looked to be about my height and thin with no ass in baggy jeans and a baggy hoodie. He was nondescript from this angle, but I kept finding my eyes drawn to him. He handed the taller of the two something that I'm positive was a dime bag of pot.

When he turned around and saw me, he looked slightly startled and jumped back a bit.

"Whoa. Didn't see anyone come out here." He had shoulder-length, messy, Viking-blond hair with a bushy mustache and goatee. His skin was much darker than would be expected with the natural, platinum hair. His eyes were also a deep, dark brown that looked almost black. He had a great smile with large bright teeth and a very nice nose – *a solid seven.* He had a thick layer of blonde hair on his arms and poking out of the top of his shirt. He looked to be in his early twenties, and his combination of features gave him an exotic flair.

I had the same level of instant chemistry that I had experienced with Jerry. Possibly more. I couldn't be sure, but the attraction seemed to be reciprocated to a similar degree. As the other two exited, he sat down on the bench much closer than was absolutely necessary.

"Can I bum a smoke?" His eyes were mesmerizing, like looking into pools of melted chocolate.

"Sure." I handed him a Camel Light, and added, "Can I buy some weed?" I shocked myself with that question, but I was entirely certain I saw him hand the other two a bag.

"You a cop?" He didn't look serious, and I think he winked at me.

I shook my head, and answered, "No."

He watched me for a few seconds, then leaned in and gave me a peck on my lips. "Wanna go get stoned? There's an alley a few blocks down where I smoke while working."

"Hell yeah, I do. I'm going to grab another beer. Can I buy you a drink?"

"Sure. Beer sounds good."

I bought four beers. Two for each of us. I hate cotton mouth. I followed him to the alley where we sat in a deep side entrance to a building that had been walled up years ago. It was out of sight without walking far into the alley which was otherwise quiet and alley-like. The width of the cubby was enough for us to sit pressed shoulder-to-shoulder with our backs against the wall. It would have been uncomfortable, but I had an over-whelming desire to sit as close to him as possible. After rolling a joint, and handing it to me to light, he slipped his arm around my shoulder and pulled me closer.

We shifted and scooted and nestled until we found a com-fortable position then passed the joint back and forth while drinking the first of our beers. Before we finished the first joint, he rolled a second, and we finished that at the same time as our second round of beers. The entire time we just sat there, with his arm around me. My head was rested on his shoulder, and we didn't say a single word. It was incredibly comfortable and so surreal, not to mention, his weed was much better than my usual fare. I was baked.

He broke the silence first, "This is amazing. I could sit there all night and not say a word, but I have to know your name."

I looked into those eyes, they were bewitching. "Jay," I replied, "Yours?"

He said something that sounded French, and I doubt I could have repeated it had I tried, but he ended it with, "Everyone calls me Bubba."

I almost laughed because I had a rapid flashback of Bubba from *Momma's Family* -- one of my first boy crushes – but I held it in and asked, "Can I call you Bub?"

"Sure. Why?"

"No reason." *Duh. Because Wolverine says bub almost as often as he stabs someone.*

He rolled a third joint, and we smoked it like we did the other two. It was wonderfully peaceful. It wasn't pitch dark, the light that made it into the cubby gave about the same amount of glow as a candle. It was a touch chilly but sitting wrapped up in each other made it comfortable. The city sounds were abundant. We could hear traffic, people talking from the street, and an occasional dog barking. But there was absolutely nothing to see from our vantage except for the side of a building.

After the joint, he turned my head toward him; and we made out for some time. It was electrifying. I loved the way his bushy goatee felt, and it was like our tongues had been practicing a choreographed routine. I have never kissed another man with the same level of intensity. When we kissed, we were perfectly in synch. Eventually, the cottonmouth became overwhelming, not to mention our rumbling, munchie-starved bellies.

"Let's go get some food," I offered.

"Sounds good. Where you wanna go?"

"I have no clue. I'm here on vacation from San Antonio. Hell, I'm hoping I can find the hotel later." I laughed a nervous chuckle. Talking to Bub wasn't nearly as comfortable as sitting in silence.

He momentarily looked a little sad, and said, "Of course you're from out of town. C'mon I know where we can get some good gumbo. Where you staying? I'm sure I can get you back there."

"Palace Hotel. Here I have a matchbook with their address."

He looked at it and told me he knew exactly where it was. We hit up the first bar we came across for a couple shots and a beer, then he took me to some tiny restaurant for the best gumbo I have ever eaten. The entire time, he got numerous pages; but when I asked him if he needed to work, he looked at me smiling and said work could wait, I would be going home before long.

He must have done his job well because he wouldn't let me pay for anything after those first four beers. After the gumbo, we went back to that nook, and I reached a ridiculous level of high, then we returned to the Video Bar. We had a few more drinks, and we had to hold each other to walk steadily on our way to the Palace Hotel.

"So, you wanna hang out more before you go home?" he asked with a drunken slur.

"Yeah, man. But you should just crash here tonight. Hopefully, Paul won't even be in the room." I had explained our lodging arrangements earlier.

"I'll walk you up the stairs and exchange numbers. I don't want you falling on your cute bubble butt." He smacked and squeezed it.

We went up to the room and found it empty. Fully clothed, we passed out.

Chapter 26

CIRCLE OF FRIENDS

Summer, 1995. San Antonio, Texas.

Bo and I started bonding by dancing on a regular basis once my first semester ended. It became an almost nightly occurrence at first. It was a very different experience than flying solo had been. I had learned that there was more to do than merely check out the men which always – *almost always* – led to fooling around. Now I had a new activity at the bar to focus on – *I need to have something to focus on.* And it was damn good exercise. Even when dancing, Bo was still difficult to spend time with because his materialism was extreme.

Kayla and I had already become quick friends before Bo began working with us. She was five months older than me, and her father was career Air Force like mine; both still active duty. She was also taking classes at UTSA. I met her the same way I met Bo, on her first day of training. What drew me to Kayla, was that she always wore a Spider-Man tie with her uniform – *our uniforms were standard fare for the time. Long-sleeved, white, button-down shirts, black slacks and shoes, and a black bistro-style apron with our names embroidered in white. The tie was our only option for individuality.* I tried, without success, to steal that tie from her many times.

Kayla and I became friends shortly after she started working. It was easy. We started hanging out regularly. When Bo started working with us, the two of them became instant friends – *Beast Boy and Cyborg* – they had an immediate bond, and it drove me nuts. Not because I was jealous of their relationship, but because she always wanted to invite him along.

After we started dancing the nights away, I felt obliged to at least hear Kayla out when it came to Bo. Although I would spend hours with him dancing, I avoided other activities. When we were dancing, I didn't have to listen to him. The drive to the bar and the drive afterward was the only time I had to endure his endless prattling. I always tried to just meet him there – *although annoying, his perpetual tardiness was a lesser evil than his snobbery.* She tried to convince me that he wasn't nearly as bad as I believed.

After an exhaustingly busy shift, and endless amounts of side-work, Kayla and I sat down together to roll silverware.

"I can't believe you don't want to see the new Batman movie," Kayla said, after inviting me earlier.

"I do want to see it. Chris O'Donnell as a superhero. Um, yes please."

"So why don't you want to go today? Because Bo is going?" *Ding-ding.*

"Duh," I replied stretching it into a few syllables.

"I thought the two of you were friends now. He says you get along great since you started going out dancing every night," she rolled her eyes. I think she was a little jealous of our late-night excursions. She was always invited, but we usually went too late.

"I don't have to listen to his stupid snobby bullshit when we're dancing," I explained.

"You won't have to listen to him at the movies either," she countered.

"True, but I know there'll be more than just the movies," I counter-countered.

"So, you don't like him? Are you just using him to go dancing? That's kinda shitty," she stated.

"No, it's not that. I just get tired of him talking shit. He can talk about his shoes for hours, and if I have to hear one more word about his Jag, that no one has ever seen, I'm going to punch him. He's growing on me, but that shit gets old."

"I don't think that's really him," she added after a few seconds of thought. "It's like he's pretending."

"What do you mean? He seems pretty sincere to me."

"No. Yeah, he is. I've been out to his parent's place. It's a beautiful house. And I've seen the Jag. I think there are three of them out there."

"Yeah, so he's a snobby bitch that has gotten everything he's ever wanted. He's funny, and he's smart, but it always comes back to how much money he has. Although he never seems to have any money," I pointed out.

"I think there's more. He seemed awkward around his parents, and they don't seem like the type to just give their kids whatever they want. I think it's some kind of defense mechanism."

"What, his materialism? How do you figure?" I hadn't thought too much about his motivations. He just seemed like all the rich-kid snobs from my high school.

"Yeah. He uses it like a shield. If I start talking about doing well in school, he'll start talking about his car or clothes or something. Or if I point out some hot guy, he'll comment on their cheap shoes or shitty car. You know, shit like that."

"That kind of makes sense. Why doesn't he ever have any money then?" I asked.

She laughed at that one, "He spends everything he makes on new clothes. He's gotta keep up the appearance."

"I thought his parents were loaded?"

"Maybe they cut him off or something. They were really nice when I met them, but not what I expected. I really don't think he's very judgmental, he just likes to talk shit."

"I dunno. Maybe. When he's not talking about his clothes, he is usually fun to be around, but it always comes back to that."

"I know. It gets old. I keep hoping he'll stop," and she actually looked hopeful.

"You should come dancing with us. He's a blast to dance with."

"Isn't it just gay dudes though? Plus, I don't have an ID, so I can't get in."

"It's eighteen and up, you just can't drink. But we could have some before we go or get stoned. And maybe you could meet a guy there. At least he wouldn't be a douche bag if he was cool enough to go to a gay bar." The dancing would be far more enjoyable with Kayla around, she could serve as a buffer when I had to listen to Bo talk. "And there are always fag hags there..."

"I'm not a fag hag," Kayla, interrupted.

"Fine. Fruit fly then." I started laughing.

"Asshole," she started laughing too. "So, you going to the movies with us? We'll probably get dinner too. Then I'll go dancing. You can watch for when he gets all snobby. It's when he's feeling threatened or if he has to show off."

"Fine. I hope you're right. Maybe we can find some way to get him to stop."

She was correct; it was a defense mechanism. Okay, sure he was a touch of a snob, but all three of us like to people-watch and talk shit. Everyone has an inner mean girl. Well, the three of us do, at any rate. He was fun to be around about sixty percent of the time, but I really enjoyed spending time with Kayla, and Bo was quickly becoming part of a package deal.

We didn't confront him that night. The two of us went on the case like the dynamic duo. Bo only got snobby when he felt threatened. We just couldn't figure out how to bring it up. We decided to call for reinforcements.

Both Kayla and I regularly spent time with Michelle, one of the hostesses. Michelle and Bo had started to become quick friends as well. It seemed I was destined to get to know him better. We approached Michelle with the subject, and she decided like I did, that Kayla was right about Bo. She was absolutely no help in deciphering a way to tell him either. But the four of us became a regular clique, and Michelle provided us with a headquarters. Her place was virtually always available for our use, even if she was absent.

The four of us often went dancing as well, and Michelle developed a taste for the ladies without losing her love for the boys. Kayla always wanted to go dancing at the straight bars, but Bo and I would find some way out of it. Kayla had the entirety of the breeders on staff to party with, so it's not like we were depriving her of her fun. Our summer days developed a routine. Once any of us got off work, we headed straight to Michelle's. There we gossiped, and listened to music, and talked about boys – *and Michelle occasionally about girls* – drank beer and wine and smoked pot. Around midnight we would head out to dance, sometimes the girls would join us sometimes they wouldn't.

One evening, the girls and I were sitting around Michelle's waiting for Bo's arrival so we could go to dinner, and the four of us were planning to go dancing afterward. Bo arrived in his uniform with no sense of urgency although all of us were famished.

"Would you just go change clothes, Bo," shrieked Michelle. She was not pleasant to be around when she was hungry.

"Fine." He disappeared into the bathroom, and after twenty minutes finally emerged. Of course, he had on a polo shirt,

Nautica jeans, three-hundred-dollar shoes with a perfectly matching belt.

"About time, bitch. Can we go? I'm starving," whined Kayla. Michelle was pouting on the edge of the couch.

I looked at Bo and asked like a catty bitch, "Are you really wearing that shirt again? Didn't you just wear that last weekend?"

"No! Oh my god, now he's going to have to change!" Kayla was eye-balling me like a bag of Lays. Bo just looked down at his shirt.

"We need to go to the mall, so I can get a new shirt. He's right, I can't be seen in this shirt again tonight. I have a reputation to uphold..." he chattered on about not having time to shop, and this was the only shirt he had for the current season, and he didn't want to wear a winter shirt or some other bull shit along those lines. He was putting up the walls because I had teased him about his clothes.

"Just stop," I told him. "Seriously. Just stop. We all like you. You don't need to show off. You could wear Wal-Mart shit, and we wouldn't care."

"Wait. What?" His mouth was literally hanging open; he looked like a moron.

"He's right, Bo. Nobody cares, and if you're spending all your money on clothes to impress *us*, you can stop. Hell, look at Jay, he's a wrinkled mess, and you don't ever say anything about it."

"The hell he doesn't, he's always threatening me with an iron. And neither my jeans nor t-shirt are wrinkled," *it was a favorite. The Dare Devil double Ds in dark red on a lighter-red background.*

"That's only because he bought the t-shirt today," Michelle chimed in, and we all started laughing.

Chapter 27

EVERYTHING IN 2s

Late December 1994 – Early January 1995. New Orleans, Louisiana.

I woke up to the smell of coffee and the clinking of ice being stirred against a glass. It took me some time to get my bearings, but when I saw Bub, the night before came flooding back. I feigned sleep and watched through barely-opened eyelids. There was a brown paper bag on the counter, a carton of orange juice, and what looked like a bottle of champagne. I glanced towards Paul's bed and was happy to discover it empty.

Bub was mixing the two awful drinks together in a pair of mason-jars, and all I could think was *please don't bring me one of those – I can't think of two beverages I hate more than OJ and the bubbly.* The coffee smelled great though, and fresh. I couldn't remember telling Bub that I preferred my coffee iced, but I watched in secret as he filled two more mason jars with ice and poured coffee over the top. He even left enough room to add more ice after much of it melted. He opened the brown paper bag and produced a box, which he dug into after fishing two plates from the cupboard.

He placed the beverages on the nightstand, and the plate had some square pastry covered with powdered sugar. Pretending to awaken, I realized I was still fully clothed – shoes and all – from the night before; peeking at Bub, I noticed his overly wrinkled attire and realized he too had slept fully clothed. Sitting up, I was greeted with a smile and a good morning from Bub, and a small queasy knot in my stomach and a terrible headache.

He looked to be feeling much the same as me, and he handed me a mimosa explaining it would kill the hangover. I wasn't looking forward to tasting it, but I was sure it would help. I was shocked by how much I enjoyed it. Mixed together, two of my most hated drinks combined into awesomeness – *mimosas are the Wonder Twins of the cocktail world.* The mimosa worked like a charm; before finishing the first one, my nausea had faded, and the headache had retreated to a dull thud. By the time I had finished my first cup of coffee and my second mimosa, the brief hangover had vanished; and I was curious about the strange square pastry. Beignets are like light and airy doughnuts, and they are delectable.

After our breakfast and a shower, Bub asked if he could show me around the city. I quickly agreed, but he told me it would have to wait for that evening as he had to go out to his parent's house. They lived more than an hour from the city in the middle of nowhere, and after I told Bub I had always wanted to explore a swamp, he looked at me in disbelief. It was one of the few environments I hadn't seen growing up in the military. I had doubted I would get the chance to get outside the city during my vacation, but he invited me to come with him.

The ride out was in a beat-up, old Jeep Wrangler, but it was too chilly to put the top down. *I have always been a Jeep guy, and even his rusted-out off-roader moved him up a notch or two in my eyes.* We smoked a couple joints as I got a bit of his story.

Turns out, I was the first guy he had ever kissed. He said he had always been gay but had never met anyone he felt comfortable to share it with. He was completely closeted except for his best friend and his "employer." He said his best friend had always known and had dragged it out of him at an early age. Everyone else in his life assumed he was straight, and he wanted to keep it that way.

I told him I had no issue with that, and I would "bro" it up with his friends and family. We got to his parents' house just before noon, and his mom prepared fresh-made-pimento-cheese sandwiches and fried okra for lunch. *My third amazing meal in less than a day.* His parents were incredibly friendly but almost impossible to understand; they both had thick Cajun accents.

Their house was old and had been in the family for several generations. It was well cared for but had a "lived in" vibe, and Bub wasn't lying when he said it was in the middle of nowhere. It was surrounded by what I would mistakenly describe as thick swampland. I even kept my eyes peeled for gators hiding behind tall grasses.

After disappearing with his father for a time, Bub came back and asked if I really wanted to see the swamp, explaining we could use his dad's boat and go exploring. About four miles of twisting channels deeper into the marsh, his family had a hunter's cabin we could use for the night if we wanted to camp out. I don't think he believed me when I told him I really wanted to experience the swamp, but it was quite evident by my reaction. I almost shrieked with excitement, and I had an overwhelming urge to kiss him, but I noticed his mom watching from the kitchen window.

By the time we reached the hunter's cabin, I was enamored with the marshland. The dichotomy of life and death everywhere was fascinating. Surrounding sounds were ever present but quickly turned to white noise. I had seen a few gators and tons of different birds. One of the alligators was huge, and I made a point to keep an eye out for them even though Bub assured me they couldn't get in the boat and none had ever been spotted by the cabin. The smells were an intoxicating mix of fresh and decay. I loved the swamp. It was a mix of life and death. Danger and peace. Old and new. Loud and quiet. It was like I was under a spell; it felt like home.

We explored the swamp and smoked a great deal of pot until the sun went down. We made out often, which eventually led to fooling around. I was happy Bub was too afraid to explore anal sex, as I wasn't comfortable enough either. The bedroom chemistry was phenomenal and our vibe, when we weren't all over each other, was serene. Like the mystique of the swamp, the dichotomy was enchanting. The day was magical.

Before the sun went down, we found ourselves back at the cabin where we cooked hot dogs and mac n' cheese on a camping stove – *my first unamazing meal in Louisiana, but enjoyable just the same.* Afterward, we sat mostly in silence and drank a few beers while smoking copious amounts of weed. It was hard to believe the night before I was in the heart of the French Quarter staying in an old house. It was one of the most peaceful nights of my entire life.

The next day we boated back to his parent's, where we had a lunch of fresh boiled shrimp that were then coated in a thick coating of some lemon-peppery blend of seasonings. It was a pain to shell all the little bastards, but the reward was heavenly. Maybe the best shrimp I have ever eaten.

We spent the entire day touring various parts of the city and surrounding areas. It was a whirlwind expedition remembered only in a foggy haze. We ate great food. We drank cheap, terrible beer. And we smoked weed. A lot of it. The endless supply of marijuana was a wonderful perk.

Throughout the day, we talked more and more frequently, but most often we enjoyed the same comfortable silence – *I have yet to meet anyone that I can spend such lengths of time without needing words to fill the void.* The more I got to know him, the more I liked him. He was uncomfortable with any kind of touching when there were other people around, even at the gay bars, but that didn't bother me in the slightest. Whenever we were alone, however, his hands were all over me, and that didn't bother me in the slightest either.

His day was filled with numerous pages, and I told him I was understanding if he had to "work." I wasn't exactly comfortable with him selling drugs; but who was I to complain since it was only weed. Especially since I broke the same law buying it on a regular basis. Additionally, I was confident that were he to get caught, I could claim ignorance, and he would support it. It was never an issue.

We headed back to Video Bar which was his base of operations. I spent most of the evening there, while he came and went and did what any good dealer does. At least once every hour he would come back to the bar and buy us both a drink. As the night progressed, he became more comfortable and would sit with his arm around me or with a hand on my thigh. He even would peck me a quick "goodbye" when he left for a delivery.

Unbeknownst to me, during one of his "check-ins" he caught the tail end of some drunken fool hitting on me; one that was handsy and determined. No was not an answer he was ready to hear, but it was nothing I couldn't handle. Bub walked up and clocked the guy in the face after watching for a few minutes. He later half-apologized for his jealous nature. It was disconcerting, not so much the jealousy, but the violence. After his outburst, his demeanor quickly reverted to the laidback one I was familiar with, but I was wary.

The rest of the night was spent much like my first night there. Bub worked in small spurts throughout the evening, and we retreated to the magic smoking cubby from time to time. We stayed at the Palace since it was closer than Bub's apartment, and luckily Paul had found other arrangements. We had the place to ourselves again, but we did get caught mid-blowjob by Ray who came in to borrow some shoes or jeans or something of Paul's. It was an embarrassing moment for everyone involved as Ray walked in when Bub was shooting his load.

We met up with everyone else a couple of hours before midnight on New Year's Eve, and Bub's best friend Junior joined us. By then the bars and the streets were standing room only. There were far too many people around. As the crowds grew thicker, Bub got rather possessive, he was constantly holding me close and sending his death glare towards anyone showing me the slightest interest. It was overtly possessive, especially considering I had known him only days, but it really didn't bother me. I was enjoying all the time we were spending together, and I liked the boyfriend vibe.

Junior was obviously uncomfortable being surrounded by so many gay men that it was almost impossible to move, but he seemed to have a good time, nonetheless. The two of us got along instantly which seemed to bring Bub a great deal of pleasure. Paul even came to Junior's rescue and pretended to be his boyfriend to help ward off roaming hands. I didn't think much of Paul before this trip, but as I got to know him more, my opinion changed. I was surprised when Ray disappeared, and Paul decided to remain in our company.

Shortly after midnight, the four of us concluded that the crowds were entirely too overwhelming and decided to pick up a few pizzas and a case of beer and welcome the new year back at the Palace Hotel. We ate, we drank, we got high. We played stupid drinking games and had a wonderful time. Bub was like a second skin, sitting as close as possible at all times. Unlike his other possessive tendencies, this aspect was trying. We all crashed eventually, and when I awoke the next morning, both Junior and Paul had disappeared.

For the rest of my vacation, Bub and I spent every moment together except for his occasional jaunts to sell some product.

I was able to visit a large portion of the city and its surrounding area. We developed a better rapport, and the conversations got more profound, and the sex was great. He seemed like someone I could get serious with, but I was leaving the next day.

Early in the evening, Bub got busy with customers. I was flying solo at Video Bar. He came in rushed, planted my lips with a kiss, and pulled me out to the tiny patio.

"I hate to ask this. But can you do me a huge favor?" he asked me.

"Probably. What'cha need?"

"Could you drop off a dime bag for me? Low risk. Quiet bar. Musician. No need to get money, just drop it off with him." He looked uncomfortable even asking.

"Where's the bar?" He wrote down directions and told me he would meet me there.

"How do I know which dude?" I asked him.

"He'll come to you when they finish playing. I told him you would have an X-Men hat on. When he walks by you, he'll comment on it. Offer to buy him a beer and pass it to him at the bar. Easy peasy. The dude is chill, and I think you'll enjoy their music." He planted a long kiss, and when he pulled away, he grabbed my shoulders and looked as if he was going to say something.

"What?" I asked

"Nothing," he turned me around, swatted my ass, and added, "I'll see you soon."

Chapter 28

CLOSER

Summer 1995. San Antonio, Texas.

Our intervention with Bo worked; he dropped his guard, and he became much more bearable to be around. Sure, he still talked constantly, and sure, he still talked about clothes and still only wore Polo, and sure, he still had snobbish tendencies; but the materialistic bullshit was taken down to a three or four. I could deal with that.

The more he came out of his shell, the funnier he got. He always had a snappy comeback and a one-liner lying in wait, but he was a good sport about taking as good as he gave. The four of us became a clique of mean girls. We sat around and talked shit about all our co-workers and people we encountered throughout the day, but mostly we talked shit to each other. Unlike most mean-girl cliques we didn't do it behind the others' backs – well that's not entirely true, but anything we said in secret was typically used as ammo the next time our target was sighted. Although rare, sometimes feelings would get hurt, but we quickly repaired the damage before the dam could break.

We gossiped about everyone, and we weren't nice about it – it simply couldn't be stopped. We were never malicious or mean to the people we slandered, it was more of an inside joke. All of us would have been mortified to have said these things to anyone outside our syndicate. We were never about hurting feelings, it was always just catty, bitchy fun. *We have often wondered if we are bad people.*

All of us were kind, but not a single group member was nice. We all genuinely hoped for good things for the people we knew, and we would all go out of our way to help those we cared for – *but we'll be bitches about it because it's fun.* Kind and nice are not the same thing.

The dynamic of the four of us was amazing. We rarely fought, and everyone seemed to like everyone equally, there were no petty jealousy issues, and we all helped the others grow. Bo was easy, the three of us attacked his snobbery whenever it reared his ugly head. For Michelle, we helped her find her inner diva. She was gorgeous but downplayed it in her dress; we encouraged her to embrace sexier and better fitting attire. And when she did, the attention she received was immediate. She also had a bubbly and vivacious personality; she could convince almost anyone of anything. Kayla, we helped keep reined in. She loved to try new and odd things, but she tended to get in over her head; sometimes she just needed encouragement to slow down and think things through. *Of course, it was more than that. We all emboldened the others to be themselves, especially our faults. We all learned to embrace yet combat the negative aspects of our personalities.* I would like to think that I was as influential on those three as they were on me because without them, I would never have destroyed my low self-esteem.

I had gone all in with my friendship with Kayla and Michelle, but with Bo, I still had my reservations. In our catty-bitch session, Bo was incredibly fond of disparaging those who lived in trailers. He loved to make trailer-trash jokes, and he had since the day I first met him. Once our friendship began to strengthen, I was worried that if I told him my family lived in a trailer his opinion of me would plummet. In no way was I ashamed of living in a trailer – ours was a new model double-wide and was nicer than much of the military housing we had lived in throughout my childhood.

A rare day working an afternoon shift without any of my mean girls led me to believe they would all be at Michelle's when I got off. The rare day got rarer when I found Bo there alone, having declined to go shopping with the two of them.

"I'm bored. And hungry. Or I'm hungry because I'm bored. McDonald's has their twenty-piece Chicken McNuggets for two bucks. We should go get a bunch," Bo practically whined. I had thought Michelle was insufferable when she was hungry but compared to Bo, she was Hell Cat to his Magick.

"I have to go home. I'm out of clean clothes. I just stopped by to get stoned before I go." The boost in confidence provided by actively participating in my dress and general appearance had the bothersome side effect of requiring far more work than finding my cleanest t-shirt balled up in my small pick-up truck.

"So, let's get high, and I'll go with you. We can eat McNuggets on the way. I've never been out that way. And I want to meet your parents. Do your parents know you smoke weed?"

"I don't think so, but I doubt they would care much so long as I stay in school and keep working."

"Why don't you tell them then?" he wondered aloud.

"No way. Mom would freak if she knew I was driving stoned," I explained.

"She can't tell?"

"I doubt it. I've been smoking since the summer before my Junior year, and I never got caught. My allergies help cover it up. They always suck."

"That's true. It's weird to see you clear-eyed, even when you're not stoned. And I can tell the difference. So, smoke up. Let's get going before traffic gets bad."

I hesitated. I didn't want Bo to see where I lived, but I couldn't think of a convincing reason to tell him no.

Picking up on my hesitation, Bo asked, "What? Your parents know you're gay, so I doubt bringing a gay friend home will bother them," when he stopped talking, you could practically see the light bulb appear over his head. "Are they racist or something? The don't like brown people..."

"No. Fuck, no," I expeditiously interrupted, "They're not racist at all. My sister's girlfriend is Mexican." I looked at his suspicious expression and started laughing. "I know, I know. I'm not racist, my best friend is black." He joined in the mirth.

I handed him the joint I had been rolling, "Spark that up, and we'll get rolling."

I was slightly fretful about his reaction, so I offered to go the back way out by the lake. It was a nicer drive, and we wouldn't have to backtrack. He wanted to see my high school and where I spent my time when I lived out there, and to do that I would have to take him to a few different small towns. This route also took a half an hour longer. I convinced him by explaining there was a Mickey-D's on the route.

We ordered three twenty-pieces, both of us were suffering from a severe case of the munchies. Bo is very particular about food, even cheap chopped-up-and-reformed-fried bits of chicken. He wouldn't let me have a single nugget until he had opened at least one of each flavor of sauce. Additionally, he had to mix a variety of sauces together until they were just right. It took him at least ten minutes, and when he was done, we had at least a dozen distinct dipping sauces, and he finally handed me one of the buckets asking which of his creations I wanted to try first.

"I don't use sauce," I explained.

"What? What?! You've got to be fucking kidding me." He started slapping me like a pimp on the side of my head and torso. His voice raised an octave or two as he shrieked, "What?

What is wrong with you? The only reason to eat these is for the sauce!" He continued his assault.

"Um, driving here." I started fighting back with my right fist.

"Truce. Truce. You're going to spill my sauces." *We have had thousands of truces over the years. I think our longest armistice was maybe two hours.* "Here you have to try my mixes at least."

I tried them. They were good, but I prefer my McNuggets naked. After politely – *okay, as cattily and sarcastically as possible* – tasting every sauce I resumed eating them as God intended. He started shrieking and smacking me again. *One minute forty-five-second truce. Not bad.*

Before I could swat him back, he began his stall tactics, "Wait. Sorry, sorry. I forgot we were on truce. Sorry. Sorry. I only hit you once." *He hit me dozens of times.* "It was a mistake. And if you hit me back, you'll make me spill sauce all over the place." His eyes squinted mischievously, "And you wouldn't want Trucka getting all dirty. She's so *sucia*, she's a dirty, dirty girl."

He resumed his assault while adding, "Don't hit back. I won't be able to keep all of these wonderfully delicious sauces I invented from spilling all over the place."

"Fine. Give me one of the sauces." It worked. His offensive abated.

"Which one? Which is your favorite," he asked in a sugary sweet tone; much like a Care Bear.

"I don't care. I don't want any but if it'll get you to stop, just give me one." Again, the assault resumed. "Fine, the hot mustard BBQ one."

Attack stopped. Care Bear voice reactivated, "Which one? With or without sweet and sour? And what was the name I gave it." He held his hand at the ready and swatted my hand whenever I reached for a nugget.

Shit, what did he call the damn sauces? "Um..."

"No ums. Answer or I won't let you eat any of them." This provoked a few jabs in warning.

"Fine. The *hot-b-que*," I answered hoping that was right. Bo smiled and handed me a little white cup of sauce. I placed it on my thigh and slugged him with as much force as I could muster in the tiny cab, "Sexy barbie is a better name though." He rolled his eyes and grew silent as the munchie monster took control. I was finally able to eat and only had to use the sauce when he was paying attention.

We stopped by Medina Lake on the way out and walked out on the dam – *long before it was gated. It was a favorite destination for marijuana intake when I was in high school. The height of the dam was enough to cause slight vertigo when looking down its sloping side, but it was usually deserted, and the sounds of the lake and sparse woodlands were serene. From the far side, you could see anyone approaching with enough time to dispose of any paraphernalia if a cop happened to walk that far. Perfect smoking locations are few, and that dam will always be my favorite.*

We smoked a joint there, and after showing him the dam, I drove him all around my high school stomping grounds, saving the reveal of my "trailer-trash" status. I no longer thought it would cause a rift in our friendship, but I was concerned that it would give him endless fodder.

As I pulled into the trailer park, I was shocked by Bo's reaction. "Wow. I didn't know trailer parks could be nice. This place is clean, and all the trailers look good. Is this why you drove me here? To prove that not all trailer parks are trashy?" I might not have told him I lived in a trailer, but I did argue with him constantly that not everyone from a park was trash.

I pulled up in front of our house, shut down my truck, and turned to Bo, "I live in a trailer. Okay?" I said it more testily than I had planned, and my volume was also increased. Bo just looked at me and didn't say anything until we walked inside, and I introduced him to my mom.

"Holy shit, this place is immaculate. You keep a beautiful home," Bo said to her. *He was right, one of Mom's many powers is Super Cleaning.* He never said anything about trailers again, and he began using "white trash" in place of "trailer trash." It was a silent apology, and I believe it was an eye-opening situation for him. It helped humanize him a little more.

From that point forward, Bo was the best friend I have ever had – *and still is more than two decades later.* Kayla and Michelle were a very close second, and I finally found what I had really needed: friends. Friends who I could be completely real with.

With those three I didn't have to closet any parts of my life. They not only accepted but embraced my geeky side – *embraced might be a stretch. They teased me about it all the time.* No, we never sat around playing *Dungeons & Dragons*, but Bo would often go to comic and gaming shops with me and never complained when he grew bored. He kept his eye out for t-shirts as well, and my collection grew due to his regular trips to the mall with Michelle. When Bo found an appropriate t-shirt, he would describe it as well as he could so I could decide if I wanted to purchase it – *if only we had taken-for-granted-constantly-accessible-pocket-sized-computers-with-built-in-cameras.* I would wait until he had found a few before I would let him drag me to the mall – *those were easily all-day affairs.*

As our pack bond grew tighter, our troop started to feel like the Beatles, so of course, it was only a matter of time before we encountered our Yoko Ono. Instead of a small Asian hippie, our band breaker came in the form of a six-foot-five, muscular, wavy-haired blonde with green eyes, beautiful smile, and a magnificent beak of a nose – *a solid eight.* He embodied the boy-next-door demeanor and had the good-looks of a B-list

Hollywood star. He was friendly and funny and understood the mean girl vibe we had cultivated and joined in. We would never have met him had Kayla not decided she wanted the four of us to go dancing for her birthday.

Chapter 29

DIRTY WORK

Early January 1995. New Orleans, Louisiana.

Bub was correct; the band was phenomenal. The front man was a mimic, and when they played covers, he sounded as good as – if not better than – the original artist. Their original songs were even better. I didn't catch the band's name, but I figured they were a local group that I would never see again. I made it to the venue just after they started, so I was able to catch most of their show. The place was crowded but not packed. I was able to find a tall table with a good view near the bar.

Like everyone, I have always enjoyed music – *in fact, it seems stupid to even write those words* – but I have never experienced music that I had connected with on such a level. I was under a spell, and I savored every second of it.

When their set was over – *unfortunately short* – one of the band members walked towards the bar in my direction.

"Is that the X-Men symbol?" he asked pointedly.

"It is. You guys were amazing, I'd love to buy you a drink."

"Thanks, man. I appreciate it." He smiled and looked a little relieved.

We walked to the bar, and while we waited for the bartender, I slipped him the dime bag and asked him what he wanted to drink.

"It's cool man. You don't have to buy me a drink," he replied.

"Yeah, I do. I meant it. You guys were incredible, and it would be my pleasure to buy you a drink," I said with full sincerity.

"Oh. Thanks. I'll take a Heineken then." *Gross.*

When the bartender walked up, I ordered two Heinekens and handed him one. "Thanks for the killer show. I hope to catch another sometime," I was serious, even though I doubted I ever would.

I headed back to my table as the equipment on stage was being torn down. I was somewhat surprised to see that roadies were doing the work. He wandered to the table with me and made small talk for a short time.

"Join me?" he asked, patting the pocket he stashed his stash in.

"Sure. Sounds great," I replied with a smile on my face.

"C'mon, there's a shed out back." I followed and discovered the shed was a refrigerated building that housed the kegs for the bar's draught beer.

"Would you mind rolling one for me? My hands are still vibrating from our set."

"I can do you one better," I fished out a joint from underneath my X-Men cap – *it's the best place to carry them. They don't get broken that way.* I handed it to him with my lighter. He lit it up took a few puffs and passed it to me.

"So, you're Bubba's boyfriend?" he asked me. "I didn't realize he was gay."

I passed him back the joint, and asked, "Boyfriend? I just met him a few days ago, but we have spent almost every minute together since I did," hearing the word "boyfriend" was startling.

"Maybe I misunderstood. When I talked to him, I could 'a sworn he said to look for his boyfriend in the X-Men hat. Didn't mean to freak you out." The look on my face must have been telling. He passed me the joint and chuckled a bit. "Good shit. Bubba always has the good shit."

"Yeah he does," I took a hit, and while holding it in my lungs, I added, "In more ways than one." We both started laughing. The musician – *I never asked his name, whoops* – was easy to talk to, and didn't seem to have any hang-ups with my sexuality. We shared that joint and talked about rather innocuous topics until the joint was nearly burnt out.

"So, do you like him? Do you want to be his boyfriend? I know it's early, but what does your heart tell you?"

I started laughing. "I haven't given it much thought, I go home to San Antonio tomorrow. I was only here for New Year's. I've had an amazing time with him, and if I lived here, I could see it getting serious. Maybe. I've never had a boyfriend before, so I don't know. We seem to have a great connection though. To be honest, I'm kind of bummed to be going home." The pot made me chatty and seemed to have a similar effect on him.

We finished the joint, and he offered to buy me a beer to kill the cotton mouth. We reached our destination just as Bub walked through the door. He approached and gave us both a quick "bro" handshake. The musician bought Bub a beer as well and bid us farewell. We took our beers back to the smoking-cubby.

"Did you like the band?" he asked.

"You were right. Loved 'em." I smiled at him, "Even smoked a joint with the guy I delivered to."

"Right on. He's a mellow dude. Talk about anything interesting?"

"Not really. Can't believe I have to go home tomorrow," I said as Bub snuggled close to me. It was a chilly night. "I'm glad I met you though. It's been fantastic." I held him closer.

We sat in our accustomed comfortable stillness as we finished that joint. I pulled away from his embrace, "I'm hungry, and another shrimp po' boy wouldn't hurt my feelings."

"You could stay," he replied. "I could take you to get your stuff, and you could move in with me. Or get your own place; however, you'd be more comfortable."

"What? Are you serious? I start school soon," for the second time in a short interval, I couldn't believe what I was hearing. Too fast doesn't describe it – *warp 9 Lieutenant Data* – but I'd be lying if I didn't consider the idea.

"You could go to school here," he offered.

"Not this semester, and I've already skipped one. Plus, out-of-state tuition is crazy expensive. I doubt I could afford it."

"I could help you, and after a year you would qualify for in-state," he was looking at me with an intensity I was unfamiliar with. It looked odd on him.

"Whoa. We just met, I don't know if I could make such an abrupt decision. My mom would freak."

Much too quickly, he added, "I could move to San Antonio. I doubt I could make the money there that I do here, and I'd probably need to get a real job. But I would help with school." I got the impression that he had been giving this a lot of thought. "You could stay another day or two, so I could wrap things up here and pack and drive there with me. I'll get you there before your first day of class."

"Wow. That's a lot to process. And maybe it's too fast. If you want to move to San Antonio, I wouldn't tell you no. These days have been unlike anything I've ever experienced. Being near you just feels right. But I don't think I could move here. Not now. What's the rush? Why don't you come visit first?"

"That doesn't feel right. I've gotta know before you go. I've never met anyone like you, and if we don't leave here together, I'm afraid I'll lose you."

I didn't know what to say. I liked Bub, and in different circumstances, I could see it developing into something. He seemed obsessed though, and that was a touch frightening. I just sat there in silence.

"C'mon. Let's go get you that po' boy." He stood up and pulled me up in an embrace. He kissed me extremely passionately. He pulled away and said in a soft whisper, "I think I love you."

The touch of fright I was feeling climbed. *What? I liked Bub, and I felt a strong connection to him, but in no way had love crossed my mind.* I pretended not to hear him and pulled him by the hand out of the alley.

After our meal, we decided to head to the Palace, and on the walk there he asked, "So? Did you decide?"

"I just don't know, but I don't think I should be the one to make the decision. If you want to move, then I am totally interested in seeing what can develop, but you need to make that decision for yourself. I need to go home tomorrow, and I think you should at least visit the city before making such a big decision."

"Yeah? Maybe you're right. How soon can I come out?"

"Whenever you want. I start school soon and my new job next week, but outside that, I'm all yours."

"Awesome."

Bub never did come to visit, but he had my phone number and address. Two days after I got home, I received my first letter from him. Over the next week, I received many more. Sometimes three or four a day. Most were declarations of love, but the last few I received dripped with venom. He was pissed that I hadn't responded to his letters, and I didn't. I was freaked out, to say the least.

I didn't hear from him for a few months, and by then I was halfway through my first semester and had started dating Gabe. When he did finally get in touch with me, he lucked out.

I happened to be home when he called. He apologized for his nasty letters, and he said he understood why I didn't respond. He said he had gained some perspective after dating someone else, and he informed me that the connection we shared was missing with his new beau. He wanted to come out and visit San Antonio for a few weeks if I still wanted to give him a chance.

I told Bub about Gabe. He became enraged and screamed at me over the phone. He slandered my name in every way imaginable, I think he even cussed me out in French. After a few minutes, my tolerance waned, and I hung up the phone. I never heard from him again.

Chapter 30

HELL NO!

Summer, 1995. San Antonio, Texas.

Kayla was the only one to pick up a guy when we went out dancing for her birthday. She had borrowed an ID and gotten drunk, and when she saw Eli at the bar, she took a chance. She walked up to him and told him he must be gay because he was hot. He informed her he was bi, and she dragged him back to our clique where he proceeded to dance with us all night.

He wasn't the only other tagalong that night. Bo ran into a friend also named Michelle, and she and our Michelle hit it off, to say the least. By the end of the night they were already talking about what it would be like living together. The six of us had a wonderful time. Both Eli and other Michelle were the same kind of mean girls, and we all meshed rather well.

Eli was gorgeous, but he was annoying. Not to the point where I wanted to punch his face, but enough that I often told him to shut up. The night Kayla "picked him up," he and I went back to his place and fooled around – *at this point, we weren't friends, so it doesn't break my no-sleeping-with-friends rule.*

We only fooled around one other time, and it was my only threesome. And it wasn't much of one, and it was incredibly uncomfortable. Eli quickly decided that he was interested in

Bo as well, to which I would have gladly stepped aside. Eli was decent in bed, but I had no interest in developing anything other than a friendship with him. After a night of drinking Bo, Eli, and I found ourselves alone together, and Eli initiated sex with both of us. Neither Bo nor I had any interest in pursuing that experience, but Eli was insistent. Bo backed off, while Eli and I finished up. Bo dragged him to the shower, and I disappeared. It was a horrifying experience that I never wanted to repeat.

Bo and Eli started dating, but not exclusively, and with the Michelles becoming an item, our foursome became a six-some. The routine rolled much the same except I started my second semester. Kayla and the other Michelle were also taking classes.

I think Bo was looking for exclusivity with Eli; Bo talked about him constantly. I continuously warned him that Eli wouldn't be faithful, but Bo was convinced the two would end up married – *and for those of you that may have missed it, that was sarcasm. In no way back in 1995 did I think gay marriage would ever be a thing in my lifetime.* I'm certain Eli also explained he wasn't looking for an exclusive relationship.

Bo had disclosed much to me about his first boyfriend, a relationship that lasted almost two years, and the way it ended was incredibly fucked up. I wondered why he would ever want to be in a relationship again, but he assured me except for the very end it was wonderful. Everything he told me about his ex, Jimmy, pissed me off. For the first time in my life, I had an overwhelming urge to beat the shit out of someone I had never met. When I finally did meet him, Bo pulled me out of Michelle's before I could.

Eli, while still stringing Bo along, had met and started dating Jimmy as well without knowing his connection to Bo – *not that it would have mattered.* Suddenly Jimmy was always around. Both Michelles and Eli liked him. Bo appeared undisturbed by his presence, but I'm sure it was an act. Kayla tolerated him. Barely. I loathed him and only hid it behind a façade of teasing. I was a complete and utter asshole to him, but always told him I was joking.

I arrived at Michelle's after working a shift with Bo and Kayla, and everyone else was there, sitting around the living room talking quietly.

When I walked in, I tossed my apron on the kitchen counter and asked, "What's up? Why's everyone so serious?"

The Michelles looked at one another, and Eli asked, "Are Bo and Kayla off yet?"

"They were right behind me, but you know Bo. I'm sure it took him twenty minutes to walk to the car." I expected a laugh, but all four of them just looked at me. Kayla and Bo walked through the door with Bo slapping her ass and holding her hair like a pony's mane.

"Giddy up, little filly. Giddy up."

"Ow, that hurts, you dick," Kayla slugged his arm and pushed him against the wall. "Whoa. What's going on here, everyone looks so serious," Kayla looked at the four of them, then me.

I shrugged. "I just asked the same thing."

Bo walked into the small living room, looked at the four of them, then me, then Kayla, then asked, "Who died? Why do they look like that?" Kayla and I shrugged, and the three of us looked at them waiting for an explanation.

"Is this an intervention? I told you, you smoke too much pot, Jay," Kayla chimed in. Kayla, Bo, and I started laughing. I noticed none of the others joined in.

"Oh shit, is this an intervention?" I asked in mock serious-ness. Which set the three of us laughing harder.

"Well. Kind of," answered other Michelle, "But not what you think."

"Um, okay?" Bo asked, "What the fuck is going on?" The four looked at one another, all waiting for someone else to speak up. Jimmy wouldn't look at any of us, and Michelle looked like she wanted to cry. Eli looked like an arrogant dick.

"So, we've been talking," Eli started.

"We who?" Kayla demanded.

"The four of us. We were starting to tell Jay..." Eli trailed off. Kayla snapped her head in my direction with an accusatory undertone.

"What? Don't look at me. I have no clue what is going on. Can you get to a fucking point Eli?" obviously the four needed some prodding to get this ball moving. I glanced at Bo who had grown silent. He was looking at Jimmy, and Jimmy wouldn't meet his gaze.

"So, yeah. We've been talking, and it's been uncomfortable for Jimmy having Bo around..." Eli continued.

"So, he can go the fuck away," I interrupted attempting to explode Jimmy's face with my non-existent telekinesis. Kayla started laughing.

"That's the problem," added Eli, "We've been talking and the three of us prefer Jimmy's company." They were all staring at the floor, refusing to look at the three of us. "But we all like hanging out with the two of you, but it would be easier if Bo just stopped coming over."

"Oh, hell no!" Kayla practically shouted.

"Y'all can go fuck yourselves," I said at the same time.

"No, it's cool," Bo said quietly, "I get it. Jimmy's always been more fun to hang with. I don't want you two to lose your friends."

"Fuck that! I'd rather chill with you than any of these assholes. Except Kayla, but I'm certain she feels the same as me." I growled at Bo.

"Fuck right I do. You bitches can all eat shit," Kayla glared at them, "Fucking traitors."

"Treacherous bitches. Y'all get yours." I balled up my fist and was going to fulfill my fantasy of destroying Jimmy's pretty face. Kayla noticed and grabbed my arm.

"C'mon, let's get the fuck out of here. We're the real Heathers, y'all is just bitches." She pulled me along with one arm while pushing the dumbfounded Bo in front of her with her other; it was much like the first time I met Jimmy. I was ready to destroy him, but I was being dragged out of the apartment.

Little changed with the three of us, but after we told the staff about Michelle's betrayal, she was ousted from the restaurant rather quickly. We had lost our headquarters, but the three of us grew tighter from the experience.

Now that he had stopped pining over ways to reel Eli in for keeps, Bo wanted to go out regularly. I loved the dancing, and the exercise was incredible, but we needed a new headquarters. Bo's house worked for meeting up, but not for extended stays. His parents were having difficulties accepting he was gay, but they were trying. They even liked me a great deal, but for several years, they thought the two of us were a couple. They often found excuses to check in on us when we were at his house.

The dancing was great, but it was too loud to carry a conversation, and mine and Bo's favorite thing to do while at the gay bars was people watch and tear them apart. *Not to their faces, of course, we let our mean girls out on leashes.* We needed a new bar to haunt.

We discovered Rooster's, and I swear it was modeled after the video bar I had frequented during my trip to New Orleans. There were screens scattered throughout with a large U-shaped bar that dominated half the square footage. The other half housed a pool table, and an open area that I assumed was designed for dancing. They played a fifty-fifty mix of current dance music and grunge/alternative. It was loud enough to drown out surrounding conversations but not so loud that we couldn't carry one. It was also brighter than the bar in New Orleans, but that was probably due to the floor to ceiling mirror that ran along the long wall reflecting all the TV screens

Rooster's had an adjoining bar upstairs, which was a sex bar. It was dark and difficult to navigate. There were tubes of lube for sale at the bar with bowls of free condoms everywhere. Virtually constant public sex acts were on display. Able to be joined, if desired. I went up those stairs exactly once and spent less than five minutes. If Bo got bored while I was playing pool, he would go up, see who was doing who and come back for a mean girl confab.

We would meet up at Rooster's then walk to the Moondust smoking a joint in between. One night, I sat waiting at Rooster's after I got off work, and Bo never showed up. When I left work, he had just started his side-work, so I was expecting him about an hour after my arrival. I noticed that I got hit on almost constantly without Bo there, and later found out while playing pool with some hottie that everyone thought we were a couple.

Bo never showed up that night.

I didn't hear from Bo for a couple days, and I learned that Kayla hadn't either. But he was scheduled to work a few hours after Kayla and I started our shift. I was bartending, and when he walked through the door, Kayla pushed him back to the server area of the bar so I could join in while we demanded answers.

"Where the hell have you been? You haven't answered a single page," Kayla practically yelled at him.

"Mine either. Bitch, what the hell?" I wasn't going to be left out.

"I met this guy. He drives a BMW 7 Series." Okay, so we hadn't been able to cure him completely of his materialism.

"When did you meet him?" I asked.

"The other night when I was supposed to meet you at Rooster's," he cleared his throat then added very quickly, "We met in the parking lot. I saw him get out of his car and I commented on it. Did I tell you he drives a BMW?" We just looked and waited for him to continue. "He's cute and nice, and his house is nice. He's a lawyer and seems to have lots of money. The BMW is a 7 series, and I think it's brand-new."

"When do we get to meet him," Kayla demanded.

"Hopefully tonight, if we don't get out of here too late. He wants to take us all to the Liberty Bar – *an amazing restaurant.* But I have to tell you something first," he confided.

"Let me guess," I interrupted, "He drives a BMW?"

"How old is he?" Kayla demanded.

"Forty," Bo said shyly.

"That's the same age as my mom," Kayla blurted out.

"Ha. That's a year older than mine," I contributed.

"I know, I know," Bo countered, "But he's very cute and nice. He seems to have lots of money, and he..."

"Drives a BMW 7 series," Kayla and I said together, which made us all giggle like school girls.

"That's not what I was going to say," Bo lied, "What I was going to say was he really seems to be into me."

"Um, duh. You're twenty-one and cute," I answered.

"Yeah. Maybe he wants a trophy wife," Kayla added.

"That sounds like the perfect job for me. But bitch better realize I don't come cheap."

"What's his name?" I asked.

"Does it matter? He's rich, and he drives a BMW." We began laughing again. "It's Robert, but everyone calls him Bob," Bo said hesitantly. We later found out he used his middle name when he first met Bo, then again with us – *something about most of his peers not knowing he was gay, and he had to make sure we were cool or some shit.* Didn't matter, by the end of the night at the Liberty Bar, he revealed that his name was Bradley, but he went by Brad.

III

ALL TOGETHER NOW

Chapter 31

ALL IN

November 1998. Reston, Virginia. West Virginia.
Tennessee. Kentucky. Arkansas.

I walked around the one-bedroom apartment one last time to ensure I hadn't forgotten anything important. It's not like I was taking much, a new Jeep Wrangler doesn't hold a lot; essentially the back seat and the limited "trunk" space behind was dedicated to my comic book collection. In no parallel universe was I leaving that behind. I had enjoyed living in the D.C. area, but I was looking forward to returning to old, familiar haunts.

San Antonio still felt like home, although my parents had relocated to the Portland, Oregon area, and my sister was currently living in Austin with her girlfriend. It had been two years since I had left, and although only the last eight months were spent on the East Coast, it felt like an eternity since I had been able to be my true self. My relationship with Doug had changed me slowly, and I was more than ready to resume a life I once again had full control over.

When I walked into the small bathroom of our basement apartment, I noticed that I had left the remainder of a baggie of pot sitting on the counter. I had planned to flush it the night before but had hesitated. I had only started smoking pot again after my break-up with Doug. Another aspect of my life given up after I met him. I changed much about myself under the illusion of working towards a stronger relationship, but it took me two long years to realize that we were always working towards Doug's ideal.

I contemplated leaving the weed and the pack of rolling papers just sitting on the counter for Doug to find but reconsidered. I just wanted him out of my life. I wasn't going to give him a reason to repeatedly call me at Bo's bitching about what a poor decision I had made by smoking pot; not to mention that he would try his guilt-trip bullshit, complaining that I could have cost him his job had he been discovered with marijuana in his apartment. It wasn't worth the headache.

I smoked as much as I could the night before with Mark, but there was still about four joints worth of shake in the bag. The plan was to flush any leftovers, but that felt wrong; however, I was nervous to bring it with me. There was no one to give it to that wouldn't be out of the way once I hit the road, so I decided to roll the remainder, smoke one of the joints, and leave the rest in the building laundromat. Hopefully whoever would find it would appreciate it.

I smoked that joint and wandered through the apartment. Part of me was bitter that I was taking very little. Almost everything in the apartment had been purchased by the two of us, but I hated the furniture, dishes, plates, glasses, artwork, bedding, and virtually everything else. We had bought it together yet, it was always the style Doug chose. I didn't want any of it, but I was bitter because I didn't want him to have it either.

My purchase of that packed-to-bursting Wrangler was the source of my last huge fight with Doug. It was also the exact moment that I realized I was finished with the relationship. It took me three months, and a visit from Bo, to build up the courage to end it, but after that altercation, I knew I could no longer go through the charade of being Doug's perfect "wife." When I bought that vehicle, I knew it would anger him, but I did it anyway. Or maybe I did it because I understood how he would react.

I loved that Jeep – *I have always been a Jeep guy* – and it was damn close to my dream car. She was a brand-new Jeep Wrangler Sport. Solid black, soft top, six cylinder, five-speed manual transmission, black rims, and a killer stereo system with state-of-the-art speakers on the roll bars. Her name was Zatanna, and I was incredibly sad the day I traded her in.

When I envisioned a drive from D.C. to San Antonio in early November 1998, she wasn't stuffed to the point that the driver's seat was stuck in an almost vertical position unable to recline. In my head, I would be driving to Texas; and once the weather warmed to comfortable levels, I would put the top down. I had put absolutely zero thought into just how full such a small automobile would be packed. I also hadn't considered that a soft-top Jeep is impossible to lock. Sure, the doors would lock, but the window's zipped off. There was no way to cover my possessions in such a way that anyone passing wouldn't recognize the vehicle was crammed to the point of bursting, and that there were few if any, security measures.

I decided I would simply stop at rest areas along the way and grab a nap whenever I grew tired. I figured I would drive for four or five hours and stop for a nap, but I assumed, incorrectly, that I would be able to recline the seat. Despite the discomforts, I was still delighted by the prospect of a road trip – *I have always loved road trips.*

On the first day, my plan worked flawlessly – *I felt like the Kingpin after a successful scheme.* Luckily the day was relatively warm – mid -60s – and overcast but dry. I wasn't in a hurry, but I couldn't stop anywhere I would have to leave my vehicle for more than a few minutes – so, only rest areas and restaurants from which I could view the Jeep. The highlight of the drive was my jaunt through the Blue Ridge Mountains. The valleys were filled with thick fog, while the peaks were bright and sunny. There was a great deal of up and down throughout. Traffic was minimal, and it was other-worldly and magical – *I have always wanted to return and explore.*

Around midnight, I crossed the Arkansas border, and I was feeling rested, as my ploy was working perfectly. Stopping and resting to avoid high-traffic times in the larger cities also kept my road rage to a minimum – *so not quite Mr. Immortal levels of anger.* Considering my seat was stuck in a somewhat uncomfortable position, coupled with the inability to stop anywhere interesting, the first day of my trip was divine.

Crossing that border was like being transported in a Boom Tube from New Genesis to Apokolips. The painted lines became faded to almost transparency, and the interstate was in horrible disrepair – *I swear there were potholes.* Almost immediately after arriving in Arkansas, it began to rain and over the course of an hour reached downpour status, complete with distant lightning illuminating the shitty road. Thankfully, there was little traffic at that time, and I was forced to drop my speed below thirty-five for safety's sake.

When I saw the sign for the rest area, I had never been so thankful in my life to see those all-too-familiar white letters on the blue, rectangular, roadway sign. I noticed the truck parking was close to full, and there were a handful of passenger cars as well. Not surprising, considering the weather and the hour. I was surprised, however, to see so many people active and moving around the entire grounds.

Despite my impression of the state thus far, the rest area was markedly nice. The building housing the restrooms was new and clean. There were even a couple of separate rooms that housed numerous vending machines. There were about a dozen picnic tables spaced a considerable distance apart, in a random pattern, and all nestled within their own covered gazebos. There was a large pet walking area, and the entire grounds were surrounded by what felt like a lightly wooded forest. I parked in the farthest spot from the light, hoping to catch some sleep while the storm passed.

I noticed one of the gazebos was stationed about twenty yards from my chosen parking space, and I felt the desire to get out of Zatanna and stretch. I dashed to the gazebo through the pouring rain and was moderately soaked when I came to a halt in the refuge. I checked my pockets and was happy to discover my cigarettes were dry, along with the three joints I stashed in the box – *I had forgotten to leave them in the building laundromat.* It was difficult to see anything in the direction of the truck parking, but I had a clear view of the illuminated area. The closest covered area was at least another thirty yards in the distance, and I seriously doubted anyone would be foolish enough to wander in the rain. I decided to light up a joint.

I retreated to the darkest and driest part of the gazebo, sat with my back against one of its two solid walls, and smoked that joint as quickly as I could. I wanted to dispose of the evidence as expeditiously as possible. Consequently, I smoked more, and more rapidly, than I usually would. I was ripped by the time I stubbed the roach on the concrete and flicked it into the rain that had impossibly grown stronger.

I lit up a cigarette as I watched an eighteen-wheeler go the wrong way, headed towards the car parking. His headlights illuminated me clearly as he slowly came to a stop across from my Jeep taking up numerous empty parking spots. I was thankful that he quickly turned off his headlights.

I walked in circles in the gazebo just to get a little exercise, at least it was big enough to keep me from getting dizzy. I was feeling incredibly relaxed from the weed, and the downpour was showing no signs of abating. I started drying off, combined with my "laps," and I was warmed to a comfortable level. I was entirely content listening to the rain beat upon the roof and decided to smoke a second joint.

I consumed it as quickly as the first. As I was extinguishing it, I noticed that the door to the truck that had parked across from my Jeep opened, and the driver hurried out. He headed straight for my gazebo moving at a rapid pace. The rain still hadn't slowed.

He bolted into the gazebo, removed his cowboy hat and shook his whole body much as a dog would. I was close enough to be sprayed, and I was surprised by the volumes of water that came streaming off his clothes. He looked at me and said, "Sorry, 'bout dat. I wuz needin' to stretch muh legs 'n this'n the closest dry spot to muh truck. Hope ya don' mine sharin','" he said – *with a thick southern drawl that I will no longer attempt to capture in written form*. He smiled and extended his hand. "I'm Hank." He was literally dripping wet.

Damn, he was sexy. A solid *day'um*. He was four or five inches shorter than me, with a thick blonde handlebar mustache. Hank looked to be in his late thirties, and he had a strong chin and brow with a square jaw and decent nose. He sounded and dressed like a cowboy, but the real kind. His Levi's were worn out, as was his tightly fitting denim shirt. His boots weren't the fancy type but looked worn in and comfortable. He had an athletic build, which was quite visible through his soaked clothing that stuck to his body. I wished the lighting was better, as I was sure his entire physique would be visible in his present condition. What I could see was well muscled, and I wondered where a trucker found time to work out.

"I'm Jay," I responded by returning the smile and the handshake. His hands were large and strong with a powerful grip that wasn't overly forceful. "You're soaked," I observed just as there was a break in the rain. We both started chuckling. I reached into my pocket and retrieved my pack of Camel Lights.

"Can I bum one of those? I ran out but decided to get out of the rain instead of pushing to the next truck stop."

I opened the pack and noticed only the joints inside. "I'm out. I have a full pack in my Jeep though." I held my hand out from under the protection of the roof. The deluge had slowed considerably. "I'll be right back," I hollered as I sprinted through the rain. After two steps on my return trip, the monsoon resumed, and by the time I again arrived under shelter I was as wet as Hank – *I envisioned Storm floating above me laughing.* Luckily the cigarettes were still sealed in plastic wrap; otherwise they would have been ruined. I opened them and handed him one. Before I could fish the Bic out of my pocket, he lit his Zippo and held it up after lighting his.

"Thanks, I appreciate that," he said after taking a long drag and holding it in his lungs. "You didn't need to get all wet on my account."

"I didn't. Not entirely. I wanted one too." He smiled and winked at me – *seriously. He winked.*

Except for that short reprieve, the torrent remained unchecked, and before we finished that cigarette, we were both shivering.

"So, I'm gonna run to my truck and warm up in the heater. You're welcome to join me." I'm certain he winked again.

I wasn't sure it was the wisest decision, and I was surprised when I replied, "You know what? Sure." I didn't want to waste the gas to warm up, with the soft-top I'd have to keep the heater running a long time.

"Great. Follow me in a minute or two, so I can clear your seat. That way you don't have to stand in the rain." Hank smiled again, and noticeably adjusted his crotch. He took off at a slow jog.

I lit up another cigarette, figuring that would be either good timing for him to make his arrangements, or to talk myself out of what could have been another foolish decision. Retreating to the relative safety of my own vehicle seemed like a more expedient choice, but I had no idea how far it was to the next gas station. I decided warming up and drying off were more important, so I concluded to risk it, but I made sure my pocket knife was easily accessible.

I ran to his truck where he extended his hand and helped me into the passenger seat. Water was still running off of him in gushing rivulets. The interior of his truck was immaculately clean – it reminded me of my mother's housekeeping – and was quite large with a sleeper portion. He turned up the heat, and we both placed our hands in front of the vents, but our teeth were chattering.

"Wanna watch a movie while we warm up?" Hank asked with a staccato, chattering voice as he placed a portable DVD player on his dash.

"Sure," I replied while rubbing my hands together.

"I'm about halfway through *Tank Girl*, but I can restart it if you want," he suggested.

"I love that movie," I replied. "I've seen it tons of times, just start it where you left off."

"Me too. It's one of my standbys." He had a hard time pressing the small buttons with his shaking hands, but he managed.

For about fifteen minutes, we both sat with our hands cupped over a heating vent and the movie providing some background noise. Except for my hands and face, I hadn't even begun to dry yet, and we were both shivering uncontrollably still.

Once his teeth stopped chattering long enough to finish a complete sentence, Hank looked at me and said, "We're gonna catch our death if we stay in these wet clothes. I am wet all the way to the bone." He started unbuttoning his shirt.

I had rarely felt so cold in my life, and I had spent three years in Alaska. He seemed to be a straight guy, but if he had been the alpha-male douche-bag type, I wouldn't have accepted his invitation to his truck. Besides, his suggestion didn't seem sexual, just practical. I shrugged my shoulders and followed suit, but I started with my shoes.

We were both shirtless and barefoot, in our soaking wet jeans. Each of us fiddled with our belt buckles. Stalling. Hank chuckled nervously and muttered, "Umm. I don't wear underwear," as his face turned an adorable shade of red.

I responded with my own nervous laughter, "Neither do I."

Before I could unfasten my belt, his pants were down. As he fiddled with the wet denim wrapped around his ankles, I stole a glance at his naked midsection. I was shocked to see his penis fully erect. My body followed suit as my blood flow diverted to my midsection. Before my pants were unbuttoned, he caught me staring at his dick. I had only meant to spy a quick glance but couldn't look away.

He looked down at his cock and said, "Umm, yeah. Sorry, about that?" it sounded like a question.

As an answer, I yanked off my pants, presenting him with a full view of my similarly erect penis.

"Oh. Never mind then," he said, after a quick, nervous chuckle.

We warmed up by fooling around. It was fun and comfortable. Hank was one of those rare people that you feel you have known for years shortly after meeting them. At about the same time as our climax, the rain finally stopped. We hopped out of his truck completely naked and smoked a cigarette in the dark. This was followed by snuggling to warm up in his cab's bed and watching Tank Girl from the beginning.

We chatted a great deal. Hank confessed that he was a married man with two children. He explained that he didn't often hook-up with men but admitted that was his goal the moment he spied me in the gazebo. He expressed that he too had a sense of long-term familiarity and asked if we could exchange numbers.

I wasn't happy to learn about his marriage, but I gave him my number anyway. I had a great time with him, and there was no concern that it could turn in to a relationship. He was either closeted or bi, and he was adamant that his wife could never learn of his dalliances. He revealed that he always wanted to find a man on the side that he could visit when he was out on a run, but that man had to be understanding of his situation. Hank didn't want a boyfriend, but he didn't want a simple fuck buddy. He wanted a friend with benefits.

We exchanged cell numbers – *back then cell phones only made calls and you were charged for each minute used. Most plans came with limited minutes that could be used during prime hours. In the evenings and on the weekends, minutes were free.* When he found out I was moving back to San Antonio, he became excited. He did a lot of work in Texas and was usually in the area at least once a month, often more.

We fell asleep watching Tank Girl, and he woke me early the next morning with a blow job. I reciprocated, and we said our goodbyes. I told him I was looking forward to seeing him in less than two weeks when he came through.

The rest of my trip to San Antonio was uneventful.

Chapter 32

WAXING OR
WANING?

September 1995- December 1995. San Antonio, Texas.

When Bo first started dating Brad, I was incredibly jealous. Throughout my second semester of college, I had gotten used to spending all my free time with Bo and Kayla. Initially, Brad disrupted our general day-to-day activities – *like the White Queen being named a teacher for young mutants at the Xavier School for Gifted Youngsters* – he felt out of place. During the beginning of their relationship, I had lost my drinking buddy; and I no longer enjoyed frequenting the bars solo. Kayla recognized my dilemma and even tried filling Bo's role as wingman, but it wasn't the same; interactions with others at gay bars always exhibit new dynamics when there is a female in the mix.

Kayla too seemed to have feelings of jealousy concerning Bo's new beau, and the two of us began using Brad's age as an excuse to try to get single Bo back. He wouldn't hear any of it though. He didn't care about the age difference, and in the beginning, Bo was only concerned with the size of Brad's bank account. As we got to know Brad better, both Kayla and I realized that he was a terrific guy, and he practically worshipped the ground Bo walked on. Except for their age difference, neither of us could come up with a convincing argument to poison Bo's view of Brad. Bo might have tried to convince us that the only reason he was giving Brad the time of day was because of his car, house, and job, but it was plainly evident that his feelings ran deeper.

As their relationship grew more serious, we all came to realize that Brad had always been a missing member of our group. He too was a mean girl at heart, and he enjoyed how much teasing the three of us did. It wasn't long before he was joining in. His house also provided us with a new base of oper-ation – *we once again had a Hall of Justice.* Unlike Michelle or Amanda's apartment, Brad owned a grown-up house with four bedrooms and three bathrooms. It didn't take long before he offered to let me use his guest room when I didn't want to make the long drive home, and as often as not Kayla could be found sleeping on one of the couches.

Bo was perfectly agreeable with this situation, he loved having his two best friends close by, and he was even happier that our group dynamic was better with Brad around. Brad suffered from a severe case of Peter Pan syndrome; he didn't want to grow old. He cherished having the three of us close by, and for the first few months, he was a regular fixture in our lives. Brad was also an extreme workaholic, but he made the time to spend with us. He introduced the three of us to some of San Antonio's best restaurants and bars, as well as several successful gay men.

Bo decided early on that I should follow his example and was convinced I needed to land a rich boyfriend. He convinced Brad to try and set me up with a few his friends, but unlike Bo, I didn't want to date anyone my parents' age, nor did I desire to be taken care of. After the fifth or sixth blind-date, I finally begged Brad to stop trying to find me a sugar daddy. Brad was embarrassed since he had assumed Bo's prodding originated from my desire to find a rich man. He agreed to stop immediately, although Bo continuously tried to get him to resume his machinations.

During this time, Kayla also settled down with one of our co-workers. The two had begun casually dating, but over time their relationship became more serious. Both Bo and I approved of Alex, and he seemed to have a calming effect on Kayla. He was also comfortable with and accepting of gay people and possessed his own inner mean girl. His more frequent presence in our group was much like Brad's, he fit in as if he had always been there.

Outside of work hours, the five of us were usually together, and about three months into their relationship, Bo officially moved in with Brad. I don't know what he told his parents, but we were all under strict orders to not even mention Brad around his family. They had begun to become more accepting of their gay son, but Bo wasn't ready to present them with a boyfriend, especially one that was almost twice his age.

Bo kept working but dropped to only one or two shifts a week once Brad assured him that he was happy to support him financially. I was still working as many shifts as possible to save money for school. I had managed to pay for my second semester out of pocket, and I was making enough money to move into my own apartment. Brad and Bo convinced me otherwise; they both thought it would be better to save as much as possible and they were happy to let me use their spare room whenever I wanted. Essentially, I became their roommate, but I was careful to not overstay my welcome.

The five of us developed a routine. Generally, after work or class I would go to Brad's where I was sure to find at least Bo, and if no one else was present, they would arrive eventually. Both Kayla and Alex were enrolled in classes, and both worked almost as often as I did. Brad was always the last to arrive, getting home from work rather late, and it seemed each day was later than the one before. Once everyone was present, we would generally go somewhere for dinner or have a pizza or Chinese delivered. Afterward, we generally watched a DVD and had a few drinks. Of course, I would retire to the back bathroom to smoke a joint whenever I desired. Sometimes one of them would join, but most often getting stoned had become a solo adventure.

Brad, surprisingly, was the one who most often partook with me. For some reason, I thought his status as a successful lawyer meant he would be against smoking, but I became accustomed to him joining me in the lavatory and taking a hit or two on a nightly basis. He never had much, but he would sit on the side of the tub and chat with me until I was finished. We developed a deep friendship, and I concluded that he was a good fit for Bo. Brad was nurturing and protective, and he extended these traits towards me and Kayla, and to a lesser extent Alex.

Life became very comfortable. I was saving money, doing well in school, had a great job and a nice car, and I spent most of my time with my four-favorite people on the planet. Both couples seemed incredibly happy, and often I felt like a fifth wheel. After breaking up with Gabe, I was leery of a relationship, but watching everyone together got me thinking about it more and more.

Following Bo and Brad's example, Kayla and Alex set up many blind dates. Most of them were double dates, but all were terrible matches, and it was because of my geeky nature. Apparently, I just wasn't cool enough for them to waste time on. I had already learned to keep my dork side closeted in the gay world, but I figured since these were guys my friends knew, I could be myself. I assumed they would pair me with people they thought would make good matches, but I was wrong. Alex simply tried to set me up with any gay person he knew – he seemed to think this was enough for a good match.

Kayla realized his stupidity and quickly halted his attempts at matchmaker.

When Brad learned that the three had taken an active interest in finding me a boyfriend, he was amused, to say the least. He thought the blind dates weren't going to work, especially with Kayla and Alex along; he explained that I released far too much of my mean girl when I was around my pack. If one of them was with me, I was just going to be too much of an ass, too soon. He rationalized that I was an acquired taste, explaining that at first, my mean girl came across as vicious and bitchy, and it took time to acclimate to my sense of humor. Once you did, I was fucking hilarious. He assumed I was less intimidating without my posse to back me up, and he was right. He thought my best route to meeting someone was going to be at the bars.

One hurdle to overcome was that I had resumed using the bars much like I had when I first came out. Once Bo settled down with Brad, he lost his desire to go out, and since I had more fun with my friends, I stopped going too. Well, mostly. When I got horny, I went to Rooster's and picked up some guy that caught my eye. I reverted to my old ways and used the men for one-night-stands. I never took the time to get to know any of them, and I never viewed them as potential boyfriends. In my mind, bars were used for one of two things. Hanging out and/or dancing with Bo or finding a piece of ass.

I explained this to Brad, and he seemed to understand the situation perfectly. The rest of our League of Superheroes felt I was being foolish. They suggested that I should just change tactics and get to know the guys I was meeting, and more importantly, exchange numbers or set up a date rather than going home with them. I told them it wasn't that easy, but they disagreed. Brad explained it much better than I could. He said my roadblocks came in two parts. First, I was on the prowl once I entered the bar; I had become accustomed to the sexual nature, so I fell back on familiar routines. Second, since I was thinking with my dick, all my desires revolved around physical attractions. I would dismiss someone who might provide a great conversation in favor of the idiot with a beautiful body.

Unsurprisingly, Brad was correct. So, I asked him what I should do to change my mindset. Again, it seemed obvious to him. He rationalized that I needed a wingman whose opinions I trusted, and he nominated Bo for the position. Bo was taken aback, he thought it was inappropriate for him to frequent the bars, but Brad assured him that he had full trust in his fidelity. He understood that Bo wasn't out looking for anything, and he even thought it would be good for Bo. Brad was always concerned that Bo would miss out on his youth by shacking up with an older man, and Brad encouraged Bo's youthful transgressions. This declaration seemed to bring the two of them closer, but it was also the start of their infinitely slow separation. They realized that they had complete trust in each other, which allowed them to spend more and more time apart. Brad's workaholic nature became more and more evident – *but I digress.*

Bo and I explained to Brad that if the two of us again started frequenting the bars, everyone would again assume we were a couple, but like many things he had an answer for this too. He disclosed that when we went out, we ignored everyone else around us in favor of our own company; from an outside perspective, we looked like a couple. We just had to make it obvious we weren't a couple by engaging with those around us, and Bo would be able to help gauge good choices with me.

Following Brad's counsel, Bo and I again frequented the bars. Mostly Rooster's so I could meet guys, and when pickings were slim, we would go dancing. I had missed the regular work out – *I hate most exercise, but without the almost nightly dancing I had begun to develop a belly. Damn munchies.*

I met numerous men and went on many dates, but I never clicked with any of them. I followed Brad's advice and started dating before sleeping with them, but I was relying too much on Bo's input regarding my choices. Consequently, I was going out with guys that were probably much better matches for Bo, but Bo wasn't on the market. I tried to explain this to Bo, but he never quite got it, or maybe he was living the single life vicariously through me – *he was rather shy when it came to dating* – while enjoying a blissful married life.

I was convinced I was right, so I started going to Rooster's during happy hour alone when I wasn't working. I would still meet up with everyone for dinner and often Bo and I would go back out later. I tried out my new-found dating skills solo and made a concerted effort only to get numbers and set up dates. I was determined to try something new, as my policy of sex first had not been working. I had learned a lot working in tandem with Bo and was excited to experiment. The only problem was the quality of men between four and six in the afternoon was a much lower caliber and generally older.

Most of the men, I simply wasn't attracted to – *and I agree that true beauty lies below the skin, I just won't take the time to find it if I'm not attracted to the outer shell. If that makes me shallow, I'm sorry. Honestly, I think it just makes me human.* I did hone my conversation skills though, and my confidence was at an all-time high. With Kayla and Bo's assistance, I had managed to shake off most of my insecurity problems. I had come to realize that I was able to hook-up with virtually any man I chose because I was hot.

Before, I had assumed that gay men weren't particular about their sexual partners. It was incredibly naïve, but I was convinced I was unattractive. I was always surprised that men I found attractive reciprocated the feeling. I assumed they thought I was as ugly as I thought I was, so naturally I assumed that any man would sleep with any other man. I had never been turned down before. Without Bo and Kayla, it would have taken me many more years to develop my confidence.

Attending Rooster's happy hour and coming out of my shell on my own became a goal, and I felt like the Punisher, completely alone and on a mission. When alone, meeting guys always followed the same routine. Anyone I was interested in, I played the "eye games" with and made my interest obvious. I then waited for them to approach and start a conversation, and if they didn't, I would move on to someone else. I had never initiated a conversation with someone I was attracted to when I was alone at a bar.

I decided to change my tactics by practicing during happy hour, and it was a great place to start. Mostly because I was rarely attracted to anyone I met there, but I decided to chat with as many people as possible. I initiated conversations with strangers, and I found most were receptive to my intimations. Most quickly turned the discussions to a sexual nature and tried to get in my pants. Most assumed I had struck up the conversation to hit on them, or at least many took the opportunity to try. I did hear some interesting stories and made a couple of friends. And after a few weeks of regular practice, I had become comfortable talking to complete strangers, but I still hadn't initiated a conversation with someone I was attracted to. I still waited for them to approach me.

Chapter 33

ROAD TRIP TO ATHENS

November 1998. San Antonio, Texas. Athens, Texas.

I arrived at Brad and Bo's house before midnight the next day. I wasn't tired, but my body felt cramped from the drive. I was surprised to find Brad there, as he had become even more obsessed with work since opening his own law firm. He spent more nights on the couch in his office than he did at home, and the rift between he and Bo had been slowly growing in my two-year absence. It was still difficult to perceive at that time, but looking back it is easy to recognize its presence.

Both were excited by my return, and they once again offered me a room in their house. I insisted that I pay rent for it, but Brad wouldn't hear of it. I convinced Bo that it was important to me, so we made an arrangement, and I paid a small weekly amount directly to Bo.

The living arrangements were great, but I think Brad was the happiest. He knew that Bo would have someone to keep him entertained so Brad could spend even more time working. Brad was happiest when he was stressed out by work, and he had his young partner at home to meet him for dinner and take care of domestic duties.

I found a job and started working as a full-time bartender. I worked Thursday through Tuesday afternoon shifts, and the occasional evening. It was close to full-time hours once I started, which took a month after my homecoming.

During that time off, Bo and I spent practically every moment together. When I started working, Bo grew depressed, so I suggested he apply as a part-time server. He wouldn't constantly have to ask for money from Brad – *another symptom of the slowly growing rift* – and he could work as few shifts as he desired. He would be able to dictate his schedule as the restaurant was desperate for employees. He agreed and started working Sunday, Monday, and Tuesday afternoons as well. It was a decent job, and the money was adequate. The GM was an asshole, but both Bo and I were too good at our jobs to be a target of his jibes.

About two weeks after my arrival, I received a call from Hank. With few exceptions, I tell Bo everything. Hank was one such omission. I was ashamed to disclose he was married; I was uncomfortable being the paramour. Additionally, I didn't want to share someone else's secret I had promised to keep. But I was incredibly attracted to Hank, and we had a strange, instant bond, and there was no risk of developing any real relationship. And a relationship was my current Kryptonite. After Doug and the strange whirlwind affair with Mark remaining single was my only desire.

"Hello," I answered his call.

"Is this Jay?" he asked, and before I could answer, he added, "This is Hank."

"Hey, man. It's good to hear from you. What's up?" I was smiling my customary goofy grin.

"I know it's short notice, but I'm going to be in Athens tomorrow afternoon. I have to wait for a load and will be sitting around the entire next day. That's a day and a half and two nights with nothing to do," it sounded much more like a question than a statement. I didn't respond, so he added, "It'd be fun to see you if you can get away. I already have a hotel booked. It's a nice suite, maybe I'll cook you dinner," again he sounded like he was asking a question.

"Sounds like fun, but I doubt I could get to Georgia in time for much more than a quickie, then I would have to turn around and drive back." It seemed like a strange invitation.

He started laughing, and after he got himself under control said, "My bad, Kiddo," *it was the first time he called me kiddo, but it became a regular nickname. It was both a little creepy and endearing. I never could decide if I liked it.* "I guess I wasn't very clear. Athens, Texas."

It was my turn to laugh, "Oh that makes a lot more sense. I was wondering how you thought I could get to Athens, Georgia by tomorrow afternoon. Where's Athens?" I asked.

"It's up near Dallas. Probably about five hours for you if traffic is decent."

"That's much more reasonable," I commented.

"That mean you're comin'?" I could envision his bright smile framed by his sexy handlebar mustache.

"Yeah, I think I can make that work. My new job doesn't start for a couple weeks. I have no idea what I'm going to tell my best friend though. He's going to want to tag along."

"You told him about me?" I could hear the panic in his voice.

"No, but he's going to want to know why I'm going to Dallas, and he's going to want to join me," I explained.

"Oh. Thank God," his relief was evident. "Didn't you say you have a sister in Austin?" Wow, I was surprised he remembered this detail. "Tell him you are going to go see her for a couple days."

I thought about it for a few moments, "I can make that work. He's still going to want to join, but I'll come up with an excuse." I felt horrible knowing I was going to lie to Bo, but damn, sex with Hank was fantastic. He gave me the name of the hotel and told me he would add me as an occupant in case I arrived first.

I walked inside, and lied to Bo, "That was my sister. She wants me to come up and see her tomorrow. She has the day off, and the following night there is some Chanel event Sylvia has to attend." Sylvia was my sister's girlfriend. They had been together for close to five years, and she was an incredibly talented make-up artist working for Chanel.

"That sounds like it could be fun," Bo replied, "We could hang out with your sister while Sylvia does her thing." I noticed he had invited himself, but I expected it. I would have been shocked if he hadn't, and it would probably have hurt my feelings. *I don't like lying to people I love, but like most humans, I make exceptions.*

"That's what I told her, and she agreed. They only have one spare ticket though. Sylvia said she would try to get her hands on another, but she was doubtful." I tried to keep it simple.

"Oh. That sucks. You should go though. It's been a while since you've seen your sister. Get it out of the way." We both started laughing.

"What're you gonna' do if I go?" I asked. He looked a bit bummed.

"Probably go see my parents. It's been awhile." He didn't look all that enthused. "You should go though. It's important to see your sister, but we are going to have to go find you something to wear if you are going to a Chanel party. Sylvia will be mortified if you show up in your usual attire." He was right, but I wasn't going to a party. I hadn't thought out the lie far enough to account for this inevitability.

"Yeah, you're right. Better take me shopping." I wasn't excited to spend money on clothes I would wear on an infrequent basis, but I knew it would cheer Bo up. He loved to go shopping, and he was incredibly effective at finding clothes that looked great on me. I knew I was going to be required to try on and model a great many outfits for him over the next few hours, but to be honest, I think I was just as excited.

It had been a long time since I let him take me shopping, and we had nothing better to do that afternoon. I asked, "Can we get stoned first?" He had found me a new pot connection, and Brad even stocked up a great deal before my return. They knew me well, and it was the best homecoming present any-one could have gotten me.

"I'll have a puff or two, but you know we'll have to go eat first," he conceded.

Naturally, food was our first stop. Food has always been Bo's first love, and he's always had a roller-coaster relationship with it. We went to three different malls, and I tried on dozens of pants, shirts, ties, belts, and other accessories. It was a five- or six-hour affair, and in the end, we returned to our first stop to purchase an outfit that was the third or fourth that I had mod-eled. It was comfortable, and it looked great on me. We even found an X-Men tie that only a true fanboy would recognize. It was the symbol repeated in miniature, a red and black herring-bone pattern on first inspection. I had already spent more money than I wanted when he pointed out I would need new shoes. I convinced him that brand-new red Converse would be acceptable. *I hate spending money on shoes I never wear.*

When I awoke the next morning, I was excited when I checked the weather and learned it was forecasted to be sunny and in the mid- to upper-seventies. I was going to get to do the road trip I had envisioned for my move home. Nothing stacked in the seats, and it was warm enough to put the top down. When I removed my new Chucks from their box and attempted to put them on my feet, Bo wouldn't allow it. Not until after the party. He warned if I got any scuffs, they would ruin the entire ensemble.

The drive to Athens was precisely what I had envisioned. The traffic was minimal, and I stopped at anything that caught my eye. The weather was pleasant, I had plenty of sunscreen – *I burn very easily* – and I got to choose whichever CDs I wanted. I turned my volume to max and sang at the top of my lungs along with my favorite songs. My only complaint with the road trip was that it was over too quickly, but there was a prize at the end.

When I found the hotel, it was close to four in the afternoon, and Hank's truck was nowhere in sight. I checked in, received my key and found the room. He wasn't kidding, the room he booked was a gorgeous suite. It had a large bedroom with a king-sized bed and its own separate bathroom that contained a shower with numerous spouts large enough to comfortably house four grown men.

When I opened the door, I was greeted with the smell of a fresh shower and wandering through the suite I discovered Hank completely naked, asleep, atop the bedding. My arrival didn't wake him, so I decided to follow his example and took a shower myself, and afterward snuggled up beside him and promptly fell asleep.

He woke me in the fashion I expected, and after we finished, he ordered a pizza and flipped through the pay-per-view movies on the hotel's cable.

"Any problems getting away from your friend," he asked me.

"Not really, but I didn't think the lie through," I explained how the lie had taken form.

"So, you gonna return the clothes when you get home?" he asked, and to be honest, I hadn't considered the option.

"Probably not. I might need it for some function he drags me to," I rationalized.

"Well, I'd hate to see it go to waste. How 'bout I make reservations at a nice restaurant in Dallas tomorrow. I've never been on a date with a dude before. I wonder if there's anywhere I could take you dancing." I had expected a couple days locked up in a hotel room. I figured Hank was so deep in the closet, he wouldn't want to go anywhere gay. "I think I know a bar that will fit the bill. Do you dance?"

"Of course," I answered.

The rest of that day we spent in the room, and the sex was great. We had similar tastes in movies. We watched a couple, forgetting to pause when our attentions were diverted.

I wasn't surprised that he had chosen a steakhouse for dinner, but I was impressed by the quality and the cost. He also requested I drive him to a western store where he spent a great deal of money on new jeans, a jacket, new hat, boots, belt, and buckle. We were dressed to the same level, but we couldn't have been more mismatched. Dinner was amazing, and we shared a great bottle of wine. He was true to his word about dancing.

I hadn't considered that his idea of dancing was two-stepping. When we walked into the bar he had found, and I was assaulted with country music, I felt slightly stupid.

"C'mon Kiddo, let's grab a drink, then we'll hit the dance floor." Apparently, he hadn't considered that my idea of dancing was completely different.

"Sounds great, but I have to warn you. I don't know how to two-step." I was studying those on the floor though.

"What? You said you dance," he replied.

"I do. But real dancing, not country dancing."

He pulled me close and kissed me hard. "That's okay I'll teach you. I was wondering who would lead, and who would follow anyway. It'll be easier to teach you to follow."

"So, I have to be the girl?" I asked with a chuckle.

"Not with that cock, Kiddo" he replied and grabbed mine, pulling me close once again.

We made out for a bit, which elicited some attention, which Hank seemed to enjoy. I dragged him to the bar and ordered two shots of Beam and two Shiner Bocks. I was happy to receive exactly that.

"A man after my own heart," he smiled as he reached for the beer and shot.

He taught me to two-step, and I loved it. It was fun dancing in such proximity, and it was possible to carry a conversation. It was also easy to press our midsections close together, and honestly, it helped me learn the basic steps. We danced for a couple of hours then headed back to the sanctuary of the hotel room.

It was a wonderful secret rendezvous, and it was the first of many. Hank even started taking more jobs that brought him closer to San Antonio. It was rare I went more than ten days without seeing him.

Chapter 34

LONG LOST

Autumn, 1995. San Antonio, Texas.

After Bo moved in with Brad, my work life lost its luster. Bo was only working a couple shifts a week, while both Kayla and Alex were working opposite schedules from me. I only worked with each of them once or twice a week. The restaurant had gotten boring without my mean girl clique to make it fun. I still had many friends there, but it wasn't the same. I needed a new work buddy.

When Shannon arrived for his interview, even the straight guys were checking him out. He was as handsome as any A-lister and could have been a model. Six-three with penetrating blue eyes, auburn hair, square jaw, prominent brow, broad shoulders, narrow waist, muscular arms and chest, and an easy, carefree smile that was essentially ever present. He was also one of those guys that were completely clueless as to how attractive he was, which of course only made him hotter.

As the universe likes to keep things in balance, Shannon wasn't as gifted in the intelligence department as he was with his looks. He wasn't a complete moron, but brightest crayon would never have been used to describe him.

Although his primary superpower may have been spreading cheer, his secondary one was severe bitchiness. If he didn't like you, he was an alpha mean girl. With the brutality of Sabretooth, he would go for the jugular and destroy a person's confidence without batting a beautiful eyelash, and he rarely apologized for it. Being on Shannon's bad side was as horrifying as being on his good side was remarkable. Although I didn't complain about the eye candy he presented, his mean girl was what I most loved about Shannon.

Shannon was also incredibly funny, mostly because he wasn't afraid to make a fool of himself. He lived by the philosophy that it was better to have people laugh with you than at you, and if he could make you laugh, he didn't much care how the goal was achieved. He was full of life, kindness, merriment, and energy. He always seemed happy, and it was contagious; it was difficult to remain in a lousy mood around him.

To balance his sunny outlook, Shannon also had a macabre sense of humor. He liked to take things to a dark place, and he regularly joked about death. Shannon loved disgusting slasher flicks, and he enjoyed trying to gross people out talking about blood, guts, dismemberment, and decay. He wanted to go to school to become a mortician, but he didn't have the grades. His morbid nature was my least favorite part of his personality, but it was a small part of his temperament that was generally easy to overlook.

Within a few shifts, Shannon disclosed to everyone that he was gay. I believe every single woman on staff cried herself to sleep when they heard the news of his sexuality. They had all been putting their best flirting skills to work, and all were disappointed by their efforts. At least they could tell themselves it wasn't them; it was him.

Except for his catty nature and bitchy attitude, Shannon was miles away from any gay stereotype; if any, he would be the all-American boy next door. In high school, he played on the varsity football and basketball teams, was the president of the student council, and even sang in his church's choir. He was an avid hunter and fisherman, a diehard Cowboys and Spurs fan, and enjoyed fixing old cars with his father. He was an all-around guy's guy; a model of the patriarchy. Except for his sexuality of course.

Virtually every night, there was an impromptu party at one of our co-worker's homes. Shannon was always invited, but he wasn't allowed to attend. His dad dropped him off at the beginning of his shift and picked him up when it was over. Shannon's only time away from his home was when he was working; consequently, he worked every single shift possible.

After a shift like most others, Shannon sat down to help me roll my silverware after finishing side work. "You should come to Amy and Ginny's house-warming party this weekend," I told him.

"I wish I could, but I doubt my dad would let me," he replied.

"Dude, you're almost twenty-one. Why do you need your dad's permission?"

He looked uncomfortable, "It's like I'm grounded. My dad's been a bitch since he found out. Sometimes I just want to stab him in the eyes, but mostly I just want it to be like it was."

There was a lot of unknown information in his response; I wasn't sure which question to attack first. I settled on, "Stab him in the eyes?"

"Yeah. With a little cocktail fork. I'd twist 'em slowly 'til they popped out."

I just stared at him with my mouth hanging open. "Not that you've thought about it much, huh?"

He started giggling, "I'm just so damn tired of his judgmental stares. If looks could kill, I'd be dead."

"What the hell did you do? Or is your dad just a dick?" many of the military dads I had known over the years were control-freak assholes. I was lucky, that was about as far from my father's personality as possible, but I figured I understood Shannon's dad; I expected him to be the stereotype.

"Nah, he's actually super cool," he disclosed. "Or he was, anyway. We used to do everything together, but when he found out I was gay, he freaked. I think he hates me now."

"Did he walk in on you with some guy or something?" I asked.

"One of his friends saw me at the Moondust and told my dad he saw me making out with some guy. Which I'm sure he did, 'cause I'm a slut," he started laughing. He wasn't kidding, slut was probably an understatement, he even bragged that he regularly gave blowjobs to his football and basketball teammates throughout high school. His face took on its all too familiar dark countenance, and he added, "I've probably got AIDS already, and I'll be dead in weeks."

"Shut up! You don't use condoms?" I was flabbergasted. Close to an entire generation of gay men died from ignorance and unsafe sex practices, while the bulk of society sat by, watched, and did absolutely nothing.

"Why? It's not like I'm gonna live to be old. Might as well have fun while I can." He smiled his infectious grin. "Who wants to get old anyway?" he asked.

"Me for one, but I'm in no hurry." Something seemed off, and like the thought was implanted by Professor X, I asked, "What was your dad's friend doing at the Moondust? Your dad is cool with gay friends but not a gay son?"

"The Moondust is blacklisted for military personnel. Dad's friend supposedly was on duty and raiding blacklisted bars. That's bullshit though, he's closeted. But I'd do him, he's hot for the daddy type."

"So why don't you move out?" I questioned.

"I'm trying to fix shit with dad first," he looked as though he might cry, but quickly put his happy face back on. "He used to be my best friend, and we did everything together. But he keeps trying to fix my gay."

"By grounding his twenty-year-old son?"

"I'm not really grounded, but he knows I'm not out at the bars if I'm home or at work. And he's started talking to me again. Kind of. But he acts like suddenly I'm different. Like I no longer like watching football, or working on cars, or going fishing. Now I'm just some freaky gay kid living in his house. He acts like he doesn't know me anymore just because I like dudes."

"I can relate," I told him. "My D&D group got all hung up on me being gay, and they all forgot I was still a person."

"D&D? For real? You really are a dork, aren't you?"

"Guilty," I replied.

"Does it get better? Did they get over it?" he asked.

"I don't know, I stopped going. It got too weird. All you need is a few good friends that don't care that you're gay. And don't sleep with them." We both started laughing. Shannon had tried to get in every male co-worker's pants. Gay or straight. His mission was focused, and that was to sleep with as many men as possible. He even solicited me once, by grabbing my crotch; but I explained that I don't sleep with friends, it slowed him down although it didn't wholly deter his efforts.

Shannon was the eldest of four siblings, and the only son in the family and most of Shannon's accomplishments were performed merely to please his father. He even admitted that aside from his locker room rendezvous, he hated playing sports; but his father was the type that lived vicariously through his son. Shannon may have hated playing on the teams, but he loved the adoration it provoked from his father. Playing sports may have been low on his list, but he enjoyed the other activities he did with his father. He loved to hunt. He loved to fish. He loved to work on old cars. He loved to watch football and basketball. He loved his dad, and he loved spending time with him.

I was jealous of the relationship he painted with his father. Although my dad was completely accepting of my sexuality, he and I were never particularly close. The relationship that Shannon described between him and his dad was something foreign to me, but the fact that a dad that was completely accepting and supportive of his gay son was foreign to Shannon. We both wished that we could experience some of what the other seemed to have in spades.

The dedication Shannon showed with his job allowed him more freedoms from his father. Shannon was "allowed" to start attending parties and events that were thrown by co-workers, and he used this opportunity to ditch the gatherings in lieu of the gay clubs. He rather suddenly missed almost a week of work, and when he did return, his fading black eye was curious.

"Whoa. Looks like someone beat the shit out of you," I told him the first time we worked together after his impromptu leave of absence.

"Yeah. I got discovered at the Moondust again," it was one of the first times I had seen him without his perpetual smile.

"Your dad's friend again?" I asked.

"Yeah. But I didn't think he would say anything to Dad after I sucked his dick in his car. Guess I was wrong."

"He the one that punched you? The closeted ass feel guilty afterward?"

"I wish. My dad did this. After his friend said he saw me at the bar again," Shannon looked close to tears, but this time he didn't try to cover it up with a smile. "I don't get it. I'm still his son. I'm still the same person, why does he give a fuck who I fuck?"

"Well, it was one of his friends..." I started.

"Okay, yeah. I get that, but otherwise..." Shannon trailed off as a single tear streaked his cheek. "I told you that fucker was closeted, but he lied to Dad and said nothing happened between us, and when I called him a liar, Dad attacked me."

"Wow. I don't know what to say. Maybe it's time to get out. You work all the time, surely you could afford to get your own place. Maybe find a roommate?" I suggested.

"What's the point. I don't want to live without my father in my life. I just wish he could get over this. He told me I had to either go to straight camp or join the military or he never wants to see me again."

"Straight camp. Ha! What a joke. Pretend to be burly, manly men all day while doing your bunkmates every night. That oughta 'cure' you." We started laughing; we had both heard stories of these types of camps.

"That sounds like a hell of a lot more fun than boot camp." His laughter sounded genuine, but his eyes were sad.

"What? Did you enlist?" I asked shocked. He had been avoiding his father's dream of his career as a soldier before I had even met him.

"I had to. Dad was going to kick me out if I didn't enlist or sign up for some Baptist straight camp. I think I picked the wrong one."

"Holy shit, man. Which branch did you join, and when do you ship out?"

"Air Force. I'm scheduled to start boot camp a couple months after I turn twenty-one," he had a faraway look on his face, and his cheeks were stained with more tears.

"Well at least we can party before you ship out," I told him. "We'll have a gay old time," we both started laughing again. "And maybe that jackass friend of your father's won't discover you at the other bars. I don't think they are blacklisted."

"Doesn't matter. I won't make it to twenty-one. I don't want to get old, and I've always known I would die young," Shannon was trying to tell me much, but I wasn't listening.

"Shut up, Shannon. You always say stupid shit like that, and you'll be twenty-one next week. You'll see, you're gonna love the other bars, and maybe the military will be good. It'll get you away from your dad, and maybe he'll realize how much he misses you and can get over his idiotic hang-ups."

"We'll see. I doubt it though. I'm sure he hates me now, but I don't know how to live without him. I could just join the military, marry some stupid girl and have men on the side. Wouldn't be too difficult considering how many soldier's dicks I've sucked over the years."

"You should find some lesbian to marry," I suggested. "Y'all can put on the show for your families and do your own thing on the side."

He thought for some time before dismissing the idea, "Then I'd have to live with a woman. I guess it could work though..." he trailed off with a faraway gleam in his eye. I thought he was contemplating a future he hadn't considered.

That was the last time I spoke to Shannon. I had the next week off, as Kayla, Bo and I were taking a vacation on the beach in Corpus Christi. We were due to return home the day before Shannon's birthday, and we had plans to make a night of it. When my shift ended that day, I was too focused on a much-needed vacation with my two best friends. I never heard Shannon reaching out for help. I wrongly assumed that he was wrapped up in his dark side as a defense mechanism for the bullshit he was going through. I thought he would join the military and get away from his father. I was convinced that would repair many of their problems. I was wrong. I didn't listen.

When Shannon didn't show up for his shift on his birthday, our manager called his home concerned. He was informed that that morning, Shannon had taken his father's car to Canyon Lake and shot himself in the head. He didn't leave a note, and he never said goodbye to anyone, but I recalled our last conversation. I was confident I knew what had driven him to such an extreme act, and I was devastated that I hadn't listened to him. After talking to many co-workers, I discovered that he had reached out to many, but no one had taken notice.

Everyone assumed it was Shannon being Shannon. He talked about death so regularly; none of us saw the warning signs.

I realized then, that hearing what a friend was saying is not the same thing as listening. I didn't listen to what he was telling me, and I lost him. I felt guilty. I felt sad. But mostly, I felt angry. For the next twenty years, whenever I thought about Shannon, I was pissed. I thought he took the coward's way out. I thought he was weak. I thought he was a little bitch for taking his own life. I was mad, and for a long time, I never forgave him.

Turns out I was wrong. I didn't need to forgive Shannon. I needed to forgive myself. If only I had taken the time to listen, this world might still have Shannon in it. Assuming our lives were similar was a mistake. Just because I had an amazing father didn't mean that he did. I assumed deep down his father was like mine because they were so similar on the surface. I assumed that eventually, he could have a happy ending with his dad, but I think Shannon knew better. He understood he could never repair the rift that opened when his father learned of his sexuality, and Shannon knew he couldn't live without his dad in his life. He may have been wrong, but I'm convinced he thought he was out of options.

I didn't know Shannon long, but we had a great kinship in that brief time. For the longest time whenever I thought of Shannon, I couldn't get past the anger. Mostly because I was mad at myself and I didn't want to admit it. I've forgiven myself, and I've forgiven Shannon. I hope he has found peace and acceptance. I can now recall Shannon for the wonderful person he was instead of the selfish act he performed. I thought I had lost him forever, but I have learned to celebrate his memory and the lesson he taught me. He was the best alpha mean girl I have ever known.

Chapter 35

LIVE AGAIN

February 1999. San Antonio, Texas.

I have always been a creature of habit, and I thrive when I can settle into a routine. It didn't take long after returning to San Antonio to find a comfortable, habitual pace. I had most evenings off, which was nice, but the money I was making wasn't great for the hours I had to put in. With few exceptions, I didn't much like the staff. Bo worked a few shifts with me which made it more bearable, but that restaurant was one of the worst I have ever worked in. Most work days ended by six, where I would return home, smoke a joint or two, and spend my free time with Bo. Except for my first night back, it was rare to see Brad. And Kayla was mostly absent, as she was doing a great deal of soul searching and contemplating moving to New York City to pursue her dream as a photographer. Generally, it was only Bo and me, but neither of us seemed to mind.

While I was in D.C., Brad had opened his own law firm, and he and his partners were very successful; mostly because Brad was spending all his time at the office. Almost literally. He slept at the office except for a couple nights a week and was only home in the morning to take a quick shower and leave his dirty clothes. Maybe three times weekly we would meet him for dinner somewhere. He and Bo had even stopped taking trips together.

After her break up with Alex, Kayla was living out the single, straight woman lifestyle, and Bo had basically become a housewife. The two were still very close, and I did see Kayla regularly, usually at dinner before she went out with her girl-friends to dance the night away and patrol for dick.

Occasionally, I wanted to follow Kayla's example, but Bo never wanted to play wingman anymore. Bo and Brad had been together for three years, and Bo had put on weight – *he always does when he's in a relationship* – and he was mostly happy playing housewife. After a couple solo excursions to the bar, I realized that it wasn't enjoyable. I didn't have Bo to play mean girl with, and after my two-year absence, I soon realized that it was mostly the same faces at my old familiar haunts. Been there, done that. Bo was shocked that my newly-single self wasn't spending more time living the nightlife, but he didn't know about Hank.

"I'm surprised you don't go out more often. I thought for sure you would be a slut when you got home," Bo observed, as we watched some Iron Chef competitor making squid-ink ice cream. Friday evenings had become a favorite. We ordered Chinese food from up the street and watched Iron Chef – *the original, that was dubbed over in English.*

"Eh, it's no fun going by myself," with few exceptions – *Hank for one* – it's always been difficult for me to lie to or keep things from Bo.

"I know. I'll go with you tonight if you want," he didn't look enthused by the idea.

"No, it's cool. Unless you want to go dancing," I missed dancing immensely. After the night I first met Doug, I never could get him to dance. Plus, the two-stepping with Hank had been magical, but I couldn't tell Bo about that, and he hated country music. I was also in desperate need of regular exercise, and my last four months in D.C. taught me that I hated gyms.

"Fuck no. I'm a fat beast, and I'll look like a beached whale on the dance floor," he reasoned.

"Bull shit. And you're a bitch, not a beast, and you'll look fine. Wasn't it you that taught me it doesn't matter how you look when you dance?"

"Duh. That only counts when you already look good. You never pay attention."

"It'd be great exercise. You've already lost a few pounds going back to work. If we start going dancing once or twice a week, you'll lose more," I was doubtful, but I hadn't tried the exercise angle.

"You're a bitch. That's actually a good idea..."

"And I'm the one that never listens?" I punched him in the arm, which caused a ten-minute battle that involved bottles of soda, the salt and pepper shakers, and about five gallons of water all over the kitchen floor.

"Truce, bitch. Truce. Oh my god, you're cleaning all that water off the floor," he was drenched after I sprayed him with the nozzle attached to his kitchen sink.

"Fine. Housekeeper come tomorrow?" He nodded his assent, so I went to retrieve a pile of bath towels. While fishing them out of the closet, he snuck up behind me and dumped a bucket of ice-cold water over my head.

"You fucking bitch!" I screamed at him and chased him through the house. This led to another skirmish.

"What the hell? I'm going to have a giant bruise. Why does it always end in violence with you? And we were on truce," he whined like a petulant child.

"Yeah, until you dumped water on me." I was laughing at his pantomimed pout.

"That wasn't violent. You looked hot. I was just trying to be a good friend and cool you off. You never appreciate anything.

You're worse than Brad." And of course, at this point he started assailing me with the wet towel he was using to clean up the water in the bathroom.

"I thought we were on truce, bitch," I had dashed to the kitchen to procure my own weapon.

"Fine, fine. You're right. You're right," as he popped me one last time with his soaked, cotton whip. And he got me good. That blow was the only one to leave a bruise that night.

"Yowch! Mother fucker!" I grabbed my upper thigh in pain.

"Oh my god, holy shit. I didn't mean to get you that good. Please don't get revenge. Please, please, please. I'll go dancing," he offered, as he stood in an awkward defensive position, but he looked more like Solomon Grundy attempting yoga.

"Really?" I asked, trying to ignore the welt growing on my leg.

"Yep. Two conditions though."

"In other words, we're not going dancing," I was completely familiar with his use of "conditions."

"Shut up, bitch. Yes, we are, and I think you'll like the conditions," his evil smile had already returned to his face.

"Fine. What are they, your majesty?" I bowed graciously.

"Oh. Oh. You wanna be like that, huh? Bitch. I guess you don't want to go dancing then. Why must you make everything so difficult?"

"Right. I'm the one that makes things difficult. Please, Princess Beached Whale, please tell me how to save your kingdom."

"Beached whale, huh? You really don't want to dance do you?" he again came at me with the wet towel.

"Just tell me. We won't get to the bar until late, and we'll only have thirty minutes to dance, and all the hotties will be gone. Or is that your plan?" I was keeping a safe distance from that towel.

"Hotties? In San Antonio? I didn't hit you in the head. You must be losing it, bitch."

"Are you going to tell me your conditions or not?" He kept me from reaching the towel I had dropped when he connected with my thigh earlier.

"Not until you apologize," his assault hadn't slowed.

"Wait. Aren't we on truce, and don't I owe you a revenge for this?" I yanked my jeans down exposing my thigh. We were both amazed by the size of the welt.

"Oh shit," he looked worried. He wasn't going to like my revenge, "Yep, truce. Remember?" he dropped his towel, "Fine. If you promise to not get revenge for that, I'll tell you, without making you apologize," his concern for my wound had already faded, and the evil gleam had returned to his countenance.

"Deal," I was ready to put this conflict to rest. But I was already contemplating my revenge, and he would have to be a complete moron not to know something was coming.

"Really? No revenge?" he asked, disbelieving.

"Really," I lied.

"Okay. We can go dancing, but first, we are going shopping..."

"No." I interrupted, stretching the word out for five or six seconds.

"God. Let me finish," he paused and stared at me expectantly.

"I'm sorry, Princess. Please continue." I was already trying to come up with something to counter his proposal.

"That's Princess Beached Whale, her holy, royal majesty," he paused again.

"I'm sorry. Your holy, royal majesty, the Princess Beached Whale, duchess of squid-ink ice cream."

"That's better..." he started.

"Baroness of bitches, pain in the ass..." I added, under my breath.

"What was that? Did you say something? You peasants need to learn your place and not speak out of turn," his voice climbed and reached imperious tones. We both started laughing.

"What's the second condition? I'm not going shopping," I told him.

"Oh, you are, and you'll be happy to. Now say you're sorry and mean it this time, servant," he commanded.

"Just tell me, dammit," I threatened him with a balled-up fist.

"Truce, remember. You promised," I just stared at him. "Fine. God, you are no fun at all. We're going to go dancing..."

"Yes, we've established that already," I interrupted.

"We're going to go dancing," he repeated. "But first we are going to go shopping. At the outlet mall in San Marcos..."

"What? We're not going to San Marcos, just to go to the Moondust," I cut him off again.

"It's the Sanctum now," he replied and paused once again. I refused to take the bait, and this time just waited. "We're going to go dancing. But first, we are going shopping," Bo paused and looked at me, daring me to interrupt again. "At the outlet mall in San Marcos," he continued. "Then we are going to drive to Austin and maybe get a hotel that Brad's gonna pay for."

"Oh, hell yeah. That sounds great!" I exclaimed.

"Told you, bitch. If you wouldn't drag things out, we'd be on the road already. Go get ready." Refusing to accept the challenge in his voice, I did what he said and practically skipped to the bathroom to start running a shower.

"Did you call Brad already?" I asked as we climbed into Zatanna.

"Oh. Whoops, no," he replied. I waited for him to return to the house and dreaded the time it would take. "What are you doing, let's go bitch. God, good servants are hard to come by."

"Aren't you going to call Brad?"

"Why? He won't even know I'm gone. Wanna bet? Don't say anything about tonight, and watch. If he notices anything, and I doubt he will, it won't be until the credit card statement comes. He's paying for a nice-ass room, and we're going somewhere expensive for dinner. He still won't notice. I could be having an affair, and he'd be clueless."

It was the first time I realized that Brad's work habits really did bother Bo. He had started finding ways to get revenge for Brad's perpetual absence, and these ways usually involved spending a great deal of Brad's money. It was obvious Bo was annoyed by Brad's behavior, but I don't think even Bo realized how much of a problem it would eventually become.

"Are you ready then?" I asked.

"Bitch," he slapped me in the face, but with little force behind it. "What did I tell you? Servants only speak when addressed. Now drive me to San Marcos, Hoke."

"Yes, Ms. Daisy."

Chapter 36

HUNG THE MOON

Spring, 1996. San Antonio, Texas.

Shannon's death was the first in a rapid series of events that sent my young life spiraling. My daily routine changed little, as I finished up my second semester of college. My grades had slipped as my social life became more important. I wasn't failing or anything, mostly Bs, maybe an A thrown into the mix. I still wasn't convinced that college was the right path, and it was quickly sliding down my priority list.

It seems the universe was aware that this was the wrong time for academics. Three weeks after my third semester began, I dislocated my knee. I contemplated fabricating some wonderful story as to how it happened, but I was dancing. Nothing crazy; it was a rather tame remixed cover of "Total Eclipse of the Heart," by Nikki French – *every time I hear any version of the song, I get phantom pains in my knee.*

I was virtually immobilized for a couple weeks, followed by a series of braces that got progressively more flexible. I was stuck at my parents' house for about six weeks before I was in a brace that allowed me to bend my knee to drive. It was over three months before my knee had healed well enough to go without support, but I withdrew from classes, shortly after the injury, in time for a full refund of my tuition.

Once I was mobile again, life picked up where it had left off, but without the pressure of school. With that refund and an increased availability for hours, I decided that I wanted to find my own apartment. After looking at a few, Bo convinced me to wait; he and Brad were looking to buy a new house and turn their current one into a rental property. Bo wanted me to find a place near their new house, once they found it.

It was an amazing two-story traditional, in an eclectic neighborhood in excellent repair. It was beautifully landscaped, had a huge hot tub and surrounding patio, a yard large enough for a pool, and a converted garage apartment. The additional apartment was a selling point. More so for Brad than Bo. Brad had learned that when I was around, Bo was happily occupied, which allowed him to work more hours. Bo fell in love with the house, and the apartment was a bonus. Brad liked the house but loved having an apartment for me to move into.

So, yes, there was an apartment. Barely. It was more of an unattached bedroom with its own bathroom and kitchenette. It was a fifteen by fifteen-foot square room, with a sink, a two-burner stove/oven combo and dorm-room sized fridge along one wall. There was a tiny bathroom nestled in one corner. The only counter space was about a foot and a half long between the oven and the sink. There was a single window above the kitchen sink that sat about four feet from a neighbor's privacy fence that was in significant need of repair. The apartment had never been used since its conversion from a garage; consequently everything in it was brand-new. It was nice, but it was tiny.

I wasn't convinced it was a good fit, but Brad pointed out that I would be spending most of my time in the main house with Bo, but I would still have a completely private space to retreat to. It was better than a bedroom down the hall from the two of them, even if it was roughly the same size, but with a "kitchen" and bathroom crammed in the same square footage. He reminded me that the hot tub was also on the property, and they had plans to add a pool.

When I still hesitated, even though he made convincing arguments – *hello, he was an incredibly successful lawyer* – he told me I wouldn't have to pay rent. He was shocked when this had the opposite effect. I always made a point to never stay more than a few days without a break, and I have always loathed the idea of being a freeloader. Brad quickly back-tracked and stated that rent would be low if I wanted to move in, but I told him that I would rather pay a fair rent. Although I didn't mean to, during that negotiation I agreed that I would rent it as soon as Brad discovered what fair market value was – *damn he could argue.*

They bought the house, and I moved into the apartment. The money I had saved to furnish a new place from nothing, mostly sat in my bank account. I did furnish the apartment, but it took little. I decided to buy a bunk bed that had a queen-sized mattress on the bottom. I used the top bunk for storage and never purchased a mattress for it. After adding a dresser, a small TV stand with a brand-new PlayStation and TV, and two incredibly comfortable – and surprisingly expensive – beanbag chairs, the main room was completely full.

I found a small table with two chairs and stand-alone cup-board that barely fit in the "kitchen." After a shower curtain, trash can, small rug, towels, and toothbrush holder, the bath-room was at capacity. Furnishing an apartment from scratch turned out to be easier than anticipated.

On the same day Brad signed the paperwork to buy the new house, the entire staff at our restaurant was called in for an emergency meeting. Due to some business mistake, the owner of our restaurant lost the lease on the building. The restaurant was still doing very well, and we were always busy, but we discovered it would be closing in three days. The owner did what he could for the staff, and some of us were offered a position at our sister restaurant downtown. I was one of the few.

I had already worked many times at the downtown location when they were short-staffed, and I already knew much of the staff. Bo was also given a job there, but within a couple weeks he quit. The vibe was completely different, and he had no need to work. Kayla and Alex found jobs closer to the university, so I was on my own at the new place. It was busy, and the money was fantastic, but Bo was right, it just wasn't the same. On the bright side, my new apartment was less than ten minutes away.

I quickly grew to dislike the job but hesitated to look for a new one. When you work for tips, it's very difficult to walk away from a restaurant where the money is good; even when it makes you miserable. I loved living in the tiny apartment behind Bo and Brad, but I lacked direction. Although I told everyone I planned to register for classes the following semester, I had no intention of doing so.

During the house hunt, Bo had all but stopped playing wingman for me at the bars, but I was still frequenting Rooster's happy hour and had even begun to go dancing on my own for the exercise it provided. My confidence had grown, and I had started to approach people I was attracted to.

Bo always told me I could land any guy I wanted, and so far, my experience matched his assessment. With my new-found confidence, I began to approach men who hadn't already shown obvious interest, and I started getting turned down. When I told Bo about this, he was afraid that it would crush my emerging self-esteem, but I had learned at an early age that not everyone would like me and had come to terms with that long ago. Being rejected at the bar was simply an extension of this, and I enjoyed the game more when there wasn't a guaranteed win.

The week before moving into their new house, Brad and Bo took a vacation in Santa Fe. Most of their possessions were in boxes piled around the old house, and they were fearful it would be burgled while they were gone. Naturally, I house-sat while they were away. Brad convinced me that if I decided to hook up with anyone while they were away to bring them to the house, so it wasn't vacant overnight.

I had no intention of bringing anyone home to their house and planned to take a week off from the bars, so I wasn't tempted. After work, on the second day of their vacation, the cable was disconnected in anticipation of the move. Additionally, all their DVDs were packed away in unlabeled boxes. All my books and comics left at their house were also packed away. I quickly grew bored and decided to go dancing.

After a few drinks, and a couple rejections, I noticed that I was being noticed. He was attractive, looked to be in his mid- to late-twenties. Honestly, there was nothing terribly distinguishing about him. About five-ten with light-brown hair, blue eyes, average nose, and slightly stocky and muscular build; the type of person you easily forget, but attractive enough to grab your attention.

What really drew my attention to him though was the way he was looking at me. It wasn't the same aggressive and overly sexual eye games. He was looking at me with googly eyes; he had a slight look of wonderment on his face, and I pictured that I had a similar expression when I was staring at Chris's crotch in high school. The other thing that attracted me was that he didn't look familiar. San Antonio may be a vast city, but it was always the same familiar faces at my same familiar haunts – *including mine.*

About the time I decided to approach him, he walked up to me and extended his hand, "Hi. I'm Doug," he introduced himself.

"I'm Jay," I stated as I shook his hand. He had an annoying handshake, the kind that is trying too hard. The grip is too tight, and the pumping too jerky – *I get it, you're a manly man.*

"Can I buy you a drink?" he asked.

"Only if you dance with me," I replied. He had been watching me dance for the last twenty minutes.

"Um. I don't know. I don't really dance..." Doug stammered.

I smiled as coyly as I could manage, shrugged my shoulders, and turned to walk to the bar. His eyes grew sad rapidly, and I learned then that his emotions were plainly visible in the way he looked at you – *it's hard to explain, but if you have known anyone similar, you will understand completely.*

I walked to the bar and ordered two Bud Lights and two shots of tequila, but unlike Ray, I was able to carry the four drinks without any problems. When I turned around, Doug wasn't standing where I expected him to be. I looked around everywhere, saving the dance floor for last. When I did start peering through the bodies, I noticed him dancing – *terribly* – and smiling with a goofy grin while staring directly into my eyes.

I couldn't stop myself; I started laughing and motioned him my way by jerking my head.

"Still want to dance with me?" he asked as I handed him a beer.

"Do you like tequila?" I offered him a shot.

"My favorite," but his eyes looked conflicted. We tapped glasses and downed the liquor. I quickly chomped down on my lime, while he sat his glass down. I snatched his lime and repeated my action.

"Hey, that was mine," he held out his hand.

I smiled, so the rind was covering my teeth in response. Doug leaned in and kissed me to retrieve it, and I started laughing again. And he did too. "And, yes," I answered him, "I still want to dance with you."

"Damn, thought being that adorable would get me out of it."
It was hard to disagree. He had made a terrific first impression
on me. He stood out a great deal from anyone I had met at a
bar. He was clever, funny, personable, and attractive, and he
seemed very into me from the moment he saw me – *and let's
be honest, that never hurts.*

I shrugged my shoulders and mimicked my performance
from earlier, turning around to leave. He stopped me by grabbing my hand and pulling me towards him. "Fine. But first,
more tequila," he thrust his arm in the air as if he were holding
a sword, and I was reminded of Wulfgar. This guy was something new and had my full attention.

We danced together for quite some time interspersed with
breaks for shots of tequila. Doug still looked uncomfortable
dancing, but he was starting to loosen up, and we were both
having a smashing time. Taking a break, we both realized we
were also smashed.

"I can't drive tonight," he slurred after taking a long swig of
beer. "I think a hotel might be cheaper than a cab though."

"I'm only a few minutes away. You can crash there if you
want," I was slurring my speech as well.

"Trying to get in my pants," he asked and winked overdra-
matically.

"No, for shafeties shake," I replied. Normally, he wouldn't
have been wrong, but Doug had piqued my curiosity. I decided
to try a new tactic. I decided to get to know him before sleeping
with him. I had even been keeping my hands to myself mostly,
and he seemed to be following similar tactics. I'll admit, it
became harder and harder to keep my hands to myself shot
after shot, but I was determined. *I have no idea where I heard
this, but if you keep doing what you've always done, you'll keep
getting what you've always got.* I didn't want a night of sex,
possibly followed by a date or two; Doug had intrigued me, and
I wanted to get to know him first.

"If you're sure it's okay, but we can't sleep in the same bed. I don't think I can control myself after this much tequila, and I really want to get to know you first," he said smiling with the googly eyes again.

"Deal," I held out my hand, and he replied with the overly masculine handshake, as I wondered if he was Professor X and had been reading my mind all night.

Chapter 37

NIGHTCLUBBING

Late Spring 1999. Austin, Texas.

It may have been a mistake for Bo to take me to Austin that night. I was enamored with the change in scenery. Austin is an eccentric city that has always been a little strange. It's the Texas equivalent to Portland, Oregon; Baltimore, Maryland; and Savannah, Georgia; all four places are just a little *off*. And I love all four of these cities for that exact reason.

I had been to Austin dozens of times before, possibly hundreds. It was always my favorite place for nightlife activities, and with few exceptions, the nightlife was always my justification for going. Only an hour's drive from San Antonio, the scenery was much better – *by scenery, I am referring to the population that could be found frequenting the gay bars.* It became a regular destination for Bo and me and became the standard rendezvous point for Hank and me.

Austin was home to one of my favorite gay bars ever. The Rainbow Cattle Corral. Even the name is fantastic. It was a country bar with a giant dance floor, a separate side bar that sometimes played grunge and alternative music, an immense patio, and plenty of standing room for those that didn't dance. It was a relatively new bar, and the décor wasn't overly "western." And the cowboys – *of course, most of them were the rhinestone variety* – were there in force. Most gay bars, regardless of theme, generally have a huge variety of "types," and you generally find a similar ratio. TRCC was unique in that about eighty percent of the clientele were in Wranglers, boots, and Stetsons. I have always had a thing for cowboys, although to be honest, I prefer the posers. Real cowboys – *and I have known many* – tend to be assholes. I suppose I enjoy the aesthetic more than the reality.

After Hank and I discovered TRCC, we always went two-stepping; and as my skills increased, so did my enjoyment. Two-stepping can be an easy dance and can be kept quite simple for beginners, but so much can be added to it to ramp it up – spins, extra steps, double-time, half-time, etc.

We had just finished a great meal at a hole-in-the-wall diner on the south side of Austin, and Hank had been quiet through most of the meal.

"You alright?" I asked, "You've been pretty quiet since we met up."

"Yeah. I'm good, Kiddo." He didn't look "good," but I wasn't sure if I should push him or not. Our "relationship" was something foreign to me. On the one hand, when we were together, it felt as if we were dating, with the cuddles, kisses, and whatnots. On the other hand, I knew he was married and had a family and had expressed on multiple occasions that he didn't want to lose that part of his life. If he were gay and single, it seems that we would have been at the stage where things were about to get serious.

"Cool," I replied. "If something's buggin' you though, you can get it off your chest. Or if you just need to vent or anything," I offered with my goofy grin.

"Well, since you brought it up," he started but paused. "I think my wife might be suspicious," he just trailed off.

"Oh," was all I could manage to reply. "If we need to cut things off, I understand. It's been a ton of fun getting to know you," it was my turn to let my sentence trail off. I meant what I said, too.

"No way, Kiddo. Not gonna happen. My life is perfect since I've found you, even my relationship with my wife has gotten better," his face flushed. It was rare for him to talk about his wife and family. "I think that's why she's suspicious. Well, that and the hotel rooms."

"What? Does my name show up on it somewhere or something?"

"No, umm..." he looked uncomfortable, "It's just that I rarely stay in a room, especially the ones I've been getting. Normally I just sleep in my cab."

"Oh. That makes sense," I replied. "I could start booking the rooms, if that would help," I offered.

"It would, but that's the other thing. It's getting expensive, even splitting the costs," he added.

"Agreed. You could always come stay with me in San Antonio. Bo wouldn't care, and the two of you would get along great. And trust me, he would never say a word," I still hadn't told Bo about Hank. He had become a personal secret. For me alone, and I didn't want to share, I enjoyed having something in my life that no one else knew anything about.

He shook his head in negation, "I don't know. I like things the way they are. You know the sleeper in my cab is big enough for the two of us. We could just sleep there," he offered, and I think he was embarrassed to suggest it because his face again turned red.

"That sounds perfect," I replied. It solved the financial dilemmas.

"Oh. Awesome," he was smiling ear to ear. "You wanna go dancing tonight?" he asked.

"Of course, but where are we going to get ready? I need a shower after earlier," I winked at him. Sex was always how we greeted each other. Usually followed by food, then dancing.

"Oh, that's easy, Kiddo. I have a membership to a chain of gyms, you can come in as a guest, and we can use their showers." That explained a physique that was strange for a trucker.

"Sounds good. Shall we?" I asked.

Our visits became a routine that was as rigid as any country line dance: 1 – Meet up at random truck stop – *clap hands and kick out with right foot.* 2 – Have great sex – *swing left hand as though twirling a lasso while taking a quarter revolution to the left.* 3 – Get dressed and head out for dinner – *clap again, followed by another quarter turn to the left.* 4 – Go to gym, shower and get dressed – *eight quick kicks alternating left and right feet, followed by another clap and quarter turn.* 5 – Go to TRCC for beer and dancing – *repeat lasso twirling pantomime.* 6 – Back to Hank's truck for another round of sex, followed by sleep – *a final clap, accompanied by another quarter revolution, bring us back to starting position.* 7 – Repeat – *repeat.*

Hank came through Austin at least once every ten days, often more, and our bond grew to the point where our sex life transformed from the "fooling around" type to real sex. Unlike every other sexual partner I have ever had, I had no inhibitions with Hank in the bedroom. Our sex life was intense, and I have never been less guarded with a partner, nor as vocal in expressing my needs.

Even when I wasn't going to Austin to meet Hank, Bo and I regularly went to enjoy the nightlife. At least once a week, we would make the hour-long trek to dance where we could enjoy the better eye-candy; but Bo was "married," and that once-a-week journey was the most I could coax out of him. I started heading to Austin at least twice weekly, by myself, when I couldn't convince Bo to join me.

This worked to my advantage, however. When Bo and I went together, I always tried to talk him into going to TRCC with me, but I couldn't tell him it was because I wanted to go country dancing. I couldn't explain how I had learned to two-step without also telling him about Hank. I was able to convince him that I learned how to two-step on my solo trips. He was shocked by how much I enjoyed it.

I became a somewhat regular fixture at TRCC, and like my early days at the Moondust, I achieved some notoriety. When I moved back to San Antonio, I resumed wearing my geeky attire – *Doug had persuaded me to give up many things he found juvenile, and my clothing was one of the first to go.* Considering almost everyone at TRCC was at least dressed up as a cowboy, I generally stood out from the sea of starched Wranglers and western shirts. Before becoming a regular, I often got strange – and sometimes dirty – looks from the patrons.

On my first solo excursion to Austin, I headed straight to TRCC. I had a goal, and that goal was to attempt to two-step with someone other than Hank. I headed to the bar in a white t-shirt that was dominated by the Marvel Comics logo – *white block letters surrounded by a red rectangle* – baggy jeans, brown work-style boots, and an Astros baseball cap.

I stood by the dance floor and watched the chaos. I wasn't afraid to initiate a conversation, but I didn't want to ask any-one to dance. I had only learned how to follow from Hank, and I figured if I made the invitation, it would be expected that I lead. I had gotten many "interested" looks from some of the cowboys, but none had asked me to dance, even the ones I had seen on the dance floor.

I decided maybe I appeared too eager and found an empty bar stool where I could sit and sulk. I was surprised that the bartender came over to take my order immediately when I sat down; it was a busy night, and I noticed many people standing around waiting for drinks.

"What'cha having sexy?" he asked. His thick Texan accent coupled with a thick dark beard – *which was a rarity in the '90s, a decade devoted to manufactured hairlessness and the razor* – and amazing – *close to a ten* – nose had me instantly attracted. His worn-in, tight Wranglers and matching Astros cap didn't hurt either.

"Shot of Beam and a Shiner Bock, please," I flashed the goofy grin – I learned long ago it was one of my best attributes. It hides my mean girl and gives a trusting and comfortable impression.

"You got it." He turned to grab my order but quickly turned back to me. "I'm about to go on a break. You wanna join me on the patio for a cigarette?" My grin had done its magic – *when it works, it always elicits a similar goofy smile.* "Drinks are on me," he added.

"Sure," I responded. Anything was more interesting than staring at the dancers waiting for an invitation. Plus, he was a hottie.

He grabbed a couple of beers, and a bottle half full of Jim Beam, along with a couple of shot glasses and motioned for me to follow him. The patio had a separate employees only section hidden away from the public, where we sat down at a table and had a couple of shots before opening the beers.

"Are you lost or something?" he asked with a chuckle, "This doesn't seem like the right bar for you."

"I just want to dance," I confessed to him. "I love to two-step and my usual dance partner is out of town," I supplied.

"Oh. You have a boyfriend?" he smiled in a feral manner. Like it was a challenge.

"Nope. Just a dance partner," it wasn't a lie. Even if Hank was more than a dance partner, in no way was he a boyfriend.

"Oh," the bartender looked dejected, as his desired challenge dissolved in front of him. "Why don't you just ask someone to dance then? You don't seem particularly shy to me," he asked.

"I don't know how to lead," I confessed, "I've only ever danced with the one person, and so far, he has only taught me to follow. I figured if I asked someone to dance, it would be expected that I lead," it came out more like a question than I planned.

"That's true if you ask you should probably expect to lead," he answered. At least I had confirmation.

"See my conundrum?" I asked, and when he just stared at me, I stated, "My problem."

"Yeah. I'm sure no one has asked you because of the way you're dressed. Put on some Wranglers and tuck your shirt in to start..."

"Yeah, no," I interrupted. "This is me, and I shouldn't need a new wardrobe to dance."

"Don't get me wrong. You're a hottie, and part of it is you stand out from the drones of cowboys I see day after day. It was more an observation. They just need to see that you know how to dance, and you'll have more invitations than you can handle." He poured us another shot. "Drink that, finish your beer, and we'll go show 'em what's up."

I downed the shot, followed by the rest of the beer – *close to full* – in a single gulp. Of course, that was followed by a giant belch. I stood up and said, "Excuse me. Ready when you are," my signature goofy grin had reappeared as rapidly as the Vanisher can disappear.

The bartender started laughing, "Slow your roll, Speedy. I still got forty-five minutes. We only need one dance to show you off." He reached into his overly-starched western shirt and produced a joint. "This'll help. You smoke?" he asked.

"Are you Superman or something?" I asked. "You're my fucking superhero," I stated, and he started laughing.

"Well, my name is Clark," he extended his hand, and I realized that we hadn't yet introduced ourselves.

"Shut the fuck up!" I exclaimed.

"Seriously. My name is Clark. And my middle name is Kent. Needless to say, my dad was a super fan of Superman," he looked slightly embarrassed. "I don't usually tell people my middle name," he declared, "it always leads to questions."

"That. Is. So. Cool. If it helps, my dad wanted to name me Bilbo," *my dad really isn't a geek, not like me at any rate, but The Hobbit is his favorite book. Mom threatened to divorce him if he named me Bilbo Baggins Bailey.*

"Who's that?" he asked, he was still holding out his hand.

"It's from a book," I supplied – *before the movies few understood the reference.* I shook his hand, "I'm Jay."

We smoked the joint and headed to the dance floor just before his break ended. We had just enough time for one song, but he was right, it only took one. Clark was a much better dancer than Hank, and he had me performing moves I didn't think I was capable of. We spun around the dance floor at a much faster pace than I thought would be possible to Faith Hill's "This Kiss."

Clark later told me he was "showing me off," and he greeted practically everyone on the dance floor. I learned that he was a regular dancer when he wasn't working. Most patrons seemed to know him by name. He was the best damn country dancer I have ever known, and he seemed to garner a lot of respect at TRCC.

Later that night he told me he was pushing me to see how well I could dance. He disclosed that he was trying to trip me up with more and more complicated steps, spins and thrusts, and he was pleasantly shocked that he couldn't get me to stumble. Sure, I stepped on his feet from time to time trying to keep up with the changes, but his talent came from his ability to lead; once I stopped trying to keep up and went with the flow, I truly learned what two-stepping was. He was amazed someone who looked as out-of-place as I did could dance better than most there.

After he returned to his work duties, finding dance partners was a cinch. When I wasn't actively dancing with someone, I was being approached with invitations. Clark saved a stool for me at his bar, and during his breaks, he would find me for a few songs. His shift ended about two hours before last call, and from that point until the bar closed, he was my only dance partner.

Chapter 38

BAG OF COBRAS

Spring 1996 – December 1996. San Antonio, Texas. Laredo, Texas. Huntsville, Texas.

It turned out that Doug was in town visiting his parents for Easter. He had grown up in the area but was living in Laredo, Texas working for the INS. He was practically a prodigy with languages, and when I met him, he spoke close to a dozen, and he learned a half dozen more in the time we were together. I can't remember what his job title was, but in practicality, he was a translator for the odd immigrant coming through the Laredo border that didn't speak Spanish. He was a fully trained law-enforcement officer, carried a gun and badge.

He was staying with his parents for a few days before heading home and asked me on a date. It was generic fare. Dinner at a decent Mexican joint followed by a movie. During dinner, he asked me what I wanted to see, and *Fargo* had recently released in the theater. He mentioned that he hated Steve Buscemi so wasn't interested in the film and suggested *The Birdcage* instead. I explained that I generally found Robin Williams annoying. He rationalized that since I didn't hate Robin Williams, *The Birdcage* should be chosen over *Fargo*. I suggested a different movie altogether, but he insisted that would be worse, as neither of us would get what we wanted. It was the prime example of what became a common tactic.

He wasn't nearly as succinct when arguing about which film to see. In fact, he was quite devious with his reasoning. I found myself happily going to see his choice after we finished our meal. During dinner, most of the conversation was dedicated to him talking about his job, but there were a couple interesting turns. When he learned that I was twenty years old, he was appalled to find out I was using a fake ID. He said he couldn't drink with me in public and encouraged me to destroy the ID. I shrugged it off, as I took a drink from my margarita.

During that conversation, he told me he was twenty-seven; the night before, I had explained to him that I wouldn't date anyone in their thirties. I wasn't looking for the type of relationship Bo and Brad had – *don't get me wrong, I loved Brad, and the two had a great relationship. It worked for them, but I didn't think it would work for me.* It was months later, after I had moved in with him that I learned he was in fact thirty-two.

He explained that he was sure that the age difference wouldn't bother me once I got to know him better. He was right, but that doesn't justify the lie. This double standard concerning dishonesty about our ages was the first of many. His controlling nature was insidious. He never told me what to do, he "guided" me towards making the "right" decision. It took me a couple years to catch on – *I'm somewhat embarrassed to say* – but he was a control freak. I may have been making the decisions I thought I had reached of my own volition, but almost every decision I made was "for the good" of our relationship. *But I am getting ahead of myself.*

From my parents' house, Laredo was only about a two-hour drive. I rearranged my schedule in order to get three consecutive days off every week. After work on the day before my weekend started, I would go and visit my parents and get up the next morning to drive to Laredo. Doug convinced me to do this as often as possible, even though he was working grave-yard hours at the time. In the two days spent in Laredo, I would spend maybe four hours with Doug; the remainder of the time he was working, or one of us was sleeping.

Only once before I moved to Laredo did he come back to San Antonio, even though every two weeks he would have five days off. When he did come, he only stayed in my little apartment once. He said it was too small and felt like a college dorm room. This seemed natural to me, considering up until this semester I had been in college and Doug was already encouraging my continued education

He convinced me to come and stay with him at his parents' house instead – *and again I'm getting ahead of myself.* On our second date, which was the day after our first, which was the day after we met, Doug took me to meet his parents. He didn't tell me until we pulled into their driveway. He explained that he told his mom about our first date and she really wanted to meet me, and he assured me that the two of us would really like each other.

I wasn't happy that he wasn't upfront with his plans, nor did I think it was appropriate to meet the in-laws on date number two – *we aren't lesbians after all* – but he was right. His mother and I were instantly friends, so I quickly overlooked his transgression. Everyone in his family was wonderful in their own way, but his mom and I grew close.

Three months after I met him, I decided to move to Laredo. He had complained that my tiny apartment looked like a college dorm room, but his place wasn't better. He had a single couch facing a TV that sat on a coffee table and a standing lamp in his living room; a Bo-Flex in his dining room; and a twin-sized futon lying on the floor across from a small dresser in his bedroom. I offered to bring my bed, but he wasn't comfortable with having a bunk bed; he said it was too juvenile.

Apparently, my queen-sized mattress – *which I was allowed to bring* – lying directly on the floor was more "grown up."

I started waiting tables in Laredo two days after I arrived and worked as many hours as they allowed. It wasn't a great job, but it wasn't a terrible one either. I continued to save money for an eventual return to school. I still wasn't sure that it was the right time, but Doug had been incredibly persuasive on that front. Mostly because he didn't want to be with someone that didn't have a degree, so I was expected to remedy that situation.

I had received my acceptance letter from Texas A&M International University in Laredo the same day Doug told me that he had gotten a new job and promotion, but he was required to relocate to Huntsville, Texas. He never informed me that he applied for the job, nor did he ask my opinion on an upcoming relocation. Granted, it was early in the relationship, but when he delivered this news, I was told I would be joining him, not asked. I hadn't been in Laredo long, and it turned out Sam Houston State University in Huntsville was a cheaper alternative.

I talked to Bo at least once a week, but we rarely saw each other, and Doug always devised an excuse to keep Bo from visiting. The only time he was "allowed" to visit was when Doug was away for work – which happened only twice the entire time I lived there. Bo and Doug hated each other, but both were meticulously careful to keep their feelings to themselves. Both were fearful they might alienate me and send me to the other. Bo backed off but made sure I understood he was always there waiting if I wanted to come home. I was oblivious to their mutual antagonism.

For my twentieth birthday, Bo and Brad bought four tickets to see my favorite band in concert. I had fallen in love with their current single, which was often played on the radio, and it took me little time to purchase both of their albums. I loved each song as much as the radio-played single that drew me in. They were touring to promote their second album, and Brad bought tickets knowing I had never seen them live. Or so I thought.

That concert caused the first real fight between Doug and me, and it almost sent me packing. The show wasn't until after my birthday and during the semester. It was on a weekday, but we were planning on staying through the weekend. About a week before the concert, we learned it was at a twenty-one-and-older-only venue. I no longer had Jayce's ID as Doug had convinced me it could be detrimental to his career if I were caught with that. *Never mind that it was 1996 and the two of us had no legal connection whatsoever.*

Brad was unconcerned. He planned to tell the doorman, and manager if necessary, that he was my step-father. As my supposed parent, it would be perfectly legal for me to attend the concert with him. Of course, we wouldn't have the "necessary paperwork" in tow, but Brad was convinced he would be able to talk circles around whomever until I was allowed in. Doug didn't want to go.

He made the excuse that he wasn't comfortable with the deception, citing his job in law enforcement. I told him repeatedly that he didn't have to go if he didn't want to, but I had every intention of attending with or without him. He argued that going without him would be unhealthy for the relationship. He always used the "good of the relationship" to rationalize and get his way. He almost pushed it too far, but luckily for him, we had driven my car to town. I simply grabbed my keys and drove away.

When I arrived at Brad and Bo's, I was angry and annoyed; until Bo produced a bag of weed that I had left with him. I had stopped smoking pot because Doug convinced me it was for the good of our relationship and could be detrimental to his career – *I can hear you gasping in shock.* The three of us got ripped before heading to the venue where we watched Brad confuse the doorman and the manager, but in the end, I was allowed through the door.

After the opening act finished their set, my jaw practically hit the floor when I watched the headliners take the stage. They were the same band I had seen in New Orleans. The same guy I delivered marijuana to and smoked a joint with, in a keg cooler, was standing on stage. When I "discovered" them on the radio, I thought they sounded familiar. I told Brad and Bo, but I'm not sure they believed me. I had to admit most of that trip was spent in a pot-smoke- and alcohol-induced haze. Much of that trip was blurry, but I'm convinced it was the same three-piece alternative band.

Remembering the significance of my hat, I reached up and realized I didn't have it on. I had forgotten it at Doug's parent's *– well not exactly forgotten, but I didn't want to go back into the house when I realized I didn't have it on.* That X-Men cap was starting to become a little threadbare, but it was on my head daily. When I returned to Doug's parents' house the next day, the hat had mysteriously gone missing. I never saw it again, and Doug insisted I was wearing it when I left.

Life with Doug wasn't all horrible, in fact, most often it was very comfortable, and I enjoyed living with someone. Doug practically worshipped me, he often told me that he couldn't believe I was with him, and that I was out of his league. What Doug liked most about me was his vision of how our future would be, and he was constantly subtly molding me to fit his fantasy. But he was always generous with praise and words of love and encouragement.

He was comfortable with my geeky nature and had no problems with me spending money on comic books, sci-fi novels, and gaming paraphernalia *– mind you, we kept separate finances, yet he always told me how to spend my money –* but he didn't like that I wore comic book t-shirts. He eventually convinced me to start "dressing my age." I was only twenty, but I think in his mind we were always ten to twenty years in the future. It was okay to be myself, just not in public where someone might judge him because of my interests. Don't ask, don't tell from the onset of my first long-term relationship.

We were also closeted to my co-workers and his alike. We told them all we were cousins when I moved in with him. We spent much of our free time with his work friends, whom I hated, but he convinced me it was good for his career. I didn't disagree with him, but I never understood the point of my presence, which always raised questions. Ironically, before I moved in with him, he was adamant that he meet my parents first, and this was before I discovered his true age. I had planned to tell my parents I was moving to Laredo to go to school, as I wasn't ready to introduce them to a boyfriend I had only known three months. I wasn't "allowed" to move in with him until this condition was met.

He also had a woman friend that he dated from time-to-time over the years. He would date her when he felt he needed to hide his sexuality for whatever reason. She was his "beard," and Ann had no idea he was gay, but he still considered her a "close" friend. He wanted me to meet her because she was an important person in his life, but to do so, I would have to remain closeted and was forbidden to exhibit anything that might be construed as affectionate. I refused, to his chagrin, but he insisted on seeing her occasionally even though I was aware of their sexual history.

Once we moved to Huntsville, our lives found a satisfactory routine. He still worked as a translator for INS, but at an extensive prison complex. I started classes, taking more than full-time hours, and worked close to forty hours weekly at the chain restaurant next door to our apartment complex. I enjoyed the domestic life, it was extraordinarily ordinary, but it was comfortable.

Chapter 39

FAVORITE BLANKET

May 1999 – November 1999. San Antonio, Texas. Austin, Texas. San Antonio, Texas.

It didn't take long to become a regular fixture at The Rainbow Cattle Corral, and I never again had any problems finding a dance partner. Clark and I went out on a couple dates, and we did have a connection, but I was avoiding anything that could lead to a relationship like the plague. I was still regularly seeing Hank, but he no longer wanted to go dancing at TRCC, he didn't seem to like that I knew people there. But I didn't need him to get my country-dance fix anymore.

I started spending most of my free time in Austin, and I would occasionally crash at my sister and her girlfriend's spare room. I didn't see them often, but provided I didn't wake them, they were accepting of the arrangement. They even offered to let me move in if I wanted to find a job in Austin since I was spending so much time there anyway.

Before the offer, I hadn't even considered the idea. Being around Bo again was wonderful. He was a much happier human having me around, he was even picking up more shifts at work. Brad was also glad to have me back, as it took the pressure off him to keep Bo entertained. I was living in the main house with the two of them as the tiny garage apartment was being rented, but I never felt like a third wheel – *but it would take both of them being around to make a third wheel; as it was, usually it was just the two of us.*

When I moved home, I was shocked to learn their tenants were the "other" Michelle and her current girlfriend. She and Bo had superficially repaired their friendship, at least enough for Bo to rent to her; although it was evident he no longer trusted her. It was like having a rival mean girl living behind the house. I never forgave her, and I was never nice to her, which caused her to look for a new place to live.

On a rare occasion when Brad was home for dinner – *instead of meeting us then returning to his office* – Bo told him of Michelle's intention to move.

"She still has three months on her lease," Brad noted. I was surprised, he never even brought up the subject of a lease when I rented the place. "And she's two months behind on rent."

"Are you fucking serious?" Bo asked. "She just borrowed twenty bucks from me."

"She's probably smoking crack," I said viciously. "Stupid bitch." We later found out that she was indeed spending her money on drugs. I'm not sure what exactly, but it caused her girlfriend to leave her.

"I was going to let her out of her lease. She's been an awful tenant, but that was before I knew she was behind on rent and borrowing money." Bo told Brad.

"I didn't know she was borrowing money from you," Brad stated. "And I didn't want to stress you out, so I didn't tell you about the rent."

"Bullshit. You didn't tell me because you forgot. If it's not work, you don't care."

"I know, honey. I'm sorry," he had learned when not to poke the bear.

"You're lucky you make a lot of money. I don't know if I would put up with a broke-ass, absentee boyfriend," he often said similar things, but this time it didn't sound much like a joke.

"I know. It's been crazy, but I can sneak out early on Friday. We can go to Houston for the weekend?" he asked.

"Yeah right. Jay and I are going to go to Austin, and you'll say you'll go to Houston. But you won't. And I will have missed out on going with Jay. Where I'd probably have more fun anyway."

"He should come with us. Can you get your shifts covered?" Brad asked me.

"Maybe. If not, I'll call in sick," I started laughing. "Unless the two of you want a romantic getaway. I don't want to be a third wheel."

"Fuck that," Bo answered, "Like I want to be all romantic with a stranger," I noticed he was giving Brad one hell of an evil eye – *it was so powerful, even the Watcher would have turned away from it.* "And just so you know, we are staying at a nice hotel, and eating at expensive restaurants all weekend," I cringed when he said this. I had been spending a lot of time and money in Austin. "And you're paying for all of Jay's shit too. And you are buying both of us new outfits to go out in. Scratch that, Kayla's coming too. And you're paying for her as well."

"Whatever you want, honey," Brad replied hugging Bo and kissing him on the forehead.

Kayla did come to Houston, and the four of us had an incredible time. During that trip, and the conversation that acted as the catalyst for it, I deduced that Brad and Bo's relationship was under some strain. They argued often, and Bo was constantly annoyed with him. He had been feeling neglected and was starting to develop bitter feelings towards Brad.

When I returned home from D.C., my presence helped mask the growing rift. Bo was happy to have someone to spend time with; he was able to ignore Brad's absence, and I was quickly becoming a crutch for their relationship. Both were growing reliant on my proximity to keep their relationship running smoothly. I don't think either of them realized how much my presence swept away their problems.

I didn't want to be their buttress though, and most importantly I didn't want Bo to grow resentful towards me because I helped make a bad relationship bearable. If he needed out, I didn't want to be the reason he stayed. I'm in no way saying their relationship was bad, they were both committed and mostly happy; my concerns stemmed from a worst-case scenario type of thinking.

I contemplated finding an apartment in San Antonio, but I was fearful that it wouldn't be enough. I came to realize that I had to get away, so I didn't inadvertently stunt their relationship. I was torn though. I didn't want to leave my best friend, and I was happier than I had been in years. But I was convinced it was the right thing to do for the good of their relationship.

I decided to move to Austin since it was close, and I had a place to stay – *although, as my sister likes to say: I never stayed with her, only my stuff did.* When I got to Austin, I found a job at a great local restaurant where I made great money. I had very few bills and started spending all my free time at the bars. I started my second slut phase.

When I returned to San Antonio, I realized that most of the faces I saw at the bars were familiar; it was all the same people, and I had already slept with the men who had struck my fancy for the most part. Little had changed in my two-year absence, and I quickly grew bored with the nightlife there. Austin, on the other hand, presented a population that was mostly new and exciting. Or so I thought.

I spent about six months in Austin, and in that time, I realized that the nightlife was virtually the same everywhere, only the faces were different. The most significant difference in Austin was TRCC and my love for country dancing. I became a fixture there and got to know the staff and other regulars. I was even given a new nickname; I was affectionately referred to as the closeted cowboy. This wasn't a reference to my sexuality, but rather to my dancing. I was told often that I was a great dance partner and deep down I must be a cowboy. Many tried to convince me to dress the part, at least when frequenting the bar, but to be honest, I enjoyed the individuality and the attention it brought. New patrons were always surprised by my two-stepping skills.

During my last couple months in Austin, I started dating a cowboy I met dancing. He seemed to want it to develop into something lasting, but I wasn't interested in a serious relationship. I kept some distance, but I did like him well enough to stop seeing other people. Even Hank.

After a rare dinner spent at home with my sister and her girlfriend, my phone rang, and I headed outside for some privacy.

"Hello," I answered.

"Hey, Kiddo," Hank greeted me. "I should be getting into town late tonight. What's your schedule look like for the next couple days?" he asked.

"Um, well..." I stalled. I wasn't sure how to tell him.

"You okay?" he asked when I trailed off into silence.

"Yeah, I'm great, but uh..." again I trailed off.

"What? You shack up with someone?" he sounded disappointed.

"Not exactly, but I've started dating someone. I'm not really comfortable with the 'behind the back' stuff. And I didn't really want to tell him about you..."

"And that's why I like you so much, Kiddo. Don't sweat it. I want nothing but the best for you. I'll sure miss seeing you, but I don't want to get in your way," he sounded sincere.

"You're the best, Hank. I'm glad you understand," it was the truth. I worried that he would be upset, and I didn't want to be the source of his unhappiness. I cared for Hank, even if our relationship was a strange closeted thing. Not to mention the indignation I felt playing the mistress.

"Can I still call you when I come to town?" he asked. "You never know when you'll be single again," he offered.

"Yeah, of course," I answered.

I expected that to be my final conversation with Hank, but true to his word, he called just as frequently. These conversations always went one of two ways.

Option A:

"Hey, Kiddo. This is Hank. You single yet?"

"Nope, not yet."

"Alright. You take care of yourself. I'll try again later."

Click.

Option B

"Hey, Kiddo. This is Hank. You single yet?"

"As a matter of fact, I am."

"Wonderful. You wanna get together?"

"Of course. When do you get here?"

I didn't date the dancer for long; I ran away before I could develop a substantial attachment, but I always thought he would have been a good match. I grew tired of the nightlife, and even though I saw Bo on a regular basis, I missed seeing him daily. My intuition regarding my presence as a crutch for their relationship was validated after I left. Brad and Bo started arguing more and more without my company being a distraction. I don't think Bo realized the situation, but I'm convinced Brad was fully aware. He all but begged me to move back whenever I saw him.

Bo had always had a dream of owning and raising Arabian horses, and he convinced Brad to buy a large enough property to pursue that vision. Brad capitulated, and they sold their house in the heart of the city, trading it in for a twenty-acre, turn-key property ideal for Bo's desires. The property contained a six-bedroom, three-bathroom house with an attached, but separate, two-bedroom, two-bathroom, walk-out, basement apartment. There was also a ten-corral barn with accompanying pastures and areas separated by elaborate fencing. Everything on the property was in slight disrepair, but before they moved in, they spent a great deal of time and money bringing everything up to date.

Bo was able to get horses. He started with two, but his herd quickly grew to capacity for the property. Bo was in heaven. He had an opportunity to pursue a dream. He became an incredibly dedicated equestrian; he committed everything to his vision. Once Bo dropped his housewife persona, he became a much happier person, and his and Brad's relationship turned from the nosedive trajectory it had been on. Of course, the horses were a new distraction, a new crutch. But that meant my presence would no longer fill that role.

When Brad and Bo offered up the apartment, I jumped on the opportunity faster than Toad blindsiding a hero. I had learned a valuable lesson by moving to Austin. I learned that the nightlife scene was practically the same everywhere. The same tired faces going through the same tired motions. Sure, the faces were different, but the motions weren't. It didn't much matter where I lived if my only criterion was the gay nightlife. That was always the same.

-Side note – horses have always freaked me out. Deeply. I find them to be beautiful and magnificent creatures, but a large and sturdy fence between them and me is a requirement. And I won't get any closer than five feet from one, and I rarely touch them. It's not so much an irrational fear of the creatures, although

they are scary beasts, it's more an inherent distrust of them. They are vile, deceitful, and murderous. And they are smart. Too smart. Horses remind me of people who purposefully play dumb; they can't be trusted and always seem to have an ulterior agenda. I have had this feeling towards horses for as long as I can remember, and considering my aunt and uncle have a cattle ranch in Montana, where I have spent a fair amount of time as a kid, I was regularly around horses from a very early age.

Although not a fan of the horses themselves, I was happy to do "horse" things with Bo. So long as he observed my fence and distance rules – *and he always has. He has never once tried to force me into an interaction with a horse that I wasn't comfortable with.* I often went with him to feed stores, to pick up hay, to look at horses on other farms. Hell, I even went shopping with him as he started dressing more to fit the lifestyle. He never got to the point of a cowboy hat and obnoxiously shiny and overlarge belt buckle. But he came close.

I even rearranged my work schedule when necessary so I could go to horse shows with him. Most were in Dallas, Houston, Austin, and other parts of Texas. We would always go to the bars and nightclubs in the evening, plus the horse shows themselves had a larger than average gay attendance. I met a lot of men at these horse shows, and it presented a unique avenue as this slut phase was winding down.

Bo encouraged me to reconnect with my geeky side. Doug had all but squashed all outward appearances, and whenever I have been caught up in the "gay lifestyle," I have closeted that aspect of my personality – *except for the t-shirts.* He would go to comic book and gaming stores with me and even helped me find a *D&D* group that was incredibly gay-friendly, but I never went – *most of my geek activities took a back seat when I was single.*

I often wondered why Bo never went to college. Brad had always encouraged it and had the means to pay for any school

Bo was accepted to. Bo always said school was never for him, he explained he just didn't like it, but when he got his first two horses, he became a scholar. The two of us spent so much of our free time at different bookstores and libraries. He would head straight to wherever horse books lived, while I beelined to the science fiction and fantasy section. Bo became an expert on Arabian horses in so many aspects. Self-educated, but truly expert.

Chapter 40

FIT

December 1996 – December 1997. Huntsville, Texas. San Antonio, Texas.

We lived in Huntsville for a year, and until my twenty-first birthday little changed. He worked. I worked and went to school. For my twenty-first birthday, he took me to dinner at the restaurant where I worked. He ordered me a margarita, without asking what I wanted, and I wasn't carded as my co-workers were aware it was my birthday.

I had made some friends in Huntsville, and was even allowed to be open about my sexuality, both at work and in class, and they all wanted to take me out drinking for my birthday. They decided upon a gay bar in College Station, which was only about a thirty-minute drive. Huntsville had numerous bars, but none were exactly gay-friendly. Doug didn't think it was a good idea, but that's where his reasoning stopped. We had a designated driver and the next day off.

Doug just plain didn't want to go. He didn't want to be surrounded by college-age kids celebrating a twenty-first birthday. He complained that I would get wasted and be hung over, and my friends would act like fools all night, and the bar would be nothing but more kids. I argued that that was the point.

When I asked what he had done for his twenty-first birthday, the picture he painted was the one he wanted to avoid. When I asked if he enjoyed it, he confessed it was one of his favorite memories. When I asked why he didn't think I should have a night like that, he replied that the circumstances were different and that I would have my drunken party in a few days. To avoid a pointless fight that wouldn't end until Doug had his way, I agreed not to go. I suppose his dinner plans were my consolation prize.

Bo and Brad were throwing me a party the weekend after my birthday. They finally added the pool they had always wanted, and the fiesta was both for my birthday and an end-of-summer blowout. Of course, Doug started to discuss reasons to stay home, but I put my foot down and refused even to argue any of his points. I simply told him I was going with or without him. He had learned the year before, and he dropped his arguments, painted a happy face, and went to my party.

I left Doug with his parents and went to help Bo and Kayla with last-minute preparations. I tried to convince Doug to come help, but he declined and half-heartedly told me to have fun. Bo, Kayla, and I had a blast that day with the final touches for the party. There were many. Close to one hundred people were in attendance that night; about half, I had never met.

I was already drunk before the first guest arrived. Not to mention that Kayla, Alex, Bo and I had been smoking pot all day. They were all under strict orders to not tell Doug, as that was a fight I wanted to avoid at all costs. The party was amazing. I got to see many friends I hadn't seen since moving to Laredo. My sister and her girlfriend came, and even Kayla's sister and parents were there. My parents were upset that they couldn't make it, but they had moved to Portland four months previously after my Dad retired from the Air Force.

With one exception, the party was amazing. Kayla and Bo had decided weeks ago that this party would also be my "coming out" party, or some similar nonsense. When the party was in full swing, they drug me upstairs, where they forced me into a used wedding dress that was so small the sleeves had to be ripped off to make it fit. They bought the dress at the Goodwill, and Kyla also procured a plethora of cheap cosmetics so they could give me a makeover. They settled on an '80s prostitute for theme, complete with bright-red lipstick, caked-on, powder-blue eyeshadow, and rosy cheeks that made me look like I'd been on a ski slope all day.

During their machinations, Doug must have noticed our absence and came looking for us. When he found us in the master bedroom, my make-up was about half finished, and I had a joint hanging out of my mouth. At the time, I thought he believed it was a cigarette because he didn't mention it until our drive home. Looking back, I'm certain he just filed it away in favor of addressing what he believed was a more immediate problem.

He was appalled that Bo and Kayla were dressing me up in drag, and demanded I take it off immediately. I refused, and Kayla informed him that he was expected to dance with me during my "coming out" number, and she was serious. She and Bo had been talking about their plans the entire time they were making me over. The song was picked out, and Bo was even teaching me moves that made the dress twirl the best when I spun in a circle. All three of us were excited and looking forward to the ridiculous spectacle.

Doug stormed out and left the party telling me that not only was I making a fool of myself, but I was letting "supposed" friends take advantage of me. I was pissed when he took off, and it almost put a halt to Bo and Kayla's plans. Brad was required to take Doug's place for my dance number, and he did so happily. The two of us laughed and giggled as he twirled me around his living room – *thank god this was a decade before smartphones, otherwise, I'm sure this footage could easily be found on the internet.*

On the drive back to Huntsville, I was lectured the entire time. I was ruining my future and risking his job by smoking pot. I looked like a fool, and more importantly, made him look like a fool. I had allowed myself to be taken advantage of. I drank way too much. I embarrassed him. I didn't care about our relationship. I never thought of anything but myself. His biggest complaint was some far-fetched idea that I had some-how *made* him drive drunk. I listened in silence because I knew if I said anything it would lead to pointless fighting where he just repeated himself.

As punishment, Doug told me I had to go see an Astros game with him in Houston. He had been trying to convince me to go since we moved to Huntsville – it was less than a two-hour drive to the Astrodome – but I hated sports. I never tried to stop him from going and encouraged his attendance with friends and co-workers.

I hate to admit it, but he was right. I loved the Astros game, and have been an Astros fan ever since. We went to a gay country bar of his choice afterward; I hated the old-school country music they played, but he loved it. I enjoyed contem-porary country music, but it was rare to hear Garth Brooks, Tim McGraw, or Reba there; instead, I was assaulted with Conway Twitty, Loretta Lynn, and Hank Williams. The bar also drew an older crowd, mostly forty plus, and Doug enjoyed "showing off" his young arm candy. I played pool while he watched and chat-ted with random patrons, always introducing me as though I was his property.

Between the baseball game and the bar, we both drank too much beer. I suggested a hotel room, but he insisted we drive home. And by we, I mean me. He rationalized that if I got a D.U.I. it wouldn't be as detrimental since it could cost him his career. He also assured me he could pull strings if I were arrested. I'm ashamed to admit it, but I bought into his reasoning and drove us home. Luckily, we arrived safe and sound, and I hadn't caused an accident or killed someone. It was incredibly stupid, and I knew it, but Doug convinced me regardless.

Astros games and the terrible bar became a regular occurrence, and always followed the same script. Fast food in the car during the drive. Beer at the Astrodome. More beer at the awful bar. Me driving us home. Drunk. I never hurt us or anyone, and I was never pulled over; I was lucky. I was stupid.

Over time, there was one change; we started fighting the entire drive home. Everything I suppressed would bubble-up when I was drunk. Sober, I would continue my practice of ignoring any problems I had with our relationship. Like everything with Doug, these arguments became a fixed routine. I think he even planned what we would fight about. He often attacked my smoking, calling it the root of all our problems; never mind I was a smoker the day we met. He even used a fight as an opportunity to destroy a favorite hat. It was light gray and featured Pinky and the Brain, but most importantly, it fit my head perfectly. He always complained it made me appear immature. He yanked it off my head and threw it out the window on the interstate. He replaced it with an awesome Astros cap, but I still hold some resentment for the loss of that hat.

Even our sex life became a scripted routine. Once every other week on his first day off – his schedule rotated – at 2:00pm, we would have sex like clockwork. I was always the top, and it was always the same position, and he treated it like a chore. That routine started the day I moved in with him in Laredo and continued unchanged until the end of the relationship. He used sex as a form of control, and although the sex was passionate at first, it became boring after I moved in with him. Quickly.

I know I have painted Doug as a control freak asshole, and it's true. He was. But he was also affectionate, devoted, and most of the time a joy to be around. He always had a picture of his perfect life in his head. That life included a partner that met specific criteria. I don't think it mattered who filled the role so long as they molded to his ideals. I don't think he ever stopped to consider if I wanted the same life as he did.

Chapter 41

STALL

November 1999 – December 1999. Fort Worth, Texas.

Coming back to San Antonio was one of the best decisions I had ever made. I was planning to go back to school in Virginia but coming back to Texas meant waiting a year to qualify for in-state tuition – if I had intended to go to school, which I didn't. Part of Doug's plan for my life involved my completion of at least an undergraduate degree, but ideally an advanced one. He planned for me to become a teacher – *at least he left the choice of grade and subject to me.*

I no longer sure what to do with my life, and my focus after returning to Texas had been mostly of a carnal nature. I was sure that teaching was not the route for me. Plus, I made great money bartending and waiting tables, and those jobs allow a great deal of flexibility in scheduling, and I enjoyed traveling, which I did as often as possible with Bo; generally, to one horseshow or another.

I had been living the single life for about a year, and I had again grown bored with it, but I was still actively avoiding any men that I felt could lead to a relationship. Hank was still a regular, secret part of my life, so I was having sex on a regular basis. I was generally happy, but my life grew stagnant. I mistook it for a healthy routine.

I spent a year doing the same thing. I worked. When I wasn't working, I was with Bo. When I wasn't with Bo, I had snuck off to see Hank. I still went dancing two to three times weekly. The exercise was invaluable, and it kept me in great shape. But my favorite part was traveling with Bo.

The day before we left for a show in the Dallas area, I received a call from Hank.

"Hey, Kiddo. It's Hank. Still single?"

"You know it. When you comin' around?" I asked.

"Day after tomorrow. Maybe day after," he replied.

"Damn. I'm gonna be in Dallas." I was disappointed. I had missed his last visit because of a horse show. But I wasn't going to skip it. Dallas was a fun city. "Fort Worth actually," I muttered.

"Really? Me too. I have a couple days off, so wanted to come see you. What are you doing in Fort Worth? Will you be busy?"

"I'll be with Bo..." I started.

"Horseshow?" he asked, interrupting me.

"Yep," I answered.

"Think you can sneak away?" he asked.

"Possibly, but I'm not driving," I said bitterly. I had traded in Zatanna. I didn't want to, she was my dream car, but insurance rates in South Texas were ridiculously high for a single, male driver under age twenty-five. My insurance rates tripled. I traded her in for a base model Dodge Neon, dark blue without a single frill. It was a brand-new '99 model, but it was a manual transmission with a cassette player and manual windows and locks. I named her Aeon the Neon – *after Aeon Flux; the cartoon, not the terrible movie* – and I hated her. That isn't fair. I hated not having my Jeep. *I drove Aeon for the next twelve years, and never had a single problem with her. It was the most reliable car I have ever owned, but she was destroyed in a severe hailstorm.*

"What if I met you at the show?" he offered.

"That'd be great. But Bo would figure us out, about three seconds after I introduced you to him. And he would probably be hurt that I've kept you a secret for so long."

"Yeah. That wouldn't be good. Will you be with him the whole time?"

"When we're at the show, no. Afterward, yes. He always ditches me at the shows to go talk horse with the other horse freaks," I stated.

"While he's busy at the show, you could meet me at my truck. There should be plenty of parking. We wouldn't be able to do much of anything else though. So, just sex, you know. I'd love to take you to dinner and dancing if you could find a way to sneak off for the evening."

"I don't know about that part, but hell yeah on the sex. If you don't mind sitting around on your day off parked at a horse show."

"I ain't been to a horse show in ages. Sounds fun. Maybe we can hang out while Bo is busy," he added.

It was a fun weekend at that horse show. It was exciting sneaking off to meet Hank when Bo was occupied. At the first opportunity, we met up and headed for his truck. He explained it was easy to find parking large enough for his truck, but it wasn't exactly close by. He thought a walk across the extensive grounds would provide a short cut, but he was wrong. We did find a group of vacant stalls in a separate building where we stopped and fooled around. Instead of a thirty-minute walk to his truck, we found inventive places for cuddles, kisses, and sex. A few times we were almost caught, which only added to the excitement.

It didn't take long for Bo to notice my more-than-usual absence, and he had spotted me with Hank enough times to realize something was up. I would signal Hank to disappear whenever I spotted Bo.

"Who's that guy?" Bo asked after Hank disappeared into a restroom.

"What guy?" I played dumb.

"The dude with the handle-bar mustache. I've seen you with him a few times now."

"Oh. That guy, um," I hesitated.

"You find some new piece of ass?" he asked. "I haven't gotten a good look, but he looked cute. I wanna meet him," he stated.

"Um, he's straight. I think his girlfriend is here too," it was a sort of a half-truth – quarter truth maybe?

"Oh. Have you hooked up yet?"

"A few times. I'm hoping for a few more," that was the full truth.

"What's his name?" Bo asked, and followed with, "Does he have a big dick?" Bo and I talked about everything.

"Hank. And yes. Huge." I didn't see how the truth here would hurt.

I have no reason to believe that Bo disbelieved the story, and I had told him as much of the truth as I could. Bo agreed to give me space that weekend to pursue the "straight" guy he thought I had just met. I explained to Hank, and he wasn't exactly comfortable with the situation. Until he met Bo.

On the second day of the show, we looked for even more adventurous places to fool around. We found an empty stall in a somewhat trafficked area for a tryst. When we exited, flushed and covered with enough hay to make it apparent we hadn't been on our feet, we ran right into Bo and a couple of his horse buddies. Both of which were gay, one I had fooled around with.

"What do we have here?" the one I had fooled around with asked coyly. Hank's discomfort was palpable.

"Did you guys find it?" Bo asked, looking right at Hank, without missing a beat.

"Huh?" He answered.

Bo introduced his friends and followed with, "You both know Jay. This is Hank. He's my farrier's brother. His fiancé lost her engagement ring in here when she was brushing her mare before dressage this morning. Jay is helping him look for it. Any luck?" he again looked at Hank.

"No," Hank said angrily, "And that ring cost me a fortune." He caught on fast.

Looking embarrassed, the guy I had fooled around with asked, "Do you guys need any help?"

"No. Appreciate it though," Hank smiled at them, then covertly winked at Bo in thanks. "Too many cooks in the kitchen might make things harder," he added. He looked at me, "Back to the haystack?" he asked.

"Yep. Let's get to it," I answered, as Bo and his friends walked away.

Bo continued to give us space the rest of the day, and he and Hank had no further interactions. But Bo had earned a great deal of respect from Hank, but he still asked me to keep his secret. I think it made things more real between us somehow if he got to know my friends. I agreed, and I didn't want to ruin what I had with Hank by it developing into something deeper. A relationship was still very low on my priority list.

Life continued with little change. That Dallas horse show was in November of 1999, and the Y2K scare was on everyone's mind. We were waiting for society to collapse, but jets didn't fall from the sky. Electrical grids didn't fail. And missiles with nuclear bombs attached didn't suddenly launch from their silos. Before computers in the first time zone past the international date line reset their clocks, and nothing happened, those fears were real and palpable, and on everyone's mind.

There were disbelievers, of course, that went about their daily lives confident that nothing would happen. And on the other side of the spectrum, there were the Y2K preppers, convinced the world would end. These preppers stocked-up fallout shelters with as many supplies as they could hold, and they retreated to them on the day before New Year's Eve, content in their knowledge that they would be the last bastions of humanity. Like most, I fell somewhere in the middle. I honestly didn't think technology would come to a crashing halt, but if it did, I hoped to be one of the first to go because the alternative sounded worse.

The '90s had come to an end, but I was still on my journey towards self-realization – *although as I write these words, I realize that journey will only end when I take my final breath* – and I still hadn't fully come to terms with my sexuality. Although I was happier than I had ever been in my life, I realized my life had stalled. I had no long-term goals.

I was happy, but I had nothing to focus on. The only thing I was certain about was that I wanted to travel. I had loved moving to the east coast, and Doug and I had visited as many places as possible while there. I loved moving to new places as a child. And I loved the small trips to horse shows with Bo.

I know the title of this book implies that the story should come to an end here, but my life doesn't quite line up to arbitrary dates. You're going to have to bear with me as we push into the new Millennium; at least for a couple of years.

Chapter 42

ROLLING

December 1997 – August 1998. Huntsville, Texas. Reston, Virginia.

The day I got my final grades for my fourth semester of college – my second semester at SHSU – I was excitedly waiting for Doug to get off work. First, we were headed to San Antonio to celebrate the onset of 1998 with Bo and Brad. Second, I had received straight A's for the first time since starting college – *straight A's were easy in high school, but college required more dedication* – and I was excited to share the news with Doug. I was sure he would be excited too, and maybe he would be less of an ass on our upcoming mini vacation.

When he walked through the front door, he was smiling ear-to-ear. It was the happiest I had ever seen him.

"I've got some great news," I told him, curious why he looked so happy.

"Me too!" he exclaimed. "Yours first. Mine will blow it away." I was hoping he was going to tell me he had won the lottery.

"I got my grades today. Straight A's..." I started.

"Yeah, yeah. That's great," he interrupted, completely disregarding my declaration.

"I just found out today I got my dream job. We leave in March so I can start my training." I was totally in the dark. I didn't know he had applied for another job, nor had he ever talked about a dream job. "I already accepted it, and you will have your interview next week. I can't wait to tell Mom." He was bubbling with excitement. I had never been more confused in my life.

He explained that he had gotten a job with one of our federal intelligence agencies, and it was a dream of his to use his language skills as an undercover agent. He had never told me about this dream, nor the multiple interviews. He never asked how I felt about relocating. He did explain that he disclosed our relationship during the interview process and that I had already passed an extensive background check.

It was a great deal of information to process. When I asked about my schooling, Doug replied that he had already taken care of it. He had secretly applied to a few schools in the area using my personal information when he started the interview process. He always checked the mail, so I never saw any correspondence from any of these schools, but he informed me that I had been accepted to four schools. I explained that I wouldn't be able to afford out-of-state tuition at any school. To which he had a solution as well; he also filled out all my financial aid forms and told me it would be necessary to take out student loans.

I told him he could stick it. I had been putting myself through college, and I planned to continue doing so. I warned him that if he accepted the benefits in my name, I would press charges; I wanted him to understand how serious I was, and I didn't trust that he wouldn't do it anyway as it was "in my best interest."

We argued about my future schooling, and it served as a perfect distraction from all the other things Doug had decided without my input. During that argument, I somehow agreed that he had done the right thing in accepting the job without consulting me first. He finally agreed to me taking a year off while establishing residency and saving money. I think he manufactured the argument to get me to overlook everything except my schooling. He was a master of control.

Never once during our relationship did Doug help with school financially. He tried to convince me, early in the relationship, to take out student loans, and when he couldn't, I was punished to figure it out myself. We always kept separate finances. Sort of.

After moving to Huntsville, we came to an agreement – *of course, the idea was Doug's.* Since I worked for tips, I always had cash. Doug rationalized that he should pay all the "real" bills – except any tuition or school fee – and in return, I would pay for virtually everything else. While we lived in Huntsville, this arrangement worked slightly to my favor; I spent about one hundred dollars less each month than when we had wholly separate finances. Some months I may have spent more, but it averaged to a small savings on my part. I think Doug did this to help me with school without admitting he was wrong.

Doug used his "great" news as an excuse to avoid Bo and Brad on our trip home, instead deciding to spend the time with his family since we would be moving far away in a few months. When I elected to keep plans with them, Doug tried to guilt-trip me, telling me that family was more important. The guilt-trip didn't work – *my mom is a master, and Doug was way out of his league.*

Doug also tried to convince me to lie to Bo about why we were moving. He had explained that we could only tell our immediate family the true nature of his future employment. I knew I could trust Bo explicitly, and I refused to keep this from him. Doug eventually capitulated and allowed me to tell Bo. He only made the decision after he realized I was going to tell Bo, regardless of any argument he made; this allowed it to be his decision so he could maintain control.

When I told Bo and Brad – *Doug never knew that I had disclosed the secret to Brad as well* – they both put on their best happy faces. They acted excited and told me it would be an excellent opportunity to see a new part of the country. That part was true, but neither told me they thought it was the worst decision I could make. They had both discerned Doug's true nature, but I was slow to the party. They both knew that I had to make the discovery myself, so they focused on the good parts of the move. Unintentionally, they increased my excitement to an all new high.

The entire time we spent together during that trip, Doug prepped me for my interview. He pumped me full of so much useless information, and the right way to answer questions. His machinations had me incredibly nervous. Nothing he belabored was addressed. Looking back, I think it was a simple psyche evaluation. After I relaxed and answered the questions, it all went smoothly. Doug told me a few days later that I had "passed," as there was no need for a follow-up polygraph test. He took credit for my success, convinced that it was his extensive mentoring.

Life in D.C. became routine about two weeks after we arrived. Doug had found an apartment, sight unseen, once he accepted the job. He never asked my opinion on his decision. We lucked out, it was a great basement condo that was an affordable, well-kept sub-lease from someone who also worked for the "company." It was in a quiet neighborhood in Reston, Virginia. I absolutely loved living there. Thankfully. I was often alone in that apartment.

Doug's training was a two-year program and incredibly extensive. It required a great deal of travel, and consequently, the bulk of his time was spent elsewhere – *he never told me where he had spent his time away and shared very few details of any aspect of his training.* His only time home was every other weekend. He would get home Friday afternoon, and leave Sunday evening. It was the only time I saw him or talked to him. It was rare for him to call home.

Under the pretense of his new job, there were many things that I was told to keep secret. The first was my sexuality and our relationship. I wasn't allowed to tell any co-workers that I was gay and was supposed to say that he was only a roommate. It was obvious that I shouldn't disclose his actual job, but he repeated that point constantly. I was to tell people he worked for the State Department, but only if they asked. I was also told that I couldn't bring anyone to our home and that I should avoid making friends outside of work in general. It was okay to have friends at work, but I wasn't allowed to spend any personal time with them. I'm not sure what he was worried about. How did he expect me to make any friends when I was required to lie about everything?

My new employment was a restaurant in Tyson's Corner. It was always packed, and constantly understaffed. I was able to dictate my schedule – *to be honest, it was the schedule Doug demanded* – and worked doubles Monday through Friday. On the weekends Doug wasn't home, I would pick up shifts. In the six months, I worked there, I had made more than double what I had the entire previous year. It was a demanding and difficult restaurant to work in, but the financial rewards were well worth it.

I tried to squirrel away as much money as possible, my chosen school was more than triple the tuition I was accustomed to – after I qualified for in-state tuition – but I was certain I would be able to save enough money. Moving to D.C. didn't change our financial agreement. Doug still paid the "real" bills, while I picked up everything else. With Doug only being home six days every month, coupled with my usual fifty plus hour work week, it would be logical to assume my savings account was growing rapidly. But it would be a wrong assumption to make.

Doug may have only been home every other weekend, but those weekends were filled with travels. We went and visited any place that struck our – *his* – interest that we could drive to. Numerous places fit those criteria. I was financially responsible for gas, hotel, food, entertainment, and any other incidentals during these trips. And they were expensive. My monthly expenses rocketed. I managed to save very little money, but I rarely addressed the issue with Doug. Since I only saw him every other week for a couple of days, I did everything I could to avoid a fight and bringing up finances always resulted in an argument.

His training schedule seemed like it was customized for the sex life I had been experiencing for more than a year. Except it moved from Saturday afternoons to Friday evenings; that way it wouldn't interfere with our weekend trips. It was still the same position, and I was always the top, and it was even more boring than ever. Outside my right hand, it was my only sex life.

We rarely fought, I had doubled down on my policy of bottling things away and just going with the flow. Plus, the trips every other weekend to places where I had never been were invigorating, if expensive. Our friendship was better than ever, but the romance and our sex-life had all but disappeared.

My social life also disappeared. One of my managers was a geek of the same magnitude, and the two of us became friends. Doug allowed me to disclose my sexuality and even tell him I had a boyfriend. When he found a higher paying job at a competing restaurant, he said he could guarantee my same hours and schedule if I wanted to follow him. Considering the other managers were dicks, I happily changed jobs.

At about the same time, Doug made the final payment on She-Hulk – my green Ford Ranger – and I brought up finances with him. I expected him to get angry, and I would have a fight on my hands, but instead, he agreed that we would have to make new arrangements. But we never made the arrangements, he always delayed the conversation until his next weekend home.

When I received the title for my truck in the mail about six weeks later, we still hadn't reached a new agreement. With title in hand and a couple grand I had put aside for our next weekend excursion, I drove to the nearest Jeep dealership. After a few hours, I drove away in Zatanna, with her top down and the speakers blaring my favorite band. My payments were only fifty dollars more than before, but the loan took a year longer to pay off. My insurance rates in Virginia climbed less than twenty dollars. I didn't think Doug would care, especially considering that when he had bought a new vehicle after getting his current job, he never consulted me about it.

Doug was irate. He couldn't believe I didn't first ask for permission. He actually used the word "permission." He told me he was amazed that I could be so irresponsible and place an additional financial burden on his shoulders without first talking to him about it. I happily offered to give him the seventy-dollar difference each month.

That infuriated him, and he declared that we would again separate our finances. I readily agreed and told him that our trips would also be split down the middle. He laughed and told me those trips were cheap. When I called him a fucking moron, his infuriation boiled over into sheer rage. He said he would show me what a real vacation was and threatened to book a trip to Savannah, Georgia for his next weekend off. He declared that I would be responsible for my half.

I just stared at him. I still had fifteen-hundred in cash, and I couldn't imagine a ticket being more expensive than that. I called his bluff, and told him to book the tickets, even challenging him to upgrade to first class. I told him I would give him the cash for mine as soon as he did, and I had two weeks to hide away enough money to match anything he wanted to spend once in Savanah.

He thought he was calling a bluff when he placed the airline representative on hold and told me first class would be just shy of eight-hundred bucks. I smiled and declared that I had always wanted to fly first class. I retrieved my money from its usual hiding spot and paid him. I started with the small bills first.

Chapter 43

COLD YEAR

November 1999 – October 2000. San Antonio, Texas.

I lived in that attached lower-level apartment for almost a year, and although I was coasting, I was happy. There were few highs that year, but there were also few lows; I was consistently content. There were also few notable events in that year. I suppose that's the nature of stagnation. Little change. In that year, I did have three back-to-back reencounters with my three firsts. My first – *male* – sexual partner, my first boyfriend, and my first live-in boyfriend.

Bo and I were sitting on a picnic bench listening to the live music. The place was packed, and our only view was a sea of lesbians' asses jammed together between us and the stage. All were dreaming of U-hauls and long talks with the band's lead singer – and if she wasn't a lesbian, then I don't like dick. Stuck in our prison of mom jeans, neither Bo nor I were paying much attention to the people squeezing by. The live music on "gay night" drew a large crowd at Tycoon Corner, and it was often difficult to navigate.

We were sitting facing away from the table, and I was startled when some man I hadn't noticed sat down on my lap and wrapped his arms around my shoulders. He was looking at Bo,

267

and I couldn't see his face, but I recognized his voice when he told Bo, "You know he's too hot for you, right?" He turned and planted a long kiss on my lips before he started laughing.

Both Bo and I joined in his mirth, and I pulled him in for a closer hug. It had been a long time since I had seen him, and I harbored no more negative feelings. Compared to Doug, Gabe was as mild as the Power Pack.

"Yeah, I had that stick surgically removed from my ass," he said after returning my embrace. Bo genuinely laughed at this, but when I looked at Gabe's smile, I doubted he had changed much. He still seemed overly serious.

He too had recently ended his first live-in relationship. He hadn't squashed down his geeky nature as much as I had, but I could tell that he had followed a similar strategy. He wasn't quite the geek he had been. He spent the evening with us, and we all became reacquainted. Gabe and I compared war stories and got drunk, and I brought him back to my place that night.

We went on a couple dates, which were great because we talked about comic books that we had read since our last correspondence. *Fun fact: shortly after moving to D.C., I received an email out of the blue from Gabe; at an email address I had never given him. I had a letter printed in Marvel Comics* Alpha Flight *volume 2 #12. I even gave a shout out to Northstar – Marvel's first gay character – and mentioned that Marvel should include more gay characters. The rest of it is just fanboy gushing about the reboot of one of my favorite super teams. It was the only letter I have ever sent to a comic book letter page, and I was excited when I saw it in print. I suppose it was the first time my words were published. My email address was listed with my name, and when Gabe read the letter, he wondered if it was the same Jay Bailey so sent a note.*

After catching up on comic books and discussing our mutual excitement for the upcoming X-Men movie, we ran out of things to talk about. We fell out of contact until the advent of Facebook.

Shortly after my run-in with Gabe, I had an encounter with Jerry, the first guy I ever fooled around with. Bo and I were at one of the large, chain bookstores. He was sitting somewhere thumbing through a book about Arabian bloodlines that had just released, and I disappeared to the fantasy and science fiction section.

I found some graphic novels that I hadn't read and found an empty seating section. Two oversized armchairs facing each other separated by a low coffee table. I noticed an attractive guy in the thriller section. He looked vaguely familiar, but I couldn't place him. His hair was shoulder length and covered much of his face. When I noticed him, I thought *damn, he's hot, but he needs a haircut.*

Before long, I noticed that he kept looking at me. I shrugged my shoulders and played along. After about ten minutes, the seat across from me vacated, and he dashed to it immediately.

"Jay?" he asked as he sat across from me.

"Yeah?" I still couldn't place the face, but I recognized it. For some reason, I kept thinking it looked older than it should, even without knowing who I was looking at.

"You don't recognize me?" he asked. Then he smiled.

"Holy shit. Jerry. How are you?" I asked.

"I'm doing well." He didn't look well on closer inspection. He looked about ten years older than he was and he was much thinner than I remembered. "So, yeah..." he started, as he started scratching his arm obsessively. "Sorry I was a dick to you. You seemed like a cool guy. It shouldn't matter if you're a nerd," he glanced at my reading materials.

He paused, and I think he was waiting for an apology for my performance as a crazy stalker. I didn't offer one.

"So, yeah," again with the arm scratching, "You look fucking great. Wanna go out sometime?"

"No, not really," I admitted.

"Oh. So, yeah," this time it was the other arm. "Do you have ten bucks I could have?" he asked.

"Will it make you go away?" I couldn't believe how far he had fallen.

He smiled. This time I noticed all the blackened spots on his teeth. It was a rotted version of the smile that had excited me six years earlier. I pulled out my wallet, drew out a twenty and handed it to him. He tried to hug me in thanks, but I reached out and shook his hand instead.

Bo saw the interaction, and when Jerry walked away, he asked, "How much did you give the crackhead?"

"Just a buck," I lied.

"Whatever, pussy. You're too nice, you probably gave him a twenty. He was hot for a crackhead though."

"Whatever, bitch," I replied. I didn't divulge his identity, but Bo was perceptive.

"You okay?" he asked me, later that day. "You seem..." he paused, "I don't know. Sad?"

"No idea," I offered. "Just an off day, I guess."

Hank called the day after I ran into Jerry. "Hey, Kiddo. It's Hank, still single?" his greeting was robotic, and we often joked about it.

"You know it," I answered. "When do you get to town?" I was unsure why, but I had a primal urge to see Hank.

"I'll be in Houston this weekend. Can you get away?" he asked.

"Maybe. But doubtful," I was instantly disappointed. "When you gonna make it out here?" I asked hopefully.

"Following weekend. At the latest. I just wanted to see you sooner. Astros are even playing at home this weekend. I was hoping we could catch a game at their new stadium."

"Damn. That would be awesome. I might be able to swing it, but I won't know until Friday night at the soonest," I offered. "Are they selling out on tickets?" I asked.

"Not sure. I'll pick up a couple. If you can't make it, I'm sure I can scalp one."

"Awesome. I'll see what I can do, but I'm not overly optimistic," I warned.

"No problem, Kiddo. Do what you can. Hope to see you this weekend," and he hung up the phone. Conserving minutes most likely. The call was during prime hours.

Walking back into Bo's house, I heard his phone ring, followed by him hollering, "Can you answer that, Jay? I'm taking a shit," he loved to share.

"Yeah, I got it," I hollered back. "Take your time," I added. Knowing he would.

"Hello?" I answered after picking up the receiver.

There was a short pause, followed by, "Is this Bo?"

"Nope. Can I take a message?" I offered.

"Jay?" the voice asked.

"Doug?" I asked in reply, although I was certain.

"How are you? I've tried to get in touch with you a few times you know..."

"I know. Bo told me," I interrupted him.

"You never called back," his tone was accusatory.

"I was busy, I guess," I supplied. "And I'm doing great, to answer your first question."

"I'm sorry. I sounded like a dick, and I didn't mean to," okay, that surprised me. He paused, but I just waited. "Do you hate me?" he eventually asked.

"What? No," I answered without much thought, and I realized that it was true. Sure, I resented him, but I didn't hate him.

This time he waited for me to break the silence. "Was there something you called for specifically?" I asked. "Or did you have a burning desire to know whether or not I hated you?"

I tried to sound playful, but I'm sure my mean girl was in control.

"So, I'm going to be in Houston this weekend. I was wondering if you could get away. We could see an Astros game at their new stadium." I almost started laughing. "I'd really like to see you. I have many things to apologize for, and I have a few of your things that you forgot as well."

"I don't know..."

"The weekend is on me," he offered. "The 'company' booked me a suite. I'll sleep on the couch. Or I'll get you your own room if you prefer. Drinks, food, game. Everything. It's on me. I think it'd help me move on if I had some closure," the last part sounded like a guilt trip.

"I don't know..." I started again.

"I think it would help you move on too," he stated.

"What makes you think I haven't moved on?" I asked, and I couldn't keep the amusement out of my voice.

"Oh, are you seeing someone?" he asked.

"No. But what in the hell does that have to do with moving on?" I didn't try to hide my annoyed tone.

"You're right," I'm almost entirely certain that was the first time he had ever said those words to me. At least in that order, and not surrounded by other words, "I'm sorry. I'd really like to see you, and you'll be happy I held on to this stuff for you."

"What is it?" I asked with little enthusiasm. I had combed through that apartment numerous times.

"You'll have to come to Houston, to find out," he answered. He tried to sound playful, but it sounded fake.

"I'll see what I can do." I was curious about his true intentions.

I managed to get the weekend off, and I waffled between seeing Doug or seeing Hank. After telling Bo about the phone call, he said I should go see Doug. Of course, he didn't know there was another option. He wanted me to go, he too thought it might provide me closure. I insisted that I was completely over it and that I had moved on. He rationalized that I hadn't, as I had refused to date anyone longer than a month. Again, I couldn't bring up Hank, although I'm not sure trying to use our arrangement as an argument for a healthy relationship would have helped.

Chapter 44

HOLD ME DOWN

July 1998. Reston, Virginia.

For two weeks before our trip to Savanah, I worked every single shift. I had a goal to have at least four-thousand dollars in my pocket before I stepped off the plane in Georgia. Two days before the trip, I reached my goal.

Despite Doug's protestations, I didn't closet myself at my second job in Northern Virginia. I even managed to make a few friends. Mostly the work type, but it was better than no friends at all. My sexuality was a non-issue at that restaurant, which was a nice change. Even the guys I expected to be homophobes seemed accepting.

Viktor and Abel were best friends, and the two were always together. They often went to a bar down the street at shift's end, and before long, I started joining them three or four nights a week. The two were always jovial, and I always had fun drinking with them. They both had the personality of alpha male douche-bags, and they reminded me of Dan; without the homophobic tendencies – *I thought of them as Hawk and Dove; young, gorgeous, friendly, and fun.* They were dedicated friends, and each seemed to make the other better. Although it wasn't much of one, I actually had a social life after I started working there.

During the two weeks leading up to the Savanah trip, my infrequent social activities came to a complete halt. My only concern was to have enough money to cover any ridiculous expenses that might crop up on our vacation. I was convinced Doug planned to outspend me, to teach me a lesson about finances and how easy I had it before deciding to buy a new car without his permission. I planned to demonstrate how much money he spent on his weekends home.

Doug had booked us separate tickets. He was flying directly to Savanah from whatever location, and I was flying in from D.C. scheduled to arrive a couple of hours after him. I was looking forward to the trip, but I wasn't looking forward to seeing Doug. We had spent the entirety of his last weekend home fighting about my irresponsible nature, and my selfishness. After two weeks apart, my anger hadn't even begun to subside, but I had heard some great things about Savanah, so I was still psyched.

The day before I was scheduled to fly to Savanah, I was close to five hundred dollars over my goal, and when Able invited me for a drink, I agreed. The closer the upcoming vacation got, the more my anger bubbled. I was feeling vicious and vindictive, and I was on a mission to make Doug pay for his couple years of control. After our fight regarding my new Jeep, my eyes had finally opened to his true nature.

As the three of us walked towards the entrance of our usual watering hole, we noticed that the parking lot contained fewer cars than usual; and upon reaching the front door, we saw a large sign that read "Closed for employee meeting. Sorry for any inconvenience." Viktor and Abel lived in an apartment close by, and Viktor suggested picking up beer and enjoying our libations there. I shrugged my shoulders thinking, *fine by me, it'll be cheaper anyway.*

At the liquor store, I was shocked to find Shiner Bock, so I bought a case in my excitement. Abel purchased a bottle of tequila and a few limes, while Viktor purchased a case of beer I had never heard of. He too was excited, as it was the brand he drank when he was visiting family. I understood the sentiment, even if my beer of choice was of a domestic nature.

Viktor was a first-generation natural U.S. citizen. His parents had immigrated from one of the old Soviet republics; one of the "Stans," Kazakhstan, Uzbekistan, or Tajikistan, I can't remember. He was the same age as me, and he was the first in his family born in the U.S. And he was beautiful. Viktor was also charming and funny. He was one of those people that everyone strived to please. I took the opposite approach and ignored – it wasn't easy – these impulses. I strived to react to his personality rather than his looks. Besides Shannon, I have only ever personally known one other person that came close to matching the physical beauty of Viktor.

Abel was Viktor's henchman. I don't think he ever had an original thought in his head. He followed Viktor with blind devotion, and the two had been friends since they met in the fourth grade. Abel wasn't funny, nor was he charming. His best qualities were his loyalty and his protective nature, and these he gave wholeheartedly to Viktor, but he also exhibited these traits to other friends. He was almost as attractive as Viktor.

Where Viktor was tall – almost 6'6" – with a somewhat trim – but incredibly muscular – and lanky body, Able was built like a tank. He was a few inches shorter than me, but about 280 pounds of pure muscle; I swear his biceps were larger than my thighs. His short, conservatively cut, platinum blonde hair, pale complexion, and clean-shaven face were in direct contrast to Viktor's olive-colored skin, jet-black, wildly-spikey, short hairstyle and chin-strap, close-cut beard. The only physical trait they shared was their nose. Both had large, Roman-shaped noses that were nearly identical – easily a 9. They were both incredibly attractive, and I secretly drooled over them. Although I don't think it was much of a secret; everyone drooled over them. Male. Female. Gay. Straight. It didn't matter, they were undeniably gorgeous.

As my sex-life had been incredibly boring for almost two years, my self-exploration had never been more extreme. Although Doug had a few pornography videos, that he thought were hidden away, I have never been much of a fan; but I have always had an overactive imagination, and from my first day meeting them, my fantasies revolved around Viktor or Abel. Or both.

I followed them to their apartment, and when we got there, I quickly changed from my uniform into a pair of khaki cargo shorts, flip-flops, and a plain light green t-shirt – I no longer had my signature t-shirt collection. *Doug had convinced me that they were juvenile and gave a poor first impression. Of course, when I replaced them, I was sure it had been my decision, but that was how Doug operated. He always got his way, but he manipulated conversations until the desired outcome seemed to have been my idea. It was a gift, and I think it was related to his mastery of languages.* Usually, I would have changed in the employee restroom at the restaurant. I hadn't planned to have a drink, and only accepted Abel's invitation when sitting in my Jeep about to start my drive home.

I didn't notice Viktor walk up to my Jeep while I was changing – which is slightly embarrassing considering the top was down. He walked up just after I had pulled off my black slacks and had my first foot in my short's opening. I finally noticed him when he started laughing and commented on the fact that I wasn't wearing any underwear. I think he commented that he was a fellow freeballer, but I can't be sure. He scared the shit out of me – not literally – and my heart was racing, and my adrenaline was pumping. *I had once again abandoned underwear because Doug didn't think it was proper. When I met him, I wore boxers. He tried to convince me to switch to tighty-whitey's, so in protest, I stopped wearing underwear, altogether. He was never able to make a convincing argument as to why his opinion of my underwear was important. The comfort of my dick and balls is my concern alone.*

I finished pulling up my shorts and waited for my heart to return to a reasonable pace. I grabbed my beer and followed Viktor to the apartment. When I walked through the door, I was amazed. The place was new, huge and loaded with high-end finishes – it was obviously expensive. It was also furnished with expensive furniture and electronics. It looked like a palace. Viktor started laughing at my literally slack-jawed expression and explained that his parents were loaded, and he only worked to meet women. He supported Abel too, they worked part-time, worked out full time, and used their outrageously good looks to convince women to sleep with them.

After this quick explanation, they both disappeared into their bedrooms to change clothes. I wasn't surprised, as they both shared the same hatred I did for uniforms. Whenever we went out for drinks, they both first went home to change. Unsurprisingly, they both always wore the most stylish clothing; they were hipsters that could afford the ever-changing fashions.

I wasn't prepared to see them dressed so casually. Viktor emerged in gray sweat pants. Nothing else. And I was sure I had heard him right earlier, it was obvious he wasn't wearing underwear – *largely obvious, if you get my drift.* Abel stepped out in a low, V-neck tank top that exposed more of his torso than it hid, and a pair of lycra-work-out shorts. It was also massively obvious that Abel proscribed to a freeballing lifestyle. It had always been evident that the two were gym rats, but I think for the second time in five minutes my jaw was on the floor. Viktor chuckled, but this time he didn't offer an explanation. None was needed.

I had only planned to drink one or two beers, which was always my limit when I had to drive. But the Shiner Bock tasted like home, and Abel convinced us all to partake in the top-shelf tequila he had purchased. Before long, we were all drunk and having a great time. I drank with the two of them often, and we had always got along well, but I usually left after two.

Abel played DJ, and I was happy to discover we had almost identical taste in music. He even started his playlist with my favorite band's newest album. Viktor and I played a slew of video games. He was competitive and a gifted trash talker, and I was having more fun than I had in a very long time. I loved the trips Doug and I took when he was home, but it had been two long years since I had just chilled with friends.

When Viktor asked if I smoked, I couldn't believe my fortune. Considering my opulent surroundings, I shouldn't have been as bewildered as I was by the quality. It was the best weed I had ever smoked, and it had been quite some time since I last partook. Within ten minutes, I was ripped, and when I went to grab a beer to cure the onset of cotton mouth, I was amazed to learn I had already finished a six-pack. Not to mention the shots of tequila. I hadn't let loose like that since my twenty-first birthday party almost a year before.

Before long, Viktor started asking the all too familiar "gay" questions. They started benign, like: *When did you first realize you were gay? When did you come out? How did your parents take it? And, did you ever date women?* They were all familiar question that I had answered hundreds of times. I'm sure every gay person in the U.S. can relate. I answered them happily; it shows the breeders that we're just people.

It's not uncommon for this line of question to turn to a more sexual nature. I wasn't surprised when the questions changed: *Have you ever slept with a girl? How do you decide who fucks who? With guys it's only about the sex, right? And, the common misconception that gay men are attracted to all men and will have sex with any guy.* I wasn't unfamiliar with this line of interrogation either and had answered these questions dozens of times in the past.

Not as often, these questions become much more personal, and I was only accustomed to being asked by close friends. But my inhibitions were down, and these were two of the only friends I had made in D.C, even if I hardly knew them. *So, do you like dick? Do you like to suck dick? Do you like to take it in the ass? And, how many guys have you been with?* I was comfortable with the two of them, and I answered the questions honestly. I had heard all these questions before but had answered them only a few times in my life. Viktor seemed genuinely curious from an intellectual level. None of his questioning was aggressive, and it wasn't done like an interrogation. The questions just cropped up conversationally, and I forgot them as quick as I answered them. Until Abel, who had been silent throughout most of the evening, spoke for the first time since the questions started.

"I've always wondered what it would be like to fuck a dude," he said. It seemed to be directed more at himself and was spoken quietly.

Viktor grabbed my empty beer bottle along with his and disappeared to the kitchen. It seemed to me that he was avoiding his friend's declaration. He reappeared with the bottle of tequila and a handful of lime wedges. He poured a single shot, downed it, and made a horrible face as he bit down on the lime. Silently he poured three more shots and sat one in front of Abel and me, leaving the third in front of himself. He looked at the two of us as he stood up.

"Go ahead. I'll grab us a chaser," and he made the same disgusted face.

The two of us complied, and while I'm sure my countenance wore a similar expression to Viktor's, Abel swallowed his drink without the slightest grimace and waved away the lime I offered him.

I felt a cold beer tap me on the shoulder, and I turned around to see Viktor extending a Shiner Bock in my direction. I also noticed that he had ditched his sweat pants in the kitchen and his penis was half erect and hanging inches from my face.

"Go ahead," he said as I robotically took the beer out of his hand and sat it on the coffee table.

"What?" I asked dumbfounded.

"You said you liked to suck cock. Go ahead," Viktor repeated as he waggled it in my face.

"Yeah, no," I said. "I have a boyfriend. And yeah, no," I repeated. To be completely honest, I'd had numerous fantasies that begun this exact way. But those were fantasies, and I was not the cheating type. "Besides, I don't do straight dudes," I glanced around the room and spied my flip-flops by the front door. Maybe I should have seen the warning signs. My daydream of their secret identity as Hawk and Dove was as far off base as possible. Black Tom Cassidy and the Juggernaut would be much closer to the truth; two powerful friends that confuse their villainy as comradery.

"Go ahead," Viktor repeated for the third time as he thrust his pelvis forward until the head of his penis touched my lips.

I pushed him backward as I tried to stand up. Abel placed his hands firmly on my shoulders and held me in my seated position without saying a word.

Viktor stepped back to his previous spot, and his dick was now fully erect; it had been growing since his first proposal. "Go ahead, you know you want to," and he slowly inched his penis closer to my mouth.

I turned my head and struggled with Abel as Viktor continued his forward momentum. Abel let go of my shoulders and grabbed my head holding it steady – although half his size, Abel was every bit as strong and sadistic as the Juggernaut. I realized in no universe could I overpower Abel, much less Viktor even if he had been alone. Abel's grip on my skull was in no way gentle, and I realized that fighting was going to do little more than cause me pain. During my struggles, I distinctly remember my hand falling in his lap to discover a second fully erect penis. By the time Viktor's penis touched my lips I decided to do what was necessary to end this encounter as quickly as possible. I got the impression they would be gentler if I were cooperative; it wasn't my first wrong assumption that night. It was also a painful realization that my earlier assumption was correct; both were hung like horses.

After Abel got a turn orally, he disappeared as Viktor took his place and resumed the aggressive thrusting he had started before being nudged aside. When Abel returned, he again took Viktor's place, and forcefully grabbed my head, turning it towards his erection. I glanced up and saw Abel tear a condom off a long strip and hand it to Viktor.

"No way," I stated, as I pulled away from Abel's hands that were gripping the back of my head.

"I thought you liked to get fucked," Viktor said with a smile and using his most charming tones. He really was Black Tom. Tall, handsome, and charming but evil and twisted. He was going to get his way, no matter what, but at the same time he going to keep up the friendly guy façade.

"No way," I repeated. "It's been a long time," I grabbed each of their dicks. "And c'mon, both of you are huge. My jaw is already sore," I forced a joking tone and added a smile. Their behavior had already been far from gentle, but I was still hopeful.

"But you like to get fucked," Viktor repeated.

Abel again grabbed the back of my head and turned it for a better angle to resume the thrusting I had interrupted. I watched Viktor tear open the Trojan Magnum with his teeth before my view was dominated by smooth six pack abs. My thoughts were dominated by gratitude that they had at least put on condoms.

Viktor, surprisingly, was very gentle and slow at first. He even used adequate amounts of lube. I was expecting rough treatment, and my only desire was their completion so I could get the hell out of there.

When my body reacted for the first time, and Viktor noticed my growing erection, he said, "See. You do like getting fucked." He was completely wrong. I wasn't enjoying a second of it. The entirety of my being was only concerned with doing whatever was necessary to get them to cum as quickly as possible. After his observation, Viktor's gentle treatment ended, and Abel was even more brutal.

They both finished on my face within seconds of each other, and after their heavy breathing died down, Viktor gathered my clothes and belongings as Abel roughly walked me to the front door with his huge hands digging into my biceps. Viktor dropped my clothes on his welcome mat just before Abel shoved me out the apartment's entrance. I heard them both laughing after they shut the door as I stood there stark naked.

I quickly dressed and ran faster than I thought possible in flip-flops to my Jeep and sped out of there drunk, stoned, and beyond sore. Halfway home, I realized that Viktor hadn't dropped my hat with the rest of my belongings, and my first thought was dominated by the fight I would have with Doug regarding its disappearance.

On the drive home, I rationalized that I had cheated on Doug – of course, looking back I realize it was rape, but I needed a coping mechanism and settled on denial and self-blame – and I felt horrible because cheating is something I abhor. I contemplated telling him but decided against it. Our fight over buying my Jeep had begun to open my eyes, and I didn't want to give him any ammo.

I truly convinced myself that what had happened was simply cheating. I blamed myself. I had been fantasizing similar scenarios for the last few months, and once I decided to go along with it, I was an active, though reluctant, participant. Surprisingly, it reminded me of my relationship with Doug; in which I was an active, if not eager, participant.

Chapter 45

PULL

October 2000. Houston, Texas.

During the three-hour drive to Houston, I considered going to see Hank instead of Doug, but in the end, my curiosity won out. I couldn't think of a single thing of mine he might have. Nothing I gave a damn about anyway. Aside from the phone call, I hadn't spoken to Doug in almost two years; and the last time I saw him, he punched a hole in the wall.

We met at Chili's. I was forty minutes early. He was forty minutes late. It was late afternoon, and there were few people there. I sat at the bar, drank a couple beers, and watched the Astro's game to kill time. I was trying to keep an open mind, but I was reminded of his lectures on punctuality. Lectures that made no sense, it wasn't that I didn't understand what he was saying, I just didn't understand why he was wasting his time – *I am never late for anything; usually I am early. That habit started long before I met Doug.*

When he finally arrived, I tried to hide my annoyance. No, I tried to not be annoyed. I didn't want to be annoyed, because I didn't want him to be able to affect me. I didn't care if he knew I was annoyed; I was annoyed at myself for being annoyed

285

at him. Before he noticed me, I settled on not showing the annoyance; I decided to show no emotion.

I turned my attention back to the game and pretended I hadn't already seen him. I was startled when he sat down next to me; I was expecting him, but I never noticed his approach in my periphery.

"You're still an Astros fan?" he sounded surprised. He was looking at my baseball cap.

"I am. I guess it's one thing I should say thank you for," I answered. I smiled, but it felt half-forced.

"Hopefully not the only thing," his smile looked less forced than mine felt. "You look great," he added.

"Thanks," I replied.

"I like your t-shirt," he finally said, after an awkward silence.

I laughed. Sarcastically and robotically, "Ha. Ha. Ha." It was a line drawing of a cityscape with a small silhouette of Spider-Man swinging through it.

"What?" he asked, "I do."

"Really? I find that hard to believe," I countered.

"Why wouldn't I? That color blue looks great on you, and the artwork in solid white is a cool effect."

"What about Spider-Man?" I was astonished.

"What about him?"

"On my shirt." I pointed to the figure.

"Oh. I didn't notice that." His eyes looked sad, and he ordered a beer from the bartender. We sat in silence and watched the game for a few minutes.

"When you stopped wearing your t-shirts, you lost your shine," he finally said.

"I think I lost it before that," I noted. I meant to say nothing.

"That was my fault. Until you stopped wearing them, I never realized how much your clothing affected your confidence and demeanor. I shouldn't have discouraged your self-expression."

"You're right. But only on the last part," I was shaking my head sadly.

"What do you mean?" he asked, looking perplexed.

"You're right that you shouldn't have tried to discourage my self-expression. But the rest is bullshit. I only stopped wearing the immature attire when I gave up. Fighting about it just wasn't worth it anymore. My demeanor changed first. You won. I looked defeated because I felt defeated, not because of what I was wearing." I kept my tone even. Like I was explaining a simple recipe.

"Oh. I never saw our relationship as a fight. There was no winner or loser."

"That's because I surrendered. We always did things your way. Trust me, you were the winner," I informed him.

"Maybe I won the battles, but I lost the war. I've come to realize how I chased you away..."

"Then obviously you don't," I interrupted.

"What?" he asked.

"You think you chased me away?" I asked.

He looked at me like I was speaking Klingon, the one language I was sure he was unfamiliar with. "Obviously," he finally answered, "Why else would you have left?"

"Because I wanted to."

"Obviously," he answered, "You wouldn't have ended things if you didn't want to. I don't understand."

"That's the problem. That was always the problem. By your reasoning, you chased me away. It was something you did. Something I reacted to. I'm sure you've told yourself that it is all your fault, and I had no other options but to leave..."

"It was all my fault," he interrupted.

"You're a jackass. And an idiot." When the bartender headed towards us, I chugged the remainder of my beer and ordered another. Along with a shot of Jim Beam.

"Want one?" I asked Doug.

"Umm..."

"Go ahead and get him one," I told the bartender, and added, "Please," as he turned to fill the order.

"I thought you'd be happy. You tried to explain the last time we saw each other. And it pissed me off. You were right. About all of it. It was all my fault."

I shook my head at him sadly. "Two years later and you still have to control everything in our relationship." The bartender returned with my order. And the check.

"Even my decision to leave you. To leave the relationship. To take control of my own life. It was all because of you?" I asked him.

"Yes? No? I'm not sure what I'm supposed to say."

I sighed, "Yes. I know." I took a shot of Jim Beam. "I really do hope you are happy, and I wish you nothing but the best." I took the second shot, then downed my Shiner Bock. I handed him the check and belched loudly.

"Excuse me," I said quietly as I stood up. I walked to my car and drove away. I thought I would never see him again. I certainly didn't think it would be hours later. Houston is a very large city.

I was unfamiliar with that area of Houston; I only found the restaurant using printed directions from MapQuest. Before going a few blocks, I realized that driving was probably a bad idea after the drinks. Sure, the shots hadn't begun to work their magic, but they would soon. I had no destination, but after a few minutes, I became familiar with my surroundings. Not my first choice, but I had a target. And it was close by.

I pressed the big red button and waited for the yellow box to spit a ticket out of its slot. After retrieving it, I watched the gate rise. I drove into the familiar parking garage and hunted for an open space. There was still an hour left before the work day ended, and I began to doubt I would find one. The garage was almost completely empty every time I had used it in the past, but that was always much later in the day, and this was a business district. I didn't find any open spaces until I reached the top floor, which was almost empty. I took a spot in a corner away from any other cars.

I fished a joint out of my backpack and smoked it quickly. I kept thinking that I should be angry. Or sad. Or vindicated. Or something. I felt nothing. I realized that he was unable to see his manipulations as controlling. He had to control everything in his life, and I wasn't going to deal with that mess any longer.

I considered calling Hank but decided against it. I was feeling light and airy – *floating like Pixie.* I realized that I learned a valuable lesson from Doug. I had always deferred to his ideal, keeping silent to avoid fights that I couldn't imagine "winning." That was my fault, and I decided to no longer squash my opinion or my feelings for the "good of a relationship." I was feeling a profound sense of freedom, and I didn't want to share it with anyone.

I exited the garage after spending some time searching for the elevator. Between the pot and the alcohol, I was incredibly relaxed, and I had a wonderful sense of freedom that I hadn't felt for quite some time. I walked the three familiar blocks hoping the old-school country music bar was still there and was open at 4:00pm.

Walking through the door, I was amazed to see it filled with more people than I had ever seen there. I was also pleasantly surprised to hear contemporary country music instead of the fare I had expected. The crowd was exactly as expected. Mostly working-class gay men aged forty plus.

I marched up to the bar and ordered two shots and a beer. The bartender set them down and pointed somewhere towards the opposite side of the bar.

"He got those for ya," I had no idea who he was pointing at.

I glanced in the direction he had pointed and lifted the first shot in thanks to no one in particular.

"He wants to know if you're working," the bartender told me.

"Huh?" I asked, "I'm just here to dance," he looked at me doubtfully. "What do you mean, working?"

"Never mind. It's nothing," he said with a grin.

"Am I missing something?" I asked him. "Thanks," I said as I grabbed my second shot and beer, turning towards the dance floor.

"He thought you were a prostitute," he said. "I told him he was an idiot, but he tipped me a twenty when he asked me to find out" he chuckled, holding up the bill.

I grimaced as my whole body shivered, "Well, tell the disgusting prick, thanks for the drinks." I headed towards the dance floor.

I started watching all the bodies spinning around. I was looking for the best dancer, and this time I didn't plan to wait for someone to ask me to dance. No, I still hadn't learned how to lead, but I didn't care. I finally picked out my target and waited for him to exit the dance floor. He wasn't an attractive man, in fact, if I had to characterize his physical appearance in a single word, that word would be ugly. But damn could he dance. It didn't matter who his dance partner was, he was the star on that dance floor. He reminded me of the dancing bartender from TRCC, a gifted lead.

I watched him step off the dance floor and head towards the restroom. I planned to approach him after he settled his business and stationed myself between the restroom door and the dance floor. I didn't want to give him the opportunity to find a different dance partner. I was going to convince him to dance with me, and I didn't think it would be too difficult considering the amount of attention I had been receiving since I walked through the door.

When the ugly dancer left the restroom, he walked towards the bar instead of the dance floor. I hadn't considered that possibility, so I grabbed my beer and walked in his direction. I planned to buy him a beer, hoping the bribe would help convince him. Before three steps, someone bumped into me from behind with enough force to knock me to the floor. This set off a chain reaction involving a few more patrons that ended with a full pitcher of beer falling on my head and soaking my head and torso.

The three-hundred-pound man with a two-hundred-pound afro that had bulldozed me to the ground extended his hand to help me stand, and he had a look of horror on his face. I started laughing, and as I reached for his hand, he did too. My shirt was literally dripping with beer, and it felt like one of those movie moments – I swear all activity in the bar had come to a sudden halt, along with every conversation and the music. Everyone was staring at me, and the ridicule was about to begin. At least that's what my head was telling me.

Only those close to the scene of the accident saw anything, and before I started laughing, most had a similar expression to the giant that had bowled me over. The cascading events were so precise that I still had an empty, plastic beer pitcher perched up-side-down on the top of my head. I was thankful that my hat had been knocked off in the scuffle and was still completely dry. Once I started laughing, everyone that had seen the incident joined in. When I grabbed the hand proffered to me – *I felt like Ant-Man being lifted by the Hulk.* I swear his index finger was thicker than my wrist.

With very little thought, I started lifting the shirt trying to free it from my torso, as Hulk reached out and removed the pitcher that now looked more like a wizard's cap. He started apologizing profusely, but I was still laughing.

"Don't worry about it," I told him. "These things happen."

"Who's going to replace that pitcher?" asked a short Hispanic man, that reminded me of a toad, in a bitchy tone. He was the only person not laughing.

"Don't worry, Princess," said the bartender who had stepped up with a stack of dry, clean bar towels in his hand. "I'll get you another. Let me clean up this spill first." He sounded more than annoyed until he noticed me standing there shirtless; one hand gripping a sopping mass that was dripping all over the floor, the other delicately holding my hat out to keep it dry. Then he started laughing too. He glanced at the floor and noticed the Shiner Bock bottle I dropped when I fell over – at least it didn't break – and said to me, "I'll get you another too, you probably need one."

"That's okay. It was already empty," I admitted. "I was headed in your direction to get another." I took some of the towels from his hand and began to help him mop up the puddle on the floor.

"Oh, I don't think so, Sweetie," said Hulk, as he took the towels from my hands. "I got this, you go clean up," he motioned towards the restroom with his head.

I received a lot of attention walking to the restroom, many puzzled looks and numerous chuckles once people pieced together what had happened. When I looked in the mirror, I started laughing again. I wet a clean bar towel that I swiped from the bartender, pumped some hand soap onto it from the wall dispenser, dropped my t-shirt into the sink under the streaming, steaming-hot water, and began to sponge bathe myself.

The sinks were directly in front of the restroom door, and when the bartender walked in and saw me, he too started laughing. Again. He had a stack of clean bar towels in his hand, and a plain white t-shirt slung over his shoulder.

"How in the world are your jeans completely dry?" he asked when his revelry abated.

I looked down and realized he was right. "Just lucky, I guess," I replied. We locked eyes through the mirror's reflection, and the ensuing laughter had us both practically convulsing.

It was one of those times when the chortles wouldn't stop. For minutes we stood there and laughed – *every time I have had uncontrollable fits of laughter, I always think that it has been too long since I've laughed that hard. Even if it happened the day before. I guess that means that no matter how much laughter you have in your life, it's never enough.* Once we were able to control ourselves, he wet a towel and added some soap. He scrubbed my back for me, as we fought back rising giggles.

After removing as much sticky residue as I could, I rinsed off the best I could with the bartender's assistance. I picked up my t-shirt out of the sink and cleaned it with hand soap as well.

"Here, this should fit," he held out the t-shirt he brought in with him.

"Thanks," I was extremely grateful. I pulled it over my head, after drying off with the last of the clean bar towels.

"Yep, looks great," he commented, looking at me in the mirror. It was much tighter than I normally felt comfortable wearing, but I agreed, it looked great. "My shift's over. Still want to dance?" he asked as he gathered up the bar towels.

"Hell, yeah," I answered. I held up my wet t-shirt. "Don't know what to do with this though."

"C'mon," he gripped my hand and pulled me through the restroom door, "We'll put it behind the bar, so it can dry. And I'll grab us a couple beers."

We almost bumped into someone entering as we exited the restroom. The bartender pulled me out of the way to avoid the collision, and in the process, I jostled another patron; which resulted in a full draught beer being dumped. Right on my crotch. The bartender and I looked down at my midsection simultaneously, and the resulting fits of laughter lasted longer than the ones that happened less than ten minutes earlier. My first thought was, *it's been too long since I've laughed this hard.*

The bartender handed me the towels he was carrying and took my wet t-shirt from my hand. "Yep, you might be the luckiest person I have ever met," he stated. "Sorry, I don't have another pair of jeans with me," and of course, our laughter resumed.

"That's okay. I have a packed bag in my car, filled with clean, dry clothes," I stated, and headed towards the door.

"Hold up, I'll go with you," he offered.

"That's okay," I said. "Can I take these?" I asked, holding up the bar towels. I planned to use them to sponge off my midsection.

"Yep," he answered. "I'll be here waiting if you still want to dance," he walked away still carrying my t-shirt.

When I stepped outside and looked down, I realized that it looked like I'd pissed myself. I hurried to the parking garage. I noticed that there were fewer cars, and I didn't see a single person. I decided to smoke a joint before cleaning up while I was alone. I finished the joint then opened my trunk to find clean clothes in my backpack.

Since I still hadn't seen anyone, I stripped out of my wet jeans and cleaned the sticky residue as well as I could. Before I could finish, a car turned the corner and headed in my direction. I was standing there in a too-tight t-shirt and baseball cap. Nothing else. I covered my dick with a bar towel as the car pulled up behind mine and stopped.

The passenger window came down, and I heard a familiar voice, "Jay? What the hell is going on?" he asked.

"Hi, Doug," I replied. "It's a long story," I started laughing. I tossed the towels in the trunk, put on a pair of clean boxers, socks, and jeans, and finished by tying my shoes.

Doug stepped out of his obvious rental car, and said, "When did you start wearing underwear again?" he asked. I ignored the question. "Sorry," he said, "You don't have your Jeep anymore?'

I shook my head in negation but didn't offer any further explanation.

"I don't think you're going to want this as much as I thought you would." He handed me a heavy, disk-shaped, metal object about half an inch thick and the size of my palm.

I looked at it and said, "I thought this got stolen."

"It did," he stated, "I was the one who took it." He handed me an olive-drab baseball cap. "You forgot this too," he added. I hadn't forgotten it. I left it on purpose. It was a Savannah's Sand Gnat's cap – their local minor league baseball team. He bought it for me in Savannah with the last of his money to replace the Astro's cap that I never got back from Viktor and Abel.

"Thanks," I replied as I took it from him.

"I've been thinking about what you said since you left Chili's earlier," he told me. "You're right. I tried to control everything, and I tried to change who you were. And I'm sorry. I didn't think I would get the opportunity to tell you that."

I didn't answer him, I just toyed with the object in my hand; turning it over and over and rubbing my thumb against its smooth surface.

"I only did it because I thought I was helping," he said, "I don't think you realize how much potential you have. You can do anything, and I was just trying to help you become a better you."

"I know. But it was always your version of a better me. Not mine."

I closed my trunk and started walking towards the elevator. Again, I looked down at the object in my hand. I was holding a die-cast metal, X-Men insignia, key-chain, attached to a carabiner that I had used on the driver's side "window" of my Jeep as a zipper pull.

Chapter 46

GOOD

July 1998. Savannah, Georgia. Reston, Virginia.

By the time I got home from my encounter with Viktor and Abel, I had completely convinced myself that what had happened was my fault. I reasoned that if I didn't want it to happen, I would have fought harder to get out of there; not to mention the hundreds of fantasies I'd had about them. I told myself I must have wanted exactly what I got, and I felt horrible. I felt like I had cheated on Doug, and it took me many long years to realize that I was raped. It was shortly after getting back from Savannah that I began having broken dreams of a uni-browed teenaged boy and a dog house – it took almost twenty years before those disparate images coalesced into a horrible memory.

When I turned the faucet to start the shower, I was still drunk, stoned and sore. Sure, I had been sore after sex before, but never like this. I cleaned myself, dried off, put on a pair of sweatpants and crawled into bed. I forgot to set the alarm clock. When I awoke, I realized my flight was scheduled to take off in less than an hour.

I had to run through the airport, but I made it to the gate just as the flight attendant was about to close the door to the boarding ramp. I sat down in my first-class seat, and I was hung over, and sore didn't begin to describe how I was feeling physically. I ordered a mimosa from the flight attendant to kill my hangover and hoped it would also numb my pain. Both physically and emotionally. I drank half a dozen on that flight.

Doug was waiting for me at the airport and had already gotten the keys for our rental car. The first thing he noticed was my naked head, without its usual Astros' crown. This led to a fight when I told him I lost it. The second thing he noticed was that I had been drinking. This led to a second fight before we arrived at the baggage carousel. But for the first time in over a year, I didn't back down. I didn't want to fight, but I didn't surrender to his wishes.

By the time we drove away from the airport, we had reached an impasse. We had stopped fighting, but we had also stopped talking to each other. Doug finally broke the silence when we got to the hotel room – opulent, and expensive – and he told me of all the activities he had planned for the day, starting with a room-service breakfast.

When he handed me the menu, I offered an alternative. He seemed angry that I didn't just go along with his plans, but he humored me. I convinced him to let me plan all the first day's activities, and we could do all the expensive jaunts he had just finished telling me about the next day.

We spent the day doing the same kind of activities we normally would on a weekend getaway. I made it painfully obvious that nothing was out of the ordinary. I even chose the same chain restaurants we always went to.

My plan was successful on both fronts. First, we had a great time once we fell into a familiar routine. We didn't have a single argument for the remainder of that day – well, until that evening at any rate. Second, he was able to see just how much these weekend trips cost me. I had a tertiary motive as well. Some of the activities that he had mentioned were of an overly physical type, and I made a concentrated effort the entire day to hide how sore my ass and jaw were.

After dinner that evening, we returned to the hotel room. We were going to see a drag show – something Doug abhorred, but he agreed to my choices the entire day – this was the first thing I had chosen that was out of the norm. But only by the venue. The first night of every weekend trip was capped off with drinks, we just went to the bar of his choice. It had been a hot day exploring the city, and we both needed a shower.

I was thankful when he didn't try to initiate sex. On any other trip, this would have been the exact moment. I had been trying to come up with excuses to avoid the encounter and was happy that I didn't have to. I still hadn't thought up anything remotely convincing.

When I got out of the shower, I noticed Doug was counting the money in his wallet. As I got dressed, I asked him what was on the agenda the next day. I listed all the expensive activities he had mentioned that morning. He closed his wallet and said he had changed his mind and wanted to continue with a similar plan the next day.

"You're out of money, aren't you?" I asked.

"No," he responded far too quickly. "Today was so much fun. Why ruin a good thing?"

"Bullshit. You promised an elevated vacation."

"You can afford your half?" he challenged.

I started laughing, "Get dressed. I need a drink," I replied.

"Fine," he huffed.

We went and watched the drag show, and he whined that I was tipping the queens too much and lectured me about drinking. Mind you, he was matching me drink for drink. I had a great time, especially when I started needling him about the next day. He wouldn't commit to a single activity he proposed. He finally admitted that he had already spent what he had budgeted for the weekend before we had even gone to dinner that night.

It really pissed him off when I offered to pay for everything the next day. Even the most expensive things he had proposed. He couldn't believe I would be able to afford it, he even accused me of being a drug dealer and/or prostitute. He couldn't believe how much money I was making bartending and waiting tables. I didn't get the impression he was joking, because he said it was impossible for a lowly server to make twice what he did. And yes, he said "lowly."

"You gonna be home in two weeks?" I asked him. His schedule had been erratic the last couple months.

"Yeah, why?" he practically spit the words at me.

"See you then. Have fun in Savannah," I said as I walked towards the front door. Luckily there was a vacant taxi waiting out front. When I sat down, I saw Doug storm out of the bar towards the rental car. I told the cab driver my destination. Up the street, I saw the rental car aggressively back out of its parking spot and speed down the road.

I pointed out the car to the cabbie, "And I need to get there before him," I informed him.

"No problem. I know all the shortcuts," he replied.

True to his word, I arrived at the hotel with enough time to pack my things and return to the cab before I spied the rental car pull into the parking lot. It was easy to spot, Doug had chosen a convertible Mustang when he still thought he could outspend me. I ducked down in the seat before he could see me and asked the driver if he knew of any nice hotels near the bar I had been at earlier. He made a few recommendations and drove me to my choice.

The hotel that Doug had booked was nowhere near the bar that staged the drag show. The cab ride there, followed by the ride to my new hotel, then back to the drag show was expensive. Very expensive. But it was worth every cent. I had gotten all my belongings and the ticket for my return flight out of the room without having to see Doug again. Plus, the driver was funny and friendly and helpful. He looked shocked when I handed him a hundred-dollar bill as a tip – *tip karma, baby.*

I spent the rest of my time in Savannah alone. And it was exhilarating. It was the only time I had ever been on vacation by myself. I didn't do anything terribly exciting, but I did what I wanted, and with the schedule I chose. I fell in love with the city that day, and my favorite part was visiting the cemeteries. There were so many old, ornate, beautifully creepy statues and mausoleums. And these resting places were always in the most picturesque part of its surroundings.

Fighting another hangover, my final morning there, I again turned to the mimosas on the flight back. In my three days in Savannah, I had come to three decisions: I needed to go to the clinic to be tested for HIV and other STDs, I needed to call Bo, and I needed to end things with Doug. The first two were easy and were done before the day's end. I had no idea how to accomplish my third task though. *Concerning the first task, I am happy to report that all results came back clean, which caused positive side-effects. First, it helped alleviate a portion of the guilt I was feeling for believing I was a cheater. Second, it started a practice of being tested for HIV and STDs every four to six months; a practice that didn't end until my partner and I had lived together for a couple years.*

I didn't tell Bo that I wanted to break things off with Doug when I spoke to him that night. Nor did I tell him about Viktor and Abel, in fact before putting the awful experience into words here, I had never shared those events with anyone. Another thing I kept to myself for years – *Mephisto, Thanos, Jerry, Bub, Hank, Viktor, Abel. I didn't realize it then, but that list was getting too long.*

The only thing I told Bo was that I had to see him, and if he wanted to visit D.C., he would need to do it soon. I'm sure he deciphered the meaning, and he must have been able to sense that I needed his presence as soon as possible. Less than an hour after that conversation ended, he called me back telling me he would be there in less than two weeks. He was coming in on a Tuesday, and staying through the following weekend, with a return flight the following Monday. When I told him that was Doug's weekend home, he asked if I wanted him to change his plans. When I told him no, his reply was surprisingly short. Only a single word. Good.

I wrote down his flight information, and seconds after ending that call, the phone began ringing.

"Hello," I answered.

"Good. I just wanted to make sure you were home safe and sound, but the line has been busy every time I called," Doug was trying to sound like nothing had happened, and every-thing was normal. "Who've you been talking too," his tone was a calculated casual.

"Bo," I answered. I wasn't trying to disguise my tone.

"How is he?" Doug asked.

"Good," I replied. "Still coming home in two weeks?"

"That's why I was calling," he interrupted.

"He'll be here that weekend," I counter-interrupted. "What were you going to say?" I asked.

"Nothing," he replied, "I look forward to seeing him," he lied.

"Oh? Good."

Chapter 47

I FLY AWAY

October 2000 – December 2000. San Antonio, Texas.
Vancouver, Washington.

I went back to the bar, found the bartender and danced. And danced. And danced. The bartender wasn't the greatest dancer, but he was good enough. I saw Doug standing by the pool table watching me on the dance floor. I didn't much care, I had finally shed the chains that still controlled me. I realized that our relationship hadn't failed because Doug tried to change me, and it hadn't failed because I didn't try hard enough. It failed because I had failed to stand up and be myself. I had said what I needed and realized I had moved on. I hoped Doug would find happiness, but for me to find mine I had to let it all go.

Like cockroaches when surprised by a sudden light, the crowded bar emptied out shortly after seven. Vance, the bartender, asked me to go to dinner with him. I told him I'd had too much to drink to drive. He offered to drive since he was sober.

We had dinner at a fantastic pizzeria, then went to a black-light bowling alley, where everything was aglow. I told him my shoe size and excused myself to the restroom, while he made arrangements with the attendant. I snuck off to my car and smoked a joint as rapidly as possible. On my way back to the entrance, I thought I saw Doug sitting in a parked car. When I did a double-take, the car appeared to be empty, but it was an identical model, make, and color as the rental I saw him in earlier – *I think.*

I spent the night at Vance's. On his couch. If he was disappointed, he didn't express it. He even made breakfast the next morning. He let me use his shower, and when I got to my car, I drove back to San Antonio. *It was the last time I visited Houston.*

Not long after that jaunt, I flew to Portland, Oregon to visit my parents and various members of my enormous extended family, living in the area. It was a typical vacation of its type. I spent most of my time with people I barely knew but was expected to be comfortable around since they were related.

Most of Mom's family lived there, but we never had. We would go to visit whenever possible, but aside from a couple aunts and uncles, and a handful of cousins, most of my family were strangers, and most I hadn't seen in at least ten years. When I visited my grandparents, I finally got to see how affected my grandfather was by his rapidly progressing dementia. I was thankful that he remembered me, especially since I had almost thirty cousins. The rest of the trip was uneventful, but Mom tried to convince me to move there. Of course, offering me a place to stay.

The day I returned to San Antonio, I got a call from Hank.

"Hey, Kiddo, it's Hank, still single?"

"Yep. When you coming to town?" I asked.

"Here already," he answered, and explained where he was parked. Bo wasn't home, so I went to see Hank.

After our usual greeting, we went out for a late lunch.

"So, what's new?" he asked, sounding genuinely interested.

"Nothing really. Went and visited my parents in Portland. Just got back a few hours ago."

"Sounds fun?" it was definitely a question.

"Yeah, it was great to see my parents..." I started.

"They know you're gay?" he interrupted. "And they're okay with it?"

"Yep. And, yep," I answered. "But yeah, there's another horseshow next week. I don't know if I'm going to go though."

"Where? I had a lot of fun at that one outside Ft. Worth. Don't know if I'll ever see a show the same way again," followed by a chuckle.

"Same place, I think. Or maybe closer to Dallas. Up there somewhere at any rate."

"Why don't you wanna go? I thought you enjoyed the shows?"

"I did. Before we started going back to the same places all the time. I liked seeing the new places. But it's always the same now. Show. Dinner. Bar. Hotel. Repeat."

"You should become a truck driver," he said. "You like to travel, and you like road trips. I love the freedom it provides."

"Something to think about," I said. "I need to get home. I haven't seen Bo since I got back, and I don't want him to get worried. I'll try to sneak back if I can."

When I got home, Bo was standing in the garage, changing a light bulb.

"Where the hell have you been?" he asked. "I knew you'd already been home," he glanced at my bags sitting by the door that led to my apartment.

"I was starving, I had to go get something to eat," not a complete lie.

"Bitch. I was waiting for you. I'm starving."

"Let's go. I'll get a milkshake or something," I offered quickly. I didn't want to deal with a starving Wendigo.

"You're driving. You can tell me about your trip." By the time we got to a local hamburger joint, I had filled him in on my trip.

"What do you think about me becoming a truck driver?" I asked him while he ate.

"Bad idea. Bad, bad idea. You get road rage too easily." He stole my shake, and added, "Where'd that come from? Do you even know any truck drivers?" he asked.

"Duh. My Grandpa drove trucks forever. Most of my mom's brothers too."

"Don't truckers have to do a lot of their own repairs too? Especially on the side of the road, in the middle of nowhere? I don't know, Jay. Why not go back to school? Don't you qualify for in-state tuition again?"

"Meh," I answered, "I don't really want to be a teacher. Or maybe I do, but Doug was pushing me towards that, so I don't want to. For whichever reason. Plus, teachers don't get to travel much."

"Yeah, but you'd have summers off. You could travel then. You wanted to be a teacher when I met you, didn't you?"

"Not really. It was what I was going to school for, but I wasn't convinced. I need to do something though. Restaurants are getting beyond tiresome."

"You should become a flight attendant. Then you could travel and give me buddy passes. Where's Vancouver, Washington?" he asked, and I didn't understand the connection. "Is that close to your parents?"

"They live in Vancouver," I told him.

"I thought they were in Portland," he sounded confused.

"Same thing," I explained. "One big metro area, separated by the Columbia River."

"Then why do you tell people your parents are in Portland?"

"It saves time. I say Vancouver. They assume Canada. I explain Washington state. They ask if it's near Seattle. I tell them it's closer to Portland. Real close. Same city, essentially. Then they ask why I didn't just say Portland then." He chuckled. "Why? What does that have to do with anything?" I wondered.

"My cousin went to a flight attendant school there. When my mom told me, I assumed Canada, but Mom told me it was in Washington, but she didn't know where in Washington, Vancouver was. I don't know how much it costs or anything, but something to look into," he offered.

I did investigate it and discovered the school was much more expensive than I anticipated. After talking to Bo, he encouraged my newfound sense of direction. I planned to move to Vancouver, find a job, save money then enroll in flight attendant school. I was also happy to be near my grandfather as his health was failing. When I was a small child, I always felt a special bond with him, and I wanted to spend as much time with him as possible before his memory deteriorated to the point that he could no longer remember me.

When I told my parents about my plans, they were excited and agreed with Bo that the job would be a good fit. I made plans to make the move before winter set in and arrived in Portland a week or two before Thanksgiving 2000 after an uneventful drive.

I began looking for a job almost immediately. I wanted to move out of my parents' two-bedroom apartment as soon as possible, and start saving money again. Few places were hiring, but I managed to get an interview at a restaurant where a cousin worked. I had spent some time with her throughout the years, but I hadn't seen or talked to her since I was a young teenager. She put in a good word for me though.

I couldn't start until after the holidays though, so I had about a month with little to do and utterly unfamiliar with the area. I knew there were gay bars, but I had no idea where. I loved being near – *it was too near, but still* – my parents again, but I was going stir crazy. My only real diversion was going to the bookstore up the street every evening after dinner and thumbing through novels.

After carrying groceries in for my mom on a cold, rainy day, she casually mentioned, "Did you know there's a gay tavern downtown?"

"Portland? And what's a tavern?" I asked.

"It's a bar, but no alcohol. Just beer and wine, I think. And no, downtown Vancouver. Your aunt told me it was a couple blocks from that comic store Dad told you about."

After dinner that night, I went to find the comic store, and in the process looked for a gay tavern to which I had no name, no address, and the casual observance of a couple blocks away. The comic book shop was easy to find, Dad's directions were more concise. I found it, but it was closed. I spent half an hour driving back and forth on the one-way streets looking for anything that might look "gay."

I finally gave up, and as I turned down a block, I had been on a hundred times that night, I saw someone open a heavy, solid, commercial door and as they slipped inside, I saw a rainbow sticker on the inside of the door and figured that must be it. I made a mental note and drove home, where I explained to my parents that the comic book store was out of business.

"Your cousin called, while you were out," Mom informed me. The cousin that helped me get the job. "She invited you to a party at her house tonight. She told me it was mostly co-workers, that you'll be working with in a few weeks."

"That's cool," I said.

"Are you gonna go? The two of you always got along as kids, it might be fun." She was wrong. She and my sister got along well as kids. They were the same age and enjoyed teasing me. "I can give you a ride. And pick you up," she offered.

"That's okay. I won't drink much. If any," I told her.

"If you do, just call. I don't mind getting you if I need to. Does that mean you're going?" she asked.

"Sure. Sounds fun. Did she say what time?"

"She just said everyone would be there after work, but she'll be there all night. What time are you going to go?" she asked.

"I don't know. Probably around eleven," I informed her.

"Why so late?" she wondered.

"If it's an after-work party, eleven will be early," I stated. "Does she know I'm gay?" I asked her, "Is she one you told?"

"I don't know if she does. I didn't tell her father, but that doesn't mean she didn't hear from someone else. Does it matter?" she asked

"It never has. Not to me anyway," I answered.

I'm glad I decided to go to that party. I met, and actually liked, a few people there. And I made a pot connection. My cousin's cousin. From her other side of the family, so not my cousin. But he gave me "family" prices anyway. I smoked a lot of pot that night and learned that my status as pothead didn't make me unique like it did back home. Everyone smoked pot, and I impressed a few of the more devout future co-workers by maintaining their pace.

"We should set him up with Becca," the tall blonde guy said. I had already forgotten everyone's name. He turned towards me, "And she's easy," he explained. He pointed towards someone in the distance.

"Want me to go get her?" the cook with a lazy eye asked me.

"Um," I answered. I had no intention to keep my sexuality secret at work, but I didn't like feeling cornered.

"You two are idiots," Angie said – *okay, I remembered one name.* "He's gay," she stated. Then looked at me and added, "Aren't you?"

Before I could answer, Lazy Eye asked her, "How do you know?"

"Because I'm a fag hag," she told him. "And my gaydar is pretty refined."

"He doesn't seem gay to me," Blonde said.

"How do gay people seem?" Angie asked him.

"Yeah, we're all sorts of different people." I joined in the conversation, reminding them I was still sitting there. At least I didn't have to decide how to tell the co-workers.

Chapter 48

UNDENIABLE

August 1998. Reston, Virginia.

The first thing Bo said when I picked him up in front of the airport was, "Oh my god, I'm starving. Food. Now, Hoke." He was beyond hungry. He was beyond hangry. He was beyond angry. He was a downright pissy bitch, but he was finally there, so I was happy. It had been one of those days of travel that requires a therapist to heal from. I didn't say much, as he regaled his day of woe. It was almost 10:00pm, and he was scheduled to land before noon. Without wasting any time, I drove him to the closest restaurant.

We sat down in the Denny's and waited for our breakfast platters. I had already meticulously chosen which restaurants to take Bo to, as his favorite part of any vacation revolves around eating great food that isn't easily found back home. Denny's was not on that list, but it provided immediate triage for Bo's "condition."

The simple act of taking his first bite of food improved Bo's mood drastically, and he was finally ready to get to the heart of the matter.

"So, what's up?" he asked. "You seem happier than I've seen you in a long time. You having an affair?"

"What? No," I answered far too quickly.

He watched me for a moment, "Something's different." I could tell he wanted to continue his line of interrogation. He understood there was more there than a simple, no. But I think he saw something that told him I didn't want to talk about it. Without a single doubt, I'm sure he could have pulled the information out of me, but I had already squashed down those feelings. Without knowing anything, Bo seemed to understand everything, and he let it drop. And he never brought it up again. Well, that's not exactly true; he brought it up numerous times, but never again after that day.

"I'm done with that control-freak asshole," I told him.

"Wait. What?" Bo asked, but he knew exactly what I was talking about.

"I'm ending things with Doug. I want to come home. Can I stay with you and Brad until I find a place?" I said it all quickly, I had been waiting for days to talk to Bo.

"Of course, you can. You know this already. But are you sure? Have you really thought about it?"

"I've never been more sure of anything. It's already done, I just don't know how to go about it," I admitted. "That's why I had to see you."

"Something tells me that's not entirely true, you don't need me to figure out how to end things. I don't think you'll have any problems with that." I was fearful he was going to start probing, but he didn't. I think Bo intended to let me know that he was there to listen if I wanted to talk about it. He didn't know what "it" was, but it really didn't matter.

"So, what happened?" he asked. "Last month, everything seemed fine."

I told him about the Savanah trip and everything else I had kept from him about our relationship. I told him about the fight over my new Jeep, and the financial issues, our awful sex life. Everything. Everything except Viktor and Abel. He noticed a hole in the story and asked a few more questions, but again, he let it drop.

"I don't know. I don't want you to make such a big decision because you are pissed at him, and I don't blame you for being pissed. I'm super proud of you though," he stated but didn't elaborate.

"Yeah? Why?" I asked.

"Because you didn't put up with his shit, and finished your Savannah trip by yourself," he said smiling. "You're such a bitch."

"I'm done," I declared. "It's over, and there's nothing else to think about. This has been a long time coming, but before the Jeep..." I started.

"He actually used the word 'permission?'" he interrupted. "He was mad because you didn't ask for permission first? Un-believable."

"Yep, those were his exact words. After that. And then Savannah shortly after, my eyes were finally open. I'm done. Done, done, done."

He watched me for a minute or two and didn't say a word. It's always slightly disturbing when Bo grows silent.

"It's more than that. There's something else. I'm sure of it," he was looking directly in my eyes, refusing to break the gaze. I shrugged my shoulders, thinking *just let it go.* "But maybe you're not even sure what that something is," he finally said. "But I believe you," he stated.

"Believe me?" I asked. "About what?"

"That it's over. I just wanted to make sure it's what you really wanted." He again looked me in the eyes, like he was trying to see my soul. "I had to be certain it wasn't something reaction-ary. You shouldn't make a decision like this just because you are mad." His gaze somehow became even more penetrating. "Or because something happened," and he grew silent again.

"You don't think I should leave him?" I asked. I thought he would be excited.

"Oh, fuck no. I'm not saying that at all. You should have left him before you even moved to Laredo. It took you long enough, but I'm glad you finally woke up."

"Why didn't you tell me?" I asked. "You could have saved me almost three years."

"Because it was something you had to learn for yourself. When you called earlier this week, I was fairly certain it was over, but I had to make sure you reached the decision for the right reasons. I didn't want to be the cause of your break up. I didn't want you to resent me, or worse yet, push you even closer to that piece of shit." It was the first time since I met Doug that Bo said a single bad word about him. He was always careful to keep his feelings in check, but now that it was over, he made up for lost time. I heard some of the most inventive name-calling during Bo's visit.

"So, what made you sure I was over it?" I asked, with his sudden change in demeanor. He was letting his mean girl take control, and the target was Doug. Before that moment, I had no idea how Bo really felt about him.

"Just talking to you mostly. I've seen you like this before. With this kind of determination. I couldn't change your mind if I wanted to. Which I don't, by the way."

"What do you mean?" I asked, "Seen me like this before? Am I acting weird?"

"Yeah, a little. But that's not it, that's something else," again, that look. "But you had the same demeanor the night you broke up with Gabe. When you've made up your mind about something, really made up your mind, there is no changing it."

"So, when are you coming home?" he asked. "I could skip the flight back, and just drive with you," he offered. "Hell, we can go pack and leave tonight if you want."

"Really? After your flights today, you're willing to travel again already?"

"Okay, fine. You're right. I want to see D.C. first anyway. But seriously, if you're ready now. I could probably even stay another week or two to help you wrap things up."

"I haven't told Doug yet."

"Duh. I know that. Fuck it, leave him a note, or just take your shit and disappear. If he doesn't understand that message, then he's an even bigger idiot than I thought."

"You don't think I should tell him first?" I asked.

"Actually, yeah. Yeah, I do. I'm just ready to have you home. After you show me D.C., bitch. When does Doug come home again?"

"This weekend," I told him.

"Are you going to end it while I'm here?" he looked both horrified and fascinated.

"I wasn't planning on it. I figured we'd avoid him over the weekend, and I'd end things the next time I saw him."

"Oh. I was looking forward to a road trip in your Jeep."

"Right? That would be awesome. But that's the other problem. I've already paid my part of the rent for the next three months. There's no way he's gonna give that back to me, especially after Savannah."

"Oh well. Fuck it," Bo declared.

"That was my thought too, but I don't want to give that fucker anything though."

"Hmm. Don't blame ya. We'll figure something out." He pushed his plate away from him. "Let's go get a drink. I think you need one."

Bo's time in D.C. was amazing and felt all too comfortable. It was very similar to the weekend trips with Doug, except I got to be my old, true, mean girl self. Considering all the places I've seen on the East coast after moving there, Doug and I never explored D.C. Not really. We went a couple times to the obvious sites: the Washington Monument, the Lincoln Monument, the White House, and Capitol building, a few museums. But almost all our time together we spent in other towns and cities, and when he was gone, I was working.

When Bo expected a guided tour, I was at a loss after the first couple of days. When we went for a drink, I couldn't even take him to a gay bar. I didn't know where any were. I suggested picking up a bottle and bringing it back to the apartment.

"What. Are you high?" he used his most offended tones.

"I wish," I confessed. "I've only smoked once since you threw me my twenty-first-birthday party."

"Why the fuck would you want to go home? It's still early, and all you ever do is sit in that apartment." He wasn't entirely wrong.

"I don't know where to take you. I've been researching restaurants, but I didn't think you'd want to go to the bars."

"Again. Are you high? Of course, I want to check out the scene in D.C. You should too, you're single now."

"Not technically. I don't know where to take you though."

"You haven't been to a single gay bar since you've been here? Seriously?"

"Are you kidding? Doug had a fucking fit when I told him I'd told everyone at the restaurant I was gay. I was even in the closet at my first job here. His cover, or some bullshit."

"Okay, fine. We'll figure it out before I go home. You don't know where a straight bar is?" He said straight as though repulsed, which made me genuinely laugh for the first time since he arrived. It really wasn't that funny, but I needed that laugh.

"I've literally been to one bar since we've moved here. It's down the street from work. A bunch of my co-workers go there. It's mostly restaurant employees from the area after they get off. Stupid breeders. Everyone is in a terrible uniform.

Hardly any eye candy worth a second look." I was trying to paint as ugly a picture as possible.

"That'll work. Maybe I'll get to meet some of your co-workers. Maybe those mega hotties you told me about will be there." That's what I was afraid of. I had told Bo all about them when I started that job. Including a few of my fantasies, but I had recently learned that fantasy and reality were two completely different things. "Let's go there," he stated in the tone he used when he wasn't going to take no for an answer.

Since getting back from Savannah, I had been avoiding Viktor and Abel at work. Pointedly ignoring them. Literally, I had only said hi to them after they greeted me first. I told myself that I was feeling guilty for cheating and didn't want to be reminded of a poor decision that I was actively trying to forget about. When we walked into the bar, Bo noticed them immediately. He started poking my ribs and grabbing my arm roughly.

"Holy shit! Did you see the guys at the end of the bar," he whispered to me as he motioned towards Viktor and Abel with his head.

"That's them," I admitted.

We got a couple drinks and sat down at an empty table. Before long the two wandered over.

"Hey Jay," Viktor said. "Who's your friend?"

"This is my best friend, Bo," I answered. "He's visiting from San Antonio." I introduced the two to Bo, who's jaw was practically hanging on the floor.

"If you guys wanna get high, just let me know," said Viktor in his most charming voice.

"We're good," I answered quickly. Bo looked at me in total disbelief.

"That's cool," Viktor replied, "We had fun getting high last week, if you ever wanna do that again, just let me know." He adjusted his crotch as he said it.

"Thanks," I answered robotically, as they walked away.

"What. The. Fuck. Is. Wrong. With. You," Bo groaned in annoyance after they were out of earshot.

"They're alpha male douche bags," I answered, "Nobody I want to spend time with," I admitted truthfully.

"Who cares? Those two could do whatever they want to me. I wouldn't complain."

"Yeah, but they're dicks," I responded.

"I bet they have nice ones," he said. "I can't believe you don't want to get high," he was looking at me in total amazement.

"Not with them," I answered. Bo just watched me for a few minutes.

"Okay, I gotcha." That was all he said, but after that night, he never spoke of them again. I'm not sure if he had pieced it all together, but he acted like a mystery had been solved. So, maybe? "We should get high, though. Do you know where to get some?"

"Maybe. Shouldn't be too hard." More of my co-workers had arrived, and I was sure I could procure a bag. Hopefully the same night. I introduced Bo to my co-workers, and he too went on a mission. Before we left, I had a bag of weed and a new pot connection, and Bo had gotten the skinny on which gay bars to go to and where we could find them.

Chapter 49

BREATHLESS

*January 2001 – August 2001. Battle Ground,
Washington.*

Being near my parents again was great, but in a very short time, it was just too much. I needed to move out, before being near them slipped from great to tiresome. I was also spending much of my free time with my grandparents. It was terrible watching Grandpa's health deteriorate, but it was the price to pay to spend time with him. Taking every opportunity to spend time with him was one of the main reasons I had moved, and I wasn't going to waste the opportunity. I'm unsure if he was ever told that I was gay before his dementia took control, but I think he knew even when I was a small child. I never told him though.

When I started working, I started saving money immediately. I needed an apartment and furnishings for it, and I had decided I was going to enroll in the flight attendants' school as soon as I had the tuition squirreled away. I never told anyone of my intention. I'm ashamed to say that I was somewhat embarrassed by it. The gay flight attendant is a very common stereotype, and I didn't want to be judged because of it.

I started going to the Tavern after dinner when I wasn't working, but otherwise, I didn't have much of a social life. I quickly discovered that it was always the same handful of people there. Most of them were nice, but they spent almost every minute of their free time there.

I relied on making friends at work, but that took longer than anticipated. The restaurant was already overstaffed, and many wanted more hours. They were resentful that another person had been hired. Naturally, they took it out on me at first. I never understood that initial cold-shoulder treatment; I was able to work a consistent forty hours every week, which meant they could do the same if they desired. I was only scheduled for twenty hours each week, and they didn't allow overtime, but I never had any problems picking up shifts to fill in the hours. Eventually, the staff warmed up to me, and it was there that I met my last, and best, roommate. She wasn't at my cousin's party, but she was there on my first day of work. I loved her the moment I met her.

On my first, and only, day of training, I was standing in one of the server stations when Sabrina walked in, muttering under her breath.

"Stupid mother fuckers," she uttered. "Why can't these stupid assholes fucking tip for the fucking service they fucking get. Don't those fucking morons know that I fucking have fucking bills to fucking pay? Ten fucking percent. This is fucking ridiculous." She wasn't just muttering, she was also incredibly animated. Arms thrown in the air in exasperation, head shaking, balled-up fists. The works.

"Well aren't you just a ball of sunshine?" I said when she looked up at me for the first time. It was just the two of us standing there. She started laughing. Uproariously.

"I don't know who the fuck you are," she said to me. "But I think I fucking love you."

And just like that our friendship was solidified, and from that day forward her name was Sunshine to me. The two of us started spending most of our free time together, but that time was usually spent drinking. Sunshine was dealing with her own demons.

Once I had enough money socked away to find my own place and start furnishing it, I started looking at apartments; which meant time spent touring vacant units. I always set up the tours before work. On the day that I found what I thought would be my first apartment in the Pacific Northwest, my scheduled tour was running late. I fell in love with the apartment, and I was ready to sign the lease, but I was quickly running out of time before my shift started. I told the property manager that I would be back after work to sign paperwork.

When I pulled into the employee parking lot, I was already ten minutes late for my shift. Very little makes me angrier with myself than running late. I grabbed my apron and sprinted for the front door, and as I clocked in, I was struggling to catch my breath. My parking spot wasn't exactly close to the front door, and my usual exercise routine – dancing – was nonexistent.

"Did you find a place yet?" Sunshine asked as I was tying my apron behind my back.

"I did. Found it this morning. Great place. Perfect size, not too expensive, and close to my parents and work."

"Oh, damn," she said.

"Why damn?" I asked. "I can't wait to get out of my parents' place. I'm going to sign the paperwork after I get off," I informed her.

"You haven't leased it yet?" she sounded excited.

"No. Why?"

She explained that she was moving into her parents' house in a couple months. It had been a rental property for years, but it would be vacant after the current renters moved out. Her parents were planning to move back to the area in about a year and planned to move into the house she was telling me about. Sunshine was going to rent it from them until their return and was looking for a roommate to keep costs down.

It was a two-bedroom, one-bathroom single family home, but it was in Battle Ground, which at the time was in the middle of nowhere. It was a thirty-minute drive to work, and slightly further to my parents' home. But once she told me how little I would have to pay in rent, I jumped at the opportunity.

She was the best roommate I ever had. Period. And she also had everything needed to furnish the house; everything but furniture for my bedroom. I didn't have to worry about buying much, so I loosened up my self-imposed saving policies and started to explore the area. I decided it was time to discover the gay scene in Portland, but I had no idea where to start – sure, we had the internet, but we didn't have Google yet; no instant answers.

I had become a regular at the Tavern, and when I started asking the bartender where to find the other bars, he offered to show me around. On his next day off, true to his word, I picked him up, and he gave me a tour of Portland's gay bars. What he did was point out all the bars, but we didn't actually step foot in a single one. He told me he was showing me where they were, but he had a specific destination in mind after the tour. He said it was the easiest place to find someone to hook-up with. Although that was very low on my priority list, I went along with his plans, I figured we would end up at a crowded bar after he showed me around.

I was correct that the place he took me to was crowded, but it wasn't a bar. Instead, he took me to a porn theater. The front part of the shop sold sex toys and the like, but the back portion was filled with viewing booths each with a glory hole connecting to adjacent booths. The place was packed with men looking for anonymous sex. Not at all what I had in mind.

I wasn't looking for disgusting, easy sex with a stranger. I just wanted to be surrounded by like-minded people.

After exploring the shop, I quickly decided that was the last place I wanted to be. I went out to my car and waited for my bartender friend to finish his business. I rolled a joint, smoked it, and waited. When he finally walked up to my driver's side window, he was out of breath stating that he had been frantically looking for me for some time. I doubt that was the actual reason for his breathlessness, but I was happy to leave that parking lot. I had been sitting in my car for close to an hour and had lost count of the number of times some random guy walked up to my car and proposed some kind of sexual encounter.

The bartender asked if I had fun, and I lied and told him yes. He was happy to hear the news, as he had no desire to go to any of the bars. He explained that the porn shops were the easiest way to meet guys, but I don't think he understood that wasn't the type of encounter I desired. I drove him home, then returned to Portland to check out the bars he had pointed out.

I went to a few different bars that were all in close proximity to one another, and they were exactly what I expected. They were about the same as anywhere else, but it was a sea of new faces. I wandered around by myself for a few hours, but I didn't talk to anyone.

After finding the bars in Portland, I stopped going to the Tavern in Vancouver, and before long I even made a few bar friends. I found a great dance club and resumed my favorite exercise. I spent a lot of my time at the bars dancing, and I started my third, and final slut stage. This was the shortest-lived of the three, and by the time I moved in with Sunshine, that stage ended.

The revolving door of sexual partners was unsatisfying, to say the least. Although I was no longer actively avoiding a relationship, I wasn't actively looking for one either. I was happy being single, and I was spending most of my free time with co-workers. Once or twice a week, I would go by myself to the gay bars to get my "gay fix." Mostly, I went to get my exercise and wished there was a gay country bar in town so I could get my favorite kind of exercise. But there wasn't.

After my short-lived slut phase, my sex-life all but dried up, but it affected me far less than I thought it would. Even when I was with Doug, I had regular sex, even if was mind-numbingly dull. For the next six months, little changed. I did meet two stand-out guys that I dated exclusively during that time. One was obsessed with me and desired more. But I didn't. The other, I was obsessed with, and I wanted more. But he didn't.

A couple months before the attacks on the World Trade Center, I first laid eyes on the first, and only, man I would ever love – *of course, I loved Bo, but that was different. And I had loved both Gabe and Doug, but before Joe, I didn't know what true love was.*

With a couple of exceptions, that night was like most others when I ventured to the gay bars. The first exception dealt with time. Instead of staying and working as late as possible, I left when my shift ended, right around 8:00pm. I drove home, showered, changed clothes, and headed to the bars. It was about 9:30 when I arrived, much earlier than I was used to. At that time, the bars were mostly empty, as the crowds didn't typically arrive until after 11:00, but that suited my mood just fine. I wasn't looking to hook-up. I just wanted to relax.

I ended up having a great conversation with a bartender at my first stop. He was probably about the same age as my parents, and attractive would never have been used as an adjective to describe him. But he was funny, and he was a mean girl. I sat at his bar chatting with him for about an hour, and I had a great time making fun of all the other patrons with him. When my phone rang, I was of a mind to ignore it, but curiosity won out.

"Hello?" I answered.

"Hey, Kiddo. Still single?" said a voice I hadn't heard in close to a year.

"Hank?" I asked. "Holy shit. How the hell are you?"

"I'm good. But I'd be better if you answered my question the way I want you to." I started laughing.

"Yeah, I'm single," I told him. "Not that it matters though," I added.

"Do you know where Battle Ground, Washington is? It looks like it's close to Portland. I have a load to deliver there, and I should get in around two or three in the morning."

"Are you fucking kidding me?" I couldn't keep the excitement out of my voice. "I live in Battle Ground," I informed him. And it was his turn to laugh.

"Must be fate," he said. "Can we get together," he asked.

"You better fucking believe it" I answered.

"Want me to call you tomorrow morning, and we'll figure things out?"

"Oh, hell no. Call me when you get in. I don't care how late it is."

"Can't wait to see you, Kiddo," he said before hanging up.

I echoed his sentiments, and when I glanced at my watch, I realized the next two hours were going to feel like an eternity. I decided to have a couple drinks in celebration, hoping it would make the time move faster. I returned to my seat at the bar, and the bartender handed me a beer.

"That one's on me, Darlin'," I'm pretty sure he had forgotten my name because every time I saw him, that's what he called me. "It was fun chatting with you, but my shift is over. Thank God."

"Quitting time always feels great," I said, realizing that the goofy grin that had been absent for so long was once again plastered on my face.

"Good news?" he asked.

"Huh?" I responded drinking half my beer in a single gulp, which of course resulted in a long belch that elicited a chuckle from the bartender. "Excuse me," I apologized, still smiling. Thoughts of Hank, running through my mind.

"Good news?" he repeated. "On the phone? You've been smiling ear-to-ear since you came back in," he explained.

"Oh. Yeah, good news. Great news actually." I looked at my watch again and realized less than five minutes had passed since hanging up with Hank. It was going to be a long night. "I just have to kill about two hours," I added but didn't offer more of an explanation. It was second nature to not talk about Hank.

"I was thinking about grabbing a drink. Pretty shitty day, mostly," his face morphed into an expression diametrically opposed to mine. "Want to join me?" he asked.

"Sure, sounds fun," which was the absolute truth. I envisioned a couple hours of releasing my mean girl with a kindred spirit. I truly hoped it would make me stop checking my watch every five minutes. "Where do you wanna go?" I asked him.

"Anywhere but here," he replied as he grabbed his jacket. Taking his cue, I downed the second half of my beer. As we walked out the side door, my ensuing belch again garnered some laughter from him. "My feelings about this place, exactly," he said.

We walked across the street, but it felt like more of a forced march. I'm sure he only had one criterion: proximity. Before that night, I didn't even realize our destination was a gay establishment. To my eyes, it was rather unique; it reminded me of the bar from *Cheers*. It was dominated by a massive U-shaped bar with tons of barstools. Surrounding the bar were numerous tables and chairs, and off to one side, there was a pool table, a few electronic dart boards, and about half a dozen video-poker machines. It was large, and two of its walls were almost completely clear glass windows. It felt like a "normal," neighborhood bar, except it obviously catered to gay clientele.

We sat down at two vacant barstools, ordered our drinks, and resumed the mean girl, shit talking we had started earlier that night. There were many targets to keep us occupied, as the bar was rather crowded. I drank my first beer faster than planned, as I was trying to kill time, not get drunk. Before I could ask for a glass of water, the bartender sat a new, full beer in front of me.

"That's from him," he said gruffly and motioned towards my left.

I looked in the indicated direction and saw a tall man holding up his beer in greeting. My eyes opened wide, as all the air exited my lungs. I was breathless and thought I was hallucinating. It was Chris. My high school crush. I was absolutely positive. It had been about seven years since I last saw him at graduation, and I could tell that he was balding prematurely, and had aged in that time, but I was certain. And I was shocked. I held up my beer signaling thanks and turned back to my new mean-girl friend.

"You look like you just saw a ghost," he said.

"I went to high school with that guy," I explained. "I had the biggest crush on him." He looked down the bar to get a better view.

"You went to high school with him?" he asked. "How old are you?"

"Twenty-four," I replied. "Why?"

"There's no way you went to high school with him," he said. "He's at least ten years older than you. Are you sure?" he asked.

I was sure, but I started covertly studying his face. I came to realize that it wasn't Chris, there were subtle differences. But I couldn't believe the similarities. The attraction I had for him was unlike anything I had ever felt before, and it was instant. I don't know if it was because he looked so much like the very first person I was attracted to, or because of something that was entirely unique to him.

The only thing I knew for certain was I had never felt this way before when looking at a complete stranger. And when he caught me checking him out, I was instantly embarrassed. My emotions were in a chaotic jumble, which was causing me all sorts of anxiety because it didn't make any sense. I tried to flash him my goofy grin, but I'm sure it came out as a look of confused horror.

"You should go talk to him," said a voice, seemingly out of nowhere. "I need to be getting home anyway." I turned away from the source of my turmoil and looking at the bartender putting on his jacket I was instantly returned to reality. I looked at my watch and realized I still had much time to kill. I contemplated his advice, but when I thought about talking to the Chris look-alike, my stomach twisted up into knots; I felt like I was going to puke. I immediately understood that I wouldn't be able to talk to him. In order to talk, I needed to breathe.

"Actually, I have someplace I need to be," also reaching for my jacket.

"You should give it a few minutes," he advised. "Otherwise he'll think we're leaving together."

I shrugged my shoulders. I had to get out of there. I felt flushed, my heart was racing, and I was having trouble catching my breath. I really started wondering if there was something physically wrong with me. I said goodnight to my new friend, and by the time I reached my car, I decided I didn't need to go to the nearest emergency room. I felt fine again and decided that it was the alcohol that had caused the symptoms, that and my excitement to hear from Hank.

To kill more time, I went to a lovely twenty-four-hour restaurant up the street and ate some food to settle my stomach and absorb some of the alcohol. I thought the time would drag because I was still incredibly intoxicated by the thought of seeing Hank. After finishing my meal and starting in on another cup of coffee my phone rang.

"Hey, Kiddo. I just got into Battle Ground," Hank said when I answered my phone. "I'm parked in an Albertsons' parking lot."

"That's right by my house," I said. "You made better time than I expected. It's going to take me about forty-five minutes to get there."

"Looking forward to it," he said.

I paid my check and looked down at my watch. It was 2:30, and I was mystified. Where had all the time gone? I realized that I had spent two hours daydreaming about Chris, remembering the countless fantasies from my adolescence. And when I saw Hank, the sex was wilder than ever before. Afterward, I thought it was because it had been a long time since we had seen each other, but I changed my mind when I realized I had been thinking about Chris the entire time.

The next morning, I ended the affair with Hank.

"It was great to see you," I told him as he was getting dressed after a shower. We slept at my place the night before. "But I think we need to end this."

"What? Why? I finally found jobs that bring me this way. The last nine months have been awful," he looked heartbroken, which surprised me, considering our lasting arrangements. "I've missed you," he admitted.

"I've missed you too. But this isn't healthy, whatever it is we have. It's not healthy for me. It's not healthy for you. And it's definitely not healthy for your marriage," I told Hank. When the conversation started, I think I was as surprised as he was. I hadn't given it any thought and couldn't believe my own ears.

"Oh," he said. "I'll leave my wife if that'll help," he offered.

"I don't think it will." I hugged him goodbye and watched him walk across the street to where his truck was parked.

I felt sad and even expected to shed a tear or two, but I didn't. In fact, once Hank was out of sight, my mind became obsessed with a different man. It wasn't Chris though, it was the guy that bought me that beer.

Chapter 50

SINCERELY, ME

August 1998 – November 1998. Reston, Virginia.

Over the next few days, Bo and I explored the D.C. area. Tourist destinations, great restaurants, and museums were our daytime fare. In the evenings we explored the gay scene. Unsurprisingly, it was the same as everywhere else except for location and faces, but it was fun. Amazingly fun. We smoked, we drank, we danced, and most importantly we talked so much shit about each other, about everyone we saw, and most importantly about Doug. It was cathartic.

Although most of the gay establishments were in the Dupont Circle area of D.C., we learned of a secondary hub in an area of town I was completely unfamiliar with. We were told of a handful of seedy bars in that area, but we also heard that one of the bars staged a fantastic drag show on Thursday nights. The man that imparted the information informed us of a bonus at the drag bar, there was an attached Go-Go bar. Neither Bo nor I were quite sure what a Go-Go bar was, but our informant told us to check it out; he was confident we would enjoy ourselves.

We decided to go to the drag show and make plans for the weekend. Doug was due to come home the next day, and we wanted to avoid him as much as possible. I knew I needed to end things, but I wanted to do it without Bo's presence. I didn't want Doug to think that my decision was influenced by him; I wanted him to understand it came from me alone.

Planning was one thing we didn't do until sometime the next morning. The drag show was incredible. The queens were talented, the MC was hilarious, and the place was packed with some wonderful eye-candy. Although I had come to terms that I was single in all but name – my mind was set to task – I had no desire to meet anyone, but that didn't mean I wasn't going to enjoy the view. As the show was dying down, Bo's curiosity got the better of him, and we went in search of the Go-Go bar.

When we walked in, we realized it was a gay strip club. Sort of. There wasn't a central stage featuring a single dancer; instead there were many podiums scattered throughout that each held a single dancing man. All were completely naked, and most were sporting erections. The podiums were at a height that placed their crotches right at eye level, and as we looked around, we saw that the usual "no hands" rules at most strip clubs were not enforced here. Dancers were molested continuously by the patrons' hands and mouths. The dancers were all gorgeous, but the patrons were all disgusting. It was such a stark contrast. Bo was mostly fascinated. I was mostly disgusted.

We explored the other bars in the area afterward, and on our way back to the Go-Go bar, we passed a huge, windowless, warehouse-style building. We noticed a rainbow flag on the front door, and it reminded me of the Moondust. Completely non-descript.

"What's that place?" Bo asked.

"No idea," I replied. "A bar maybe, but I don't hear any music. And there are no signs or anything anywhere." We watched an attractive guy, about our age, ride by on a bicycle. He turned into an alley and emerged a minute or two later walking towards the mystery building. We watched the door close behind him without any indication of what was inside.

"Whatever it is, it's open," Bo noted. "Let's check it out."

We walked into a completely walled in square ten foot by ten-foot room. It was bisected by a long, glass-top, hollow, display counter; the kind you would see in the jewelry section of any department store, except it was completely covered with black cotton fabric. Directly across from our entrance was a closed door. There was a cash register on the empty counter and a nondescript man in his forties sitting in a comfortable-looking recliner directly behind it. When we stepped up to the counter, we could see the cabinet was filled with computer monitors. Obviously, the screens were monitoring the building. The only other feature in the room was a giant mirror on the wall beside the door.

"Got your cards," he asked as he stood up from the chair. "Or do you want to buy a membership? I've never seen you two before."

"Is this a gym?" Bo asked, and the cashier started laughing.

"No, but you can get your exercise," he chuckled.

"What is this place?" Bo asked.

"It's a private club," he answered, as though that were an adequate explanation.

"What's that mean?" I asked, which invoked further laughter from the attendant.

After looking down at the monitors, he said, "Go on in, you boys are already getting some attention." He waved towards the door as we heard a loud buzzing sound. "There are condoms and lube supplied throughout. We stress that you need to use them. Have fun."

We walked into a locker room. There were rows of coin-operated lockers and built-in benches. Directly ahead were showers, and there were two doors on both the left and right walls. When I looked behind me, I noticed that the mirror in the lobby was of the two-way variety. There were about a dozen men in the locker room. A few were naked, but most were clothed. We watched them disperse through the various doors. Many were giving the "interested looks" that were familiar from the bars. Suddenly Bo and I were alone.

"Oh. It's like a bathhouse," Bo said. "Or a porn theater, maybe? Fuck it, I'm exploring," and before I could say anything, he disappeared through one of the doors. Moments later, a separate door opened. The guy that walked through seemed to be the guy we watched on the bicycle not long before. When he noticed me, he smiled and walked towards me. I was instantly attracted. It was the same feeling I experienced when I first saw Jerry and Bub. Instant, animalistic chemistry. By the look on his face, I assumed it was mutual.

"Hey," he said. "What are you doing here? You are too hot to be in here, you're going to be attacked," he started laughing.

"What are you doing here then?" I asked in return. If I was too "hot" to be there, then he was doubly so.

"I hate the bar scene, but sometimes I need to get laid," he said rather matter-of-factly. "I just made the rounds, and I didn't see anything remotely interesting. I was about to leave," he gave me a hungry look. "Until now."

I explained to him that I was in a relationship and not there looking for sex. Within minutes, I was reminded of the instant bond I had the first time I met Hank. I felt like I had known Mark my entire life in very little time. We sat down on one of the low benches and talked for some time. I told him about Doug, and my plans to end our relationship. I expected him to grow bored and expected him to leave in search of someone else. I was surprised when he started disclosing aspects of his life as well. We had been sitting there talking, ignoring everyone else, for longer than an hour before Bo finally re-emerged. I still hadn't left the locker room, and neither had Mark.

"Ready to go?" Bo asked when he approached the two of us.

"You must be Bo," Mark said, "I'm Mark," he extended his hand. I had already told Mark a great deal about Bo. "Get lucky?" he asked Bo, mischievously. I realized then that he also had an inner mean girl.

Bo started laughing, "Yuck, no. These guys are gross." He seemed to really look at Mark for the first time. "What're you doing here?" Bo asked him. Which made the two of us chuckle. "Besides, I just like to watch," Mark looked at Bo dubiously, but I believed him. I knew what a prude Bo was. He turned and looked at me and repeated, "You ready?"

"He hasn't even seen the place yet," Mark stated. "We've been sitting in here talking about what a bitch you are," he was challenging Bo already, which only made me like him more.

"I'm good," I answered. "I wanna get stoned and find some food," I told him.

Bo looked at me then Mark, and said, "You should join us," Bo liked a challenge.

"I'd love to. But I rode my bike," he said.

"That's okay, Jay drives a Jeep, and the top is already down. I'm sure we can fit your bike too."

Bo and Mark also had instant chemistry, but not the same kind. The two were instant friends and attacked each other ruthlessly, but they both loved it. The three of us did as I suggested, and Mark even came back to my apartment with us. Mark and I ended up fooling around that night, and when I awoke the next morning, I expected to experience a familiar sense of shame and guilt. But I didn't. What happened with Viktor and Abel felt like cheating, but what happened with Mark didn't. Doug and I were already separated in my mind when I met Mark.

The next morning, after Mark and I repeated events from the night before, the three of us went to breakfast. Bo and I concocted plans for how to avoid Doug that weekend. I expected him at the usual time, late afternoon. We decided to find a hotel for the weekend, and I was going to leave a note with Doug telling him we went to Baltimore. Mark offered to let us stay with him over the weekend instead, insisting he would make an excellent tour guide for the city. Bo and I agreed. After breakfast, we dropped Mark at the closest train station and agreed to meet up with him at his apartment sometime that evening.

We enacted our plans, but before I could write the note for Doug and get out of there, he walked through the front door and almost tripped over the bags we had placed there.

"Hello," he called out, "What's going on?" he asked when he spotted me.

"Bo and I are going to Baltimore this weekend," I explained, hoping to get out of there quickly.

"Wait. What's going on?" Doug asked again. I expected him to be angry, but he looked sad and resigned.

"We're going to Baltimore," I repeated. I was trying my hardest to keep my voice even and casual, but I'm sure some of my anger was showing through. Explaining my position to Bo for the past days had given me a feeling of righteous anger.

"That's not what I mean," Doug said. "We need to talk." He was still standing by the door, and Bo disappeared to the bathroom.

"You're right, we do. But not now. Bo and I are going to Baltimore," I repeated.

"No. We need to talk, now," he said and walked into the living room. "I shouldn't have tried to keep you two apart," he muttered.

With Bo listening in the bathroom, I ended things with Doug. He repeatedly asked if I had been cheating on him. I told him no, even though I felt I had. I don't think he believed me, because he wouldn't let it go. He seemed sure that I had been having an affair since our arrival in D.C., but he was wrong. I thought I had made a mistake once but looking back I realize that wasn't cheating. It was rape. The night before with Mark was technically cheating, but I had no guilt concerning that. So, technically I lied. I didn't feel much of anything when I told him, and I didn't cry until he got up and left. And even when I did cry, it was only a couple of tears before anger again became my dominant emotion.

I don't know if he came back home that weekend, but I didn't. I didn't want to see him again, but I never got the chance to tell him why I was leaving. He was convinced that I had met someone new and was leaving to start a life with him. Two weeks before I left, he came home early for his weekend off, before I could get out of the apartment. We had an identical conversation, but this time he was demanding to know who my new boyfriend was. He even punched a hole through the drywall in his anger. It wasn't until I saw him a year later in Houston, that I was finally able to tell him why I left.

True to his word, Mark gave us a tour of the city. Places I didn't know about. The three of us had an amazing time. Amazing. Our dynamic was quite like what I had always experienced with Bo and Kayla. Except that Mark and I had a short-lived but astonishingly passionate affair. Before moving back to Texas, I spent most of my free time with him, and on Doug's weekends at home, I stayed with Mark in his apartment.

Our chemistry was comfortable yet intense, but our friendship grew in a very short time. I was relaxed enough around him to be my true self, and he seemed to feel the same way. I didn't let myself get attached though. I was moving back to Texas, and I didn't want a new boyfriend. Although I became enamored with both him and the city that I had spent little time in, I had to get away.

At one point he offered to let me stay with him until I could find my own place if I wanted to stay in the area, but I declined. He never expressed it openly, but shortly before I left, I got the impression that he would be willing to move to Texas if I asked. I never did. Of all the men I have ever been intimate with, Mark has always been my "what if." *What if I had met him at a different time? What if I wasn't ending a relationship when I met him? What if I stayed in D.C.? What if I asked him to move to Texas?*

I spent such a short amount of time with him, but our bond grew so strong in that time that I count him as an ex. I believe what I felt towards him was love; we burned brilliantly but briefly. While I may wonder what might have been, I'm sure I met him at the exact time I needed to. After two years of a passionless relationship and a mostly hollow friendship with Doug, I was reminded of passion and friendship and kinship at the time I needed it most. I was able to emotionally heal much more rapidly because of him.

I thought my last night in D.C. would be the last time I saw him. We had a few drinks with some of my co-workers then went back to my apartment to try and smoke the remainder of my baggie of pot. We tried, but we failed. I drove him to the train station and said goodbye. I was sad to see him go, but I was thankful for the time I spent with him.

He came and visited me in Texas a few months later. During his vacation, we even drove to Laredo, where I took him across the border and gave him a tour of Nuevo Laredo. It was his first time in Mexico, I think. While he was visiting, we had a continuation of the passionate affair we had started in D.C., but before long we fell out of touch. He and Bo have remained in contact and have even seen each other a few times over the years.

Chapter 51

HEY LOVE

August 2001 – January 2002. Battle Ground, Washington.

I went back to my familiar routine, but whenever I went to the gay bars, I always went and sat at the *Cheers* lookalike hoping to see the Chris lookalike once again. After a couple months, I gave up hope but didn't think too much about it. In fact, once I realized I had saved up enough money to pay tuition in full for flight attendant school, the last thing I wanted was to meet someone I might get attached to. With that realization, I stopped going to that bar completely.

After calling the school to find out when I could start classes, I learned it would be at the turn of the year, mid-January. Before that could happen, the terrorist attacks on September 11 changed everything. Suddenly, my dream of becoming a flight attendant was dashed. I could have followed through with it, but among numerous other reasons, I was certain my mom would chain me in a basement before she would let me spend that much time on airplanes.

Suddenly I again stalled. I wasn't sure what to do with my life. I liked the proximity of my parents and grandparents, and I had made a couple of good friends. Mostly, I was happy with my life, but I needed to find a direction again. Something new. I hated living in the Portland area but mostly because I suffered from terrible allergies there, and the endless days of grey skies slowly ate away at my soul.

I still hadn't told my parents, but I planned to return to San Antonio. I had six months left on my lease, even though I'm sure Sunshine's parents would have let me out of it. I planned to ride out the lease, and during that time I went through the same motions I had been performing since arriving at my parents' home about two years earlier.

One thing had changed though. I was again comfortable in my own skin, a sensation I hadn't felt since the first time I got an erection when fantasizing about a classmate's penis. I felt whole, and more importantly, I had learned to love myself. I didn't know what I was going to do moving forward, but I knew who I was. I wasn't opposed to meeting someone, nor was I opposed to falling in love, but I had come to the realization that love was most likely a myth.

On a night like any other, I drove into Portland after my shift ended. I had changed into a pair of jeans, and a brand-new t-shirt – one of my all-time favorites. It displayed Iceman on a light blue background, along with the words "Iceman says be cool, stay in school" – and a pair of black low-top Converse. I was wearing a red baseball cap featuring a Flash symbol embroidered in yellow thread. I was comfortable. I was me.

I ran into Fatty-J, my very first bar friend in Portland. His nickname was a pot reference and not at all related to his size, he was actually rather thin. He was a blast to hang out with, and he loved to dance even more than I did. He worked at the *Cheers*-ish bar, but I rarely saw him there. I was shocked when he suggested we go there for a couple of drinks before dancing. He was also acting mischievously.

We sat down at an empty table, and Fatty-J ducked behind the bar to grab us each a beer. He sat them both in front of me, and said, "Watch those, I'll be right back," and he disappeared up a staircase to the bar's office.

I could only see their feet when I heard him tell someone, "Just c'mon. You'll be happy you did." When the two bodies came into view, I was completely floored to see the Chris look-alike standing beside him. I felt my face turn red as my goofy grin made its customary appearance.

"Joe, this is Jay. Jay, Joe," he introduced us to one another; I felt like I was going to puke.

"Hey," I said. It was the best greeting I could come up with.

"Hey," he replied.

I was feeling tongue-tied but didn't want to look like some mute idiot, without much thought, I said, "Can I buy you a beer?" I chugged the rest of mine thinking a buzz would be helpful. I even did something almost unheard of; I suppressed the resulting belch in fear that I might offend him.

"No. I got it," he turned towards the bar. I can't be sure, but Joe appeared to be as flustered as I was feeling.

"But I owe you one," I replied.

He chuckled, "You don't owe me anything," he flashed me his first genuine smile. He was in obvious need of dental work, but I distinctly remember being mesmerized by it. "Besides, I work here, you can buy me one later," he added.

The three of us spent the next four or five hours together. Fatty-J seemed to recognize our awkwardness and provided us both with a comfortable presence. If he hadn't been with us, I think I would have puked all over Joe sometime that night. We all had a great time.

Joe and I spent the next twelve to fifteen hours alone to-gether at his apartment, and I only left because I had to work. He did too, and I learned that he had worked at that bar the whole time. Sort of. I never realized that there was a small, attached martini bar through the door by the pool table. He bartended in the martini bar on weekday evenings as well as taking care of the books for both bars. When I got off work, I raced to his bar and waited for his shift to end. We've been together ever since.

Like Cyclops and Phoenix, our relationship bloomed. We quickly developed a physical and emotional bond that would rival their psychic rapport. From our first meeting, we spent every minute of our free time together. On the weekends, Joe and his dog Memphis came and stayed with me in Battle Ground. On weekday evenings after work, I would join him at his bar until he was off, and I would stay with him overnight. To be as upfront as possible, I set a few ground rules. I didn't sit him down and dictate these rules to him, but as things became more and more serious, I was clear.

I explained that I wouldn't be willing to live with him until we had been together for at least a year. I explained that I would never be okay with an open relationship, nor a three-some or any other type of group sex. And I explained there were precisely two things he could do that would cause me to end the relationship without a second thought. 1- I would not accept cheating, and I promised to be faithful in return. 2 – I explained that if he ever became addicted to hard narcotics, I would walk away, no questions asked.

There was a single time that our young relationship almost came to a screeching halt, and oddly enough it wasn't related to any of my rules. I decided to give him the benefit of the doubt, however, and I'm glad I did. Although our relationship developed fast, and I was certain I loved him, I refused to completely commit until I saw him interact with Bo and Kayla. Without their consent and approval, I refused to entirely drop my walls and put my almost superhero focus into a healthy relationship where I wasn't afraid to be myself.

Kayla was the first of the two to meet him. Shortly before Joe moved in with me, we saw her in Seattle; she was there for a business trip and had a free day to explore the city. I was fearful that Joe would be rejected and had decided that if Kayla didn't like him, I would end the relationship swiftly. Before the trip, I made it clear to Kayla how crucial it was for her to tell me her true feelings towards him. She promised. About two minutes after the two of them met, my fears dissolved completely. I could practically feel the instant kinship the two had. In fact, our dynamic that day felt almost identical to the one Kayla, Bo, and I shared. Kayla assured me by day's end that Joe had her approval and she was certain Bo would feel the same about him.

The first time Bo and Joe met, it was the exact experience but in a different location. I was worried that they wouldn't like each other, but once I saw the two together that fear abated. Again, the dynamic felt so familiar. It was like when Brad invaded our group, he fit in as though he had always been there.

As this tale ends, I have come to realize exactly why Joe is my perfect partner. He is the perfect amalgamation of those that most influenced my emerging sexuality in a time of silence and secrecy. I had found bits and pieces amongst the people I connected with along the way, but in Joe, I have found the perfect combination.

In high school, Chris was the first person I ever thought about sexually. He was my first crush and my first fantasy. I suppose on some level, he is exactly my type. I've already explained that Joe and Chris could be long-lost brothers, sometimes when I look at him, I still get flashes of Chris. It's not just their physical similarities, it's also Joe's gait, his demeanor, and the sparkle in his eye when he shows his true smile. It's uncanny how many physical characteristics they share. I've often wondered how Joe would look in a western-style shirt, skin-tight wranglers, and cowboy boots.

Like Murry, Joe isn't afraid to show his true self on the surface. He has been open about his sexuality since an early age, regardless of stereotypes.

Like Dan, Joe is sexy. He isn't just attractive, he oozes sex appeal. I understand it is completely subjective, but he is down-right sexy.

Like Amanda, Joe accepts and emboldens me to show my true self. He encourages my geeky interests and has been known to read an occasional comic book or play Magic the Gathering with me for hours on end. He knows how rarely I share things with others – outside my Inner Circle – so he brags about my accomplishments to keep me from bottling them up inside.

Like Jerry, Joe's smile electrifies me. When Joe flashes his true smile, he has dropped his walls, and you can practically feel his soul.

Like Gabe, Joe is a fellow geek. No, he doesn't read science fiction and fantasy novels regularly. He only touches the occasional comic book, and he has never played *Dungeons & Dragons* with me. But he is a band geek. Complete and total band geek. Joe even marched with the Troopers Drum and Bugle Corps during his last few years of high school. Geeks come in many flavors, but deep down we are all still Skittles.

Like Ray, Joe and I share sexual chemistry. We are almost always in sync, and he can read my needs and desires like an Archie comic – with an easy understanding.

Like Bo, Joe regularly reminds me of the little things that make me wonderful. Don't get it twisted though, neither of them sit around recalling all my amazing feats and regaling me with stories of my superhuman greatness. Frequently their lessons are difficult to decipher and painful to realize, but in their own ways, the two are constant bulwarks for my self-esteem. They both constantly reassure me to be myself without any reservations.

Like Kayla, Joe inspires me to push harder artistically. Kayla has a passion for photography that I have never seen rivaled. She is a talented artist in other mediums, but when she found photography, she became wholly dedicated. Joe shares this exact same passion artistically, except his focus is mutable. Whenever he expresses himself through art, the results are sublime. Music. Drawing. Painting. Sculpting. Stained Glass. Airbrushing. Carpentry. Photography. Gardening. The list is everchanging. He attacks each of these with the same passion as Kayla, but moves from one to the next, rarely returning to a previous medium. They both inspire me to express a similar passion through my words.

Like Bub, I can sit in comfortable silence with Joe. There is never a need to fill the air with idle conversation. I also have a deep sense of security and safety when he is near, that is intensified when in physical contact with him.

Like Brad, Joe's work ethic is borderline insane. He has workaholic tendencies that could possibly rival Brad's, but I help him keep them in check.

Like Shannon, Joe is an alpha mean girl. Unlike Shannon, he embraced his much later in life, and he still hasn't realized his full potential.

Like Hank, Joe is reliable. He is always there when I need him.

Like Doug, Joe pushes me to better myself in every possible way, but he doesn't try to dictate what exactly constitutes a better me. He encourages me to use my focus to its fullest potential, but he never tells me where to aim it.

Like Mark, my relationship with Joe flared quickly and deeply, and our connection was instant, and for the last seventeen years, those flames have grown to a conflagration that would outshine the Phoenix Force.

When I accepted my own sexuality, I started on an epic quest to discover what it meant to be gay. What I discovered was that my story really wasn't much different from anyone else's.

Everyone must come to terms with their own sexuality and grow comfortable in their own skin. Gay, straight, transgender, bisexual, queer; it doesn't really matter.

The problem with closeting practices like "Don't ask, don't tell," is it robbed an entire generation of their voice. We were told not to talk about our sexuality, and so long as we didn't, we were free to be ourselves. I didn't realize back then that those things that I equated to gay are really universal discoveries that all people must find. Love, lust, pain, betrayal, friendship, confidence, the list goes on and on.

Since I believed that society didn't want to know about my sexuality, I closeted away so many things. So much of this story are those things that I didn't share, even with those I am closest to. Over the years it has become increasingly easy to hide aspects of myself away, when it makes life easier. Much like I hid much of my geek side while discovering my gay side.

By sharing my tale, I fight back against years of conditioning. "Don't ask, don't tell" only works if you play by its rules. Closet your voice. Closet your inner demons. Closet your desires. Your hopes. Your dreams. Your passions. Your fears. Closet yourself. Just blend in.

Instead, do ask. When you encounter someone who is different, someone that might make you feel uncomfortable, ask them to tell you about themselves; what you will find is they really aren't very different at all.

Instead, do tell. Stand up and be yourself; show everyone that your life is as valid as everyone else's.

Closets are for clothes, not people.

EPILOGUE

TURN UP THE BRIGHT LIGHTS

For eight years much of my life was placed on hold as I discovered what it meant to be gay. I started that challenge alone and finished it the same way. Once I was able to fully accept and love myself, it was easy to give my all to my relationship with Joe. This tome is not a complete representation of my life during those years, but rather a collection of experiences and people that helped me shape my identity as a gay man. When I started that adventure, I was completely clueless about what awaited me. Although the journey wasn't always pleasant, I wouldn't change anything in those years; without the good and the bad, I wouldn't be the person I am today.

My mom remains in the Portland, Oregon area, where my parents moved after my dad's retirement from the military. After two horrible years combating an aggressive form of cancer, we lost my dad about five months after I published the first edition of this book. The death of my dad was one of the hardest things I have ever experienced, and I miss him every day.

My sister is currently living in Cheyenne, Wyoming with her wife of ten-plus years. The two of them seem happy and dedicated to one another. We don't talk nor see each other nearly as much as we should.

I have tried to find Chris many times on social media, mostly because I'm curious how he looks all these years later. I wonder if he and Joe actually look alike or if my memory has played tricks on me.

I am Facebook friends with Julie, and she is happily married with children. She is still living in South-Central Texas. I have had no contact with Eddie since I punched him in the face, and the last time I saw Skye was when I made her cry. I have made no attempts to contact either.

I haven't had any contact with Murry since I stopped attending his weekly *Dungeons & Dragons* gatherings. I have searched for him on Facebook and other social media sites, but so far, I have been unsuccessful.

Amanda and I had a falling out many years ago. She wasn't there for me when I truly needed her, and she took our friendship for granted. I haven't spoken to her in almost twenty years. I will always cherish the friendship we had, but I have never been able to overlook her betrayal. Both she and her mother have made numerous overtures to contact me through social media, but I have blocked their attempts. That part of my life will remain in my past for now.

The last time I saw Ray was at a bar in San Antonio. At the time he was in a serious relationship and had a great job. He seemed incredibly happy, and I wish him all the best.

I have often wondered how Bub's life took shape, and I have been curious to find him on Facebook, but I can't remember his real name, and I doubt I could spell it even if I could.

Gabe and I have had sporadic contact throughout the years. Mostly through social media. He is living in California and seems to be happily "tied down" there. He is still a fellow geek, and I wish him all the best.

Bo is still my best friend in the world. We talk regularly and see each other as often as possible. He is currently single-ish, with a twenty-acre property in the Hill Country of Texas. He still has a handful of horses but has given up the "lifestyle." A few years ago, he decided to pursue his education, and he is slated to receive his undergraduate degree in May 2019. He is currently applying to various dental schools and plans to become a dentist.

Kayla is still my other best friend. She followed her dream to become a successful photographer in New York City. She succeeded. She has lived there for the last fifteen years, and her career has been amazing. *Of all the people represented in this book, Kayla's role is the least fair. She has always been an important part of my life, but her contributions to my "gay awakening" were surprisingly minimal. Her contributions towards my personal life, however, have been monumental. I love you Kayla and want you to know your importance in my life aren't fairly represented in this tale because of its focus.* Kayla and I are regularly in contact. She settled down with a great guy shortly after moving to New York, and the two have been together since.

Brad died from cancer in 2016. He spent the last few years of his life as a hermit and even gave up his work life. He was always uncomfortable growing old, and as the disease destroyed his body, he hid from the world. Sadly, he died alone. His influences on my life were immense, and I miss him every day.

When Alex and Kayla split, I never heard from him again. That break up was fucked up on so many levels, and we discovered that Alex wasn't the person he presented himself as, but that is Kayla's tale to tell. Not mine.

I haven't spoken to Doug since I last saw him in that parking garage. In 2004 or 2005, he managed to track my parents down and sent me a letter through them. I responded to that letter, but we haven't had any contact since. About six months ago he sent me a friend request on Facebook. Every time I log in, I see his face and the two familiar boxes: Accept or Decline. I still haven't made a decision one way or the other.

Once I left Virginia, I have unsurprisingly had no contact with Viktor or Abel. I am certain that the machinations they used on me have been used on many others. I hope one of their victims had the bravery I didn't and reported them. Hopefully, the two are in jail somewhere receiving the same treatment they doled out.

Mark and I have remained in contact throughout the years. Mostly through Bo, as the two of them have maintained a friendship. Even he and Kayla are friends now. He is a successful artist living in the Pacific Northwest. He seems to have successfully battled his demons and seems happy. He's even sent Joe and me some of his artwork. I wish nothing but the best for him.

I haven't heard from Hank since I ended our whatever-it-was. I have never looked for him through social media, and honestly have little, if any, desire to do so. I hope that he has been able to come to terms with himself, and I hope he has found the courage to be honest with his wife and family.

Joe and I moved to Cheyenne, Wyoming in 2007 to be closer to his parents – *I have won the in-law lottery. Joe's parents are both two of the most amazing people I have ever known, and I am happy to call them Mom and Dad.* I decided to return to school in 2015 and finished my undergraduate degree in English, December 2018. I decided that it was time to share the stories that constantly traipse through my head and am currently pursuing a career as an author. In May 2016, Joe and I were legally married. We only told two people and went to Vegas to tie the knot. Bo was my best man, and Kayla was Joe's. It was only the four of us, and it was amazing. We didn't tell anyone else until after the ceremony, and we had no guests. I wouldn't want it any other way. After 12 years in frigid Wyoming, Joe and I moved to the heart of the Texas Hill Country – less than 20 miles from Bo – where we are currently living our "happily ever after" with our furry-and-four-legged children.

Acknowledgments

First, I would like to give a thank you to everyone out there who reads this book. This was often a difficult book to write, and in so many ways it was even more challenging to share. If you enjoyed the book, please take the time to share it with your friends and family. As a brand-new, independent author anything you can do to get this book into the public's hands is immensely appreciated.

Second, I would like to thank everyone mentioned in this book for giving me the fodder needed to tell a compelling story. Joe, Mom, Dad, Bo, Kayla, and everyone else. Thank you for the influence you had on me; both the good and the bad.

Third, I need to give a shout out to Jessica Andrews - for both the support and hard work - alongside a special thanks to all of my beta readers, thanks for your feedback and support.

Lastly, I would like to extend my warmest thanks to Sarah Noffke – with a casual remark, she provided the spark of inspiration I needed to write this book.

About the Author

To learn more about the author and to find his other works, please visit, jaytbailey.com.

APPENDIX - GRATEFUL

May, 2024. Kerrville, Texas.

I wrote the following story specifically for my dad when we learned his death was imminent after his two-year battle with cancer. I'm happy to write that he was able to read the tale only two days before going into hospice care. He said it meant the world to him – and it meant the world to me to write it for him – and he expressed his desire that I share it with the world.

Although the story isn't thematically tied to my journey of coming to terms with my sexuality, it does demonstrate how my relationship with my dad influenced my life. As such, adding it to the 2nd edition of Don't Ask, Don't Tell, seemed like the perfect place to share it. You can read it as "prequel" as it all takes place before the beginning of this book. Or you can think of it as an expansion of Chapter 2, R3WIND, as it expands on the relationship between my parents and me. Regardless, it is told in the same voice and supplements my memoir – alongside my life – wonderfully.

The Bellyache

I

Yesterday, I got a visit from an almost forgotten apparition; a barely remembered ghost from my childhood. A bellyache. It isn't a nauseas sensation, nor does it feel like I've overeaten, in fact it doesn't affect my appetite in the slightest. It isn't a cramp, or a stabbing pain, or a burning sensation. It's like a rock or a knot, but that isn't quite right either. Although it has a solidity, a weightiness, it also feels like a pit. A bottomless chasm or a galactic blackhole. It doesn't really hurt, at least not in the physical sense, but it's a constant discomfort, and I can't help but wonder how long my phantom intends to haunt me this time.

It was more than thirty years ago, when I first felt this malady. I was nine years old, and my father had just left for his assignment in Okuma, Japan. I don't really remember the day he left, and I'm not sure if he got on a commercial airline or a military plane; in fact, I don't even remember if the last time I saw him that day was at home or as he stepped onto a plane, but I am certain that he flew to his post. I do, however, remember when I learned of his orders.

"JT, there's something we need to tell you and your sister," Dad said, one day during dinner. Until my sister and I grew old enough to begin working, we always sat down at the dining room table for dinner. It was guaranteed family time, each and every day, and I never really gave it much thought before, but I appreciate this daily interaction more than I ever thought.

My sister and I looked expectantly at him, and I wasn't overly concerned. Dad didn't look like he was about to disclose anything awful, but my dad is the perfect model for the "strong silent" type; and since he, instead of Mom, was about to convey some news, I knew it was going to be important.

"I got orders to Japan," he said matter-of-factly, with little emotion. Maybe a touch of a frown, but it is hard to say as Dad's face is usually a mask, and it was a long time ago.

My dad had already begun his twenty-plus-year career in the Air Force by the time I was born, and I had always lived on a base during my short life. I may have already lived in a few places, but I only had memories of Malmstrom AFB, in Great Falls, Montana. Unlike many other military families, I had lived in one place since beginning school. But I did grow up on base, so I was familiar with people flitting in and out of our lives. We may not have moved a great deal, but my friends did regularly. Consequently, I had an intimate familiarity with how the military lifestyle worked.

"Cool," I told my parents excitedly, and I noticed the frown and sadness on my mom's face. I'm not sure what my sister's response was, or if she said anything at all. She often followed Dad's lead when it came to silence. "When do we go?" I asked, but a slow realization was dawning.

"We don't," Dad replied, not quite cryptically, but I don't think he offered much more of an explanation. Instead, Mom has always been good at speaking up for herself, and for him. One of the many reasons the two make such great partners.

"We don't get to go," Mom piped in. I can't be entirely sure, but I think there was a touch of resentment in that statement. "It's a tiny base, and there isn't a school for you and your sister to go to. So, we're stuck here."

"Oh," I responded, and I kept it as casual and neutral as possible, but I was angry. I thought it was incredibly unfair. I wasn't mad at Dad, at least not at first, but I was jealous. And that jealousy quickly evolved into subtle anger. I tried to keep my emotions under wraps before Dad left, but he probably knew I was irritated. But I was never mad at him, although he was most likely the target of my ire before he left. I wasn't angry that he was leaving, I was angry that I didn't get to go.

That wasn't when the stomach malady began; that didn't arrive for a few months. It was the day Dad departed when the low-grade pain started, and it didn't disappear until he came home for Christmas while on that assignment. He was only home for a couple weeks before he had to return to the Far East, but during those two weeks, what had become a constant annoyance vanished.

Before his trip home, at least twice weekly, I would visit the school nurse. I always complained of a bellyache, but she could never find anything wrong with me, and after a couple weeks, my mom became involved. She took me to the military doctors, and they too could find nothing physically wrong. It was then that I was told that my ailment was all in my head, but we could never figure out what was causing it. Of course, looking back, I realize that the source was my father's absence, but at the time I don't think any of us connected the dots. That's when I started getting teased about being a hypochondriac, and although my blight may have originated in my head, that didn't make it any less real. At least not for me.

II

Dad and I never quite connected on a friendship level. We never really liked the same things, and I always thought he was disappointed in me. But I was wrong, completely wrong. He always allowed me to be exactly who I was, and he never expected anything else; but I was a kid and I thought since

I didn't like to go fishing or hunting or bowling or sports in general, and I hated the horrible cacophony of the car races that he loved, I wasn't living up to my obligations as his son. But those obligations were in my head, not his. I realized this many years ago, but I never talked to him about it.

I never really talked to him about anything, which isn't to say we didn't speak to each other, we talked often of inconsequential matters, but we both used my mom to relay our feelings and deeper messages. Maybe we would have connected more, had we opened up to each other, but Mom was always there to be our bridge. It was comfortable and comforting, and I don't regret the dynamic. I always considered our group bond to be stronger than that of father and son or mother and son. I always feel at my best when I have them both near me. I never needed him to be my friend, but I always needed him to be my dad. And it was a job he excelled at.

Dad always encouraged me to follow my interests, which fell decidedly in the realm of geekdom. Comic books, fantasy and science fiction novels, Dungeons & Dragons, school, the works. For the most part our interests never lined up, but he always tried to include me in his hobbies, as well as asking questions and taking a small part in mine. Sometimes it was torturous trying to carry a conversation with him, and I believe he often felt the same, but it was always comforting to have him nearby.

"I'm going fishing this Saturday. Wanna come with me?" Dad asked during summer break, while we were living on Elmendorf AFB, in Anchorage, Alaska. The silver salmon were running, and Dad being the consummate fisherman loved salmon season.

"Sure," I replied, noncommittally. Shortly after Dad returned from his post in Japan, he got orders to Alaska, but this time the entire family joined him. We had been there for a year or two, and I was about twelve years old and beginning my teenaged-angsty years.

"Are you sure? It will probably be an all-day thing," Dad responded to my unenthusiastic reply. Since his return from Japan, our disconnect grew. At least it did for me, and I believe I had built up some resentment during his absence, not to mention the confusion of adolescence.

"Is Mom going?" I paused *Super Mario Brothers* on the original *Nintendo Entertainment System.* It was a prized possession, and I was obsessed with completing the game to rescue *Princess Peach.* I had finally made it to the second level of the eighth world – an all-time best – and I was annoyed that he was continuing the conversation.

"I don't think so," he answered. As a child, my tendencies ran towards the "momma's boy" stereotype. The two of us were close and grew closer during Dad's year-long AWOL from the family.

"Okay," I held the small, rectangular controller, waiting for him to leave, so I could return to my 8-bit adventure.

"I'm planning on leaving early..." he started, as he turned to leave. I almost laughed aloud at this bit of information. Of course, we'd be leaving early; he was always up early. "If you change your mind," he concluded.

I was about to press the start button to continue my game, when I realized something didn't add up. "What?" I asked.

He turned back to look at me, his face the usual mask but slightly annoyed. "If you change your mind, and decide you want to go, I'm planning on leaving early," he explained.

"Why would I need to know what time you are leaving, if I change my mind?" I asked, confused.

His exasperated countenance morphed to slight befuddlement, "Huh?" he asked.

"If I change my mind, and decide to stay home, why would I want to know what time you are taking off?"

"Oh," his face returned to its familiar visage, "So you're going?"

"Yeah," I'm sure I sounded annoyed. I thought I had been clear with my single-syllable-vague responses.

"Does that mean you're going to fish?"

"Maybe," again, my answer loose and undefined.

Barely, almost imperceptibly, he shook his head in bewilderment. "Don't stay up too late playing your games, it'll be early when I wake you," he warned. I've always been grouchy when facing a day without a good night's sleep, and I'm sure he didn't want to deal with a grumpy pre-teen. He turned and exited my bedroom.

Before my attention returned to the old, black-and-white television screen, I heard my mom from the living room. She wasn't speaking loudly, nor was it a whisper, but it was clear she didn't think I could hear her from my room.

"Is he going?" she asked Dad.

"I think so." His reply too wasn't exactly confidential, but they were talking to each other in the way that parents do when they think their children aren't listening. "I don't know why though?" he confessed to her. At the time, I thought he sounded disappointed, but honestly, I believe it was sheer confusion. "He doesn't like to fish, and he'll probably just read or sit against a tree and doodle in his drawing pad."

"So?" Mom asked.

"So, he probably won't say more than ten words to me the entire day, and he'll be bored," he answered.

"So, you don't want him to go?" Mom sounded irritated. Where Dad's expression and tone was almost impossible to read, Mom was the opposite; her emotions were always clear.

"No. It's not that," Dad reasoned. "I just don't want him to be bored all day, and if he stays up all night playing that damned Nintendo, he'll be an asshole."

I felt a twinge of anger bubble up inside me. Not because he called me an asshole, because he was right. If I had stayed up all night, "asshole" would be a gross understatement. I was angry because he didn't understand why I wanted to go fishing with him.

I always liked being around my dad. I have always felt at peace when he was nearby. Sure, talking to him was often more painful than not, especially at that age, but that never really bothered me. I have always enjoyed the comfortable silence shared between the two of us. I have never felt the need to chatter aimlessly with him. In fact, I preferred it when we didn't talk. That doesn't mean I didn't want him close though.

I went to bed early that night, and the two of us spent the next day somewhere in the wilds of Alaska fishing for salmon. Well, to be fair, he fished all day. From time-to-time I would pick up my pole and cast it into the river, but these instances were few. For most of the day I sat, with my back against a tree, either nose-deep in a Piers Anthony novel, or with a mechanical pencil furiously scribbling away in an over-used drawing pad.

He asked me a few times if I was bored, and if I wanted him to take me home. I told him no every time, but I don't think he believed me. I was perfectly content going on trips such as these. Dad was able to enjoy something he loved, and so could I. I loved to read and draw, and I could perform those activities anywhere. Since Dad's hobbies involved some travel, I would just pack up my supplies and go along. I've never told him that the most important part of these journeys was simply his presence.

Whether he meant to or not, he taught me to enjoy the silence in the world. The unspoken connections. And when he is gone, I will miss that hushed bond most of all.

III

Before we left Alaska, my parents gave me the best gift I have ever received. My very first best friend. Moose. Throughout my entire childhood, at any given time, we always had at least one four-legged brother or sister. Our animals were never pets, and we always treated them as part of the family. Moose's mother was a pure-bred Siberian Husky, and his father was a German Shepherd / Husky mix. His mother belonged to a family whose house was on my path to school every morning. I'm not sure where his father lived, as this wasn't a planned pregnancy; he wasn't a stray, as there is no such thing as a stray dog on an Air Force Base, but when he impregnated Moose's mom, he did so after breaking loose from his home. I never even saw Moose's dad, but his mom and I were already great friends by the time she had her litter.

On my way to and from school every day, I would always stop and play with Moose's mom. She wasn't an overly friendly dog, but she liked me a great deal. In fact, after she had her puppies, there were very few people she would let near them, but I was one of the lucky ones. And once Moose and his three littermates came along, I would leave early for school and spend as much time with those five dogs as I could.

Moose was my favorite from the moment I saw him. He had one brother and two sisters. He and his brother were solid black when they were born, and the girls were a medium gray. I liked all four of the puppies, but Moose and I had a special bond from the moment we met. He was always the first to greet me, and he would chase off his siblings so he could have me all to himself.

I talked about those puppies, especially Moose, as often as anyone in the family would listen. I don't remember asking if I could have one – we already had a family dog – nor did I have any idea what the owners were planning to do with the puppies once they were weaned from their mom. I was clueless that my mom had gone and talked to the owners in this regard.

When Mom took me to pick out one of the puppies, I couldn't believe it. I was flabbergasted. Dumbfounded. And I was more excited than I had ever been. When we got there, and Mom asked me which puppy I wanted, there was no hesitation. I picked Moose up and hugged him close to me. I explained to his mom and siblings that I would give him a wonderful home and that he would be loved his entire life; I didn't want them to worry about him.

His original family gave my mom a large, brown-paper sack filled with the food the puppies had been eating, along with records of his first shots and other incidentals. I'm unsure if my parents paid anything for Moose, or if he was happily given to a happy home. I had gotten to know his first family fairly well, and I think they were glad to give me one of the pups after all the time I had spent with them and their mother.

On our walk home, with my newest furry-brother, I yammered on and on about all the things the two of us were going to do. All the tricks I would teach him. It was one of the happiest days of my life.

"So, what are you going to name him?" Mom asked, interrupting my incessant babbling. She too had a giant smile on her face, seeing her son so ecstatic.

"I dunno," I answered noncommittally, as I tussled the hair on the pup's head. His overly large and pointed ears still hadn't learned to stand erect on the top of his head. They were still sticking straight out to the sides, although all his siblings' ears were already in their proper position.

"Better think of something soon," Mom warned with a chuckle.

"Why?" I looked over at her. We were about the same height at the time.

"Because if you don't, then your father will," she explained. Apart from Moose, I believe that Dad named every other pet we had ever had. It has always been a running joke in the family, that once Dad names an animal, it is part of the family.

"Hmm," I replied, as I took her warning to heart. Moose was my first pet, and I wanted the honor of naming him. "I think we should call him Moose," I finally said about the time we reached our house.

Mom's initial response was laughter, but she followed up with, "I like it. Why Moose," she wondered.

"Because his ears look like antlers right now," I told her laughing, as I sat him down on the kitchen floor so he could explore his new home. If he wanted to do so alone, he was out of luck. I don't think I left his side for the next six months unless I was at school.

"Let's hope your dad likes it too," she said thoughtfully as I followed the puppy through the living room and up the stairs.

When Dad got home from work, Moose ran to him excitedly. He liked everyone in the family, even the six-year-old Pekingese, Tattoo.

"So, what are we going to call him?" Dad asked after the two played and became acquainted with one another.

"He already has a name," Mom informed him. "JT named him Moose."

"No, I don't think so," Dad said thoughtfully with that all-too-familiar, mischievous look in his eye. "He looks more like a bear to me. We're gonna call him Bear."

"What?" I practically screamed. "No way! His name is Moose; just look at his ears. They're like little antlers."

"They won't stay that way forever," Dad replied. "He's definitely Bear. He's a little black bear," Dad said in that tone that meant finality. Like all our other pets, he had named this puppy and he acted as though the matter were settled.

"Nope," I responded in the exact same tone. "His name is Moose," I looked him in the eye, unafraid to back down.

Dad returned my warrior's glare with one of his own. "It's Bear," he stated empathically.

It was a Friday, after school when Mom and I walked the couple blocks to pick up Moose, and for the rest of that evening, Dad and I argued about what he was going to be called. Dad was convinced that he would be named Bear, but I knew better. By the time I went to bed that night, with Moose in tow – until I moved out on my own, Moose always went to bed with me; he may not have stayed the entire night, but he wouldn't leave until I had fallen asleep – the two of us were still adamantly arguing our cases with one another. Additionally, we both tried to recruit my mom and sister, but the two stayed out of it.

When I awoke early the next morning, Dad was in his usual spot. Coffee in hand, sitting silently in his recliner. I flashed him a dirty look, ready to resume our battle, but he responded with a friendly smile.

"I think Moose needs to go potty. You'd better take him outside."

Dad never admitted defeat. He never mentioned the name "Bear" again, and Moose was a member of the family for the next fifteen years. He was my first best friend, and such an important part of my life. I don't know if Mom talked to Dad that night and convinced him to surrender, or if he decided on his own. What I do know is my father is stubborn, and that doesn't even come close to describing his unyielding nature. Obstinate, bullheaded, steadfast still don't equal his prodigious persistence once he made a decision.

I have always admired this trait, although it can be quite frustrating to combat. But I learned to stand up for my convictions. It was my decision to make, at least it was from my perspective, and I followed Dad's combat training, achieved victory, and won my spoils of war. Moose received his proper name.

I also followed Dad's example and didn't lord my achievement over him. Don't get me wrong, I wanted to. I was damn proud of myself that I had bested the best in a battle of wills. Maybe I had an unknown ally in Mom, but wars are never fought alone. Dad and I reached an unspoken truce, and we moved forward as though we hadn't spent hours arguing. I learned then how to stand my ground when necessary. If I am one-hundred percent sure that I am correct, or if the argument at hand is completely subjective and I am only arguing my point of view, I will not withdraw, and I will not surrender.

Like Dad, my opinions can be swayed, and although I hate to, I can admit when I am wrong. Dad's headstrong nature is both his most admirable and frustrating personality trait, and I could say the same about myself. But I wouldn't have it any other way.

IV

Every morning my dad was the first to rise, and it was early; always before the first rays from the sun touched the horizon. He would quietly prepare a pot of coffee, then pour himself a cup and sit silently in his recliner for about an hour before showering and dressing for work. Even on the weekends, he would follow this routine, except he wouldn't head out the door before the rest of his family had joined the woken world. He wouldn't turn on the television or radio, and he didn't sit and read the daily newspaper. He would relax in his recliner and sip on his coffee, content in the silence, preparing to face the day.

After a few years spent in Alaska, Dad's next orders were to Lackland AFB, in San Antonio, Texas. For our first couple years there, the entire family spent summers indoors where the air conditioner made life bearable. It took some time to adjust to the severe change in climate. I was well into my teenage years, and it was the summer before I started high school.

That *NES* system that my parents had bought for me in Alaska, with one of our dividend checks, was still my most prized possession. To call my obsession with video games an addiction seems too mild. I had long ago finished my quest to rescue the Princess and had moved on and through countless other digital adventures. My current compulsion was the classic *Tetris,* and I had stayed up the entire night trying to beat my personal best of 210 lines – although I never did, but I promise you level 21 is incredibly difficult to pass.

It was shortly before five a.m. when I exited my bedroom to relieve an overfilled bladder. I had been drinking *Shasta Cola* all night. Now that we were teenagers, my sister and I had more freedom regarding our food and beverage choices, and although Mom would get on me for drinking too much soda, there was only one rule to follow. Never drink the last one. The last pop in the fridge was always Dad's.

After performing my deed, I headed to the kitchen to grab another ice-cold can, and noticed my Dad sitting in his recliner, quietly sipping from his mug of coffee.

"Been up all night, Chicken-Neck?" Dad asked. He loved to tease, he always has, but Chicken-Neck was his favorite nickname for me.

"No," I lied, needlessly. He sounded amused, not annoyed. It was summertime, so I didn't have school, and I wasn't yet old enough to start working part time, and although I bitched about them – like all teenagers – I always finished my chores and did what was expected of me around the house.

"You're up awfully early then," he mused, the mischievousness clear in his voice.

"Yep." I was still prone to the simple monosyllabic response with Dad. When I opened the fridge, I noticed that there was only a single soda on the shelf. Although there was a full jug of *Sunny Delight* and a few bottles of *Yoo-Hoo,* I wanted the caffeine. I had been fighting off sleep all night and had come close to beating my high score. I wasn't ready to succumb to the Sandman.

When I heard the coffeepot gurgle its final drops of water through the grounds-filled filter, I had a sudden inspiration. I reached into the cupboard and produced a mug. I poured a few ounces of the dark-brown liquid into the cup and took a tentative sip. Then quickly spit the bitter fluid into the sink. From the corner of my eye, I noticed that Dad had risen from his chair and was watching me silently from the dining room. He had that fiendish look on his face, and I didn't want to give him the satisfaction of providing another avenue for teasing me.

I pretended not to notice his observation, then added a bit more coffee to my cup. Careful not to look in his direction, I grabbed the milk from the fridge and the sugar from the pantry. I added enough milk to the cup until it was a couple inches from the top, then added five or six heaping tablespoons of sugar and mixed the concoction together. When I was finished, the liquid was almost overflowing in the ceramic mug. I had to bend over to sip at it until it was safe to lift. Thankfully the bitterness had been diluted with the cream and sugar.

"When did you start drinking coffee?" Dad asked, and I turned and looked at him as though I were clueless that he had been standing there watching me.

"Now," I answered with a sarcastic smile.

"That's not coffee," he returned an ornery smirk. "If you want something that sugary sweet, then just drink a soda or some *Kool-Aid*."

"This is how I like it," I reasoned. Although to be honest, I hated what I had just mixed. I didn't mind the sweetness, but I hated milk — always have — and it was at least seventy-five percent of the beverage.

"Well, I don't want you wasting my coffee. It's more expensive than *Kool-Aid*, so if you're going to waste it to add some flavor to your milk, then don't bother." He was still acting impishly, but I refused to give him the satisfaction.

I picked up that mug, then poured its contents into the sink, before rinsing it under the faucet and filling it almost to the top with coffee. I narrowed my eyes at him, then lifted it to take a sip. It burnt my lips and tasted worse than anything else I had ever drunk. "You're right," I said flippantly. "This is much better," I lied.

Dad just chuckled at me. He knew I wasn't enjoying the coffee, and although I tried not to react, I'm sure he also knew that I had burned my lips. But I drank that entire cup of black coffee as Dad followed his morning routine. After he showered and dressed in his military uniform, I poured myself another cup of coffee, making sure that he saw. He laughed again and left for work without saying another word about it.

I don't know if he remembers that particular morning, but I will never forget it. First, it began my life-long – okay, almost life-long – love affair with that nectar of the Gods. Coffee. Coffee is the perfect beverage. Secondly, he may not be aware, but I learned something important from my father that day.

That morning, I learned that if I was going to do something, then I should do it "right." No, of course, I don't believe that there is a "right way" to drink coffee but using it to flavor some milk is clearly "wrong."

I also learned that if I wanted to do something right, then I needed to commit to the action. I had been determined to prove to my dad that I was a coffee drinker that morning, and once he dictated exactly what that meant, I committed. I choked down that awful libation and continued to do so whenever my dad was around. I didn't do it because I liked it – although I came to understand the term "acquired taste" – I did it to prove something. If I hadn't followed through, there's a good chance that I would have put that mug down, and never touched coffee again. And I would have been the worse for not acquiring the taste. Really, I love coffee.

It may have been something simple, and he might not have intended to teach me anything, but he did. It was then that I started to follow through with my interests. I stopped giving up when things became difficult. No, I didn't commit to everything I tried, but those things that interested me, I poured myself into. Without Dad's teasing and prodding, it most likely would have taken me much longer to learn this lesson, not to mention that I may not have learned it at all. But it wasn't just that morning, that was just the moment it all became clear. My dad is one of the most committed people I have ever known. He follows through with his every duty and obligation, even those that he hates. And because of his example, I have learned a valuable lesson. If I commit myself to anything than I should feel obliged to see it through to the end.

V

For at least half of my life, I labored under a false impression regarding my dad. I always thought that he enjoyed repairing old cars, after all, he spent at least five or six hours every weekend shimmied under an old Volkswagen or Dodge. And he was a great mechanic, and although I can't be certain, I never remember any of our vehicles being serviced at a garage unless there was something seriously wrong.

I hated it when Dad worked on those old vehicles. Absolutely hated it. Once I was old enough to follow simple instructions and hold a flashlight, it was always my duty to "help."

"Goddamn it, JT, how hard is it to hold a flashlight," Dad growled from underside of my sister's first car. "Shine the fucking light where I'm working," he commanded.

As I moved the beam to what I thought was the indicated spot, I couldn't help but be annoyed. For almost a decade, I had been Dad's assistant when he was playing mechanic.

Normally Dad is calm, quiet, and calculated, but there were definite exceptions, when his angry side came out to play. And fixing cars always got him into that head space immediately. I didn't say a word in response, but I probably rolled my eyes. My routine when helping Dad with the family's vehicles has always been the same: shut up and pray whatever he is doing is over quickly.

"Do you see my hands anywhere near where you have the flashlight pointing?" Dad snapped angrily. I always took his annoyance personally. I believed he was miserable when playing mechanic because I wasn't very good at playing assistant.

"I can't see your hands at all from here," I snapped back. Although silence was my typical response, sometimes I couldn't stop myself from keeping my ire in check.

"Just give me the fucking flashlight," his hand jetted out faster than a cannonball, from underneath that silver Mazda, "And hand me that goddamned socket wrench."

Handing him the flashlight, I had a brief fantasy of smashing him over the head with it, before turning to look at the chaotic array of tools piled in the grass just out of arm's reach for him. I stared at the pile of tools and wracked my memory trying to remember which one the socket wrench was. Shrugging my shoulders, I grabbed what I thought was the correct instrument and placed it in his outstretched hand. The flashlight had already disappeared, and his hand was bouncing with irritation.

After handing him the tool, his hand withdrew briefly, only to come speeding out again, as he angrily mumbled something incoherent.

"What?" I asked, although I knew what he said. I couldn't see him, but I could picture him as he pulled the flashlight from his mouth.

"Does this look like a goddamned socket wrench to you?" he barked.

"No, it looks like a goddamned hammer." He slid out from underneath the car and glared icily at me. I returned the expression.

"If you aren't going to be any help, you can just go inside," he told me calmly, although his eyes were smoldering coals.

"Fine by me," I flashed him a catty smile, then followed his recommendation.

When I walked through our front door, Mom noticed and powered down the vacuum cleaner. "You guys done already?" she asked, then followed up with, "That was quick."

In response, I just looked at her. It has always astounded me that Mom could read a person's face and body language so quickly.

"Let me guess, your father is being an ass?"

"Of course, he is," I growled. "He loves to scream at me."

"That's stupid, why would you say that?"

"Because that's all he does. Why else do y'all always make me help him work on the damned cars."

"He's not yelling at you," Mom explained. "He's just venting because he's in a bad mood. Besides, he's trying to teach you crap you'll need to know."

"How to hold a goddamned flashlight? He doesn't teach me anything, he just screams at me when I do things wrong," I didn't realize it, but I was following his example and venting my frustration at another target. I was practically screeching at Mom, as I stormed off to my bedroom.

To this day, whenever anyone mentions anything of a mechanical nature to me, my brain shuts down. I don't listen to a word they are saying, and I wait impatiently for them to stop talking so I can change the subject. I hated helping my dad work on cars, and for the longest time, I believed it was because I was stupid when it came to things of a mechanical nature. After all, I had spent a great deal of my childhood "helping," but even after years, I couldn't locate a socket wrench in a pile of tools. I have always told myself that it was one of two things. First, maybe I was an idiot in this aspect, but I refused to believe it. I did well in school and always thought of myself as "smart." Second, it was my father's fault and he was a lousy teacher. In my head I have always bounced between these two options, but I've come to realize that I was wrong on both counts.

I have come to realize that Dad hated repairing those vehicles, and because of this his worst nature came out. Since I couldn't stomach Dad when he was constantly screaming and cussing, I would tune out the entire experience. I'm certain that he spent time explaining the different tools and procedures. He probably even made me perform tasks to get a feel for what he was doing. But I didn't pay any attention. Zero. I just wanted the task at hand to be finished as soon as possible so I could get away from the raging monster.

I thought that my presence ruined an activity that he found enjoyable, because whenever he was finished, his mood would instantly return to his mostly quiet but playfully harassing self. I always believed his happy demeanor returned as soon as I was away from him, but it was because he was finally finished with his duty.

Dad did teach me a great deal, but it has nothing to do with mechanics. In that regard, I learned nothing. When I have car difficulties, I call a mechanic. It took me a very long time to learn this lesson, and like most things I learned from Dad, I'm unsure if the lesson was intended or not. I learned a great deal about duty and sacrifice, not to mention the worst way to hold a flashlight.

He didn't spend so much of his weekend under a car or stooped over the engine block because he liked to; in fact, looking back, I'm almost entirely certain that he hated the work. We didn't have enough money to drive newer cars that were under warranty, nor did we have the funds to employ a mechanic whenever repairs were necessary. Plus, my father was incredibly gifted at keeping those cars running smoothly.

He spent his time cussing and yelling because the work needed to be done, and he was the one with the skills. It was his duty to his family, and he sacrificed his time – the most precious resource of all – to make sure that our family had proper transportation. Sure, he may have been a dick while engaged in "mechanic-ing," but there is nothing wrong with venting. Maybe I was incredibly sensitive, and maybe he shouldn't have used me as the target of his ire, and I am certain that there are healthier ways to channel frustration, but I learned a great deal about life. Although I wouldn't listen to a word he would say, I would give nearly anything to hold a flashlight for him one more time.

We don't always do get to do the things we enjoy. But there is a certain satisfaction that comes with performing tasks that are required, if miserable. Since I always internalized my dad's behavior when I was helping, I felt at blame and inadequate. I hated the screaming and cussing that I believed was directed at me, but he was just yelling at nothing most of the time.

When I am feeling angry or frustrated, I tend to do just as Dad. I tend to scream and curse, but I have learned not to direct the monster at anyone, and I am usually, not always, successful in this regard. I hated feeling like the target of his discharges and have made a conscious effort to not do the same. I believe that Dad too has come to this realization over the years, and it has been a very long time since I have seen him lash out at someone over such petty issues.

VI

Technically, when Dad joined the military, the US was still engaged in the Vietnam War, but by the time he had finished basic training and his tech school, we had pulled our troops from the Far East. For the majority of Dad's military career, the

US was at peace with the rest of the world. Sure, the Cold War was still in full swing, but it wasn't until Desert Storm that we had to worry about Dad being deployed to an active war zone.

Dad came home one day after work, with a familiar look on his face, and when he said he had something to tell the family that night at dinner, I was sure we were going to be presented with new orders. I was right, partially; he did receive new orders, but like his tour in Japan, this assignment didn't include his family. When we were told that he was being deployed because of the upcoming war with Iraq, the entire family was instantly on edge. Until we were told that he was being sent to England, in order to help set up an overflow hospital in the English countryside. He wouldn't be anywhere near the actual combat zone, but his assignment didn't have any set duration, and we had no idea how long he was going to be gone. All of us were thankful that he wasn't being deployed to a combat zone.

The Shock and Awe campaign that the US used was highly effective, and as such there were "few" battlefield wounds and casualties. The hospital that Dad helped to erect didn't see many (if any) patients, except for the occasional local emergency. All-in-all dad wasn't gone for long, but during that time, Mom locked up our house, found a friend to take in our dogs, and took me and my sister to Washington state until Dad was sent home after his tour.

It was during this time that the bellyache returned, but I still hadn't deciphered that its presence was directly tied to my father's absence. As I was older, it was my first year of high school, and I had been teased for years about being a hypochondriac, I didn't tell anyone about the discomfort in my midsection. I didn't go to the school nurse, and I didn't talk to Mom about it. I suffered in silence.

While Dad was away, I was always consumed with fantasy and science fiction worlds, comic books, and doodling in my drawing pads. I wasn't in a state of depression, but I wasn't particularly talkative with peers or my family. It was also a complicated time of adolescence, so I don't think my behavior seemed out of place for a fourteen-year-old boy.

Before Dad left for England, he asked me to pick out four or five of my favorite books. He figured he would get some reading in during down time as the location of his post was far from any real center of civilization. I spent hours combing my bookshelves trying to decide which of my favorites to send along. I was excited that Dad was taking an interest in one of my favorite past times, and I really wanted him to enjoy the books as much as I did. I sent along the first Xanth novel by Piers Anthony, something by Robert Heinlein, and one of the books from The Belgariad by David Eddings. All favorites.

While Dad was away, Mom often sent "care packages." They were always filled with homemade cookies and treats and stuffed to the limits with Dad's favorite candy bars and other incidentals that were difficult to procure across "The Pond." Not as often, we would receive a care package from Dad. These would come to us after he got enough time off from work to go and explore areas of England. His packages would be filled with small knick-knacks and souvenirs from London or Oxford or anywhere else he was able to visit. The entire family loved to open these boxes to see what Dad had sent.

"We got a package from your dad," Mom informed my sister and I, after school one day before we left for Washington.

"Cool," I replied enthusiastically. I don't know if my sister shared my excitement, but I believe she did. "What's in it?" I asked.

"I don't know. I haven't opened it yet," Mom supplied as she grabbed a kitchen knife to cut through the layers of packaging tape.

We dug through the box, filled with all sorts of small items, all labeled with our names. Although there were some interesting items, it was the books in the box that grabbed my attention. The three books I had sent with him when he left were sitting at the bottom of the box. My initial reaction was disappointment; I believed that Dad hadn't read them, and since they were being returned, I also believed that he had no desire to read them. I kept my disappointment in check and focused on the various items.

Later that evening, as I was returning those books to their proper homes on my bookshelves, I dropped the hardback copy of *The Sorceress of Darshiva*, and when I did, a hand-written note from Dad fell out. I can't remember exactly what was written on it, but the message warmed my heart.

The note informed me that he really enjoyed that book, and looking back, I'm not sure why I sent that one. It was book four of *The Malloreon* series, which was the second series following the same cadre of characters. Although I'm sure I intended to send book one of the first series, for some reason this was the one that made it into his luggage.

The letter described how much dad liked that book, but now he was curious as to what had come before, and he wanted me to send the other books in the series. I was so excited that Dad shared an interest in what is probably my favorite two fantasy series of all times, that I pulled all pertinent books from the shelf and brought theme into the dining room. I explained the note I had found to Mom and told her I wanted her to place all the books in her next care package. She laughed and said it would cost a fortune to ship so many, so instead every time she sent a box, she would include the next couple books in the series.

The next time Dad called, the two of us spent the entire time chatting about that book, and I revealed far too many spoilers from the books he had yet to read. Although I'm sure I ruined many of the plot twists for him, he seemed happy to let me ramble on-and-on about the literature. It was one of the rare times when our interests aligned, and he eventually read all the books in both series. Dad and I have had many conversations regarding how those books would make wonderful movies.

During that phone conversation, I felt closer to Dad than ever. But he had never been farther away. Dad wasn't gone for a year; in fact, he wasn't even gone long enough for me to finish a school year. I started my freshman year of high school in Texas, spent a few months of it in Washington, but finished it out back in Texas. The entire time that Dad was away, I experienced the bellyache, but I never disclosed to anyone that it had returned, and at the time I still hadn't deciphered its origin. Every time the two of us talked on the phone while he was away, the stomach pains would disappear, and we spent the entire duration talking about the works of David Eddings.

When we got the news that he was being sent home, and Mom started making plans for us to also return to Texas, the bellyache vanished. It was quite some time before I felt that sensation again, and it faded from memory until its eventual return.

VII

During my freshman year of high school, I was excited to take Art as an elective. I had spent most of my childhood with a pencil in hand, and although I primarily drew in a comic-book style, everyone who viewed my artwork was always quick to praise it. Sure, everyone who saw it was friends and family, and they could easily have been offering platitudes, but when I signed up for the class, I believed I had a leg up on my peers. Luckily Art class was offered at both schools I attended during my freshman year, but I started and finished my ninth-grade year at Medina Valley High School in Texas. The months spent in Washington while Dad was away didn't cause any problems when I returned to Art after Dad's return from England.

In no way do I intend to oversell my artistic talents. I'm not the best artist, hell I'm not even a great artist, but I am adequate; most importantly, I am a dedicated artist. I spent a great deal of time inventing superheroes, aliens, and fantasy creatures as a child, and I made a conscious effort to improve my skills. I doodled regularly because I enjoyed it. On my first day of high school, I was most looking forward to the first period after my lunch break, so I could learn different techniques and try out new mediums.

I enjoyed the class thoroughly and received high grades on all my assignments. I actively attempted to master the basic techniques, and I wasn't hooked on maintaining the cartoony style I had cultivated over the last decade. I desired nothing more than to work out my artistic muscles.

My high school was a small one; there were less than a hundred kids in my class, and we had very few electives to choose from. Art was one of the classes that was offered each year, and although anyone could sign up to take Art I, to take the more advanced classes, a student was required to get permission from the teacher. As my freshman year was winding down, I approached the Art instructor to receive the needed endorsement to move on to Art II my sophomore year. When I was told that I couldn't, I was devastated.

Although he told me as diplomatically and politely as possible, my teacher basically informed me that I just plain didn't have any artistic talent and taking more advanced classes would be a waste of both my time and his. I was completely dumbfounded. Not only did I receive an "A" in the class, but I also got along with the teacher and there was a marked improvement in my artwork that year.

When I got home from school that day, Mom could tell that something was bothering me, but I didn't disclose to her what had happened. Instead, I retreated to my room and lost myself in a brightly-colored-digital nirvana – I still had the old black-and-white TV in my room, but I had procured the color monitor from our first home computer, once the family had stopped using it. The monitor was huge and heavy, but the screen was tiny, maybe half the size of my television, and I constantly shifted the *NES* connections between the two depending on the game and whether color or size was more important. Mom didn't pry and she gave me the space I desired to work out my disappointment, but when Dad got home from work, I'm sure she said something to him, because he came into my room just to chat. An almost always awkward, and assuredly rare occasion, especially in those perplexing adolescent years.

"Hey, Chickenneck. What'cha playin'?" Dad asked as he stepped into my room, still in his fatigues – it must have been a Wednesday, every other day he wore his "hospital whites."

"*Dr. Mario,*" I responded sullenly. He didn't say anything for a few minutes, but he sat down on the bed beside me and watched me play.

"I don't get it," he finally said.

"What's that?" I asked, but I didn't turn to look at him; the bright, primary-colored capsules were falling down the screen rapidly.

"What in the hell is going on?" he chuckled as he said it, but I wasn't exactly sure what he was referring to. When I didn't answer, he clarified, "What's the point of this game? What exactly are you doing?"

I spent the next ten minutes explaining the game to him, and I can't be entirely sure, but I think he even took the controller in hand to give the game a shot. By the time I had rambled on about a relatively simple game, I was more at ease, and had all but forgotten about my day at school.

"So how was school today?" Dad asked nonchalantly, once I had finally stopped talking. Instantly, the disappointment I felt returned. I didn't say anything, but Dad was quick to notice my shift in mood.

"What happened?" he asked softly. I didn't want to tell him. I was feeling incredibly disappointed in myself. I had always considered myself a good artist and being told by a teacher that I liked the fact that I had no talent had been a devastating blow to my fourteen-year-old psyche. I was afraid that Dad would be as disappointed with me as I was with myself. I felt a slight twinge of tears on the verge of breaking free, but they never did. I didn't respond but kept killing the cartoony viruses on the monitor.

Like earlier, Dad sat there in silence, offering an ear to listen to or a shoulder to cry on. He didn't demand answers or try to pry the information out of me. He offered unconditional support. He watched me play the game and even started offering his opinion on how to play the game more effectively. It put me at ease again.

"You'll feel better if you talk about it," he offered. I maintained my silence.

"If it's easier, you can talk to Mom," he suggested, as he rose from my bed about to exit the room. "But I promise it will help."

Before he could make it to the door, I told him what had happened when I asked the teacher for his consent to take the next Art class. "I guess I've been wasting my time," I finished my tirade, indicating the pile of drawing pads and pencils on my desk.

"That's stupid," Dad stated, and momentarily I mistook the anger in his voice to be directed at me.

"Who gives a damn what one asshole says," he continued. "Hell, he can't be much of an artist if the only thing he can do is teach high school. If he had any goddamned talent he wouldn't be here. How the fuck would you expect him to recognize talent in anyone else when I doubt, he has any himself." Of course, these arguments are ridiculous. Artistic talent resides in all of us, and whether we express it or use it as a means of employment isn't the only measure of success. But Dad's intent wasn't to use logic. He was angry that someone had made his son feel bad about himself and one of his passions, not to mention he was trying to cheer me up.

"Do you enjoy drawing?" Dad asked, after a long tirade filled with some wildly inventive cursing.

"Of course," I replied.

"Then you know the best thing you can do?"

"What?" I asked, smiling. It was fun watching Dad vent his ire in a direction away from me and empowering knowing that it was all done for my benefit.

"Prove that son-of-a-bitch wrong. Don't stop drawing and get better than he ever dreamed of. And when you do, you won't even care if he knows," he told me, sagely. "And if you do, you can send him a signed comic book, and be sure to circle your name on the credits page," he added, followed by an uproarious laugh.

I took Dad's words to heart, and when he left my bedroom, I powered down the Nintendo and picked up a pencil and pad, and for the most part, I haven't put them down since. I even spent six or seven years tattooing to make some extra cash.

I learned an incredibly important lesson that day. I learned that the opinion of one person shouldn't derail my focus and dreams. Regardless of their expertise or their influence, no one can interfere with my goals. In fact, the best way to motivate me to do anything is to tell me that I can't. That I don't have the talent. Or the drive. The focus. Desire. There is only one person who can stop you from succeeding in life. Yourself. Because of Dad, I have learned to never get in my own way.

VIII

After Dad returned from England, he was never again sent away for any lengthy trips. I had all but forgotten about the bellyache that had cropped up over the years. I spent the rest of my high school years in Texas, got my first job. My first car. My first girlfriend. My first apartment. Dad and I got along rather well for those awkward years, but mostly because we gave each other plenty of space. It wasn't until the summer after I graduated that I experienced phantom aches in my midsection. Thankfully, this stopover was rather short.

I moved out shortly after graduation. I got along with my parents well, but I have always enjoyed autonomy. I moved into San Antonio, about a forty-five-minute drive from my parents' house. That summer was an awakening experience for me. I came to terms with my sexuality and came out to myself and my friends. For some odd reason, it took me months to tell my parents.

Neither of my parents have ever had any issues with gay people or the "gay lifestyle." They have always been open-minded and both judge people for their actions, not for such petty ideas such as sexuality or skin color. As my sister was out – and basically always has been – combined with the fact that her many gay friends were always welcome in my parents' home, it was rather silly for me to believe that they would take issue with my sexuality.

But it was a palpable fear, and it took me months to build up the courage to tell them. When I did, my best friend was by my side, and she was holding my hand in support.

"I have something I need to tell you," I informed my parents after the two of us drove out to their house. It was a hot summer day, and my parents were relaxing in their above-ground pool, fighting the Texas heat.

"Okay," Mom said. It was obvious by her mannerisms that she knew my proclamation was important in nature; at least to me.

"I'm gay," I finally told them after a long pause. I was trying to keep my tears in check, but I was fearful that their reaction would be positively negative.

"So?" Mom said almost immediately, and when I turned to look at Dad, he simply shrugged his shoulders. Neither of them appeared to be very surprised, and by their reactions, I knew immediately that nothing had changed. They weren't at all upset, and they acted like I had just told them that the sky was blue.

When the pit in my stomach disappeared, I finally realized that it had been there since I told my Dungeon Master about my sexuality. He was the first I came out to, and when I did, the bellyache arrived. But it was gone the moment I knew that nothing would change between me and my parents.

I never really talked about "being gay" with my parents. But I really didn't need to. They recognized that it was a small part of my personality, and since they didn't make it an issue, neither did I. It took me quite some time to fully come to terms with my sexuality, but I realized early that it was my issue alone. I never needed to defend myself, and I never needed to deny who I was to my parents. I never needed to go out of my way to make them comfortable with my homosexuality. Because they plain didn't care, or if they did, they understood that it was their issue, so they never made it mine.

My parents loved me unconditionally, but before that moment I never quite understood what that meant. Because of them, I too learned to look past those things that are out of another's control, and to never judge them for those things. It was maybe the most important lesson I have ever learned, and just like all of Dad's other teachings, it was subtle instruction.

IX

When I learned that Dad had cancer in his liver, initially I was devastated. Dad had taken care of himself through the years. After thirty years of smoking cigarettes, he woke up one day and decided he was finished with the filthy habit. He never smoked another cigarette, and he quit by sheer will-power alone.

I was standing with Mom when they rolled his hospital bed back to the surgery room; it was necessary to remove half of his liver to combat the cancer. Dad survived the surgery like a champ, but before he was released from the hospital, it was necessary for me to return home to Wyoming. I was in my senior year at the University of Wyoming, after decided to return to school. When I left Washington, like everyone else in the family, I was hopeful that the surgery would remove all the cancer from his liver.

It was only about a month later that I returned to Washington; I had already purchased a plane ticket months before to spend spring break with Mom and Dad. When I arrived, I was presented with one of the most difficult sights I have ever seen. Dad was sick, and it was the first time in my life that I had ever seen him like that. It was difficult for him to get around, and he was nauseous and in pain almost constantly. The surgery had left him less than he had always been, but he refused to let it get him down. By the time I arrived, Dad had already started an aggressive regime of chemotherapy, as the surgery wasn't successful in removing all the cancer. The doctors were hopeful that this treatment combined with the surgery would add years to his life, but after the treatments, the cancer was still present. Since the chemotherapy didn't stop the cancer from spreading, Dad followed the doctor's recommendations and submitted to a round of radiation therapy. Unfortunately, this too was unsuccessful. Even through all the aggressive treatments, the cancer was still growing in his liver, and it had begun to spread through his body.

Since this nightmare started about two years ago, I have gone to visit my parents as often as possible. Every time I see Dad, his health is worse than the time before, but even this doesn't keep him down. He is still working, because like me, he thrives with routine. I know many would call him crazy or idiotic spending his final days at the grindstone, but I believe it is a comfort for him. It has been hard watching the most powerful man I have ever known succumb to this illness, but even in this there is much I can learn from him.

Just because he knows his life is coming to an end, and even though he knows his health will be on a steady decline until that day, he refuses to give up. He hasn't surrendered, and he is still living what life he has left with as positive an outlook as possible. Life can be cruel. Evil even. And what happens to us and our loved ones is rarely "fair," but that doesn't mean that we can't make the best of a terrible situation.

Dad was always a constant in my life, except for the few times when his career took him far away, but thankfully these instances were few. He has always been there for me, and as his mortality becomes more and more apparent, the best I can do is to return the favor in the time he has left.

Dad and I may never have been friends, but that was always the last thing I needed from him. I was incredibly fortunate; I was blessed with two parents that wanted to provide the best lives possible for their children. I've always been loved and accepted, and they have never treated me as though I were an extension of themselves.

I don't know if Dad intended to teach me the lessons that he did, but most likely, like all great teachers he led by example. I don't know if Dad knows how influential he has been on my life. He is the greatest man that I have ever known, and the thought of him not being there is the scariest thing I have ever had to face. But I have learned so much from him, and I know I can get past this. Not only can I survive the experience, but because of him, I can use this to make myself a better person. I can't let his death destroy me, and the best way to honor him is to live my life just as he taught me. This may be the darkest moment in my life, but that doesn't mean that there isn't any light, and no matter how dull the light may be, it will shine brightest in the dark.

I have never taken the opportunity to tell my dad just how much he means to me, but I hope that reading this will give him an adequate indication. But words fall short; there are some things that language simply can't describe. Because of Dad, words aren't necessary. Our bond has always been silent. Unspoken. But that doesn't mean that the bond isn't strong.

As the pit in my stomach grows, I have come to realize its presence isn't a nuisance. My bellyache doesn't derive from my dad's absence, like I have come to believe. I didn't realize it, but it's the place in my body that Dad has made his own. Sure, the bellyache can be frustrating, and it thrives in its persistent stubbornness. It is generally silent but can flare up with little notice. It doesn't derive from Dad's absence, instead it is a reminder that he is always nearby. I wouldn't be the man I am today without his constant presence in my life, and initially I couldn't conceive of a possibility of moving on without it. But that's what the bellyache is. It's Dad. And I hope it never disappears.